A Bernard

stima e affetto

Carlo

maggio '92

IN SEARCH OF A GLORIOUS DEATH

of that confused mass, taking shape for the first time. And the world unfolding before my eyes not only seemed different, and unexpectedly vaster than it had done before, but remote from me, and also disquietingly hostile.

Watching the trams lurch noisily down Via Labicana, my friends would sit there waiting for me on a stone balustrade at the far end of the park. We'd wile away the hours there, soothed by the sound of the water gurgling into the fountain. Giannetto Lettari's restless eyes would follow the movement in the streets below us.

'They were quick enough', he'd say, 'they were quick enough to change all right, but what are we left with? What are we now without our past – without everything we thought we were?'

If one of us didn't turn up, we became uneasy, gripped by a sense of actual mutilation, and we'd spend the whole time watching the distant gate, waiting for the moment when at last he'd show up, running breathlessly towards us from the far end of the avenue.

When we finally lost all hope of seeing them, I'd leave with Giannetto, Blondie and the two Grama brothers, driven by the hope that maybe events – as though mysteriously connected to the places where we experienced them – would work out differently now, in the unknown streets we'd approach as outsiders. We'd stand among groups of people by newspaper stands; and while the newspapers looked like the ones we always saw hanging from pegs – even the words were the same – it was as though some mischievous hand had turned them upside down, altering the meaning entirely.

And so off we'd go again, wandering down the streets, the sun beating down on us. 'They've wiped out the lot', I heard Fabio mutter, 'not a trace left . . . not a single memory of what there was before. It's like being on another planet.'

At dusk, we'd go up the deserted avenue flanked by pine-trees, and say goodbye at the corner of Via Mecenate.

'Bye.'

'See you.'

Then Fabio and Enzo Grama would speed off, running past the wall of the timber merchant's so as to be home before their father got back; while Blondie would walk away in his light gaberdine suit, shoulders held high in imitation of Giannetto's swift, resolute step.

5

As for me, all I had to do was walk in through the darkened doorway and breathe in the evil smell of the stairs – lit by one dusty shaft of light – to be gripped by utter despair. Everything seemed just waiting to attack me with hopelessness and misery, so that all the excitement I'd felt from talking to my friends would instantly evaporate.

And there they'd be, sitting under the kitchen lamp with their dullness, their works, their smells: 'Where've you been? I told you I didn't want you coming in late.'

Going towards my room, I'd hear him mutter furiously behind my back: 'Who does he think he is? What does he think he's playing at?'

His house of cards came tumbling down in a single evening – one of those infuriating evenings with him silent and grey over his soup, lifting his spoon to his mouth as he swallowed. He cheered up though, the moment we heard voices, a little uncertainly at first, rising up from the darkened courtyard.

'Turn on our radio! Quick, turn on our radio', he said, 'there's been some news!'

For days now, he'd been waiting for a stroke of the magic wand, so that once and for all he could 'put all those moaners and groaners in their place'. His little brown eyes lit up in a flash as he sat there waiting for the first signal from the radio. There was no doubt about it – what else could all that yelling and shouting be in aid of? 'It's Him! We'd forgotten about Him! He'll look after us! I knew it! I knew it!' At last here was the glorious victory he'd been waiting for – the miracle!

'It's just what happened at Caporetto in World War One. Everyone thought we'd had it – even talking about an armistice, no less – but all along I just knew we'd win!'

And instead came that slap in the face. The magic eye of the Magnadyne winked a couple of times, and as that voice broke through – reverberating around the dining-room, there, between the fake mahogany sideboard and the drinks cabinet with its six rose-coloured champagne glasses with the twisted stems – the order of the universe was turned upside down: *Rome, July 25th, 1943 . . . His Excellency, Benito Mussolini, has resigned as head of state . . .*

Like a scratched record which nobody had any intention of taking off, those few words – loaded with all their banality – bounced dully from his face (which had remained fixed for a while in that expression of expectancy, and was now crumbling as though it had lost all means of internal support), over to her eyes, which, in a flash, had grown watchful and uneasy, like those of an animal suddenly sensing danger: *Rome, July 25th – His Excellency Benito Mussolini . . .*

And as the shouting and applause rose up from the dark street, he sat hunched in a corner by the open window, biting his lips, moaning and trying to stifle his sobs, while she kept saying over and over again in this flat, toneless voice: 'We've got to hide, we've got to hide, we mustn't be seen!'

All around, windows were being flung open, casting rectangles of light, filled with wildly gesticulating shadows, on to the pavement. It was then that I saw His head – the head of the man who was supposed to protect and defend us – being hurled out into the middle of the street.

I felt something snap inside me, and I thought to myself: right, he's going to do something now, say something to stop all this and bring things back to how they were before.

But instead, as that plaster head was kicked along the cobblestones against a backdrop of jeers and insults, he just sat there – racked by sobs, weeping and shaking his head and not taking any notice of my distress.

I also remember the tenderness of those fine, almost feminine hands, his quick smile and that ready optimism which seemed to bubble up at the slightest opportunity. He was always the first to greet you: with a faint bow he'd lift his hand to his hat and raise it an inch, even if it was only Sor Ubaldo, the baker, or the caretaker of the flats.

I'd hear him open the front door, walk down the corridor and drop the keys on to the hall table. She'd greet him from the kitchen doorway – 'Hello, Tonino' – then he'd sit down beside the window with a newspaper on his knees, until she called him to supper. Sometimes, I'd sit by the window, waiting for him to appear around the corner of Via Merulana with that self-contained air of his, as though he were held together by some kind of inner reserve. Then, once he'd seen me, he'd wave, and I'd watch him cross the sun-filled street, looking up in that trustful way he had.

And it was my father's head – the head he always held high because 'he'd never done anything to be ashamed of' – which ended up being kicked along the cobblestones that evening by the crowds.

His head.

She would spy on me with ruthless determination: if the telephone ever rang, she'd be poised ready to answer it before I could get there.

'Yes, who is it?' she'd say, and it was only if I were actually there, that she couldn't bring herself to lie. 'Yes, just a moment . . .', she'd add in a different voice, bitter and resigned, then stand there behind the glass door in the hall, hoping to catch the odd word.

In the mornings she'd get up silently at dawn and, locking the door behind her, she'd scuttle off to mass. When she returned I'd still be in bed, but I'd hear her pottering around the house, stopping every now and then to listen for me. She'd discuss her thoughts out loud, and it was always at the point when she was about to be overcome by panic that she'd say over and over again: 'God no, I won't let this one get away! I'll keep him at home with me!' She'd sidle up to the door to listen, then once she realized I'd heard her, she'd half open it and poke her head around.

'What are you doing?'

She'd give one of her sighs.

'Let things be, my son, there's nothing we can do now . . . just concentrate on your studies.'

And off she'd go, shaking her head and muttering her reproaches:

'All this suffering, my sons! All this suffering you've caused me!'

Once I was about to go out, when I found her blocking the front door – she'd decided that she wasn't going to let me pass:

'Where are you going my son? This isn't the time to be going out . . .'

8

By the dim light of the eternal flame I could make out her bulky frame standing beneath the medallion of the Sacred Heart, feeling her breathy heat as she tried to touch me, to cling to my arm. She smiled.

And as I turned into the next street, I saw her out of the corner of my eye, creeping furtively out of the door with a coat slipped over her houseclothes. Then I ran and ran until I could no longer hear her trotting breathlessly on those little stumpy legs of hers, her handbag pressed close to her breast.

Another clear memory: a cloudless, sunny day, and the monastery up on the Palatine Hill immobile in the light. We'd made it as far as Porta San Paolo, taking shelter behind the low garden-walls of the houses. The noisy shots of anti-tank guns left an acrid smell in the air, as a shower of bullets skidded along the cobblestones.

It was there, in that silent neighbourhood, that we came across a group of runaway soldiers creeping furtively through the undergrowth which spilled over some railings. They looked shabby in their uniforms, and, as they turned around, we saw that their frightened faces were dripping with sweat.

In the grounds of Villa Celimontana, clothes and abandoned military equipment lay rotting behind the myrtle hedges, while high on a hill, Giannetto – agile as an acrobat – had climbed up a palm-tree. He sat there gazing into the distance.

'Can you see anything from up there?' we asked him, as he leant out from the trunk, supporting himself with one hand.

There, among luminous meadows in the higher regions of the sunlit park, we rediscovered an immense feeling of space, magnified by that silence all around us. Just then a great din rose up through the air from the direction of San Paolo, and was soon lost over towards the other side of the city. Two men came running down the deserted avenue, looking over their shoulders with terrified faces:

'Quick, run! It's the Germans – they're going to attack!'

We watched armoured trucks going into battle along Via dei Trionfi, the sun beating down onto the camouflaged sheet-metal. The roar of engines travelled along the grassy slopes of the botanical gardens towards the ruins, and over to the streets on the other side. Just a few minutes earlier, under the arches of the Colosseum, we'd been talking to some soldiers dressed in leather jackets and helmets. They sat there on broken columns, wiping the sweat from their hot faces –

'Why don't they just go home and leave us alone?'

Outside the arcade, a small group of their officers were gathered around a major, and as they stood there beside the trucks, smoking, one of them said: 'But if the king's gone, and the government's fled, who are we getting our orders from? . . . Who *are* we fighting for?'

The major didn't reply; instead he looked out towards Via dell'Impero, as if there, in the empty streets, the answer lay waiting. The surrounding roads were empty as far as the eye could see.

We were following Giannetto down past the great walls of Via Quattro Cantoni, and from there to the Suburra – a mass of narrow alleyways and silent crossroads. You got the feeling that the city had turned its back on its own streets, retreating further into itself in the face of all that had happened. We walked on, sticking close to one another, intimidated by the sound of our own footsteps . . . All those frightened faces peering out from half-closed doors; while a car hurtling at full speed down the empty street left this sense of desperation in its wake . . .

Then, at the foot of Via Pie' di Marmo came that apparition: a colonel on horseback in the silence of the deserted city, the sharp, staccato sound of the horse's hooves going clop-clop-clop over the cobblestones, as he sat on the sheepskin saddle, scabbard hanging from his side. He had a droopy moustache, like Grandfather Angelo's in the photograph hanging up in the hall at home, and a row of ribbons on his chest. Was it a dream, a mirage? It couldn't be! Just when all seemed lost, here at the last minute was this sudden lease of life – a miracle! What else could the Colonel have in tow, if not an entire regiment preceded by fanfares? You wanted to throw yourself out of the door, run after him, touch him with your own hands so that you too could be part of the regiment with its banner flying high in the wind . . .

And instead there he was, standing at the corner of the street outside the half-closed blinds of the baker's shop, alone and on foot, leading his horse by the reins towards the empty Piazza del Collegio Romano, the sun beating down on his curved back and the horse's tail swishing back and forth rhythmically to the clop-clop-clop of its hooves. All around lay that silent city, patrolled by paratroopers in dome-shaped helmets, who roamed the streets in noisy motorcycle side-cars, taking pot-shots at windows for the hell of seeing the blinds ripped to shreds by the bullets . . .

Dusk was falling as we ran from doorway to doorway: the streets were wide open now, silent and deserted, so that anyone could cross the city freely from one end to the other. One passer-by, then another – they looked so shrunken and vulnerable; and there was this feeling of worthlessness in the air, as though they sensed that they were completely at the mercy of events now, unable to offer a single word or gesture in their own defence.

It must have been a day later, maybe two – it's hard to put those events into any precise sequence – when, all excited, she came running up to me on the landing of the stairs: 'Your Uncle Gigino phoned. He wants to talk to you – says you've got to go round there right away.'

The moment I'd walked into that room, sat down by the desk and looked up at his intelligent face – fixed until now in an expression of permanent irony – I caught a flicker of astonishment cross his features, as though for the first time he were seeing me in a new and unexpected light. 'Who are they?' he seemed to be asking himself. 'What are we going to do with them?' He collected himself almost immediately though, dispelling at once any traces of unease. 'Right now', he said, 'things are in such a mess that it's impossible to see anything clearly. We can't tell yet what's going to happen, or what's the best course of action. And there's no point in making rash decisions . . . So, you see, you're not the only ones who are confused.'

His books and periodicals were everywhere – on shelves, piled high on his desk, and even on the floor. The dimly-lit room was filled with the good smell of printed paper mingled with cigarette smoke.

'Responsible men don't rush things', he was saying. 'You're intelligent – you must be able to see what I'm trying to say. In this day and age, the first duty of responsible men' – and he stressed that word – 'is to preserve themselves for the future, for when they'll be needed.'

11

It all felt a million miles from home: from the smell of mould rising up from the narrow courtyard, the sitting-room filled with the decrepit, cast-off furniture she accumulated each time a relative moved house, and the store of chestnuts she kept drying under the bed 'for all the difficult times ahead . . .'

In the mornings Blondie would come round and we'd open our books: second aorists, orthopterans, perissiodactyla, *Luigia Pallavicini came tumbling from her horse* . . . Those interminable summer afternoons! The sun filtering in through the dusty window-panes, and those tedious hours spent with our books, curling around the edges by now: *Cònticuère omnes* – caesura – *intèntique òra tenèbant* . . .

Afterwards we'd go and masturbate in the winter-linen cupboard – first him, then me. Pulling them out of our pants, we'd make them stiff, then measure them. He already had a man's one. After that he'd shut himself inside the cupboard, do it, and emerge looking resigned and gloomy, as though he'd just come face to face with some ineluctable fact of life. Then it was my turn. I could no longer contain myself. I stood amongst piles of blankets and mothballs – quick, quick now – all that confused, restless energy just waiting to burst out . . . I held it in my hand: a little green shoot which would quiver and poke up its head at the first hint of a fantasy, then stand there looking cheeky and defenceless . . .

When it was over, we'd muster up a smile in an attempt to re-establish the rituals of normality; but that expression of resignation remained on his face, as if he bore that man's organ of his with all its ineluctable pretensions like a burden, a doom . . . A little dazed and vague, we'd return to our books – back to *Àt tuba tèrribili/sonitù taratàntara dìxit:* onomatopoeic hexameter.

And that's what I had to get back to – the 'tomorrow', which, according to him, it was my duty to preserve myself for . . .

I'd been promised a world full of hope and adventure. I'd experienced that feeling of being part of some great welter of voices, warmth and human presences; and all I saw around me were deserted streets, with the few people about looking frightened and crushed. No words were exchanged between them: keeping themselves to themselves, they'd scuttled back nervously to the safety of their houses.

'We were wrong', he said, leaving his desk and going out on to

12

the terrace, 'we too were taken in.' How calm he looked with that intelligent face of his, as he stood there watering the roses, fingering the petals with delicate hands:

'It's like this', he said. 'You've just got to accept reality. Your way won't solve a thing.'

His heyday was over now, and he looked around the garden as though to emphasize quite how removed from it all he'd become. His voice had grown nonchalant again: 'You see', he said, 'I have my study and my books . . . I get up in the mornings and take care of my plants.'

But whatever it was that he perceived, I felt left out of it: me, Giannetto, Fabio – even my father – we were all excluded.

He saw me off at the door of his house in the usual way: a little joke and a five-lire coin pressed into my hand. I could see that he was already remote from our conversation, fretting about all the wasted time away from his books. But what did I have to look forward to? A journey back down those dark, silent streets, to a shabby doorway, then up a flight of dim stairs, and into the flat, where the two of them would be sitting in the back kitchen like a pair of bedraggled pigeons . . .

My footsteps crunched along the gravel, as a warm mist settled over the silent streets. 'Us', he'd said, and at that moment I'd been proud to be considered part of that 'us'; but now I realized there was an element of calculation behind his words: he, his professor-friends and all the literary and artistic people who frequented his house – they were part of that 'us'. But where was I supposed to fit in?

The street-lamps came on, each one illuminating a small patch of pavement with a pallid circle of light. In the distance, I saw a passer-by cross over swiftly to the other side of the street. So, this was where all those rousing words, the music and banners had got me, but now what? I had to turn around and go back home.

Back to what though? What was there to go back to if everything concerning my childhood now lay in ruins, completely wiped out? And the further away I moved from them and their passive acceptance of things, the more I felt any sense of belonging I might have once had being swept away, and in its place a dull rage beginning to form.

13

It was that German officer – the first person to treat me with real respect, as though I were a man – who brought out a self-respect in me which I had not known existed.

He was standing behind his desk with the stiff collar of his tunic unbuttoned, looking surprised and incredulous, but all the same doing his best to understand what we were saying. He didn't know what to think, though: it was all so unexpected, and he hadn't been left any instructions. However there was one thing he seemed quite sure about: in his opinion, with no government or army in command, Italy had simply ceased to exist. He tried to make us see that she'd become nothing more than an occupied territory, her people controlled by a foreign army – a mere pawn in the giant chessboard which Europe had now become.

We stood awkwardly in a row, in our summer suits, while from the open window we heard the raucous shouts of sergeants giving orders in the courtyard down below. What was the point of it? Who were we doing it for? he asked us in that harsh, yet clear, Italian of his, wanting to know what we thought we'd achieve by joining up. And it's only looking back on it that I can see quite clearly he, too – Captain Fritz or Karl Tannert of the German Wehrmacht – wanted to make us see that we should go home, pick up our satchels and finish our studies.

But Giulio Fasano, whom we'd nominated as spokesman, just stood there with his hands glued to his sides, his young, decent face looking tense and impatient, as he kept saying over and over again: 'We don't want to surrender! We don't care what our own people think – we just want to go and fight!'

How often have I asked myself what that officer could possibly have made of those twenty boys turning up out of the blue like that, with their request to go and fight, in the midst of that crushed, defeated nation?

He looked at us in perplexity and regret: as far as he could see, there was no other alternative, and it was here that his voice – as thought to ensure we were left with no illusions whatsoever – became thin and precise: 'So you want to become German soldiers?'

I think his eyes and hair were brown – was he an Austrian perhaps? Who knows? He certainly didn't have the military bearing you'd expect of a German Wehrmacht officer, his tunic worn carelessly, and without a belt, as though he were in civvies. And yet when he stepped down from behind desk, he buttoned up his jacket and his face grew serious: '*Bitte*,' he said, 'may I shake your hand?' He stood before each of us, clicking his heels and politely offering each one of us his hand in turn – explaining that under the circumstances – *Bitte* – it was the least he could do. Beside me, Fabio, the eldest of the two Grama brothers, puffed out his chest and stood almost on his tiptoes in an effort to appear taller and more grown-up.

And that's the image which remains of the boy I first met on the Colle Oppio in the midst of those troubled times. In those days, Giannetto and Blondie and I all used to meet in the deserted avenue of the park, and go and sit by the fountain. Then one day he showed up – this taciturn boy who almost never contributed anything to our discussions, but who every now and then would grab hold of your arm as if to say: look, I'm here too and I agree with what you're saying . . .

Who could have guessed that, beneath that quiet and mild exterior, something was gnawing away at him which ten years later would rear its head and bring him to such a tragic end!

In fact it was to find out more about that distant episode that one day I made a phone-call across the gulf of twenty-five years and went to see his brother, Enzo. He was still living there in the old family place – a house surrounded by shrubs in Via Principe Amedeo. It was raining the day I showed up: how surprised he was to see me after all that time! He held me by the shoulders as we stood at the front-door: 'Well, well, well, what a surprise! Can you believe it – here's Carlo after a quarter of a century!'

Then he led me into the sitting-room and we sat opposite each other on dark leather armchairs. He was hesitant at first when I began to prove him about the past:

'Well, what can I say . . . it's difficult to remember after all this time. You know how long it was before we were free of those memories – years and years it took . . . But for Fabio it grew into a kind of obsession: he became even more dark and withdrawn, and when he walked into a room, you'd sense this icy barrier, as though he were carrying a kind of impenetrable aura around with him . . .

'He'd spend hours in his room, brooding about the past and looking over those pictures – especially the ones with Lieutenant Mazzoni in them, D'you remember Lieutenant Mazzoni? That young officer from Zara who committed suicide? It was as though they held an evil fascination for him which he couldn't get rid of. He'd go and leaf through the old albums at the Luce Institute, and he even got a caretaker there to sell him some originals for his collection. Hours he'd spend, staring at that officer's face . . .'

Enzo's gestures were all coming back to me now: that mocking, light-hearted way of talking he had, which, at the time, I remember finding in such contrast to his brother's unwavering seriousness. Reluctantly he went on, pushing himself to react to my insistence:

'No, there's nothing more I can tell you – well, what d'you expect after all this time? After the tragedy my father wanted nothing more to do with those days, and he destroyed everything – photographs, newspapers, the lot.'

Then, as though he were really struggling with those memories, Enzo fell silent for a moment. He shook his head: 'You see my father couldn't take it – after a year he too passed away . . . a heart attack it was.' He went on: 'The poor man was tormented by remorse. Asked himself if he'd ever properly understood his son, whether he'd been too hard on him – on both of us really – when we first got back.'

And now I wondered how I was supposed to confess to him that the only reason I'd gone there in the first place and looked him up after all those years – forcing him to open those old wounds – was to have him confirm my suspicions. It was only by chance I ever got to hear about it at all: one afternoon I was leafing through the newspaper, when I came across one of those insignificant little news-fillers about him. Fabio Grama! About ten years had gone by since we'd first met and thrown ourselves into that adventure. For quite a while we'd barely been in touch, only seeing one another if we happened to met in the street on our way home:

'Ciao Carlo', he'd say.

'Ciao Fabio', I'd reply.

And then off he'd go in silence, down Via Buonarroti with his shoulders slightly bent.

16

'We tried to forget about it,' Enzo went on, 'in fact we only told our children a couple of years ago, when we thought they were old enough – my wife and I agreed on that. They already knew about an Uncle Fabio who'd died, but we never mentioned the circumstances – we didn't want to upset them, you see. In the event they took it quite well – but then what d'you expect . . . it all happened such a long time ago now . . .'

And so Fabio Grama, the taciturn boy I'd known in those far-off days when we were demobbed, had become nothing more than a distant 'Uncle Fabio who died a long time ago' to some present-day kids – part of the foggy, antediluvian past before their birth. And yet I still have an incredibly vivid picture of him in my mind, that afternoon in the Via Nazionale when we first set off after our meeting with Captain Tannert. The lorry had pulled up for a moment beside the pavement, and as though our voices were in some way connected with the speed of the truck, our singing, too, came to an abrupt halt. We were gripped by a kind of embarrassment at the sight of all those grey, silent people traipsing by in never-ending lines; who, once level with us, would step aside and leave this empty space around the truck. Then, out of that anonymous flux, an old woman with a veil over her face, holding a pince-nez, made a beeline for him, Fabio, and hanging on to his arm, she kept asking him in this petulant voice: 'Who are you lot, anyway – who are you?'

And all Fabio could do was sit there at the edge of the lorry, shrugging his shoulders, looking at us, and not knowing what to say as she kept tugging at his sleeve: 'Well, you see, we're . . .' And that's all that came out.

When we left she was still there – a slight figure in a grey dress, standing in the empty space the passers-by left around her, holding her pince-nez to her nose and looking at us questioningly as though she were still saying : 'Who are you lot anyway – who are you?'

I looked around at that suburban house with the English mahogany table and the polished cabinet. It was pouring outside, and the big hard leaves of the magnolia-tree were wet with rain. And there we were, all those years later, with cars and buses humming outside the window . . .

Enzo returned to the tragedy, and I noticed that his expression had changed. It had happened in the broom-cupboard, he told me. He was alone in the house, and when he heard the shot, he realized immediately what had happened. He ran over, but couldn't get in because the body had fallen against the door, blocking it. He kept pushing and pushing . . .

'You see, he was still alive. We took him off in the ambulance, but it was too late – I couldn't save him . . . He died on the journey before we made it to the hospital . . . I heard the death-rattle . . . I was holding his head . . . that black hole in the temple . . .'

Enzo fell silent, and I realized that he wasn't going to say anymore. Just then, his wife came in to ease the awkwardness of the situation:

'I am sorry,' she said, 'but you know what it's like over the phone – and all those questions you kept asking me! How many children did we have, how old they were . . . You know how it is, too, these days – you can't trust a soul. How was I to know you were an old friend of Enzo's, turning up like that after almost thirty years!'

The magnolia-tree I remembered though: it had been there in the days after the war, when every now and then I'd go and visit them – that and the hawthorn-bush beside the iron railings which ran the length of the garden. Even at the time you could sense something uneasy in the air: they were usually very friendly, but every time I arrived they'd greet me with a kind of embarrassment, as though they themselves felt uncomfortable in the severe atmosphere of that house – all those big, cold rooms full of gloomy furniture. Their father was a civil servant. Apart from that, you could also sense the mute reproach directed against those two.

When I got there, having puffed my way up Via Agostino De Pretis, they were all waiting for me outside the old cinema. Then Giannetto Lettari looked around and said: 'Right – that's the lot of us now.' We met up with the others in the German Captain's ante-room.

The moment the lorry pulled out on to Piazza del Viminale, we began singing. The notes sounded a little uncertain at first, as though we were intimidated by our own audacity, but as each individual voice returned mingled with those of the others, the singing grew increasingly confident and gay. People in the street

18

looked up in astonishment at the unlikely spectacle we made, but it was too late by then, we had disappeared.

And then we departed, leaving them behind – those crushed, defeated people who walked the streets with the setting sun beating down on their backs – to carry the miserable burden we left, alone with their shadows lengthening on the pavement. We had nothing more to do with it, we had chosen another road which we could not envisage leading beyond that day.

What a surprise when the lorry continued down the wide road, and into the outskirts of the city, where the street began to thin out and the empty spaces grew vaster by the minute: with a start we realized that our journey was not over yet, that there would be a tomorrow that we hadn't foreseen.

You could read it clearly on their faces: how tired and apprehensive they appeared to me. We'd made our grand show in that shaken, silent city, and in the fury of our singing we'd managed to give vent to some of the rage which had been building up in us over the last few days. Now we had abandoned the stage and it was just the beginning. This journey would go on, and there would be an aftermath to face: that evening we wouldn't be walking home through the dusk-filled streets along with all those other people, growing more disillusioned and defeated with each day that passed. No, we'd risen out of that flux, and looking about us at those empty streets where the wind blew freely through the alleyways, gathering up piles of leaves against the doors, we realized that we no longer had a public to play up to and pit ourselves against. All that remained was the falling night, the breeze which was growing chill, and my companions' faces, which I could now see for what they really were – child-like and frightened as my own.

It seemed an incredibly long journey. All that night long . . . forward, forward . . . down never-ending roads, until it acquired a mythical dimension; the voyage restored us to childhood, to the vague and fantastic world where anything was possible. History itself had stood still for a moment, and across that fracture we managed to escape.

We didn't come across a single person in those shadowy, dusk-filled streets: not cart, nor wayfarer, nor motor-car. We were the only ones around that night.

One of our lot leant out and tried to find out from the drivers in the cabin where we were going, but he got nothing precise out of them. And it was that uncertainty which heightened the feeling that we were heading for a non-existent destination, somewhere that wasn't to be found on the map – a new place and a new era where we'd all stick together and turn our backs on the world. Every now and then we'd stop, and the German lorry-driver would get down and look at a road sign with a torch: 'Ja, ja', and we'd be off again.

Giannetto lay down in the back of the lorry, his hands clasped behind his head, trying to work out where we were from the position of the stars. 'Look,' he said pointing to the sky, 'that's the Great Bear, and that's the Pole-Star – the little bright one down there. There's no doubt about it lads – they're taking us north!'

And in an instant our imaginations were fired: the world was a vast, mysterious place, and here we were, heading towards the great forests and long, bare, windswept beaches of the Atlantic – away from all this misery to a new and different life.

Perched on the edge of the lorry, I saw the dark shadow of the Cadet gazing out into the distance, indifferent to the cold. He said he recognized landmarks – this crossroads or hill, that clump of trees over there: 'I'm telling you, we're heading south,' he said. 'I know where we are: this is the road to Cassino.'

'That means we're going straight to the Front,' someone said. 'We'll be fighting right away!'

Down there lay the answer to everything, I thought to myself, imagining a long line of fire, with streaks of light darting beneath the clouds on the horizon. We were heading straight for that furnace.

Here they are, like chalk masks, my companions' faces engraved in my mind: the two Grama brothers, incredibly young-looking as they huddled close to one another for warmth; Blondie manically straightening the folds of his trousers and dusting down his jacket as it blew in the wind; beside him there was Lando Gabrielli looking tense and hard, while further on, Giulio Fasano – too wrapped up in his thoughts to protect himself from the cold air, just happy to be on a lorry heading for the war.

Those two, arm-in-arm, had been the first to present themselves at the door. They stood there nervously as the others began to trickle in in small groups, until a guard wearing army fatigues let them in. They carried on looking frightened and disoriented until they suddenly caught sight of us, and after a moment's hesitation, their faces lit up.

'I don't believe it – not you as well! What are you lot doing here?'

Laughing, we ran up and hugged them, while all around us, the same scene was being re-enacted with each new arrival. The cadet was keeping count: *Eight men went to mow/Went to mow a meadow/Eight-men-seven-men-six-men.* . . . He kept running from one group to another: slapping shoulders, pulling people aside – telling them God knows what – until a new lot would arrive, and without warning he'd be off again: *And, ten men-went to mow/Went to mow a meadow/Ten-men-nine-men-eight-men-seven-men* . . . on and on like that until he got to twenty.

Sitting at the far end of the lorry with his back against the side, Strazzani was saying: 'We've got to stick together, we'll tell them we've all got to stick together! We'll form a platoon all to ourselves – sew tri-coloured badges on our sleeves. . .' He was a dark, skinny boy with a long face and thick, steel-rimmed glasses. A tailor's apprentice, he said he'd been. Like a real know-all, he kept poking his nose into everybody's business, managing to sound pompous and petulant at the same time, while the university students who were sitting in the dark section of the lorry beneath the cabin, good-naturedly pulled his leg. But Lando Gabrielli was really laying into him in that sarcastic, cutting way of his:

'So, what makes you think you can sew anything you like on your uniform, then?' he was saying.

But Strazzani wasn't to be swayed – he had an answer to everything; besides, he'd thought about that one:

'That's okay – what we'll do is wear them inside our jackets, so no one'll be able to laugh at us. I'll sew them into the lining of our tunics, you won't be able to see a thing from the outside.'

'But what's the point?'

He looked at him in astonishment.

'Don't tell me you can't see it! This way they'll be able to recognize us when we're dead! All they have to do is open our jackets, take one look at the badge and they'll say: "Ah yes, this one was Italian!" '

And that is exactly how I too envisaged the end of that day:

21

our little band going on the offensive in the midst of a bare plain, and later on, soldiers stooping in the gloom as they removed the bodies: 'Oh look,' they'd say, 'here's another of them.'

The wind had picked up, making us shiver: it was impossible to keep warm in light suits and short-sleeved shirts. Goodness knows where we were, or how far we'd travelled: it all looked so new and different – a million miles away from everything we'd left behind us. Meanwhile, the lorry continued to race swiftly through the shadows of the dark hills, finally appearing to have found its way.

Chapter II

PERCHED up high on a limestone substratum, the village stood isolated in the middle of the countryside, squeezed in tight between great dank stone walls. Around sunset, we'd return from training with hot faces and sleeves rolled up, singing as we clattered noisily through the dusty streets. Then, breaking ranks outside the whitewashed school in the square, where a terrace opened out abruptly over dry fields, we'd sit with our mess-tins between our knees, eating our rations on a low wall at the top of a cliff, while the swallows darted through the ravine, maddened by their own speed.

Beaming, and waving his mess-tin like a censer, Corporal Michelizza came over to us with the same jovial air he'd greeted us that night when we first arrived on the lorry. 'Cheer up, lads', he said. 'War's a good laugh, but it's no bed of roses!'.

Then sitting on a rock, he gave us our first lesson, in between mouthfuls, on the art of love:

'What you do', he said, 'is stick a cushion over her face, then shove it up her until the cunt starts going plaff! plaff! plaff!'

He laughed, displaying a set of fine strong teeth, his eyes twinkling in that red and white face.

Just before dusk fell over the deserted courtyard, you'd sense this feeling of anticipation in the air, the sea glistening in the distance like a fine line on the horizon. That was when the 'Cremonesi' would sit around a cooking-pot filled with wine in their corner of the dormitory, and begin one of their interminable drinking sessions.

First, Sergeant Bonazzoli, a big, engaging grin on his face, would dip the cup into the liquid which gleamed brightly between the zinc sides of the pot, and letting it bubble sweetly for a moment, he'd display it to the assembled company, proposing the first toast in a kind of Gregorian falsetto.

'Your health!'

After that the others would each take a drink, and with a full cup, they'd repeat the formula with the same affected ceremoniousness only this time in a kind of low, suave chant.

'Your health.'

They drank without haste, lingering over each little sip, complimenting each other with a series of winks and grimaces.

After a while, their deep, sonorous voices – in such contrast to their usual stiff manner – would get freer and freer and fill the room, yet never mingling, each one remaining quite distinct.

Scattered about on straw mattresses, or on the wooden school benches which were piled up against the wall, we'd sit there watching them in silence, afraid of causing offence by interrupting their game.

Little by little, though, as the wine began to have its effect, the atmosphere would get less formal, more unpredictable, until finally hilarity prevailed over seriousness. The only exception was Carletto Ferrari, the eldest of the group, who continued to cast suspicious, sidelong glances through narrowed eyes over towards our corner of the room.

'We never dropped our machine-guns, you know! We never dropped them!' he muttered over in our direction, 'and for as long as you've still got them . . . okay, so there's a war on – Americans, British, armoured trucks, and what have you . . . but so long as you've still got your machine-guns . . . '

Then, his little face all screwed up in a grimace of rage, he got up, and stumbling over to where we were sitting, he planted himself in front of us provocatively.

Bonazzoli tried to pacify him with that soothing voice of his:

'Come on Carlo, give it a rest! For Christ's sake just let it go! Don't start acting the fool, now!'

'Because in Russia, you know,' he went on, not taking any notice of his friend, 'after a certain point they said, right – that's it, we're retreating: the Russians have broken through, and we're retreating. After all, he who runs away, lives to fight another day! But of course we had to stock up first, and so everyone heads straight for the storeroom and starts grabbing sacks of sugar and whole eighty-kilo-rounds of parmesan cheese. Fuck! And what do those bastards do next? They go home, that's what they do! They go home, just round the corner! And what about all the kilometres we'd covered by train and lorry, and that last bit on foot? What about all that, or have you forgotten about it? You,' he shouted, nodding his head and glaring at each one in turn, 'you – Carletto, Giano, Dumanesk, and Balsi and Bernabò and

Tulas: rucksack full of bombs, rucksack full of tins, rucksack full of cognac you had – we'll stick to our guns, you said, we're off!'

He paced up and down the room, swinging his calves which poked out from beneath a pair of plus-fours, and shaking his fez, which, perched on the back of his head, looked as though it might tumble off with each step he took. Every now and then he'd go up to the pot to fill up his mug, and pulling a face as he drank, he'd come back over to our side, those inquisitor's eyes of his ready to pick up the faintest hint of mockery on our faces.

'Because so long as you've got your machine-gun,' he went on, 'you can forget about all this yessir-nossir crap, you've got your machine-gun, do you understand? And Bonazzoli after you with the ammunition, and them following him. They say we've got to go home – right then, we'll go home! Are we in a tight corner? Time to retreat? Time to march? Well, we'll march till we drop. Hungry? Not to worry, we've got rucksacks full of tins, and when it gets dark and cold, there's plenty of cognac. Then word gets out – hey, the Russians are down there. Well who the fuck else d'you expect it to be – the station-master from Cremona waving his little red flag? Of course it's the Russians for Christ's sake! And if you can't go another way, you are forced to meet them face to face. While the other soldiers, not the Blackshirts, the first things they drop are the guns and hand-grenades – they're too heavy they say. And so it's all over – you're free! You won't see your hut again! When out of the forest comes this peasant – a simple peasant, d'you hear – with a stick, and tac! you're bumped off by a peasant!'

You weren't allowed to get distracted either: the moment he caught you fidgeting he'd grab you by the collar and glare at you with eyes that were beginning to mist over a little; dribbling a little and muttering curses and threats which seemed to consist primarily of that cunt! *fidec!* or you've really had it now!

The prime target for these sudden outbursts seemed to be Lando Gabrielli. Although he'd muster up this superior smile, trying to appear above it all, he stood there looking lumpish and embarrassed, until Carletto decided it was time to let of his prey.

Meanwhile, the officers were living it up in the tavern opposite the school in the square. From the open window, we could hear the shouting and singing being carried along the steep, narrow streets of that village which smelt of dankness and stables.

25

Lieutenant Matteo's stentorian voice rose up above all the others: 'It's the dog house for Platoon-Leader Sacco!' we heard him shout. 'A bucket of tomato sauce over Lieutenant Sacco's head for daring to name that villain and traitor of a king!'

Angered by these unexpected interruptions, Carletto's eyes grew wicked, and turning towards their direction, he muttered: 'Don't you worry – colonels or not, captains or not, there'll be a bullet for them too!' Then returning to his audience, he went on:

'The eighth of September was the same bloody story: the war's over, they said! Everyone can go home! Over, my arse! And what about that lot with their Panzers! And Frascati that you could see blown up into the air like fireworks by the Allied bombs! And motorbike riders arriving with one set of instructions and leaving with another: no one's to move now, they'd decided. Meanwhile, back in the tents, everyone's trying to get a word in: should we obey Badoglio? or go home? Were you meant to fire at Germans? Then this bloke comes in saying that the CO's hopped it – the officers are back in civvies, and the Germans are ready to attack.'

Every now and then one of those great hefty companions of his would give a nod of agreement, as they sat there drinking silently, and with great seriousness, around the cooking-pot. From the open window, we could just make out the ruined castle in the distance, and beyond that, the outline of the setting sun getting bigger and more distinct as it dropped towards the sea.

Carletto went on: 'In the beginning we all agreed to be united and stick together, but then people began getting itchy feet. The Southerners started asking if they'd ever get home at this rate, then one day at roll-call: "Blackshirt Allegretti!" Silence. "Blackshirt . . ." There weren't anymore any blackshirts or greenshirts! During the night they'd packed their rucksacks, taken off their badges and done a bunk!'

I have a clear memory of Giulio Fasano sitting perched on a pile of school benches watching Ferrari's antics with a taut, attentive face – mesmerized by that performance. In just a few days he'd changed from the neat, well-bred boy he'd been into a scruffy rag-bag of a soldier in an outsize grey uniform. By contrast, the Cadet, a veteran before his time if there ever was one, never missed out on the opportunity to leap to his feet with the agility of an athlete and strut around in his uniform, which he'd done his utmost to make as elegant and dashing as possible.

Every now and then Sergeant Bonazzoli would interrupt Carletto in mid-flow, addressing the Cadet from where he was sitting:

'Hey rascal, keep in line!'

Ferrari went on: 'We were in the "lion's den!"'; D'you hear? The "lion's den!" – Mussolini's lions, that is! And then the same bloody story as Russia – the same! That lot had really had it: either the Jerries would get them, or the other lot would. And so they hopped it! I'm telling you, colonels or not, captains or not, there'll be a bullet for them too!'.

Darkness was falling, and the room was filled with shadows: one of those still evenings, with the smells of cooking and underwear and bodies stagnating in the air. Someone lit a candle on the dome of a helmet, and by the weak light of the flame, Carletto's shadow rose up towards the ceiling, gesticulating wildly like some grotesque puppet. And in that heavy dusk, illuminated by the pallid light of the candle, the faces of my companions grew familiar again, each regaining the individuality which our uniforms, and the exaggerated poses they were adopting, seemed to have eroded.

'And so, Carletto and Giano and Cotti-Zelati,' Ferrari went on, 'and you – Dumanesk, Suardi, Balsi and Bernabò and Tulas – can't you see that if you lay down your arms, that lot'll think we've given in. But so long as you've still got your guns, the war's not over, and the winners won't have won yet!'

We lay there on our straw mattresses, allowing ourselves to be lulled by the fantasies which his words aroused; while sitting on the short flight of steps outside the school, soldiers in subdued voices were singing the song about the long train heading for the frontier. I lay there with my back against the rucksack, feeling the leaves of corn inside the mattress rustling beneath me: the soldiers, our slang – all those basic things – had given a new order and meaning to the world, which now seemed to hold a place for me.

Then, huffing and grimacing, Carletto lurched towards his companions, and after a quick drink came back to our side.

'Right now,' he went on, 'the Führer thinks he's got another three hundred soldiers. I saw him, you know, at the Russian Front, surrounded by the biggest load of stuffed-shirt generals you've ever laid eyes on. He was just standing there, staring down at the ground without saying a word, while the others who were looking through binoculars, explained what was happening, telling him who was who, and about the operation on the front line. Well, I'm telling you, with that little tooth-brush under his nose, he looked like the biggest dick-head of the lot! At this very moment, he thinks that Carletto Ferrari's become a German – well that's fine by me, he can think what the hell he likes! But how could I ever become a Jerry, tell me that? They eat potatoes, I eat risotto . . . They say *arbeit zum macht zarbeit*, and I haven't a clue what they're on about. They get all worked up and start yelling – while I just say : fuck off!'

They carried on filling their tin mugs, but the cooking-pot was half empty now, and much of the formality had yielded to drunkenness. 'Your health?' proposed Domaneschi in that shy, reserved way of his. 'Your health!'

We had this feeling of being surrounded by unexplored, virgin territory. Where was this village? What was happening in the outside world?

Some mornings we'd see car-loads of officers and batmen with tommy-guns around their necks, setting off into the deserted countryside on reconnaissance missions. When they returned at dusk, you'd get the feeling that they were back from some great foray into deserted villages, where the old ways of communal life had vanished, where all forms of authority had yielded to those bristling carloads of weapons now free to roam the empty streets.

Orderlies with brilliantined hair would leap down from the cars, brandishing the spoils of their adventures: red and blue carabinieri's plumes, and those heavy, brass-handled daggers. They spoke of barracks attacked, of terrified brigadiers who'd been forced to hand over their plumes 'for the platoon-leader's boots'. And before our eyes rose images of windswept cities, of deserted neighbourhoods and villas all along that bare coastline, while Lieutenant Matteo, robust and exuberant, circulated amongst them, demonstrating his approval with a good deal of hearty back-slapping and corbash-waving.

Out on the plains, over where the road turned towards the sea, a

'Republic' had been set up. There were seven of them in all, who didn't belong to a battalion and who weren't taking orders from anyone. They dressed like German parachutists in long, loose khaki-coloured trousers and light cotton shirts. They refused to recognize any authority whatsoever:

'Rank means nothing anymore!' they proclaimed. 'It was abolished during the defeat. We're all equals now, so just piss off and leave us alone!'

In a meadow, over on the other side of the rank, green canal, they'd put up a tent with a Breda machine-gun on the bridge and a sign saying: 'No one to pass beyond this point!'

In the evening they'd sit around a big camp-fire roasting pieces of mutton which the peasants had slaughtered on the quiet, addressing each other with German titles as they served the food: Brembati who was descended from a noble family, they called *Graf* Brembó, while Corporal Cerroni had become *Oberfeldwebel*. Further down, where the plains gave way to steep volcanic rocks, there were great gaping gorges filled with abandoned weapons and the dusty, windswept remains of deserted encampments.

Cerroni was saying: 'We still call it Fascism because it's a word we're used to, and it's what our comrades died for. But right now, it no longer has any bearing on what it meant in the past: Mussolini's gone, Italy's defeated, and the regime's crumbled. The others – all the traitors who laid down their arms – rejected it. But even for us, it doesn't mean anything precise or unequivocal anymore: we've each got our own personal idea as to what it stands for. And we all stayed on for different reasons, too: why did these twenty boys run away from home when all seemed lost? Who asked them to? What were they after?'

Looking down at the ground, he spoke quietly and unemphatically, choosing his words with care in an attempt to clarify his thoughts. He sat there poking the embers with a stick, his face illuminated by the glow of the flames.

'The nation? The fatherland?' he was saying. 'No! It is not that anymore, but only me, you and the *Graf* Brembó, that's all. Here we are, the only ones left, the only ones who say: we won't surrender! That's why you can't force anyone anymore: whoever wants to can come. What we've got to do is put up a table in the middle of every village square and start beating the drum. Those who are interested can pick up a gun from the pile and go off to the front. "This way now, the enemy's over there . . . ".'

He'd taken part in the Greek and the Russian campaign, and he had a few medals to prove it. He was also the eldest of the group – he must have been about twenty-three or twenty-four – but the respect he commanded from the others was due more to that seriousness of his, as if he carried some ineluctable burden of responsibility on his shoulders.

'Victory? Defeat?' he muttered, shaking his head. 'That's for the others – for the Germans and the Allies. We're out of all that. All we've got – or rather all we've been left with – is our own individual fate.'

Tall and stocky, *Graf* Brembó was going around the circle serving great hunks of omelette from an enormous frying-pan. All around us lay that warm, silent night, where not even the anguished mooing of a cow, or a dog barking in the distance, could rid us of the feeling that we were surrounded by an empty world. It was at moments such as those that I felt all the real events and circumstances of our adventure had dissolved, and I pictured myself back in the remote past of that ancient village we were there to defend: all three hundred of us soldiers would gather on the plain, and there would be one final battle to settle things for good . . .

'What you want is fair enough,' said Massimi, 'but whoever has betrayed us must pay for it.' He left long, lazy pauses between his words: 'I'm telling you, we're not having another July 25th', he said. 'A bunch of traitors from the majors upwards, they were. Backs against the wall, I say.'

He spoke in this grudging, world-weary way, as though he didn't feel obliged to explain his words, or as if you weren't worth the effort. He'd spend the whole day lying on an army-blanket in his bathing-suit, roasting in the sun, and when he was well-browned on one side, he'd turn languidly over onto the other, lying there in the heat like a cat, arms and legs stretched out in abandon. He always carried a big revolver stuffed into his trousers.

'This time we'll really wipe the slate clean', he went on in the drawling voice of his. 'If Mussolini had got rid of them at the time, back in '22, then we wouldn't be in this mess now. The first thing we've got to do is deal with the traitors of the *Gran Consiglio* of Fascism and those who fled on September 8th – then we'll see to the rest.'

Cerroni listened to him thoughtfully, without answering, while Barbati – who even in that alien uniform had lost none of his native Neopolitan elegance – nodded his head and spurred him on: 'And that bastard dwarf of a king in Piazza del Quirinale – if you can call him a king, that is! String him up from the balcony with a lead weight on his feet, and pull the cord!'

They kept themselves to themselves, all day long there in the shadow of a reed hut, only venturing out at dusk, as the torn flag they'd mounted on a pole fluttered in the sea-breeze. And the harder it blew, the wider and more frayed became the hole they had cut where the king's crest had been. Pointing to it, they'd say: 'That is our one flag, a banner, with a bloody great hole in it that you can see the sky through!'

We had no idea what was happening in the outside world – in Rome, or at the Front, or what the Germans were getting up to. And frankly we didn't care: it was as though we were living outside of the times, in a parenthesis between two eras where, deprived of any yardstick by which to measure reality, we could give free reigns to our imaginations, envisaging the future in any way we pleased.

That was why we were so stunned when we heard him on the radio again for the first time: could it really be Him? Word had got around that he'd been liberated and that he was going to make a speech that evening. We stared at one another, disconcerted at the sudden realization that we'd forgotten all about him. The Duce? It rang like a false note, out of key.

'Yes, him', someone said.

We tried to picture him, but what was left in our surroundings that could possibly conjure up the era he belonged to?

'So he's alive! Where?'

'In Germany.'

At the crossroads tavern, filled with dust and the long rays of the setting sun, no one seemed to be able to tune the wireless which was perched on a shelf behind the bar, emitting a great deal of noise. As the landlady stood there, one elbow resting on the marble counter, a rag in her other hand which she used to wipe the marks left by glasses, his voice finally broke through all that din and interference, reaching us from a long way off. We didn't recognize it at first. Could it be his, that remote, weary voice? It was impossible to visualize him in a foreign land, to picture him against such confused background, so different from where we'd first known him. There were soldiers standing up against the old wooden bar, immobile. In order to gauge their reactions, I looked at Massimi and Cerroni, who were sitting in a corner by one of those iron tables, listening intently. I realized then that the more he spoke, the more gloomy and restless they began to look. The same old words – remote as the voice itself – no longer had any effect on us; indeed all they did was to show how hard he was trying to get into the swing of things which had now been completely overtaken by events.

I remember that knot of shabbily-dressed soldiers, sitting hunched and absorbed around the dirty tables, staring down at the cement floor – covered in spit and cigarette-ends – while weak rays of sunshine filtered in jaggedly through the dusty window-panes. As we sat there in silence with our half-filled glasses on the tables, there was no shouting, no heated exchanges: instead we realized that he lay frozen at the point where his own story had been interrupted, and that his words now had no bearing on us whatsoever.

Looking through the dirty window-panes, I could just make out the deserted 'Republican' tent, standing alone in the midst of the stubble plains. The sun was already low on the horizon, casting long rays of light over the roof, while the torn flag, unmoved by the breeze, hung limply from its short wooden stake.

Cerroni, whose face has now become a mere shadow in the confusion of my memory, died a few weeks later in a run-of-the mill road accident. It happened on a bend in one of those twisty Abruzzi roads: a lorry overturned and he was trapped beneath it. I remember the convoy slowing down, while men were leaning out from the sides to see what was happening: 'What's wrong?' they kept asking, 'What's happened?'. Then someone down by the edge of the road called out his name: 'It's Cerroni.' Looking down at the lorry lying on the grassy bank, its wheels in the air, I couldn't believe that he could have been crushed beneath it. Further on, his strangely shrunken-looking body had been stretched out on the wet field.

Suddenly, how remote and unreal those September days appeared to me – days when history had not yet taken its course, and it looked as though something new might still emerge from the chaos of confused intentions and illusions which had first stirred us. And yet I couldn't rid myself of the feeling that something definite had died with him – something which was tied to the particular moment and now ceased to exist, as though all possibility of hope were bound to him, rather than to any concrete circumstances.

I also got news of Massimi, through a chance meeting with someone after the war at one of those parties people were always holding then, although I can't remember now at whose house it was. Only a few years had gone by, but it already seemed incredible that anyone could have actually known him, could speak of him as someone who had really existed. For I had relegated him, along with all the others, to an uncertain, mythical world which I felt unable to reconcile with the reality which was taking shape around us – a reality which seemed a million miles away from anything we could have possibly imagined at the time.

He was a young bloke, with a callow face, and one of those smiles which seems to be concealing something. He was talking about the Blackshirts, about 'Tupini' and all the old stories of horror and bloodshed, when at a certain point this name came out: Massimi.

'Massimi!' I exclaimed. 'What d'you mean – which Massimi?'

It was as though the curtain had been suddenly raised on a scene, which, unbeknown to me, remained intact across a gulf dividing the present from everything that happened all those thousands of years ago; and which was now exploding before my eyes with startling clarity.

It was at the kind of party where girls with sweaty armpits went around offering you sandwiches and glasses of wine – the sort of house where the walls are covered in faded wallpaper. An uneasy-looking bloke with trapped, shining eyes, he kept himself a little apart, and yet the moment I gave him the green light, then whoosh! out it all came, all those memories which were too much for us to bear. We were always on the lookout for an opportunity to glamorize the past, to raise it above the dreary reality we'd slipped back into, mainly in a bid to keep the rude awakening – perhaps forever – at bay.

He said he'd met Massimi in his home-town, Ancona, where he'd returned to get married.

33

'Married?'

'Yes, married – to Barbara of course!'

Now I remembered. His pistol, Barbara! That big revolver he always carried around with him, it was called Barbara. He must have named it after his girlfriend.

'He married her . . . '

Just imagine getting married in those days, I thought to myself, picturing the kind of Fascist wedding they must have had: a handful of his comrades forming an archway with their daggers outside the church, and all around this feeling of emptiness . . .

In a gravelly voice, the gramophone was playing *Blacky and Johnny are going a-walking*, while all around, couples were dancing beneath the yellow glass lamps. He said that Massimi had told him he'd returned, 'because the first thing you do is put your own house in order, and whoever must pay, will pay.'

'Apparently,' he went on, 'one day someone told him that the Fascist commissar was up to some funny business – nothing much, just pocketing the odd thing here and there, and taking petrol for his own use. And so what does Massimi do but go straight up to the bloke's office at HQ and in that drawling voice of his, asks whether it's true. "Come on Massimi", the bloke starts saying, "what the hell's got into you, now?"

'Apparently, he then pulled out Barbara, the big 11.2 revolver he'd picked up during the armistice from a pile of abandoned weapons – mainly '91's rifles and old leather cartridge-cases – and there and then, at his desk, he shot him.'

He told me all this in a very casual voice, at the same time throwing me sly, self-satisfied looks out of the corner of his eye, as if to say: hang on, there's more to come – I'm saving the best bit for last!

He described how, when the Allies arrived, Massimi refused to leave the city – he wouldn't run away like all the others. Instead he waited for them at HQ, just him and Barbara (the one he married) with that flag with a hole in it hanging from the window, the last of the patrols fleeing down the empty streets, and all around this silence descending upon the boarded-up houses.

'Then he took his wife by the waist,' he went on, 'and clutching his tommy-gun, he walked out of the doorway. Both of them were killed on the steps.'

What a sight: the two bodies lying bleeding on the slope out-side the open door, that torn flag hanging from the balcony . . .

Could it be true? Could it have really happened like that?

There was a fairy-tale quality to their story, which in itself was typical of the times – all the wicked villains and the heroes meeting bloody deaths.

It wouldn't take long to find out though. All you'd have to do is go to Ancona and make enquiries in certain places – goodness knows, there were enough people around who'd still remember. You'd root them out – old men now, with stomach ulcers, with prostate trouble – yet ready to spring to life at the drop of a hat, to pull out all the old stories, all the old grudges.

Chapter III

WE were meant to be going to the Front, but instead we headed north. And there was no one there at the quayside to wave us off, no one to say *Goodbye, my love, goodbye*, as there had been for my father in the First World War, and for everyone else until then, including the Cremonesi when they left for the Russian front. All the same, they were jumping up and down and winking for joy as they stood there, loading their kitbags on to the wire racks shouting: 'Hey you lot! Kiss this dump goodbye – we're going back to Italy!'

And if any of us dared say: fuck you! the way they did, then they'd get furious and reprimand us, because up there in 'Italy' you weren't allowed to use that kind of language: in Italy people knew what was what, and their opinion seemed to matter.

She sat on a wooden bench in the dimly-lit compartment, watching us with tired, incredulous eyes. I remember her thin face, her greying hair, and the way she kept mechanically gathering up the faded hem of her coat and pressing it to her lap.

'I came here like a thief', she was saying. 'How could I tell anyone I was going to say goodbye to my son? . . . And this pain I carry around with me . . .'

Then her eyes suddenly flared with rage: 'You boys don't know what it's like!' she shouted, 'It's all right for you – you can all stick together and no one'll dare say a word to you! We're the ones who've got to live with those cowards!'

However that brief flash of anger was short-lived, and soon she sat there dejectedly, shaking her head. Staring at her, Fabio Grama said:

'Don't worry about a thing, Signora, let them get on with it. Colonel Ussari, the battalion commander, says that in a month's time we'll be back to face the enemy. Then we'll deal with them, you can be sure . . .'

And yet beneath her show of resignation I could sense a dull rage gnawing away at her, full of reproach directed against me. All her cunning and perseverance hadn't been enough to keep me home, and now what use was my pity to her? All she could

36

do was return to that empty house, where the war had robbed her of the last of her three sons. 'And what about that poor man, your father, who is waiting for me?' she was saying, 'How can I go back to him without you?'

I looked at Giulio Fasano's mother, a tall, distinguished-looking woman dressed in black, who was sitting opposite him and holding his hand between hers as she gazed out of the window. When she got up to leave, she said to him:

'It won't help one bit, you know, but if it's what you've decided . . .'

Then without warning, the train lurched forwards into the darkness, and began coasting along the tracks, slowing down to thread its way between some freight carriages. My mother was still there:

'You've got to get off now,' I said to her, 'the station's over in that direction where you can see the lights.'

I watched her disappear along the rubble of the tracks with that slightly bow-legged walk of hers, stumbling every now and then between the carriages as though she were about to fall, then picking herself up and carrying on.

For three days and three nights we travelled, chugging along that autumn-filled landscape. And there were no other trains in sight, apart from the odd army-green locomotive with Gothic lettering down the sides – no passengers waiting beneath the iron canopies of the stations we slowly passed through. Sometimes, on a deserted platform, we'd see a lone station-master standing there, jerkily waving us on with his flag.

Then at one point Sergeant Acciaroli, holding a steaming mess-tin in his hand, came over to sit with us. 'A soldier's life is a good life', he announced. 'Look, you've got it made: meals all taken care of, no worries, and you get to see the world!'

He sat there on the bench with that row of multi-coloured ribbons gleaming on his chest, sipping his coffee, blowing at the edge of the cup, and observing us with this ironical, paternal look in his little blue eyes.

'Just remember,' he said, 'the trick's in dodging the first one. That one's not addressed to anyone – it'll do for troops and veterans alike. All the others'll have name-tags on 'em!'

I sat there beside the window, letting myself be rocked by the movement of the train, watching fields and suburbs and villages slowly filing past. So this was my country: Italy, that scalloped boot, which was marked in green on school maps. And I was surprised to realize that Italy, that word with all its vague, emotional connotations, had no bearing whatsoever on what was unfolding before my eyes.

In their section at the far end of the compartment, the Cremonesi were singing: *Do you remember the month of April, and that long train . . .* as dusk fell, and the setting sun painted the carriage ceiling orange. Lying on tarpaulin sheets suspended from the luggage racks, we'd spend hours watching the rays change according to the direction of the train, following the swift, dark shadows cast by the ironwork along the tracks. It was then that everything around you – your companions' faces, a mess-tin, a kit-bag – seemed to acquire a mysterious warmth or substance, becoming more intimate, more yours.

The further we travelled, the more deserted the roads began to appear, and a kind of sadness began to set in. Where were the peasants? Who'd divided the fields into the various crops – the people on those roads, flanked by dusty hedges, which wound their way through the suburbs? It was as though they'd retreated into the shelter of their own domestic walls, afraid to venture out into the bright light of the fields, where they'd be too vulnerable, too exposed.

The countryside had become flatter now, and the morning air was filled with fine layers of mist. With a single movement of our hands we wiped the condensation of the windows and looked out at rows of tall, graceful poplar-trees, at red-roofed villages dotted about on the plains.

Throwing questioning glances at one another, the Cremonesi were peering out more frequently now at those empty stations with their bare awnings. Then one morning we awoke to find ourselves on a disused railway track at the edge of a country village. And there, on the road, the lorries stood waiting.

We put on our coats and slipped woollen balaclavas over our heads. Each time we spotted a new village, there would always be someone on the look-out to get us going. 'C'mon lads, a village! Let's sing!' And we'd be off again: *Battaglioni del Duce, battaglioni . . .*

Sometimes we'd see a woman watching us with incredulous

eyes from the doorway of a house, or men's faces turning around uncertainly from behind the dirty plate-glass of some miserable café. Exulting in the disturbance, we'd sing all the louder.

Night had fallen; we realized we'd arrived as we crossed a bridge, and the convoy began to slow down. A long line of doors and windows unfolded before our eyes, and we found ourselves hemmed-in by buildings, watching the trapped glow of the headlamps travelling in swift beams across the walls, only to be interrupted by a rectangle of darkness and an increase in the roar of the lorries each time we reached a crossroads. We kept slowing down, and as we turned right into a narrow road we heard a plaintive: 'Who's there?' lose itself in the night.

The barracks hallway, illuminated by the faintest of lightbulbs hanging from a cord, was filled by the roar of engines, which, compressed into that restricted space, was now overflowing along the empty stairways. Our headlights cut through the darkness, and we peered out at what looked like boarded-up warehouses in the dark recesses of the courtyard. Later we'd try to resist the sudden sense of dismay which had overtaken us at the sight of those rooms – bare and echoing as an empty cathedral – and at the sound of our footsteps stumbling in the gloom. By the dim light of the candles, we saw shadows of unfamiliar objects: upturned wooden bunks, a disembowelled straw mattress, a table lying with its legs in the air. How cold and lonely we suddenly felt, exhausted by our long journey.

All around us, the dense, compact night was pressing hard against the windows, while beyond lay that unknown city – locked in an impenetrable shell which all our singing and travelling had not even managed to dent.

With their usual diligence and expertise, the Cremonesi were already getting stuck in, piling up weapons and equipment into the middle of the room. Like a colony of ants they moved, swiftly, shifting cots, sweeping and rummaging amongst piles of junk until they found what they were after. I was seeing them in a new light now – aware that all the determination and effort they put into what they did could not conceal the anguish in their gestures – a sort of desperate, surprising futility. Then, to shake us for a moment out of the despondency we'd fallen into, Enzo

Grama's voice rang out gaily and provocatively:

'For fuck's sake! And they call this Italy!'

By the time we woke up the next morning, word had already got around: 'Who . . . what . . . where?' people were asking, rubbing their sleep-filled eyes in an attempt to understand what was up.

'It's true – they've found the notices.'

It seemed impossible.

'Says who?'

'I saw it myself – one of the officer's batmen had one: ten thousand for the commander, it says, five for the officers, and a thousand each for one of us – dead or alive.'

We couldn't believe our ears: still in our knitted vests, the ties of our long-johns flapping around our ankles, we gathered around the sentinel. Apparently it was true: notices had been put up in certain places during the night. Now, sergeants were going around shouting orders for everyone – 'Clerks, orderlies, the lot of you' – to gather at once in the courtyard.

Beside himself with rage, Commander Ussari was standing on a pile of crates, his face purple, neck bulging.

'So those bastards thought they'd try it on, did they? This place is just one big nest of cowards and monarchist traitors! We'll show them though . . .' A great charge of pent-up rage and violence was vented in his words: 'I promise you, we'll wipe Piedmont off the map of Italy!' he bellowed. 'For each one of us, there'll be ten of them!'

We gnashed our teeth and nudged one another at the prospect: we'd put on a parade with all the soldiers and weapons out in full force – that'd show them who they were dealing with!

He sat there bombastically in the saddle, goatee beard quivering, his stiff arm hanging by his side. 'March in eights at wide intervals!' he shouted, 'and no singing! Keep in line!' The noise of our footsteps rang out ahead of us, while all around, mortars and machine-guns scattered grapeshot above our heads. 'I said no singing!'

Curious faces peered out at us from the pavement: 'Who are this lot?' they seemed to be asking one another. 'Where have they sprung from now?' People were stopping in the street, and coming out of shops and doorways to stare. Clutching the handles of our daggers, our ranks formed a tight, menacing barrier advancing towards them. And the front rows scattered, their expressions uncertain: what should they do, stay or leave? But Lieutenant Matteo was hot on their heels, charging along the walls with his heavies: whips and fists raised in the air, shouting and swearing as they hauled people out of bars and from behind shop counters: 'Salute the banner!' he thundered. 'Salute the heroes of M Battalion!'

Then here and there we began to see arms raised in salute, somewhat sparse, uncertain at first, but continually increasing – the people themselves looking a little surprised at the sight of their own arms suspended in mid-air like dead things.

And after that, when clubs and pick-axes were let loose in the street, we were given our heads: 'I don't want a single trace of the monarchist past of this town to remain!' he shouted. And so in an avalanche of glass, down came the frosted windows with their engraved Savoyard crests at the Three Kings Hotel in Corso Principe Umberto. along with all other memorial stones, insignias and plaques, including those at the post office and Café Royal.

'Fuck the House of Savoy!' yelled Commander Ussari in a rage. 'Nothing but a line of bastard kings and jezebel queens! A nest of traitors, the whole damn lot of 'em, starting with Vittorio Emanuele II, the most illiterate, alcoholic runt of them all! Even Cavour was a pimp and a pederast – like all Frenchmen!'

He looked satisfied, triumphant, as we sat in the theatre that evening with our black fez and canes gleaming amongst the gilt mirrors and crystal chandeliers. And as the little orchestra struck up the *Giovinezza* song, the people seemed glued to their seats: *Now that the battle cry/Is ringing from the trenches . . .*

The next day, too, bumping into them in the street, they stepped down from the pavement to let us pass. Some even raised their arms in salute.

Vague rumours were coming in that some lorries had been attacked. When we went to the motorised units to see if it were true, we found drivers in leather jackets standing with one foot on the running-boards of the vehicles, looking arrogant and casual, yet a little nervous too. And when we asked how and

41

where it had happened, no one seemed prepared to give us a straight answer: no, he hadn't seen them, one of them said – apparently when they'd jumped out of the car to fight back, they'd just vanished, cowards that they were. They also told us that in another place they'd come down from the mountains to requisition supplies, and that they had picked up a few of our people there. It was unverifiable information though, synonymous with the kind of legends and fables which were circulating at the time – instantly forgotten as soon as things returned to normal.

Sometimes in the evening, towards the outskirts of the town, we'd hear a sudden explosion wailing in the distance. Stopping what we were doing for a moment, we'd stand there, looking uneasily at one another: 'Just one of our boys larking around', someone would say. Then we listened to the patrols traipsing around the barracks, and that voice calling out: 'Who's there? Stop, or I'll shoot!' When they opened the front door, we'd catch the echo of footsteps, and sometimes even the murmur of voices in the cavernous hallway.

You had the feeling that beyond the city, in that no man's land where the town petered out towards the rice-fields, there lurked vague danger – an unknown, threatening presence, physically embodied in the marshlands and in the mist which wreathed the reed-thicket. It was as though out there in the darkness plots and conspiracies were being hatched which you felt unable to pin down to any kind of concrete reality. All you could picture were these shadowy, dead men's faces moving furtively in the gloom; although, come morning, as we marched through the courtyard and out into the drill-ground opposite the barracks, those ghosts would have disappeared.

In our free time, we'd stroll beneath the low arcades of the main street, filled with the sound of voices and shuffling footsteps. All those wan, inscrutable, commonplace faces . . . could they be the ones? There wasn't a single person there who fitted the vague picture you carried around in your mind . . . although, hang on, what about that chap over there? Beneath his look you caught a flicker of something which chilled the blood . . . it must be him! And yet the minute you looked as though you were about to approach him, he became all timid and servile, as though apologizing for something. No – he was just a coward, no one to be afraid of . . . how could those people ever be capable of anything, when our presence alone was enough to keep them in line? Returning to the barracks in the evenings, we'd hear a solitary bugler sounding out the retreat, the long notes of his trumpet rising above the mist-veined square.

Then one day, somebody pronounced the name of that village, and it became a real place, with a real location. Crossing the plain towards the mountain, a lorry had been hit by a volley of bullets coming from the direction of some houses – there was no doubt about it – you could actually see the bullet holes down the side of the cabin.

'They certainly fired all right', one of them said.

'But how? Where did it happen?'

'At Borgosesia', he replied.

The name meant nothing to us: 'Borgosesia? . . . What's that?'

All the same, it did have a harsh, hostile ring to it: Borgosesia – there was something final and cutting about that name.

'Where is it?' we asked.

'Right below that line of mountains.'

And immediately in our minds rose an image of some border-town, flanked by mountains, in a distant, mythical place at the edge of the plain.

Night had fallen – a dense, heavy night, which lay between the narrow streets and over the jagged outline of the roofs, while in the distance, luminous points of light were dotted about the darker bulk of the mountains.

The companies were returning: I heard the shuffling of tired feet and the sound of officers calling the platoons out to parade in subdued voices, as the wind howled among the ranks:

'Second Company! . . . Where's the Second?'

I recognized my companions' voices: that must be Bonazzoli's squad, the other one Domaneschi's. Emerging from that darkness with coat-collars pulled up, little clouds of steam issuing from their mouths, I heard them talking with their usual imperturbable voices, their thick accents. Apparently nothing had happened at their end: just the odd peasant walking along a mountain road, leading who knows where, a cartload of hay, and a few women on bicycles: 'Halt! Papers!' and that was it.

43

Word had got around, though, that there'd been some clashes, deaths even.

'Deaths?'

'Yes, Lieutenant Matteo reported it – he's been wounded too, and his arm's in a sling.'

At each stop, we dumped our weapons on to the ground – quickly picking them up when it was time to leave – while the men carrying the metal supply-boxes prised their numb fingers off the handles and let them fall with a clatter. I heard Enzo Grama swear.

Then, out of the darkness, a voice suddenly called out 'Who's there?' – hushing all the moaners and leaving a long trail of silence in its wake. By the light of a match, we could just make out the barrels of their Breda 30's machine-gun, faces tense beneath their helmets. Wrapped in greatcoats, they were sitting in the shelter of some crates, drumming their feet on the ground. As we went past, we heard muffled voices rising up in the thick air; and I saw Fabio Grama's finger tighten around the trigger of his machine-gun as he pressed the butt against his shoulder.

Meanwhile, down below in the empty, dusk-filled square, the doors of the town hall were open; and from the hallway a rectangle of light, filled with gigantic shadows, was cast on to the pavement. There beneath the vaulted roof, the sound of shivery, echoing footsteps and voices grown suddenly harsh, unnerved us, while in the brightly-lit hallway, we saw officers with shrunken faces gesticulating nervously against the white walls.

'Double the number of sentries!' they ordered. 'And bring out the patrols!'

It felt good sitting on the floor, with the radiators switched on, our backs against the walls. Crouched beneath the window-ledge me and the Paduan were dipping the ends of our daggers into a tin and fishing out glutinous chunks of meat. He'd already given me my share of the loot: pulling out the dead man's wallet, he'd counted out forty-five lire into my hand. It was amazing how quickly he'd nabbed it: the minute he got there and saw the body lying in the middle of the alleyway, he looked around for a moment, and quick as a flash, he hurled himself on top of it. Then grabbing hold of it by the shoulder, he turned it over, deftly slipping his other hand into the jacket pocket.

Our cheeks glowed with the heat and a sense of well-being, after having been at the windy checkpoint on the bridge for all that time. Now we could take off our coats, unfasten our belts, and sit there smoking in peace. Enzo Grama had removed his boots and was sitting on an army blanket, massaging his feet with a blissful expression on his face. Every now and then we heard the boom of gunfire echoing in the distance . . .

'Who're they firing at?' someone asked, as after a moment's hush the buzz of voices picked up once more. Just then, another squad came in with their coat-collars pulled up over their necks.

'What's up?'

'They got Landi up in town . . . inside a doorway it was – two shots in the head . . .'

'And Tartaglio, over the other side of the river in that village on the hill – Sergeant Acciaroli was with him.'

'Who the hell was it? Who did it? Have they got them yet?'

It was dusk: I'd been sent out on fatigues or something, and I'd walked the entire length of the city. They'd picked up the two bodies in that faint light, laying them out in the back of the lorry with the wind flapping through their jackets. Others, too, had come to look at them, watching silently as they hung over the side of the lorry.

When Lando Gabrielli sharply pulled back the sheet of tarpaulin which covered them, it was with a sense of shock that I realized they didn't move or flicker their eyelids. Tartaglio lay there like a broken puppet in his stained uniform, curly hair encrusted, his eyes still open, yet dulled like those of a dead animal. Resting against the dusty boards, Landi's face – a bluish, bruised-looking colour – had swollen up to an incredible size, as though made of rubber.

'That's what happens if you get hit on the back of the head', someone whispered.

Shadows flitted about the dim square, and a heavy sky hung over the rooftops: it was that sky which was so oppressive, making you feel there was no possibility of escape . . .

Clumsy in their overcoats and heavy boots, they came at dusk to look at the dead – the foggy air muffling all sound as they stood there for a moment, hanging on to the mudguards, dim outlines framed against the grey sky.

'We'll make them pay for it!' said Lando Gabrielli through clenched teeth. 'We'll avenge their deaths!' He jumped down from the lorry and headed back towards the town hall.

I walked away, looking down at the ground, watching the toes of my boots – first one, then the other – advancing along the pavement; while out of the corner of my eye I followed that never-ending line of doors, bolted up from one end of the street to the other.

I repeated their names over to myself – Landi, Tartaglio – trying in vain to pull them out of the murky void they'd suddenly fallen into.

There, at the checkpoint on the bridge, I remembered that there'd been that initial moment of shock: 'But how? We didn't hear a thing! How did it happen? Who did it?'

Our surroundings looked exactly the same as before: the empty stone bridge, the bare trees covering the far side of the hill, that gently winding road, and now suddenly this absurd sense of loss . . .

I searched back through my memory for traces of them: Landi was that Florentine who'd sung sentimental songs in a tenor's voice, the evening when we first set off in the carriage from the platform at Rome: *Our Lady, when the cannon begins to roar . . .* and yet it was impossible to connect him with that messy, swollen-headed corpse lying in the back of the lorry. I remembered him well: I'd never liked him much – always going on about his ribbons and red stars, the Russian campaign, and giving himself all the airs and graces of a veteran. By contrast, I had an incredibly vivid picture of Tartaglio standing outside our checkpoint, where he and Sergeant Acciaroli had stopped for a moment to talk to us. At one point, someone cracked a joke and I remember him laughing – a really full, hearty laugh: his whole face lit up as he opened his mouth, threw back his head, that lock of hair falling over his forehead. Then he and the sergeant crossed the bridge, disappearing past the bend in the road which led through the trees and up into the hills.

Coming up to a crossroads, I heard my loud footsteps echoing ahead of me in the deserted street. I was waiting for something – movement, voices – but instead all I saw was a damp alleyway, flanked by stone walls, winding its way around a corner, and up into the bulk of the village beyond. Suddenly, I grew frightened at the sound of my own footsteps . . .

I couldn't muster up any feelings for them: who were they to me? What did those events – their deaths – really mean to me? The uniforms and weapons we shared – was that what it boiled down to? I repeated to myself: they've killed a comrade, a comrade is a brother, we fight side by side, but those words aroused nothing in me – no pity, no anger. There was something deeper, more important than pity or anger but I couldn't pin it down – just this obscure sense of unease. The image of Tartaglio laughing kept coming back to me: yes that laugh – that was the laugh of a living man all right! The graceful ease of his movements, the heart beating beneath the skin . . .

What relation did that image bear to the twisted-up corpse lying on the back of the truck? We'll avenge their deaths, Lando Gabrielli had said, and for a moment it had seemed that his words had the power to drive away my bewilderment. Yes – we'd avenge their deaths, get even, make them pay for it . . . But even that was no use now: what bearing did it have on what had happened, I asked myself? What could it change? Like the roads, the sky, and everything else around us, it was on this side – it could never reach them. I pictured them again in their crumpled uniforms: twilight, and the two death-stiffened bodies lying on the dusty boards of the lorry; cold, alien objects, no longer comrades to be vindicated, no longer veterans of the Russian campaign – boys, friends, arrogant, simpatico . . . They were nothing now – nothing. Only corpses.

I was sidling cautiously past the walls with my gun at my shoulder. Out of the corner of my eye, I watched the long line of bolted-up doors, the dark rectangles of shuttered windows unfolding along the street. As I approached a deserted square, the echo of my footsteps, magnified by that emptiness all around me, rebounded off the walls and was carried back to me.

An iron fountain gurgled monotonously in the silence. I hesitated before continuing. Where were the inhabitants of that city – the people in the streets and shops? What were they doing? Where were they hiding? Were there really people to be found behind those walls and shutters? What was going on?

The night lay fixed outside the foggy window-panes – a dense,

47

sightless night which made the empty square below us appear enormous in the darkness. The room was heavy with the harsh smell of bodies and their heat. Putting together all the tables in the room, the Cremonesi had built themselves a makeshift alcove, where they sat in a circle like a kind of silent tribunal. At intervals, cries from down below rose up, then suddenly vanished:

'Halt! Who's there?'

'Patrol.'

'Patrol Halt! Password!'

Then for a second we'd hear footsteps disappearing along the pavement.

Sergeant Acciaroli was back, looking very pale, with his wound all bandaged up. He stood beneath the yellow lamp, nervously fingering the dressing which covered his swollen upper lip.

'What about the bullet, boss?' we asked him.

'I never found it.'

He spoke slowly, stumbling over his words. With difficulty, he unstuck his lips, showing us the wound in his mouth: in place of his incisors, there was a clotted black mass.

'That was one without a name-tag, eh Sarge?' said Enzo Grama, winking at him. He tried to smile, but all he could muster was a grimace, which the pain soon put an end to.

'I suppose you must've swallowed it then', someone commented ponderously . . .

By now he had regained that usual look of his, that calm, confident veteran's air. Whatever out-of-the-ordinary event had taken place up there in the alley was in the past now – already part of his memory, tied forever to that unknown place outside the city. He was back among his comrades, surrounded by their voices and the warmth of their presence – all the old, familiar things.

But I couldn't get that image of him out of my head: clear as daylight, I'd met him running down from the direction of the gunfire, just a few minutes after he and Tartaglio had disappeared over the bridge. He was bleeding from the mouth, and his hands were stained, but he couldn't wash them. How incredibly vulnerable he suddenly looked, standing there clutching his tommy-gun as though he were glued to it, staring out at the direction he'd just come running from.

48

'He didn't want to fall, that bastard,' he gasped, 'he didn't want to fall!'

Leaning against the wall, he tried to re-live what had happened a few moments before, in an effort to come to terms with it, but something had got him inside – something new and unforeseen which chilled him to the very marrow.

'I found that son of a bitch leaning over Tartaglio's body,' he went on, 'spitting and swearing at him with his pistol still in his hand, shouting bastard! traitor!'

His speech was broken, as he stood there spitting out clots of blood. He seemed to be finding it difficult to drag himself back into reality, and it seemed as though everything which until then had defined him as an individual had been crushed by some gigantic force which gripped him from within, leaving its mark on those sightless eyes, in the uncontrollable shaking of his entire body. Standing there, clutching his gun, he was trying to re-live what had happened in those terrible moments, yet at the same time trying not to reach the end, as though in this way he might somehow alter the outcome of those events.

'I only just managed to aim in time,' he said.

I remember Tartaglio's wide-open eyes, and how alive they looked despite their fixed expression. I almost felt like shaking him by the arm and saying: 'Come on, Tartaglio, get a grip!' But the way his limbs were flung out and his body hugged to the ground was so unlike that of a living man, that it was enough to dispel any illusions.

The other bloke, dressed in mountaineering clothes, was lying beside him on his back, in the same position the Padovano had left him in when he'd turned him over to rob him. What most stuck in my mind though was that first moment, when I'd gone running down the damp alleyways, gun in my hand, and I'd stumbled across them lying in front of me in those weird positions. What a feeling of unutterable alienness those two bodies exuded, stretched out in that little alleyway between those miserable, unplastered houses. It was, I thought, as though some spiteful hand had just picked them up and dumped them there in front of me in that unlikely place.

'A fiend,' the sergeant was saying, 'he was a real fiend!' as though the word somehow both agitated and liberated him.

'When I turned the corner,' he went on, 'I saw him there,

leaning over Tartaglio and swearing at him; I took him by surprise, but he still had time to level his pistol . . . I kept on mechanically firing shot after shot at him, because I couldn't get the ammo in . . . I was filling him up with bullets, but he carried on staring at me with hatred – that really vicious hatred in his eyes . . .'

Only a few moments had gone by, and yet in spite of the sergeant's efforts, it already felt as though those events belonged to some incredibly remote and unattainable past.

I remember the Paduan bending down straddled over the corpse, and going vlack! vlack! vlack! from one cheek to the other, with Tartaglio's helmet which he was holding by the chinstrap. He had picked it up off the ground, and he shook it violently, shouting: 'Son of a bitch! You son of a bitch!' The corpse's head was swinging from side to side, and the helmet was smeared with blood, but it was only when that vlack! vlack! vlack! started to really grate on the sergeant's nerves, that he said to him:

'That's enough now, pack it in!'

In the distance, a solitary burst of gunfire broke through the silence: trr! trr! trr! then nothing. I sat there waiting – no, that was all. Crossing the length of the city, it had disappeared back into the night, as the silence fell back into its place. It was a Breda all right – there was no mistaking that muffled sound, that slow, staccato rhythm. It was coming from some place which had vanished into darkness now. Where were they? Towards the mountains, or on the Sesia where the water gurgled and coursed among the stones? Or perhaps over there, where the village petered out towards the plains? Down there the darkness was vaster, more insidious, shot through with mist which lay in vaguely familiar shapes . . . Who were they firing at? I could imagine them at the corner of some house, huddled inside their greatcoats, holding on tight to their weapons, eyes rigid in the darkness. Perhaps Blondie was there – Blondie who was scared of the dark . . .

A rustling sound, a flash of light, shadows – 'Come on, shoot! For Christ's sake shoot!' The flash eliminators would be lit, there'd be a sudden burst of gunfire, then silence again. And they'd be sitting there counting the minutes till dawn, ears pricked, drumming their feet, lighting cigarettes in the hollow of their hands. Tonight's for you, my friend, all for you . . .

Set a little apart from the others, the lorry with the dead was out there in the corner of the square. I was astounded by the fact that we had left them on their own, in the back of the truck, until I realized that they no longer needed to be watched over – or anything else for that matter. After all, what could happen to them now? There they'd be, lying there in the cold and dark, not feeling a thing, no fear – nothing. No one gave a damn about them anymore; they meant nothing to anybody.

The other bloke, the mountaineer, was still lying in the alleyway outside the worn doorstep, just as we'd left him: turned over, all crumpled up . . . Coming away, I took one last look at him, and it was then that I noticed something strange: his clothes suddenly looked too big for him, as though death had unexpectedly withered the body inside.

Right now, his boots were sitting by my bedside – a good pair of mountaineering boots with double-rivetted soles. I hadn't tried them on yet. I only just got a glimpse of his face as I leant over him to get them off, but it was enough to see that the skin of his face had gone a yellowish colour, acquiring the texture of parchment. His feet were still warm and the boots slid easily off his woollen socks. I'm sure when he put them on that morning, he never once thought that someone else would be taking them off for him – that they'd have ended up right there by my bedside. What had he done in that interval? Where had he been? What had he said? Who was he? And how had he ended up there?

It was Lando Gabrielli who took them off, one by one, to be interrogated. Tripping over our legs, the prisoner in front, they'd come out of the big room across the hallway. 'Come on, move it! Let us through!' and they'd disappear into another room at the far end, filled with a great coming and going of officers and their orderlies. Every time someone opened the door, we'd catch a glimpse of their heated faces amid the cigarette smoke: there were the Commander's heavy features while Lieutenant Biondi was sitting next to him behind a table.

The prisoners would come into the hallway looking quite normal, apart from the dazed expression on their faces as they stood gazing uncertainly around the room. If I really try hard, I think I can actually remember one of them getting to the door, and standing there disoriented, looking around as if he couldn't quite work out where he was or what was happening to him.

About thirty he must have been, a skinny bloke with hunched-up shoulders. I remember he even managed to muster up this smile, as though to apologize for all the trouble he was causing us – until Lando Gabrielli shoved him from behind, saying: 'C'mon, move it.'

Someone from the political squad was standing by the door, keeping any onlookers at bay.

'Is it them? . . . Where'd they find them?' someone asked.

'Clear off! No one's to enter – Commander's orders.'

They even started getting all hoity-toity and arrogant with us, as if that duty conferred some kind of special authority upon them.

Alessandrini, and the other quartermaster sergeant from Friuli, were the ones to deal the blows. The minute the prisoner crossed the threshold, they'd throw themselves on top of him, and dragging him inside, they'd begin striking him with open palms and fists. Still hitting him, they'd push him into the chair by the desk; holding on to his collar, Alessandrini would start punching him right between the neck and shoulder bone with his enormous fists.

'I'll make you speak all right, you son of a bitch!' Then someone closed the door.

Each time there was a pause in Lieutenant Biondi's brooding, insistent voice, the beating would start up again. And as the Commander interrupted at intervals to ask a question, we'd hear his choleric voice exploding with rage:

'Two of my men were killed today! D'you hear? Two young soldiers, veterans of the Russian campaign! You filthy bastards in this nest of filthy bastards! I'll show you what M Battalion is made of!'

His voice swelled with rage, and we heard his swagger-stick come down on the table. His words stirred our blood.

When they came out of the room, though, it was another story altogether: no longer trying to smile or apologize, they seemed to

52

be having trouble enough just walking, their eyes fixed on some distant point as though they were unable to see us. They responded incredibly slowly to the orders of the political squad who accompanied them, as if they hadn't heard, or were no longer intimidated by that tone of voice.

'Would he talk?' someone asked, in a way that suggested he wasn't expecting an answer.

Arab-fashion, the Cremonesi had formed a circle, and were sitting on blankets with their backs to us. Eating and muttering amongst themselves, they were passing the bottle in their usual ceremonious fashion; yet this time leaving out the ritual: 'Your health?' Only very occasionally, with impassive, unchanging faces, would they glance over in that direction, then without comment return to what they were doing.

Lando Gabrielli had brought in another one: opening the main door, he pointed to one of them and said: 'You – come outside!' Then letting him pass, he ordered in that harsh voice of his: 'Move it! In there!'

His face looked grey and drawn, and there was a rigid, forced quality to his movements. At a certain point we heard Carletto mutter, 'Bloody shirkers – always licking the officers' boots! They never have the nerve to come out, then they stand there boasting!' But Lando pretended not to hear: contracting his features even more, he shoved the prisoner with the barrel of his rifle as we moved our legs to let them pass. The two quartermaster sergeants stood there waiting by the door.

Tall and stocky-looking, Lieutenant Matteo came out of the room, right arm bandaged in a sling. As he stood there with his jacket thrown over his shoulder, he showed us his swollen left hand: 'Bloody hell, they're a tough lot,' he said. He was red-faced and sweating: in fact they all emerged strangely glowing, moving with this kind of febrile excitement. 'Defend yourselves, I told them! Ignore my uniform – defend yourselves, man to man!'

'They're just a bunch of cowards!' someone said.

Meanwhile a patrol was returning: wrapped in greatcoats, helmets pulled down over their balaclavas, so all you could see were their eyes blinking in surprise at the sudden bright lights. As they entered, they brought a gust of icy wind with them which left a long trail of silence in its wake.

We were made to change rooms. Most people got under their blankets, forming dark twisted shapes in the middle of the room, except for Giulio Fasano, the only one who couldn't find a space. I watched him lie down in the middle of the icy corridor, ill-wrapped in his blankets, livid face resting on his rucksack, his entire body shaken by spasms.

At intervals, we'd hear bursts of shouting and blows coming from the main room. A few soldiers returning from duty had managed to slip past the political squad, and now they were getting their bit in:

'Shout "Long live the Duce," you son of a bitch!'

Then came orders and threats from the guards: 'Get out of here! I said get out!'

As he stood there in his dark blue suit, he'd lost none of the aristocratic air which had immediately struck me that evening when we went with Lieutenant Sacco to pick him up from a far-off villa. While they interrogated him, I remember feeling each one of the quartermaster sergeant's open-fisted blows, and Alessandri's great punches, resounding inside me.

Just before we set off, the Lieutenant had come up to us in the lorry and whispered in the darkness: 'He's a big fish, so mind you keep your eyes peeled.' Then, with the engine on low, the lorry slid off into the night.

The moment we walked into that villa, we were gripped by an incredible feeling of unease, standing there amidst the carpets, the antique furniture, the silver knick-knacks. The manservant came running up to stop us going any further: 'Where do you think you're going? What are you doing – I told you His Excellency was resting!'

Just then, the owner of the house appeared in a red silk dressing gown, knotted around the waist. Lieutenant Sacco, wrapped in a greatcoat which reached the toes of his boots, stood in front of him, scrutinizing him with that hairless, deadpan face of his; addressing him respectfully enough, but at the same time throwing us cold looks behind his steel-rimmed glasses, as though to say: 'Watch this one – don't be taken in by him'.

Wandering around the room, he was offering us cigarettes from a heavy silver box, which exuded a fine aroma, and at the same time listening to Lieutenant Sacco's words.

'Certainly, Lieutenant,' he was saying. 'Rest assured, you have nothing to fear.'

I can't remember what he looked like, and I'd be hard-pushed to describe him in detail, yet certain of his traits are still with me. A tall, distinguished-looking man, with black hair combed off his face . . .

One thing I do remember quite clearly though, is that when I raised my eyes from the cigarette-box he was holding out to me, and I met that affable smile, not only was I compelled to return it, but something actually changed inside me. That man, who, until a few moments before had been no more than a stranger, had suddenly become a person I knew, someone with whom I'd established a rapport. And immediately I hoped it was just a mistake, that he wasn't the person we were after. Right now, I thought to myself, the Lieutenant's going to clear the matter up, then we'll make our excuses and leave . . .

Meanwhile, cautious and aloof, yet still managing to preserve the expression of distaste he'd greeted us with, the manservant was holding out a big silver lighter towards my cigarette. That's when I became aware of my cracked, filthy hands and the threadbare cuffs of my coat, and I felt ashamed of my clumpy, mud-covered boots trampling the thick carpet. And how hateful the Paduan's lean face suddenly seemed to me, poking hungrily out of his creased fatigues, as he leaned against a long sideboard filled with silverware, making faces at me as if to say: 'Cripes! Will you take a look at this!' drawing insistently on his cigarette, which was already damp and crumpled through eagerness.

It was then that the lieutenant's voice, suddenly grown icy, broke through to shatter any illusions: 'I regret to inform you that I've been ordered to take you away with me,' he said.

Watching his hairless face, I saw that same expression that I'd noticed, when, walking out of the town hall towards the lorry, Commander Ussari had called him back and said to him: 'Lieutenant Sacco, I'd like to sort this out with your usual diplomacy and lack of fuss.'

He'd replied with a nod, the faintest flicker of a smile on his lips.

The lieutenant led the prisoner upstairs to get dressed, and as they came back down the marble staircase, I noticed that the man's face had lost its expression of relaxed affability. He still tried to look pleasant when his eye fell upon us, but it was done mechanically, out of habit.

It was when they reached the landing of the stairs, and the platoon-leader's orderly stepped down beside him, holding on tight to the strap of his gun, that I saw him throw a dazed, questioning look towards his manservant, like a mute cry for help.

'Let's go,' said the platoon-leader.

It was dark outside, and the shadows were creeping from their hiding places as the two soldiers grabbed hold of his arm. The formalities were over now.

As we walked down the short flight of steps and across a gravel driveway towards the gate, the lieutenant followed on behind, calmer now, with an abstracted look on his face, as though the matter no longer concerned him. He slipped on his gloves.

It had become icy and the night was shot through with a dense, hard cold – a cold which froze all sound and resisted all movement.

Downstairs, someone slammed the main door shut, and the echo resounded through the hallway and out into the dark, narrow courtyard beyond. A sentinel was stationed outside the closed doorway, gun at his shoulder, balaclava covering his face, while the Cremonesi, their gear tidily arranged beneath the table – machine-guns, boxes of ammunition, kitbags – were lying down in their alcove, enormous bodies composed in sleep.

There were no more footsteps going up and down the corridor, and, even in there, the beatings had stopped. In the middle of the room a guard sat dozing on a chair beneath the yellow light, while the prisoners knelt on the ground, faces against the wall, arms crossed above their heads. In the end they'd allowed them to, as they'd just stopped responding to orders: 'Lift up your arms! Higher I said – higher!' They did try, but they just weren't able.

Meanwhile, Sergeant Acciaroli lay tossing and turning on his straw mattress, unable to find a comfortable position. His wound had swollen up to an incredible size, disfiguring his whole face and preventing him from sleeping. Enzo Grama was huddled under a tarpaulin sheet, covered right up to his face.

Even the commander – Commander Ussari of M Battalion – was lying on a table in one of the rooms at Borgosesia town hall. This time, he and his officers hadn't taken over a restaurant, with plenty of wine and singing, guns resting there by their sides. Instead, like us, they were lying on top of office desks in the darkened town hall, daggers at their belts, boots rigid, snoring.

More gunfire, nearer this time, and a long 'Who's there?'
'Patrol.'

And then we heard the patrol turning in, their footsteps echo ing in those unknown streets.

Chapter IV

BLONDIE went. The minute Lieutenant Veleno made his request,
he jumped down from the lorry, and without a moment's hesitation, he sloped off in his usual, sulky adolescent's fashion. There
we were, sitting on the lorry, drumming our feet with cold, chewing those damp pieces of rubbery bread, when Lieutenant Veleno
came over asking for volunteers. The words were barely out of
his mouth, before Blondie jumped to his feet and leapt over the
side of the lorry. I felt like seizing him by the arm and saying:
'Where the hell are you going – what d'you think you're doing?'
but I didn't have the nerve. Thin-lipped, he held his head reso-
lutely and said to me: 'Can I borrow your gun?' Then, holding
on tight to his rifle-strap, he jumped down and hurled himself
forward as though doing battle with himself, with the very air
around him.

Tense and impatient, the lieutenant stood there, picking
people from the crowd which had gathered around him: 'You'll
do, and you too, back there.' A stocky, irritable figure, dressed in
a light windcheater, he'd come bursting jerkily out of the main
door in a rage. All around him they were pushing and shoving to
get noticed: there in the front row I saw the cadet. Tall and athletic, he'd come running up as though he were on a race track,
planting himself at attention in the impeccable pose of a trained
model.

'For Christ's sake – that's enough now! I don't need anyone
else – just go away will you?'

As they headed towards the church in loose rows of three,
guns at their sides, I saw Blondie's head amongst the others, that
light, fine hair of his sticking our from beneath his helmet.

The first to appear in the doorway in his blue suit, his distin-
guished manner unruffled by the night he'd just spent, was that
man. I was amazed to see him standing there on the threshold
without an escort, but then what did I expect? Unable to reconcile the occasion with that figure standing there, I kept asking
myself: 'Who is that civilian? What's he doing here?' And it took
me a while to even half-register him: 'Oh yes, him,' I thought, yet

not really connecting him with the person I'd met the evening before; nor, for that matter, to the event which was about to take place. He'd appeared matter-of-factly in the doorway, but once there he stopped, as if he'd come face to face with some unforeseen obstacle, or as though it was only then that he fully realized what was happening. I saw quite clearly the look of disbelief on his face, as if he couldn't even recognize the square he must have known so well: all those expectant faces, the troops in lorries, armed soldiers dotted about the place and, above all, that vast, empty space he had to confront. He stopped, taking a step backwards so that the men behind him came to a halt at his shoulder. Then a voice rang out imperiously from the hallway, and someone came running up, grabbing him by the arm.

One by one they filed past to the top of the steps: appearing in the doorway, they'd pause there for a moment, looking dazed and bewildered, disoriented by the lights and what they saw in front of them; until, pushed on by the people behind, they turned to face the steps, heads bowed, paying particular attention to where they stepped.

I stood there, rooted to the spot, fascinated, unable to string together a single coherent thought as I watched them file past – mechanically chewing damp bread and cheese, while a sort of febrile tremor ran under my skin from the tip of my toes, right up to the nape of my neck.

From that point onwards, everything began to take on the rarefied quality of a dream: the thin line of backs advancing slowly along that empty space, as though propelled by some impalpable force which was showing them the way in spite of themselves, the soldiers accompanying them with appropriately grave expressions, the damp sloping pavement, that heavy grey sky . . . No voices, or sounds, or movement anywhere. Four hundred men stood in the square in absolute silence.

Then at a certain point Bonazzoli's voice, coming from somewhere behind me, broke through the silence in an attempt to ease the tension: 'They're already free,' he said. But the accepting, fatalistic tone of his voice immediately rang false, out of key – showing his inability to step back from events, the futility of trying to come to terms with the situation by belittling it.

The one in front had stopped again; he was looking around as though searching for someone, as though determined to go no further . . . For, you see, when it came down to it, he just couldn't accept that absurd fate – something which had no bearing at all on his life, on his beliefs, on his position. Was it possible that from one day to the next – in the space of a single night – everything could have been turned on its head like that? Wait, he seemed to be saying – what's happening? What are you doing? Wait . . .

Who was he looking for? Whom did he want to speak to? What was there left to say? What hope, what possibility, remained in sight?

There wasn't one friendly face or object he could turn to – just us with our weapons, our desire for revenge. I remember that terrible moment of suspense, confronted as we were by the unexpected will of this man who wanted to save himself at all costs.

Then, from behind a tight knot of soldiers over on the other side of the short flight of steps, a voice broke through – a harsh, authoritarian voice which I recognized, but which sounded cutting and alien now in that charged atmosphere:

'What's going on? I said move it!'

That's when I felt the need to search the commander out, to look him straight in the face and ask him what was happening, to make him calm my fears, find some sort of acceptable justification for what was happening. Standing amongst the troops, without his usual retinue of officers – almost as though he were trying to disappear into the crowd – he looked unexpectedly solitary in that extraordinary moment, startlingly naked, too, as he did years later, when I saw him divested of his uniform and all the respect it commanded. I looked at his heavy plebeian features, which the cavalier's whiskers could not disguise, at his thighs, already turning to fat beneath his tunic, at that general air of awkwardness in his bearing and movements. All that remained of his former authority, and decisiveness was a mere outward shell: what I saw quite clearly – although I tried at once to deny it – behind his scornful exterior, behind the uniform with all its decorations and medals and stripes, was a man who had lost all his arrogance and self-assurance. Deep in his eyes there was an uncertainty and bewilderment which he was furiously willing himself to suppress. Standing there in a corner, doing his utmost to behave in a manner appropriate to the occasion – hoping perhaps to rid himself of some of the unease he was feeling with all those eyes upon him – all he could do was to tap his boots nervously and clumsily with his cane.

Then I saw the political squad come running up; hurling themselves on top of the figure in the middle of the square, they again prodding him with the barrel of their rifles, irritated by this unforeseen interruption which was marring the solemnity of the occasion. And as that brutal gesture brought him back to his surroundings, they all began walking again, each one recognizing the way to go. Isolated and intimidated in that enormous space, they crossed the square; on the other side, the firing squad stood waiting.

Step by step, their legs took them there – the same legs that had carried them throughout their lives, and which now lead them to that place. You watched the tip of each foot advancing, first one, then the other (how many were there left to go?), chilled by the thought that in a moment's time there'd be one step which wouldn't be followed by any others. You gave a start, and a sudden impulse of revolt coursed through your veins: you wanted to run, to get away from it all, but you could do nothing, nothing . . . Because you'd become nothing: just a clenched fist in the pit of your stomach, a trembling knot of fear which racked your body with useless spasms.

And no, not one of them refused to go, not even one threw himself onto the ground shouting: No! I won't go! They didn't have to drag anyone off by force, pulling their legs and clothes. In a way, it was too easy to kill a man like that: at a certain point he becomes more docile than an animal being led off to the slaughter, a kind of empty rag-doll moving along like an automaton.

And now he too, appearing to have understood the inexorability of the situation, was going along with the ritual – a ritual we needed in order to camouflage the ghastly reality of what was happening, in order to reassure ourselves that we were only performing some everyday act similar to what we'd done before. And he – the man who was about to be robbed of his life and everything in it – he too was part of that lie. He must have wanted to do it, to throw himself onto the ground and lie there kicking and shouting: 'No! I won't go! Why d'you want to kill me? Why!', so they'd have to gag him, drag him along by force, tie him up. But he couldn't do it . . . Or perhaps he wanted to try to escape, shouting Murderers! murderers! murderers! to their faces. But he couldn't do it.

Paralysed by a kind of monstrous complicity, he too was trapped in the mechanism of that hanging doom. And it was that which gave me some measure of the enormity of what was happening.

All the lieutenant had to do was take the first one by the arm and lead him to his position, for the others to line up next to him like sheep as if each one knew his place. There they stood, a row of slightly bent backs, some with their heads bowed, one or two even mustering up the strength to lift up their faces and look around.

Then the political squad, who'd accompanied them until then – making sure everything was in order, that the rows were straight – went off to join the ranks. They were young, and did everything with great seriousness.

Lando Gabrielli and Aleramo Daga were among the ones who'd set off that evening on the lorry with us. They'd spent the whole night interrogating them, they knew their names, their faces, their voices; they'd seen them looking around in bewilderment for a means of escape, and now they were going to shoot them. They had to prove themselves tough and consistent to the bitter end: the revolution had begun now, and all pity was dead.

The last to go was the lieutenant. His movements lacked their customary charge of pent-up fury and excitement, and there was a tense, rigid look about him, as if he too were performing some irrevocable act, but one which – no matter how hard he might deny it – he'd just discovered to be futile and absurd.

No, it wasn't like the movies, or when you said: 'Get them up against the wall! We've got to get them up against the wall!' It was something unbearable which gripped you by the bowels, turning them inside out as if they were about to be ripped out of you. And all I could do was stand there, rooted to the spot, saying over and over again to myself: 'Right – they're going to kill them now. They're going to kill them.'

I could add nothing to that. What was happening was so vast and immediate that it prevented me from stringing together a single thought, from mustering up even one of the reasons I knew and had repeated so often to myself. I tried conjuring up the faces of my dead friends: comrades they'd been, two young soldiers . . . But all the justifications which until then seemed more than adequate – betrayal, dishonour – appeared now to have lost all substance, swept away by the enormity of those words: 'And now they're going to kill them'. Nor did they have any bearing on the argument made up of all those words and excuses: this was another kind of truth now, a truth which was bound up to be unbearable tightness in the pit of my stomach, and all of its harrowing emotional load.

Stripped of everything which made us hate them, all the reasons which had decided their fate, they were just men now, living men like you or I, part of the same fabric of life; and yet, in a moment's time they would cease to exist.

Not a sound or movement or breath: those four hundred men stood beneath a leaden sky and boarded-up houses, gazing at those backs without moving a muscle.

It was his voice – the same voice that swore and threatened us, that joked and got angry – that gave the order, an order we'd all heard before in books and films. Standing there beside the first row, wrapped in a light windcheater, he shouted: 'Load!' I watched them manoeuvring the bolts with movements which until now had been so familiar and innocuous: track! Back again, the bolt shooting forwards and engaging the bullet which slid into the chamber. In one stroke they lowered the handles and they were ready. Then came the next order in that Tuscan accent of his:

'Aim!'

And that was it, the worst moment of all, when more than one of the volunteers must have felt this tremendous wrench inside. Because it was time now to line up the rifles and search for the target. And the target was the head of a man standing ten paces in front of you. Yes, that one. The one who'd already been pointed out to you – him. There, in front of you, there are his shoulders still rising and falling with each breath, his clenched hands shuddering. There is the man as he stands waiting for the moment to come to an end, for you to blow his brains out. Now the gaze passes over the backsight notches, and centres on the target: right there on the nape of the neck where the hair grows so fine you can see the skin beneath it. You have to shoot him there.

And that 'Fire!' wasn't something that could wipe out everything: you have eliminated them, solved the contradiction. If only it were! No, that too was something absolutely different now, and had nothing to do with anything you'd imagined, or read, or thought it to be. It was something concrete, made up of particulars and blood – above all, blood.

As the volley of bullets rattled unevenly through the air, there was a moment's pause before they began to fall, as if they themselves were surprised by the suddenness of it all, and weren't quite sure yet whether it was time to drop, or as though the life they'd been robbed of were still holding them up in some extreme act of affirmation. Then they began to fall in slow-motion, some of them toppling limply to the ground where they stood, as if their knees had simply given way; while others, as if pushed from behind, were thrown forwards in a kind of half-step; while others . . .

The line had completely disintegrated now, as if each man had found his place to die. What got me most, though, was the way they dropped to the ground – so unlike that of a living man. Passively they fell, like objects, not people, doing nothing to save themselves or break their fall, because what had happened out there had broken all bounds.

He didn't fall though. He stood there on the spot in his blue suit, as if nothing had happened. It was incredible: the echo of gunfire had faded away, and he was still there. An agonized row of twitching, writhing bodies on the ground, a lake of blood forming around them – and he was still there.

Then bit by bit it began to happen: we saw him gently lift his right foot off the ground, his leg buckled, he straightened it, then, slowly at first, but getting faster all the time, he began moving it up and down, kicking furiously into that empty space.

And in the silence, alone beside the row of dark, bulky shapes on the ground, he stood there, his leg kicking and quivering uncontrollably.

It was a long, unbearable moment.

I remember him so clearly, twisting his head as he turned, and the expression on his face. I was sitting on the lorry a bit to one side as he turned towards us, with a gesture of surprised incredulity as if to say: what are you doing? What's happening? And then he looked at us – yes, he was still alive! Still on this side, in the land of the living, like us. There was a questioning look in his face, in his eyes . . .

I don't know how many times, I've asked myself what could have been going through his mind in that final moment . . .

He could still see, though, see everything: soldiers all over the place, that row of wheezing corpses on the ground . . . A terrifying silence held us in thrall, as the solitary figure stood gazing at us. We saw that his face hadn't changed from the evening before, only there was a different kind of uncertainty on his features now – anguished, animal, interrogative . . . He hadn't given up, though: he was still alive, still on the side of the living, along with us and the rest of the world . . .

What could have possibly been going through his head? What can you think of at a time like that? Later on, I would have to face that moment myself . . . You get a rumbling in your ears, as the voices and sounds around you mingle in one gigantic, deafening roar. And yet there's a silence inside you – a complete and solitary silence which is the silence and loneliness of the world itself.

Was he aware of those dazed, uncertain eyes behind him? What was happening? Why? Who knows – maybe he thought it was a mock-execution or something, the seconds ticking by, and still nothing happening . . . Your hopes are raised: it's happened to others, you know, it's happened to others! They won't kill me – it was just to frighten me, to teach me a lesson . . . You stand there in front of that damp, scabby wall, waiting, waiting . . . what can you focus on now – isolated splashes of blood . . . one of the bodies on the ground giving its death-rattle . . . someone going delirious?

Heart in your mouth you'll clutch on to anything: it's over now, you think, they've got it out of their systems, they'll take pity on me, let me go . . . Why bother with anyone else, with me? You even find a word to cling on to: I'll be pardoned – *in extremis*: it's happened before, you know, it's happened before . . . The whole essence of your being is concentrated into that instinct of self-preservation, the final spark in its purest form . . . Let me go, please let me go . . . gradually, on my own, I'll go, around the corner on all fours, without troubling a soul . . .

Until suddenly the lieutenant's enraged, incredulous voice – back now to its usual furious pitch, the anger releasing some of the anguish he was feeling – broke through that silence.

'What are you bastards doing? What the hell d'you think you're doing! Fire for Christ's sake, will you! Fire!'

The soldiers behind him rushed to load their rifles, and the first sprinkling of shots was fired from the ranks. Then all hell broke loose as a cacophony of shots burst out from every conceivable spot: from soldiers positioned on lorries, from those dotted around the square from the foot-patrols stationed on street-corners. The deep sound of musket shot mingled with the harsh volley of automatics, as from every corner of the enclosed space they fired down at that spot. I saw soldiers who'd already fired once frantically reloading their guns and shooting again, while others, who at first had stood there looking stunned and uncertain, were now pulling their weapons off their shoulders and pointing them in that direction, infected by that fury. And all to strike down that absurd, still-rigid object propped up against the wall – to make that leg of his stop.

As the hail of bullets hit him, we saw him stagger, give a little hop – swaying from side to side as if he weren't quite sure where to fall – then, bent in two, he slid down on that leg almost into a crouch, until he lurched forwards.

And that was it: he'd fallen, it was finished now, over. But not even then did it stop: shots continued to rattle and explode from all directions as though the entire battalion had gone shooting-mad. Everyone wanted to be a part of that killing: the revolution had begun there and then in that orgy of blood and fury. The bullets bounced along the pavement, throwing up a shower of sparks. For seconds it lasted, showing no signs of abating, until the colonel came bursting out of his hiding place among the soldiers; and standing in the middle of the square, he began shouting and waving his stiff arm about like a madman:

'Stop, for Christ's sake, stop! Stop firing!'

Then silence. A tremendous, unbearable silence – a silence which contained everything: hate, anger, fear, desperation. A silence which oppressed us, which held us in its grasp. There, beneath a leaden sky in that enclosed square at the foot of the mountains: a silence; real, tangible, stony silence.

Silence.

Detaching himself from the line, the lieutenant walked over with tense, mechanical footsteps. He began with the first one on the right: one step forwards, a shot, then he moved on. I just caught odd glimpses of him between the rows of soldiers, a bulky figure wrapped in a light windcheater . . . He'd stop as though searching for something on the ground: you'd hear the shot, then moving on again, he'd stop for a moment and fire once more.

The soldiers were left there with their rifles in their hands: he'd disappeared out of sight, and it was only by following the sound of the shots that you could figure out where he'd stopped. After the half-way mark, he paused for a moment to fiddle around and change the cartridge clip of his Beretta. Then he moved on again.

The sound of his shots crackled with a dry, staccato rhythm – a harmless, foolish sound after the great din which had filled the square. When he got to the last but one, he paused longer than usual and fired twice. There was a moment's uncertainty, until a soldier in camouflage came running up with his machine-gun under his arm, and let off a volley of shots. Looking down at him, still not satisfied, he fired once again. We watched the little brass shell-cases skidding along the pavement, as that heap of bodies lay twitching on the ground.

He didn't fire at the last one though, and he signalled for the other bloke to stop too. Then, turning around to face the troops, he shouted:

'By the left, march! Quick March!'

Over? Not a chance. Even afterwards, it wasn't like in a book where you turn the page, and as the story unfolds, you forget what's just happened – as no doubt will happen here. No: frozen there at the second we'd killed them, in those unnaturally stubborn, immobile positions, there was to be no 'afterwards' – no page to turn, no sequel to the story. You wanted to do everything within your power to ignore them, to forget them: I wriggled about on the lorry, then turned my back. Some people were talking, another bloke was frantically rummaging through his rucksack. There was nothing for it, though: their presence was stronger than anything else – an enormous unmoving force right there behind my shoulders. When, in order to rid myself of that feeling of unease, I did turn around in irritation (as if to confirm or deny their presence), I found them lying as we'd left them, in exactly the same spot – a mass of dark shapes flattened by a tremendous weight which nothing now could shift. And nor can it ever change: while for you time passes, broken up into other acts and events, that moment remains static, turned forever into stone. Inert, estranged from its surroundings, it is a zone you are unable to penetrate or connect with anything else. You'll never be able to force your way through, and it will be the same story each time you think about it: you'll follow the sequence of events right to the end, where it'll break off, interrupted at a point where it can never be resumed. Because, you see, you've committed an act beyond your scope: an act you can neither cover up nor make amends for; an act which has no sequel.

Soldiers began jumping down from the trucks and running in that direction. 'Stay on the lorries!' shouted the officers. 'We're leaving!' Now one took any notice. A wall of backs had formed around the bodies, blocking them from sight. Then, without marking time, the platoon walked back in rows of three, straggling a little. A few people still had these stunned expressions on their faces, but in a rigid way, as if they'd been frozen on to their features. Not Blondie, though: his face was pale as he walked along, abstractedly clenching his jaws beneath his chin-strap. Then, jumping up on to the side of the lorry, he sat down in his place and began unloading his rifle. His lips were pressed together tightly, and he was moving mechanically, yet at the same time as though he were trying to overcome some tremendous force. We didn't exchange a single word, but he knew that he was being watched. He looked different to me, changed somehow, as if the horror to which he and the others had been privy left an empty light behind their eyes. Now I saw them for what they really were: boys still, with the same faces I knew so well, but touched by some hideous secret which lay beyond themselves and everything else, distancing them inexorably from me, placing them beyond the confines of some awful, hallowed region.

When I turned round to jump on to the side of the lorry, I saw the Cremonesi sitting in their usual spot beneath the cabin: Giano, Carletto, Dumanesk and all the other familiar faces. They

68

carried on eating – cutting the bread up into little squares, bringing it slowly to their mouths – as they sat there in that obstinate, intractable silence of theirs, a kind of deliberate absence of participation or curiosity. They felt so distant to me, that isolated little group, the last ones on the lorry, locked in their blind stubbornness as though made of stone.

Yet I couldn't bring myself to cross the square so openly, to walk over there as the others had: a kind of obscure fastidiousness prevented me from expressing the uncontrollable fascination I felt towards the whole business. And so, trying to appear calm and disinterested, I took the long way round – heading first for the right side of the square – but it was as though I were being pulled along by some invisible string which prevented me from moving of my own free will.

A group of officers was standing there: a few had already lit cigarettes, but no one was talking. They were all together in a circle, but each man looked elsewhere.

All of a sudden I saw him coming towards me, with his unnatural, twisted gait. He walked past the group without stopping, as though he hasn't seen them; nor did they call out to him. Small and graceless, yet he walked tall, shoulders held high. The first thing I noticed were the spots of blood on his light, billowing windcheater. In order to break through the wall which divided us, I felt the need to approach him, to talk to him, to try somehow to fit him back into the words 'Lieutenant Veleno' by saying them aloud: 'Lieutenant – Lieutenant Veleno . . .' He didn't turn around, so I tried to make my voice sound casual: 'Lieutenant', I said, 'Lieutenant . . .', but in order to get round those words I was forced to sound almost jokey: 'Lieutenant, you've got blood on your jacket,' I said.

He didn't react, as though the words hadn't broken through; he carried on walking, looking straight ahead. As he went past, I heard him mutter – as though to collect himself – 'I am stone . . . I am a man of stone'. He couldn't stop – he had to go, he had to get away from there. It troubled me, but then what did I expect him to do or say? He carried on walking towards the main door of the town hall, a solitary figure wrapped in an aura which now isolated him from the rest of the world.

Faced by that spectacle, I didn't know where to look. A puddle of sticky blood had formed around the twisted-up bodies, still seeping through their clothes and on to the ground. Looking from one to the other of the lifeless bodies lying on the pavement, all I could get was a confirmation of horror and emptiness. What had brought me there? What had I hoped to find? Aside from repugnant details, there was nothing else there – nothing, no answers . . .

Others were wandering around in a wary, almost circumspect manner, as if afraid of where to tread. They'd come running up with hasty footsteps, then once they were level, they slowed down cautiously and stopped. For a while they stood there, whispering the occasional word, until, hoping to appear nonchalant, they walked off back to the lorry, slowly now, as if they found it difficult to retrace their footsteps . . . down the road which had led them there, the only road left.

I found myself in a state of weightless, feverish excitement, as though I were no longer master of my own body and movements. If someone had brushed past me, I would have shuddered right to the core of my being. Then I felt a familiar presence behind me: he'd come up like all the others, but with slower, more leaden footsteps. Looking down at a pair of shapeless boots and those grey-green socks, I knew who it was – Fabio Grama. Without looking, I could see his face with its bulging forehead and staring eyes, yet I didn't dare meet his gaze: there was something inside me preventing me from looking up – the awful knowledge that if I had done, so our eyes would have avoided each other with a terrible wrench, and at that moment, all I would've seen on his face was the same false expression that I had on mine. That moment would have come between us forever.

When I did raise them, to look elsewhere, and I found the wall before me in all its surprising nudity, an unexpected image rose before my eyes. Shivering, I saw myself standing before that wall, alone and defenceless as they had been just a few moments before. And I was filled with a disturbing thought: right, it's my turn now to face the wall! Now that their line had been gunned down – and the protective screen they formed, destroyed – it was I who'd have to stand with my face to the wall!

Everyone was gripped by a frantic haste, as the officers' orders cut through the air, and the patrol returned almost at a trot. All we wanted to do was go, get away from there: we had nothing more to do in that place. Even Lieutenant Veleno had reappeared: none of the man-of-stone stuff anymore, all that had disappeared. He was back to what he'd always been until an hour ago; the same lop-sided walk, the same voice with its Tuscan accent: 'Engines on for Christ's sake!' he shouted, sitting astride a motorcycle. The spots on his jacket had dried now into insignificant brown marks.

The square was filled with the sound of engines, as one by one the trucks moved out from their positions, following the one in front. You could see everything from up there: all those bodies lying abandoned where they'd fallen. The Cadet was back in his heroic pose on the side of the lorry, while Blondie was sitting there smoking, pulling mechanically on his cigarette. As we drove past, someone from my lorry spat down:

'Bastards!' he shouted.

Chapter V

THUS we re-entered the night from which we'd emerged. Like a grey serpent, the procession slithered away, the lorries' headlamps casting a faint beam of light on to the white road . . . Croce Mosso . . . Valle Mosso . . . Strona . . . The engines rumbled as we drove into built-up areas of low houses.

A winding road, it was: one minute we'd be puffing our way up twists and turns, the next, shooting down hollows surrounded by frost-covered forests.

One by one the beams struck the shadows of the trees; as we drew nearer, they'd cross and huddle up around the trunks . . . trees, trees, and more trees, unwinding before our eyes . . .

Crouched numbly in my evil-smelling clothes, I tried desperately to distance my thoughts from those places, to drive away the images of the day, in search of what had been before, of an illusory light to illuminate the abyss into which I felt I'd fallen . . .

Oh to be able to leave, to turn one's back on that city which until the day before I hadn't even known existed! To take another road, to leave that town behind us without ever having known its narrow streets, its low sky hanging over the roof-tops . . . Away, I wanted to go back to the person I'd been before, when songs still sounded the same – away to other places and cities whose names meant nothing to me, like the names of any other places you'd never been to before.

Dragging its way through the darkness, the column went on: a succession of lorries tied together by an invisible thread, packed full of soldiers sitting in gloomy silence. They were there, too, the dead, in one of those trucks – our fallen comrades with military crosses on their jackets. I could imagine them – such alien-looking objects now – lying in the back of the lorry: hard as wood, the wind flapping through their uniforms as they bounced from side to side, marble faces covered in dust.

We'd been attacked again: unexpected bursts of gunfire exploding from the hillside, angry shots resounding on street-corners. I'd seen other comrades fall limply to the pavement, or suddenly keel over, dead, on to the lorry benches. And everywhere we went, we left corpses lying beneath a wall: Borgosesia, Crevacuore, Cossato . . .

Wherever we gathered our own, the pool of blood grew wider. At Cossato – for who can ever forget the night at Cossato – they asked for mercy. The wall was illuminated by the naked glare of the headlamps, as the gesticulating shadows of the two kneeling men grew larger, and the silent, village night was filled with their desperate cries, begging for mercy for themselves, for their children –

'Fire!' shouted Lieutenant Matteo. 'Fire!'

We lay huddled together like a herd of exhausted cattle, the wind blowing through our bent backs, ruffling the edges of the blankets and canvas sheets we'd thrown over our shoulders.

I'd fallen into a state of dull, brutish apathy: it was like following a train of thought right through till the end, but when you got to a certain point, it would just break off and dangle uselessly in a void. That's where the abyss was, where you could proceed no further. All I could do was go back again and again . . . And out of that black hole, beyond which I was unable to continue, rose this feeling of anguish, like a race without a finishing-post, a passion deprived of its object – grown painful now, untouchable as an open wound.

Blondie was sitting opposite me, looking more closed in that stubborn silence of his than he'd ever done before. I could just make out his adolescent face, illuminated at intervals by the glow of his cigarette, looking drawn and tense beneath the balaclava he wore under his helmet.

He'd gone – I hadn't been able to stop him. Pushing his fear right down to the barrel of his gun, he'd performed that irrevocable act – gone beyond that frontier, taken his revenge, seen that justice was done. But now what? Had he found the certainty he hoped to render absolute by that decision? His face remained mute, his lips pressed tightly together. At one point he muttered, more to himself, without looking at me: 'I went for the experience, you know . . . to see what it takes to become a man . . .' And I realized then that by committing that act, not only had he not found the confirmation he was seeking, but instead he'd destroyed everything – them, himself, the reasons that had first led him to it – and he was sunk even deeper into a void whence there could be no return.

Village after village unfolded before our eyes, shadowy and deserted, with long rows of houses built close together. The silent darkness was broken at intervals by roaring of engines and the lights of the trucks. Arborio, Greggio, Oldenico . . . We glimpsed the low, thick-set pillars of a colonnade, a little square cut through for an instant by the dazzling headlamps which were then immediately switched off. I was seized by cold from both inside and out – a really merciless cold that swept freely through my entire body, which I was unable to resist.

Just one week before, I'd had my eighteenth birthday! Only three months had gone by since that September day when I'd first set off, when all other roads had seemed closed to me. Now I sensed again that desperate desire to get away, to flee, just as on that morning when I'd gone running breathlessly up Via De Pretis, amongst those silent, distant people, tormented by the fear that my friends wouldn't be waiting for me outside the old cinema, for us to all leave on the first lorry.

And now those friends, scattered about on various trucks, were sitting there clutching their rifles with blood-soiled hands, branded forever by that act.

The outline of the hills was receding now, dissolving into darkness as the plains began to edge towards us. Layers of frayed mist hung in the air, pierced at intervals by rows of naked mulberry-trees, their long, whip-like branches studded with drops. Little by little, my mind was stealthily returning to its usual train of thoughts, everyday matters began to hold my attention, indicating how I might emerge from that sense of loss. I started to become aware of my surroundings: the road, the trees, the gun I was holding. All that had been dim, slowly began to regain substance and weight. I saw my friends' faces: Domaneschi's gentle smile as he winked imperceptibly at me: 'Hey rascal, what's bitten you?' The zones of emptiness inside me began to contract as things fell back into place. I felt for the bottle of wine at my side, and drank some of that purplish liquid. Even the lorries seemed to be going faster now, speeding down the straight, asphalted roads as though they'd just shed some great load.

We passed rice-fields and marshes, divided by banks of black earth which glistened with a leaden pallor beneath the cloudy sky. First one, then another, then another . . . a farmhouse stood

74

silhouetted against the opaque shimmer of stagnant water. Senses began to take over – tiredness, pitiless cold: the mechanism which had broken down began to lumber back into gear. There were words to say, gestures to make. The dust would settle over those images, life begin to close around the lacerations . . . And even if deep down there remained great stains of darkness, where all noise or commotion could be drowned in a second, by the following day you'd begin to forget about it. You'd sleep on it, and the next day go out for a drink with your friends: Bonazzoli, Carletto Ferrari, Domaneschi, Tulas, their familiar faces, their jokes, their 'Your Health?' Caught up once more by life, a kind of shell or callous begins to form around those events, with all their disturbing emotional weight. And if you were given the chance, you'd talk about it with them in order to mix the events back into the melting-pot of words and justifications. Back there it had shattered, but now, bit by bit, it began to reassert itself as the slang you knew – a slang you hid behind (even though it hadn't been able to defend you there), which now, against a background of everyday events, was regaining its power of evasion and illusion.

'Hey, Carletto, war's a fine thing!'

'That may be, but it's fucking hard too!'

You slap Carletto on the back, and he gives you a hearty one in return, because by now his expert eye has discerned the fact that you too are becoming a veteran – someone who's learnt not to lose his head in an argument, who can knock a few back without losing his cool; someone who won't linger over details, who'll get on with things, who'll press on ahead: a person who's able to cope with that monstrously trivial business of just pressing on ahead, which, in the end, is what life all boils down to.

Then there were the songs: all the songs which made up the myths and fantasies of your childhood, songs which had the magic ability to create a cloud around you in which you felt free from all worries.

Yes, we may have killed, but we carried on singing. Up there in the mountains we'd perform our bloody deeds, then on the way down, to rid ourselves of the memory, our songs would thunder beneath the arches of the porticoes and out on to the streets. It was as though we had two faces: one for the forest hunts, for the ambushes behind farmhouse walls, for the sudden bursts of gunfire which could bring a man down against the wall; and one for the part we played in the other side of that story – our version of it.

The moment the first houses began to appear, scattered around the outskirts of the town, there'd always be someone ready to call out: 'Hey lads! We're almost there!' And that was the signal: helmets would be straightened, the rows on the benches would get into place, and starting from the lorry in front, fragments of song would travel in great gusts like wildfire down the column. It was like a long shiver running along the line of trucks. In a flash you felt your voice exploding inside you and mingling with all the others: Christ, you were still alive! You'd managed to come back in one piece! Gripped by a sudden whirling sense of exultation, which left you feeling stunned and overwhelmed, your voice swelled and merged with all the others until it returned to you, immense-sounding now . . .

Shadowy doorways and empty pavements unfolded before our eyes, as we travelled through those darkened streets. And as our singing expanded and contracted according to the width of the road, disappearing finally into the side-streets beyond, I watched my companions' tense faces, those open mouths, so full of sound and fury. As our singing rebounded off the closed shutters, it was then that the contrast reasserted itself: there they were – civilians, pig-headed strangers, who'd scuttled back into their houses, to the warmth of their beds – and that's where they were staying put. I could just imagine those anxious disbelieving whispers going on behind the windows: 'Not them! It can't be! Where're they back from? What do they want?' How we revelled in the anguished silence we left in our wake, in the sense of exultant violation, of having penetrated an alien body which our singing left twitching:

'Yes it's us – we're back! We weren't swallowed up by the mountains! We're the ones who'll always be back – we'll never die!' And in the shelter of the big tent, our voices swelled in fury: *Watch out all you shirkers/ 'Cause M Battalion's back!*

And so we relived all the notes and music of that past kermesse, for ever vanished: the hymns, the songs, the marching tunes, brought back to us by the survivors of lost battalions – the Greek campaign, Abyssinia, the Russian front – the heroes of all those real or imaginary feats. And the more those songs began to sound like mere hollow, meaningless nostalgia, the more we'd go all out to fill the silence which surrounded us – to rekindle the world of emotions and illusions which had exalted our youth. Each time someone came out with one you didn't know – *The dead we left behind/At Passo Uarieu* – you'd sit there with your ears pricked, so you could store it up in your memory for later. And once you'd learnt it, you too felt as though you'd been to Kantemirovka or Maritzai yourself.

Those eighteen months of hatred and bloodshed passed by in a great sing-song. It was the very fabric of our culture, all we'd learnt in the twenty years since our birth, a means of understanding the world. We found a song for every occasion, for every mood: they were our way of expressing ourselves. We got to the bottom of those events in a kind of drunkenness which our singing invariably reawakened. Song after song, which we hurled out like provocations, like dares, to arouse now-dead echoes in those people, to reproach them for the silence – both to call out to them and blame them.

Those songs would drag you out of yourself into a world where everything grew blurred, sunk deep into a drunken mist: fear, doubts, memories.

Right till the end we sang, right till the very bitter end and that last day in Milan when all seemed closed to us; Blondie, sitting there – rigid with terror – in the attic in Milan, saying over and over again: 'Let's shoot ourselves, come on let's shoot ourselves . . . ,' looking at me with that void behind his eyes. By then it was all over: no more lorries to pick us up, no more columns on the move, no more weapons, comrades, runaway songs – nothing.

There was just that final act to face out there in the street, and we did it in the only way we knew. We sang: without conviction by now, with tight throats, voices flat with anguish, we sang – me, Blondie, the Padovano and the Cadet. We sang, while down below partisans on street-corners sprayed the walls with bullets – deep-sounding rifle-shot and crackling machine-gun fire – but taking it easy because they knew that we were trapped. And we sang: *Let us be ever-more/Worthy of our dead . . .*

We were still trying.

'Shoot ourselves? What'd you mean shoot ourselves? What are you saying?' shouted the Paduan, maddened by terror. 'You're crazy! You're off your head!'

But this time the knot didn't dissolve, the miracle didn't happen, the hand clutching our insides never released its hold: the days of miracles were over. And a few minutes later we were on the streets, in the midst of spitting, kicking crowds, shouting:

'Death to you! Death to you!'

The dormitories always had a cold, desolate look about them, which made your heart contract: burnt-out stoves, rows of wooden bunks lining the wall; the striped mattresses folded in half, the smell of mould rising up from the walls and cement floor.

When we returned in the evenings, we'd pile our weapons haphazardly in the middle of the floor, then in silence, dragging our feet in cold-hardened boots, we'd each head for our place. There, slipping off our ruck-sacks, we'd unbuckle our belts and shoulder-straps from our aching shoulders. Back to my bunk, and the damp blankets which made you shiver to the touch, to the worn out mattress, to the bulging ruck-sack stuffed full of hard objects, which served as a pillow.

Meanwhile, down at the other end of the room, someone would already be taking apart the bunks the dead men had slept on to burn in the stove. As the young wood cracked and splintered beneath each blow, the corvée would enter, dragging along the floor the iron pot filled with soup.

Still in our greatcoats, like a herd of frozen cattle, we would huddle around the table by the stove, drinking soup out of rancid-smelling mess-tins, the silence only broken at intervals by the scraping of metal spoons and the roar of flames sucked in through the stove-pipe.

Then two veterans would come in and distribute the stuff, picking up the dead men's knapsacks from the empty space on the floor where their bunks had been. There, amongst the crumbs, the wine-stains and the dirty mess-tins, they'd spread out the meagre objects on the table: a few scratchy vests made of coarse, grey wool, some long cotton drawers with knee-straps, stinking of badly-washed linen that had been allowed to fester, a few crumpled packets of cigarettes, some cartridge clips, and one of those black flannel shirts that *you wear to fight and die in* . . .

Out of one of the pockets came a pair of steel-rimmed glasses. We stared at them in silence as they sat there, amongst the crumbs and stains. Then someone picked them up, and turning them around uncertainly in his hand – as if weighing them up to decide their fate – he said: 'Well, I think we ought to send these back. We'll post them to the family.'

His glasses: he'd gone down in the first burst of gunfire. I remember that sharp face of his framed by nickel-plated wire, the iris of his eyes dilated by the thick lenses of his glasses. I can see him so clearly now, sitting on a bench in the lorry, wrapped up in blankets and a balaclava, the wind whipping his coat-collar up around his neck. I'd seen those little glass discs shatter inexplicably into small pieces, but it was only as a fountain of hot, sticky blood came spurting over my hands that I realized what had happened.

The veterans were picking things up, selecting them with greedy, expert eyes. After they'd taken what they wanted, they distributed what was left amongst the others. Balsi, with his flat, expressionless face, beside him Corporal Bernabò, veteran of the Russian campaign, thin and bony with quick hands and yellow eyes . . . It made you wonder how many times they'd gone through that same ritual, in a shelter in Albania, a stronghold on the Don . . . You felt a little guilty in the beginning, and you wanted to make them stop – how dare they touch dead men's stuff! – but after a while you thought to yourself, well, it's no use to them anymore . . .

Even I got a small fistful of tatty, half empty cigarettes – his cigarettes. He never used to smoke much: he liked to hoard them up in grey paper packets between his socks and vests, pulling them out one at a time, savouring each one with great gusto and thriftiness.

Little Strazzani – the petulant, know-all tailor's apprentice, who, that evening when we'd first set off on the lorry, had insisted we sew tri-coloured tapes inside our jackets, so as to be recognizable when we were dead: 'They'll take one look at the ribbon and say "Ah, yes, it was one of them".'

It was a strange moment, as though time itself were standing still. I remember all the faces around me suddenly growing inexplicably pale, their expressions freezing on the spot, while Bonazzoli, who'd been passing around the bottle, had a rigid smile on his thick-set features. I couldn't work out what was happening until there was a screech of brakes, and the lorry threw me on top of the people in front of me. The air suddenly became threaded through with steel wires, which stretched and snapped with a hissing sound. The everything around me grew animated: I saw figures jumping up from all directions, speeding off down the road with their backs bent. And at that moment, as if he too wished to follow them, Strazzani stood up, and gazing at me blankly, as if for support, the blood coursing down his cheeks, he collapsed gently on to the ground.

His bed, too, had been burnt. It used to be over there where the line of bunks now broke off, where the empty space had made inroads in the dorm. I tried not to look at it, but your eyes were inexorably drawn towards the spot. Only Enzo and Fabio Grama stayed on in the last bunks by the window, isolated from all the others. Nothing would make them budge: they carried on obstinately making up their beds, as if they hoped their presence might somehow negate the truth. The barracks were silent now: a mass of icy rooms, filled with platoons huddled in corners . . .

I lay beneath the blankets, forcing myself to conjure up the same childhood tricks that had once helped me retreat into myself, a way of blurring reality and all that had wounded and tortured me during the day. There I was, surrounded by tired, harsh-smelling bodies, some already asleep: my comrades . . . It was just as I headed towards the threshold of sleep that their presence most astonished me. Who were they? What was I – the 'I' that's only visible in that hinterland between wakefulness and sleep, one minute before going under – what was I doing there? Images of my friends' faces drifted before my eyes, tied to dislocated words or expressions. For it was only as evening fell that I felt sleepy enough to forget the heavy tiredness in my limbs, to halt the confused jumble of questions and images in my mind.

Putting even my head beneath the blankets, I could just see the dormitory through a chink between my balaclava and the edge of the blanket. There was Carletto Ferrari, an empty bunk on each side, fretting and muttering away to himself with a dazed expression on his face. He was looking around incredulously, waving his mess-tin about and turning from side to side as though addressing an invisible audience. He seemed surprised to find himself alone, and it was then that I thought of Bonazzoli – who'd been hit while jumping off a lorry, and had stood there clutching his shoulder with a massive hand – of Domaneschi, whom I'd seen rolling down the metalled surface of the road. Both of them were in hospital now with the others.

Then Carletto, all serious now, got up as if he'd been struck by an idea, and came lurching over to where I lay, spilling his wine on to the ground. His face was contracted, and his eyes had become narrow, red slits: 'Here you are, rascal,' he bellowed, handing me the mess-tin as it sloshed on to the blankets: 'Take it!' He rolled his eyes as though he were searching in his head for something to say – a little harder now, almost there – when out came a kind of grunt. He stumbled, furious at his inability to express himself, tried once more, and out of his furred-up mouth came a few of the stock phrases . . . villains or not villains . . . colonels or not colonels . . . Then with a gesture of irritation, he pressed his lips together, and stalked off back to his bed, where I heard him finishing the sentence in a confused, gloomy mumble.

My limbs felt tired and heavy . . . fragments were drifting through my head: the coldness in the lorry . . . Strazzani's little body curled up in the back of the truck as it had been when I'd turned round to jump off the edge . . . Blondie who'd done it for the experience, to make a man of himself . . . those two sharing out the dead men's stuff.

I rediscovered the warmth, the familiar smells of my body, bruised and tender all over, exhausted right through to the muscle and joints. That body of mine which barely seemed to belong to me any more so much had it changed, grown hard and spare after extreme hardship it had been through; and which, from one moment to the next, could become as rigid and cold as Landi's, as Tartaglio's, as Strazzani's . . .

All around me lay the silent, icy barracks, rows of stable-like dormitories filled with shadows. It was then that it felt as though we were the last men left to carry arms: this struggling little group of obstinate, useless soldiers. Would the reinforcements that the Cremonesi were so faithfully waiting for ever come, that anonymous flux of soldiers to fill the empty corners with their warm, human presences, to restore that feeling of belonging to something – some kind of larger community – which might lend a dimension of reality to our being there? Or would we always be so few, just whoever you saw around you – people whose faces, whose manner of speaking you knew, even the day they had enlisted – that frail little line where everyone had his own personal spot, and where, if anyone were killed, a void remained – an emptiness which could only be filled by the ranks spreading out and increasing the space between each man.

Little by little, sleep crept up on me as I lay there with my blankets wrapped right around my body to keep out the draughts. Even in my sleep I forced myself to remain absolutely still, as the slightest movement could let in a blast of icy air that would torment me for the rest of the night . . . Everything felt rough, hard, uncomfortable . . . I shivered a bit until gradually a little warm point of heat kindled inside my body, radiating out through my limbs, until the shivering ceased. That's what I'd been waiting for, willing it to spread out and envelop me.

Having polished our boots with a mixture of fat and soot, we brushed our uniforms and polished our helmets with a wool rag. Four men to a coffin, we carried them slowly through the city on our shoulders, cheeks resting against the new wooden boxes.

Then the guard of honour came out of the funeral chamber, and as they reached the doorway, a bugler sounded the notes, and the rows of soldiers held up their weapons. The youngest officer carried the standard. A sweetish, rank smell of flowers lingered in the deserted mortuary.

When they saw the head of the procession advancing down the street, they resignedly came out of shops and bars to line the routes and salute the dead in silence. It was for that one, final act of violence that we carried them high on our shoulders like trophies, to be able to shout out to ourselves that there *was* a point to their deaths, that they *did* mean something. Clutching the handles of our daggers, we stuck our elbows into the hollow of our neighbour's arm, muttering insults and threats: 'Go on you cowards, salute!' The noise of all our feet simultaneously stamping the pavement rebounded through the entire line with a shudder, as we filled the town with the even tread of our footsteps.

Later, we packed the narrow aisles of the church to sing the soldiers' prayer before battle: '*O Lord who lights each burning flame/ And stills each burning heart.*' Raising our voices, we filled every corner of the church from the apse to the stalls with our singing: '*We ask your cross to be the sign/Leading forth this flag of mine . . .*'

As we set off down that never-ending avenue towards the iron gate of the cemetery, people were no longer lining the route of the funeral procession. The coffins were set down in the middle, the three companies forming a quadrangle around them, as we stood there – just us and the dark cypress-trees, framed against a high, whitewashed wall.

The colonel was making a roll-call of the dead, furiously calling out each name in that harsh voice of his:

'Legionary Scimonelli, Renato, fallen in battle.'

'Present', we answered, as the song says: *'When their names are called we answer "present", looking into one another's eyes.'*

'Legionary M –'

It was in that way, through ritual, that we tried to impose ourselves on a reality which rejected us; to counteract our feelings of hopelessness. Yet alone with those coffins, deprived of a public, we were confronted with the reality of those deaths, and even ritual was unable to cover up the sense of anguish and isolation.

We raised our daggers, and stood there shouting: 'To us!' gazing out beyond the fringe of cypress-trees towards the plains, down where the mist lay in wreaths above rice-fields, and long rows of bare mulberry bushes. Questions didn't arise, but rather a feeling of dismay: dismay over all the things you weren't able to give shape to, but whose existence you were aware of in the silence around you, in the shared words and gestures you repeated to yourself, but which had now lost their resonance: the dead, those who died for the Cause . . .

Under a square patch of green, they were laid to rest – beyond the laurel hedge and beneath the tall cypress-trees which swayed like long plumes in the wind.

It was a shadowy, isolated spot, cut off from the marble tombs and chapels with their veiled angels. They were strangers even there, despite the crosses and helmets and inscriptions which made it into a cemetery for us soldiers.

The bugler was sounding the call for off-duty as we went back, hanging our helmets on the nails above our bunks, slipping off our heavy cartridge-cases which were filled with ammunition. By now he'd learnt all the fanfares: the reveille, 'grub's up', 'corporal of the day to bring in his detail'.

In the streets, our hobnail boots rang out beneath the low

colonnades, the black tassels of our fezzes bobbing arrogantly up and down behind us.

All around lay the city, divided in two by the narrow, grey-flagged main street: the market square with its rows of stalls, covered in dripping tarpaulin, and its smell of rotting vegetables; the avenue lined with lime- and plane-trees, and further down, the sleepy little railway station which was always shrouded with mist in the mornings. Behind the zinc bar of the Café Royal, Lieutenant Matteo, swagger-stick hanging from his wrist, was lording it over his cronies. At the corner of a street we ran across Sergeant Coccetta, toothpick legs poking out from a pair of billowing plus-fours, who responded with a martial air to our military salute. But where were the people: the men and women, the bar-cashiers, the restaurant-owners?

Yes, there were passers-by all right, people in shops, women behind market stalls. We walked amongst them, rifles slung around our necks, doing our best to get ourselves noticed. And yet they slithered past like shadows, absently, refusing to meet our glances, trying to make themselves – and the way they stepped out of our path – invisible.

All right, so we were there, but they wanted nothing to do with us.

'They were the ones who were going round smashing memorial stones on July 25th, when Mussolini fell, knocking down statues and shouting: Down with him!' muttered Fabio Grama grimly as he walked beside me, ungainly in his tatty uniform.

'The same ones who used to go and wave their flags at parades shouting "Long live the Duce!" ' added Giannetto loudly, so that they'd hear him beneath the damp arches of the colonnade. 'Only you see they've gone on holiday now – to another planet.'

If you looked behind those inexpressive faces, at the servility they could switch on in a flash, you sensed something disturbing which our high-handedness was merely an attempt to stamp out. So we were there in our uniforms, with our guns, our presence. Yes, we could go into a bar and say: 'Hey you – give me a grappa!' and if you gave him a dirty look, the man behind the counter would instantly switch to that grovelling manner. Yet nothing had changed: in fact their very passivity seemed to be concealing a refusal which had grown remote, and for that reason, all the more inaccessible. It had brought them together, as if everything which until then had divided them – fear, exhaustion, grief – were now coalescing (even if only negatively and temporarily) into a new solidarity, which seemed to spring into life at the very sight of us.

'It was a fine dream all right,' said Giannetto, 'to wipe out twenty years of our past in a single day. All finished now – back to home-base, hand out your flags, the game's over. A good dream, and instead, without warning, we turn up. That's why they can't stand us. We're their dirty conscience, you see, the mirror of their living memory!'

But the woman the Friulian sergeant was sleeping with – well, that was another story, a sudden rent in the whole tissue of silence and ambiguity. A machine-gun post had been placed in her house, by the window which faced over the rice-fields. I remember her coming into the empty room I was guarding and shutting the door behind her. As she leant uncertainly against the glass cabinet, I heard her panting in the shadows: that woman's smell of hers with which the whole house was impregnated, the disturbing sound of her breath in the dark . . .

The sergeant was out. Then at a certain point, she came close and I felt her brush past me, lightly. I tried to say something, but the words came out tangled, hesitant, unable to find their way. I don't know how we got talking about it, but I felt her drawn into a completely different subject which made her forget what had originally brought her there. She spoke of all the bloodshed, and out of her words grew an unexpected, reverse side of the story – an entire reality which was alien and unknown to us.

All we ever did was climb back into the lorries and leave, thinking that was that – over and done with. The only after-effects, you thought, were those inner lacerations you bore. Who would ever have imagined that those 'cowards and traitors', the villains who'd 'sold themselves to the enemy', might actually have a reason – even a single reason – not to deserve what was happening to them? And yet unbeknown to us, a whole network of whispered reports was travelling by word of mouth through the villages of that valley; and as she spoke, from those dislocated events – which already appeared so distant to me as almost to be forgotten – a picture was forming whose perspective had gone

85

awry, a story upon which none of our reasons could hope to have any bearing.

The more she went on, the more harsh and confident her voice began to sound; at the same time everything I tried to bring up – the deceit, the betrayal – began to seem increasingly inappropriate. She spoke of mothers and wives who'd gathered up the dead, using the words 'slaughter' and 'atrocity' without fear. I wanted to order her to be silent, but the images her words evoked seemed to have freed themselves from the actual circumstances I remembered, and it was a different story I was hearing now: her version of it. Now, everything had sunk to this profound level, where all I could do was stand there watching my defences crumble in the face of a pain I was unable to resist. She'd got the upper hand all right – with her adult, female authority, as though my uniform no longer intimidated her.

She'd become distant now, no longer panting, and I felt her withdraw into the darkness like an animal. Then cold and aloof, without saying a word, she walked out of the room, leaving me in a state of confused irritation. Is that what she'd come for? I asked myself. And there I was, letting her get the better of me! But what about our dead comrades: Tartaglio and Landi and little Strazzani?

She only dared talk like that because she was sleeping with the sergeant. I remember his footsteps creaking up the wooden staircase as if he owned the place. I could imagine him in the intimacy of her room: freshly laundered sheets, lights out and that warmth of hers which enveloped the whole house. But I sensed a rift now, a rift which couldn't be healed, and I realized that all she gave him was her body, her desire. As far as anything else went, she stood with the others, her people, on a different shore, utterly condemning and rejecting him.

Cowardice, weakness. What value did the words of those miserable, shabby people have, people who'd turned their backs and retreated into their houses? What weight could those whispered conversations carry in the face of us who'd chosen the dangerous way, to fight?

'At the moment they're in a kind of no man's land,' Giannetto was saying, 'but they'd be quite prepared to forget everything and change sides again. They'll always be for the winners, you see, for the side that's strongest.'

Behind our backs, we sensed hostile eyes watching us behind half-closed shutters. And if you happened to walk into a bar or restaurant, you'd hear the whispers die out, the conversations suddenly coming to a halt, and you'd see a spasm of disgust crossing faces looking obstinately at the ground. It was then that the desire to cause pain and violence flared up in you, the evil need to heighten – to worsen – the rift that divided us, to punish them for the rancour of their rejection, for the picture they had of us. Lieutenant Matteo's swagger-stick whistled through the air as he slapped it down on the bar. 'C'mon lads, let's serenade those cowards,' he ordered in that booming voice of his. 'We'll show them what we're made of!' Then he and his gang were off:

Peace, peace to the huts of the poor,
But for palaces and churches – dynamite.
We'll stab the bastard middle-classes
We'll rise against them and we'll fight.

Gradually they turned their backs on us, paid up, and one by one began to leave. The bar emptied, and again you were back amongst the faces and voices of your companions. And in the sudden silence you understood what it was that made you want to lash out and wound – that voluptuous desire to appear even worse than they thought you were, born of the realization that you'd lost all hope of removing or overcoming the obstacle of their rejection. But what lay beyond those lacerations? All you were left with was the sound of your panting breath, that slowly dying tumult. All right, so you'd pushed yourself beyond fear and rage, but not for a moment could you even scratch the reality where those who denied you stood. And so, holding out your rifle, you retreated, looking around at your friends – the people who accepted you, who spoke your language, who could be silent with you. It didn't matter who they were, or the fact that there were so few of them.

You sat by the cooking-pot, dipping your mess-tin into the wine, and slowly you began to warm up again, back once more amongst those familiar voices, the overlapping arguments, the myths and illusions being reborn.

'Hey, Giano, who'd fighting this war then?'

87

'Fuck you – us lot, that's who!'

Exactly, it was us lot: Carletto Ferrari, Domaneschi, Tulas, who could bend a tent-pole with his bare hands, and Bonazzoli with his unchanging jokes. That's all you had to do: concentrate on that side of things not look beyond.

But what about mornings at reveille, with the lacerating notes of the bugle wailing in the darkened courtyard like the pain of loss itself? The effort of finding your body and your place in reality with the sergeants' stentorian voices smashing brutally into your dreams like a fist? Suddenly you had to pick up the whole fabric of acts and words which belonged to the person you'd now become – name, surname, etc. – a being who was a million miles away from the uncertain, vague thing you'd been just a moment before, and who had now vanished along with your dreams. Then came the horror of bare feet in boots as hard as wood, the icy wind blowing in from the open windows freezing you to the marrow, and the muddy puddle of water on the concrete floor around the washbasins. I heard one of the sergeants call out: 'Big boys at night, arseholes in the morning . . .'

You sat at the old deal table with the smell of coffee rising from the thermos drums, crumbling your bread into that sour brown infusion – so different from any other drink you'd tasted before. Then scooping up the soggy pap into your aluminium spoon, you brought it to your mouth: it tasted of your eighteen aching years – a life-time condensed into one living moment, redolent only of itself.

Meanwhile, outside in the misty square, the line of lorries stood waiting. 'C'mon now, move it! Get a move on will you!' Boxes of ammunition, guns, kitbags, spares. Someone offered a hand to pull me up: 'Engines on – column on the move!'

The singing began at once: *Long live the M's, with their badges and their stripes . . .*

On the first bench behind the cabin, the Cremonesi were sitting in a row, solemn and composed, while next to them the Cadet, perched in his usual place at the edge, was practising his best legionary's leer, looking from side to side in search of admiration.

Past the railway bridge now, past livid expanses of rice-fields, the road running high along the marshes; past rows of skeletal mulberry-trees and farmhouses snuggled high among the plains; past a flock of ducks scratching in the mud with their flat beaks, who pause for a moment to watch us move on . . . Caresanablot, Oldenigo, Albano . . .

Chapter VI

Greggio, Ghistarengo, Lenta . . . villages leaden with treachery, with hostility, with mistrust and fear, as palpable as the living . . .

Emotions have remained: dislocated images, flashes of memory . . . a half-erased name on a rusty old road-sign at the corner of a house; a long, crumbling wall surrounding a court-yard; the eye flickers back to a shadowy hallway, to a face retreating behind a window . . .

How many times in the years that followed did Fabio Grama and I go over such memories in an attempt to clarify them, to give coherence to those events? It was as though our recollections had splintered, dissolving into a tangle of displaced episodes, departures, returns, unexpected encounters, amongst which we felt all the original reasons which had taken us there fading and becoming ever more enmeshed in a confusion of unresolved episodes with each day that passed.

Fabio and I used to meet up at a bar in Porta Pia. Stunned, still disoriented by what had happened, we'd sit down at one of the iron tables beneath the plane-trees. Plenty of activity taking place around us: illuminated news-stands, jeeps dotted about here and there, people walking past who were full of interests and things to do. We'd say hello – he with that mild secretive smile, that sort of infantile seriousness of his – and we'd begin to talk. Invariably we'd return to those events.

'D'you remember?' he'd say. 'D'you remember that time . . .' And we'd be back amongst those events, emotions rising to the surface with startling clarity. We'd remember a sentence some-one once said, the sound of a voice, the expression on a face. The names of one of those villages would come out, and in a flash we'd see it before our eyes: that's right – it was at that bend before the village that Taddei was killed! In our minds we saw him roll off the lorry, his head between his hands, to lie there on the grassy bank by the road.

Sitting on the lorries, we saw signs of defeat everywhere: deserted town-halls, abandoned police-stations, and a pervading sense of misery – of really piercing hopelessness – as we drove up the hills. I remember feeling as if we were penetrating an alien world, a way of life which had closed its doors to us, a whole network of relations of which we could never hope to be a part. It was something akin to nature itself – to the mountains and the meadows, to the stone houses with their long wooden balconies – as though the people, the woods and the villages were all part of this one thing which repulsed us and shrank from our presence.

And what about those shadowy presences in the hills which could materialize for a moment, leave their mark and then vanish? Sitting on a bench, maddened by the jolting of the lorry, tormented by the cold and dust, you fell into a kind of stupor: the long line of doors unfolding monotonously before your eyes, shuttered windows, rice-fields, the outline of the hills . . .

Then there'd be a sudden jolt; the lorries would screech to a halt; shouting, swift footsteps, orders:

'Over there – quick, they're over there!' Hurling ourselves up the steep slopes, breath getting shorter by the minute, weapons heavier, we would stop, panting. Feeling the blood pounding behind our eyes, we looked around at those ragged slopes, at dishevelled, windswept fields where the odd wreath of smoke from a chimney mingled with the mist lying over the streets and houses. In the distance, where the long, grey stripe of road disappeared around a bend, we could see the lorries at a standstill, motionless. What had happened? Where could they have got to?

That night at Varallo! Beyond the edge of the roof-tops, the hills were full of spying eyes. They were there all right, somewhere in the scrubland, having suddenly emerged from the gloom. They attacked us on the road running past the stream, and once in the narrow streets, overshadowed by hills, I could imagine them up on the slopes, vague presences beyond the glaring sheets of flame which the tracer bullets had lit during the day, and which now circled the village like weird necklaces at some incredible barbaric feast . . .

We'd got this far, but it was time to slip hurriedly through the deserted city, away from those oppressive hills, back to the mist-filled plains . . . I'll never forget the strange, penetrating smell of disinfectant which the wounded on stretchers left in their wake; they left the hospital almost furtively, bundled away quickly into ambulances . . .

And so we left, clutching our guns, the engines on low. There wasn't a living soul in the streets: not a dog or a voice, not a window that hadn't been closed, not a door unbolted. The lorries' wheels threw up a spray of muddy water as they hissed over the damp, asphalt roads. I smelt the acrid smell of smoke as wide, crackling sheets of flame wound their way through the hilltops . . .

We travelled slowly down the avenue flanked by little stunted trees on each side of the dug-up pavement. And as we passed over the deserted level-crossing it felt as though the road itself were physically moving away, closing up behind us. Once we got out of town, the lorries picked up speed and we drove on through the valley.

Staring into the darkness, I sat clutching my gun, fascinated by the spectacle of those fires: the wall of flame rising up, fanned and tormented by the wind, and filled with strange, contorted fire-ghosts, as though the burning undergrowth were alive, gesticulating. And as the wind tore through the wall of fire, they flitted about like shadows, chasing one another and waving their arms, as though greeting our progress with threats and derision.

A short distance apart, the lorries slithered down the dusk-filled road. No one felt like talking as we sat in the dense darkness beneath the tarpaulin – all eyes, ears, hands tuned to our weapons. Every now and then we'd hear a brief volley of gunfire exploding above the din of the engines, while higher up in the hills a sudden gust of flame would bloom in the darkness like a rose.

All around was this feeling of danger: night-time, the unknown village, and the tracks from our tracer-bullets illuminating the slopes like long swords of light. A shudder went through me then, and to this day it has left its mark on the very core of my being. I remember that my body was rigid with cold, and yet I could still feel the empty cartridge cases striking hot against my hand as they leapt from the gun. By the light of the head-lamps I could just make out Fabio's face beneath the brim of his helmet, his features contracted as though he were having difficulty in supporting his machine-gun as it spurted out little gusts of flame into the wind. Then the outline of the hills began to recede again, disappearing gradually into darkness . . .

And when the column drew to a halt in the midst of some

fields, as though to get its breath back, how strange the silence and stillness of the plains seemed after all the wind, the danger, the tension we'd been through. You could sense nature's imperturbable calm as the night hummed with a thousand soft noises – a calm which all those lorries and the whispering voices beneath the darkness of the tarpaulin could not even begin to ruffle.

In short, that road became familiar and hateful to us, a kind of looming evil lurking at the gate of the city, ready each time to wrench us out of the oblivion which wreathed our memories, and hurl us back into a poisonous reality.

Sometimes Fabio and I would look up those places on the map as though to reassure ourselves of their existence, to convince ourselves that they were real places with real locations, and not just part of the mythical world where all those events were gradually fading. And yet even finding them on the map, mingled with unknown villages – as anonymous and insignificant as any other place you'd never been to or heard of – merely heightened that sense of unreality, which was moving further away from the tangible world with each day that passed. Nothing remained now, not a sign or word to verify the experience we'd lived through, to lend even a crumb of truth to those memories. When had it happened? Where?

I watched his absorbed face as he sat there, tracing our route with his finger: Gattinara, Romagnano, Grignasco . . . places branded in the memory like some interminable way of the Cross, flooding back now with all the images and emotions associated with those names . . .

We spoke of a bridge we'd once crossed, of the red roadman's house over where the road turned and the lorries were forced to slow down. That's where it happened, right there – that's where they opened fire on us from behind those trees on the hill-top . . .

'Look, here's where we abandoned the lorries and had to run up the road. D'you remember?' said Fabio. 'D'you remember Captain Fabbri saying what whoever wasn't up to it could step forward and he'd leave them there!'

Fabio stared at me in that anxious, questioning way of his, waiting for me to show that I did remember and could confirm it for him. Of course I remembered! Dusk, the cold wind blowing through the ranks of soldiers, and the captain saying: 'I'm not taking any cowards with me.' Only one person stepped out though, that dark, good-looking boy from Ferrara. Then the captain took the rifle off his shoulder without a word and gave us our marching orders.

And so on we went . . . one step, two steps, gathering up the dead from under the trees, the bodies of our comrades, turned over, their badges and stripes ripped off.

I remember the air taut with the smells of winter: of animals closed up in their stalls, of brushwood burning in fireplaces, leaves rotting amongst the beech trees. Our feet rang out on the cobblestones in those narrow streets, hemmed in by low houses with their wooden balconies. There were orders and curses on that interminable journey: Halt! Gather up weapons, collect ammunition – onward down yet another path in search of yet another group of houses clustered in the stillness of the mountains. How many times did we clamber up those paths, pass beneath those hill-tops? Names of villages on ancient sign-posts, people fleeing and church-bells ringing on our arrival. Then you found yourself on guard-duty at the edge of some deserted village, waiting there with the wind blowing, and feeling that emptiness all around you in which even the presence of companions counted for nothing.

'Halt! Who goes there? Halt!'

Those orders became the only language we knew: we had nothing else now – nothing. And that's what made you huddle up close to your gun – the one thing left to you – feeling the coldness of the tripod between your legs, clinging on to it for dear life, gazing out with numb eyes at streets disappearing into darkness.

The first impression was always one of alienation. Where were you? What were you doing there? Then little by little you came to master your surroundings: the pile of logs by the side of the road, the crumbling parapet of a bridge, the muffled roar of the river coursing down the stony slope – all the random details which made up the habits and history of a place, so that gradually you entered into a kind of intimacy with it.

But it was like standing at an impassable frontier: what could lie beyond that point where even imagination foundered, where everything disappeared into darkness? Your intuition grappled with an utterly inviolable reality: the knowledge that if you went one step further, then that frontier, too, would shift.

And so at times I'd imagine getting up alone in the darkness, and holding my breath, I'd tiptoe out silently into the night, forward in search of the reality which had evaporated on our arrival, in a bid to grab it unawares – even for a single moment – in all its intimacy and warmth.

I knew it wasn't possible, though; with each step you took, the wall of silence would move one bit further from the barrel of your gun. And I sensed obscurely that there would always be a stretch of road to cover, one more place whose doors would remain closed to me, a part of the world I would never know.

Our passing left no trace. As soon as we climbed into the lorries and were back on the move again, a wall of silence would close up behind us. Our actions and words lacked all resonance, remaining sealed within our domain, an area which contracted with each man that fell, until a stain of silence formed in its place.

And the longer you sat there on a box of ammunition, eyes glued to the darkness, the more doubts would begin to form: why did that wood-pile look different now? What was that dark patch? Had it been there before? I hadn't seen it there before – the blood began to roar in my ears – what could it be? I'm telling you someone's there! I would wait in suspense, listening to the wind howl amongst the branches, stripping the bark from the trees, and it was then that I became aware of my absolute solitude.

I would light one of those acidic, half-empty cigarettes which left wisps of bitterish black tobacco stuck to your lips. It'd last for about six or seven minutes if you kept it tucked inside your coat pocket in the palm of your hand. When you lifted up your coat-collar, slipping your face inside to hide the gleam of the lighter, there was a second of light as the little flame spurted up – a sudden feeling of warmth and intimacy in the space between your body and the material of your coat. Your surroundings grew blurred. What kind of reality did those few seconds belong to – that little corner of the world, so warm and reassuring there beneath a wing, suddenly so full of life!

And yet with equal suddenness you found yourself back in the dark, more intense now, and shot through by innumerable points of light. After that moment of welcoming brightness, how disturbed and uncertain it left you feeling: where were you?

The cold worked its way through your clothes, rising up from your hardened boots and wedging itself right into your joints – a hard, obstinate cold which refused to let go.

Then came the sound of footsteps from behind – yes, they *were* footsteps! But the terror only lasted for a second – it was the patrol! I recognized them, heavily wrapped up, as they approached cautiously from the side of the road, knowing that for an instant their presence would re-connect me – albeit very tenuously – to the company billeted back in the village.

'Halt! Who goes there?'

How surprised you were by your voice emerging out of that silent dialogue – it sounded so different! Then you heard the squadron leader speak – of course, it was Bonazzoli, and the one with him must be Carletto! Even so, you spun the formalities out for as long as possible, hoping to make the moment last:

'Password!'

'Returned.'

'Proceed!'

They stood there, hands tucked in their pockets, looking around and stamping their feet on the ground. Carletto winked slily: 'Hey rascal – colonels or no colonels, there'll be a little one for you too!' I smiled, cracking a joke back, trying to detain them. A cigarette, and that little cloud of steam rising up from the opening in their balaclavas. Then the goodbyes:

'Eyes peeled – got it?'

'Right you are!'

Their footsteps grew distant, and quite soon you were no longer able to hear them. They'd disappeared, sucked back into the night along with their 'ammo's' and 'fuck me's', and all the rest of their jargon. Alone once more, even more alone than before that interlude, you tried to re-familiarize yourself with your surroundings. And yet with everything as alien as it always had been, you realized then that the trick was to try to re-establish the network of fragile relationships, to find reference points. Sometimes though, you just couldn't do it.

Suddenly the silence of the valley was shattered by the tremendous burst of gunfire from my Emghe. With a sense of surprise, you felt it take on a quivering kind of life, rear its head, little spurts of flame shooting out, illuminating the skeletal trees which poked out unexpectedly from the earth like hands reaching out into the darkness. And as these long razor trails of tracer-bullets rose up towards the sky, the others came rushing over:

'What's happening?'

'There's a light – down there . . .'

'Where?'

'It's not moving any more now.'

'I'm telling you, it's a star.'

Sometimes, if you happened to look up, you'd see this enormous starfilled sky there before your eyes. It was so unexpected, like the skies you'd seen at other times, in different days, that you were surprised to find it still there. It left you feeling troubled, lost.

Bit by bit that road lured us further down into the depths of the valley, drawing us into an unknown, impenetrable world. We established garrisons here and there – at Borgosesia, at Pray, at Varallo – and road-blocks at the edge of the villages. Then at night as you were out on patrol duty, the ground freezing under your feet, an order would sometimes come through: 'There's been an ambush – second company on to the lorries.' Flying through the wind, we would get to some village square full of lowered blinds and shut windows. Vague scraps of information would come through:

'Yes, they fired!'

'Where from?'

Someone pointed: 'From up there in the hills.' You looked over in that direction, at deserted slopes and a line of trees: 'No way! They were over there,' somebody said, 'they fired from the little wall behind that house . . .'

Orders were yelled out in unknown doorways – 'Open up! open up!' – and we entered the miserable houses, up flights of worn stone stairs, looking under beds and in all the wretched, stale-smelling hiding places. I remember an old woman sitting by a lifeless grate, motionless as a wooden statue, her hands folded over her apron. She didn't even stir as we burst in. In the back room we found an old man lying on a couch.

'Get up!'

He didn't move, until with a rough gesture Sergeant Acciaroli pulled the covers off him, and there on the bare straw mattress we saw two yellow, weightless, skeletal legs.

'He's my husband. He's old,' said the old woman, who'd followed us, leaning against the door-post. 'He's paralysed,' she added resignedly. In the doorway, as we were leaving, we heard her murmur: 'I know it's not your fault: you're under orders, you've got to obey.'

We got out of there as fast as we could, and there wasn't a single person – not even the sergeant – who dared say that no, it wasn't true, that we weren't under orders, that we were volunteers fighting for honour's sake, fighting to avenge the betrayal, fighting to . . .

But no words came out.

Then one day they told us they had surrendered at Coggiola:

'Yes, they've come down – they've handed over their weapons.'

We were stationed at the local school in Pray: the radiators on, a thick layer of straw spread out over the classroom floors, and the windows all steamed up. They made us get into the lorries, and when we got to that windswept village we couldn't wait to find some sort of shelter, anything to escape from those wind-driven roads.

Huddled together like a flock of unprotected beasts, they stood in a corner of the large room casting nervous glances over their shoulders. How cold and damp it was! Dusty planks covered the floor, and snow was piled up alongside the houses. There were about twenty of them, frightened boys in mountaineering clothes, who stood there looking at our uniforms as if they didn't have a clue what was happening. Could they be the ones? Those lumbering bodies, stupid with cold and exhaustion – the big working hands of people who were used to stacking hay and chopping wood? – could it really be them? In the opposite corner they'd piled up a jumbled mass of rusty old weapons – Napoleonic muskets with brass breeches and little, slender-barrelled pistols.

Commander Ussari was trying to jolly things along with a festive air, but he only managed to seem more clumsy that ever.

Standing there with that bull-necked, heavy frame of his, he gesticulated into the empty space which lay between the two camps, while we sniffed each other suspiciously from a distance. It didn't come off, though, and even for us it rang false: here was the man who was going to shoot every coward and traitor, weed out the rot, wipe Piedmont off the face of the map – now turned all paternal and conciliatory.

After that we had to sing *Fratelli d'Italia* together – one little sing-song and everything would be forgotten. It was a distant, alien song though, not part of our repertoire, and it brought out such a sadness, such a longing to throw it all in. *Brothers unite/For Italy is arising!*

They were tired and defeated; we, weary and indifferent. I watched Fabio Grama's blue lips moving mechanically without appearing to emit a sound. How were you meant to make those words mean anything . . . Italy? Outside, the wind was howling beneath the mountain tops: there were those crates of rusty weapons, our ragged uniforms, hatred, desperation – all that misery . . . Italy – what was it supposed to mean? Did it still exist? Their voices sounded strained, and one or two of them appeared to have gone off into a trance, without realizing they'd stopped singing.

Did it ever consciously occur to me to open the door, lean my gun against the door-post and leave – to just walk out? No, but I must have felt like it. What else could that torment, that sense of anguish and futility have been? Where to, though, where?

You cold leave your country, walk out of that story – out of all stories . . . Just go – along by the river maybe, watching the water gurgle and eddy among the stones, watching a brown leaf being swept downstream by the current, seeing it stop as if it were stuck, then beginning once again.

The commander was stalking up and down the room with that jerky, Sicilian puppet's walk of his: medals gleaming, dagger, blackshirt, beret, all truculent and ferocious, yet at the same time playing the angry patriarch, satisfied by the return of the prodigal son.

'Well done, lads! Well done! The nation's one for all, and all for one!'

What we'd done was to burn the hiding-places at the *Case Rosse* in the plains around Noveis. We scrambled all the way up to the big meadow, where huts were dotted about on the slopes, and behind it a dense, compact wood, filled with beeches and elms. Winter had come, bringing snow in its trail, and the kind of cold which is shot through with knives. And so they had come down.

Back on the lorry, they sat among us on the benches, looking outwards, only at intervals casting sidelong glances at us. That enforced intimacy made us even more ill at ease, until someone broke the ice by offering a cigarette. They smoked carefully, hungrily, rolling the cigarette about in their fingers, yet they were composed too, with a kind of reserve that was foreign to us. They were wearing big heavy mountain boots and plus-fours. We watched them curiously, unable to relax. All right, so they'd come down and handed over their weapons, but it didn't seem to have altered their manner, their way of doing things. That realization disconcerted us. Their faces, too, were different from ours. We sensed that they had no desire to talk to us, and in fact we were the ones who, anxious not to offend them, were doing our utmost to play down the differences between us. They weren't as I'd imagined – a kind of reverse side of ourselves. They didn't show that frantic desire to appear to be something at all costs; they behaved just like ordinary mountain folk, the kind of people you ran into in the villages. We wouldn't have been able to talk about the things we usually discussed amongst ourselves: honour, combat, our country, courage. They were different from us: simple, almost banal.

Little by little we began to exchange the odd word. Their lives in the mountains seemed to have not very much to do with the war – traipsing about from one hiding place to another, old Chassepots on their shoulders, kitbags, the weapons somehow incidental. At times they'd been forced to get up in the middle of the night 'because the Fasc -' and here one of them broke off, looking around uncertainly. 'You, that is,' he added, looking surprised. We all laughed.

'Don't worry, once you all get into town you'll find work, and no one'll bother you anymore,' someone said in a soothing, paternal voice which immediately sounded false and out of key.

The one sitting more or less opposite me had been a woodcutter, and was hoping to find a place on a Turin building-site.

'But what made you go up the mountains then?'

At this he grew silent, hesitant, and shrugging his shoulders, he tried saying:

'It was the Germans, you see . . . people were running away . . . they said they'd kill the lot of us, take us back to Germany.'

He wasn't wearing a coat; trembling, he kept his hands in his pockets, his head tucked into his jacket collar. They were looking at us more naturally now, and some even began to venture the occasional smile. At times they grew thoughtful as if they sensed something more personal beneath our appearance, a quality which belonged to us each as individuals. They asked us where we were from, what we'd done as civilians.

'Students.'

'Students?'

They threw each other questioning glances, uncertain what to make of this discovery.

But at a certain point Lando Gabrielli's harsh voice broke through, shattering the friendly atmosphere:

'What d'you think you're playing at? Stop being such idiots! There's no point in grovelling to this lot.'

We hadn't realized he was in the lorry, for usually he either travelled in the cabin or in the officers' cars; his interruption disconcerted us, plunging us rudely back into a reality we had forgotten about. Then one of their group, who was sitting beside him, tried to calm him down by answering him in the friendly tone which had established itself:

'Come on now, keep your shirt on.'

'Who the hell d'you think you are?' Lando burst out at once. 'Just remember your place and thank your lucky stars things worked out as they did. I'm telling you, if it'd been up to me . . .', and turning his back on him, he muttered: 'Can you believe it? He really thinks we're equals now! I'd just give him a shove and let him go under . . .'

Then Bonazzoli's booming voice interrupted him from the other end of the lorry:

'Hey, rascal – hold your peace and leave him alone! D'you hear – let him be!'

But they remained silent after that, not uttering a word until we got to Pray.

That evening, when he turned up at our door with a pile of blankets under his arm, hoping to stay the night, no one wanted him in with us. Without giving any specific reason, Bonazzoli just went up to him and in an unusually firm voice said: 'No, not here. Go where the hell else you like, but not in here.'

Lando, however, refused to budge: his face all contracted, he sat down on a pile of straw, and in a voice that rang false with the effort of overcoming our silence, he began to speak:

'Why won't you get it into your thick skulls that this is war – d'you hear, war! How d'you think they'd treat you if they ever got hold of you? When we found Lieutenant Melloni at Camasco, they'd poked his badges into his eyes!'

No one ever asked him anything, or wanted to hear what he got up to behind that door marked 'Political Office' – the confessions extracted during interrogation, the cries, the blows – but sensing our hostility, he obviously felt the need to justify himself:

'Oh, I know you don't want to dirty your hands, but how else d'you think we're supposed to get our information? These men are cowards, not soldiers! They'll never meet us head on – they just strike from behind and run!'

The snow was up to the window-panes now, but we were warm and dry in the classrooms with the radiators on full-blast, and the straw spread out on the floor. We'd taken off our pullovers and woollen vests, and, barechested, we were sitting around picking the lice out of each other's armpits, searching for them with obstinate thoroughness in the seams of our clothes.

We could sense his furious contempt for that mute rejection of ours: he thought we were childish and ignorant, only good for obeying orders.

'Can't you see this is a revolution! You can't start a revolution with silk gloves! This time we're not making the mistakes we made in '21 – no way! We'll wipe the slate clean. All pity's dead now . . .'

Oh yes, that was one of our refrains: '21 with cudgels and castor oil; revolution Italian-style, all blood and guts! This time it would be different, and yet it seemed to mean something quite alien and unrelated to Lando's way of thinking, his way of going about things. How much we hated him and his companions, all the shiny-eyed mummy's boys with pasty faces, forever hanging around the officer's quarters!

'We go and risk our necks,' muttered Carletto to himself, 'and then we have to hand them over to people like that!'

102

I could feel Lando's eyes searching for an audience, and sensed his stubborn desire to overcome our rejection. Then he played his last card: 'No!' he said, barely controlling his features, 'No, I don't listen when they cry out for mercy! I don't listen, I don't let it get to me! I just remember how they killed Giulio Fasano, and I see his dead body lying there in front of me! I don't listen – I don't listen to them!'

He knew that his words would disturb us: the picture of Giulio Fasano, lying on the ground with his face in a puddle, was still so vivid in our memories. It had happened in the square at Croce Mosso, on one of those mornings with the sky turning all white and swollen with snow. I'd bumped into him just a few minutes earlier in one of the narrow alley-ways: there he was with his rifle slung around his neck, his puttees – which he'd never learned to tie properly – flapping around his calves, exposing a white band of skin.

Then we heard the shot, and running over, we found him lying there, a trickle of sticky blood oozing down from his open mouth, mingling with the dirty water on the ground. Some soldiers rushed over to the boarded-up houses, shouting: 'It came from there – from over there! They fired from that window!' But nothing could be done for him now.

From their confused accounts we managed to piece together what had happened: apparently they'd been escorting a group of English soldiers who'd escaped from labour camps at the time of the surrender. He'd been leading the group, singing, when a window opened and from somewhere a shot was fired. Just one, aimed specifically at him, and it got him in the mouth.

'He died singing,' his companions told us, 'He died singing.'

Fabio and I went to get him. I remember Fabio sitting beside the already stiffened corpse, which was wrapped in a sheet of tarpaulin, bouncing up and down with the jolting of the lorry; he was going back over the evenings in the village where we had enrolled, when we'd light a candle on the dome of a helmet, and sit on our straw mattresses listening to Carletto Ferrari's 'machine-gun' and 'your health', the warm evening air filtering in through windows which looked out on to the countryside.

Small and dark, with that glowering face of his, Fabio was saying: 'D'you remember how Giulio's eyes would light up? He'd grab hold of my arm and whisper: "Grama, these are Italian soldiers – d'you hear – Italian soldiers! Italy's still got soldiers! In years to come, people'll be saying that not everyone accepted defeat!" '

Fabio's eyes wandered above the line of hill-tops unfolding beyond the edge of the lorry, towards the milky sky which was heavy now with snow. 'He came all the way to Croce Mosso to be killed by a bullet in the mouth. Shot by an Italian!' he said gloomily, looking down at the rigid shape in the tarpaulin, which was knocking against him in the wind.

Yes, that did stir the blood, but it was irrelevant. And Lando, sitting by the doorway, locked in his stubborn desire to be accepted, knew that. He realized by our silence that we didn't believe him, that we knew Giulio's death had nothing to do with what he got up to. Giulio was still alive on the night the whole sordid business had begun. I have a clear picture of Giulio lying wrapped in a blanket in the corridor of the Borgosesia town hall, his head resting against his rucksack, his face mauve with cold.

We couldn't meet Lando's gaze, and there was no mistaking the awkwardness his presence caused. Then at some point Bonazzoli got up from his place and ordered him to leave:

'You're free to go now,' he said.

With difficulty, Lando picked himself up off the ground and, gathering up his blankets, he left.

I watched him walk through the doorway, shoulders slightly rounded in his tight uniform, belt strapped around his thin waist, a few wisps of straw still clinging to his trousers as he disappeared down the corridor.

Lando Gabrielli! That wan face, the smile like a contraction beneath the skin. Who was he? Whatever became of him? We first met that morning in the German captain's ante-chamber. Arm in arm, he and Giulio arrived together, the two boys so different from one another. And forty years ago Giulio came to his end up there, while Lando had turned into that . . . The last picture I have of him is of his bent back disappearing down the corridor of the local school at Pray . . . We never saw him again. Someone said he'd been transferred to Commander Ussari's headquarters. He never returned to those villages, though, and even after the war we didn't find out what had become of him. It was as though he'd gone up in smoke, disappeared into a

void. I have a picture of him in my memory, sitting on a
wooden bench in the train next to his friend, the night we left
Rome from the station surrounded by grey apartment blocks
on the outskirts of the city. Two boys like any others, they were
– like all of us. Giulio's mother was there, a tall, distinguished-
looking woman, sitting opposite her son, looking at us from
time to time with bitter grief in her eyes. Then, as darkness
began to fall over the deserted platform, and the voices in the
carriage dropped to a whisper, she got up and said goodbye to
him: 'It won't do any good you know, but if it's what you
want . . .'

In the beginning, after the war, we'd meet at the bar at Porta
Pia in Rome, to exchange news about this and that; and to
confide how we escaped the reprisals. We never spoke of Lando:
no one knew anything about him, nor remembered seeing him
amongst the hordes of survivors, who, mingling with the
wounded and prisoners of war returning from German camps
had flooded southwards in allied trucks and open-roofed freight
trains. Even Fabio Grama, who remembered everything, never
once spoke of him. It was as though he had never existed. If, by
chance, his name happened to crop up in conversation, we'd be
overcome by a kind of embarrassed disgust, and without warning
a dark shadow which we found difficult to dispel would fall over
our memories. It was as though we wanted to wipe him – and all
he stood for – out of our minds. Could he be dead? Who knows?
Nevertheless, the thought comforted us.

Then one day he emerged from that misty past. I'd gone to
visit the elderly Signora Fasano on one of those occasions when
all those memories would come flooding back, and then I'd
decided not to stir them up anymore. I'd never have met her if it
hadn't been for that casual encounter on the train so many years
before. I'd looked her up in the phone book, and given her a
ring. She was still alive, and no, she didn't remember me. 'But
come, come anyway,' she said in a firm voice which belied her
age – eighty-five, as she later confessed.

'You can't imagine how overjoyed I am that you came to look
for me,' she said. 'Imagine seeing a friend of my Giulio's after all
these years!'

We sat down in the sitting-room on old armchairs with gilt
arm-rests and she scrutinized me, as though searching my adult

face for traces of those uniformed boys her eyes had flickered over on that distant evening.

'No,' she said, 'it was too long ago . . . you were all bunched together and what do you expect after everything that's happened, the years that have gone by . . .'

Then suddenly, right in the middle of casting her mind back over the past, she recalled an episode which, thinking back on it, had appeared strange to her.

'Ages ago I met another one of your group, years and years ago it was . . . right here at the bus-stop outside my house. He was a youngish man, in his thirties, but already greying around the temples. He had a thin, restless face . . .'

At this I pricked up my ears, seized by a kind of anxiety, almost a premonition.

'I can't remember his name – he did tell me, but it's gone now. you know what it's like . . . Anyway, he was one of the original group of twenty who'd left with my Giulio. He told me they'd known each other at school, then at university, and that they'd decided to set off together.'

There was no doubt about it – it was him, Lando Gabrielli! I recognized him at once. How strange it was to hear news of him after all that time, to have him there before my eyes in the middle of that bourgeois house on Via Salaria!

'He told me that he'd got on in the world,' she continued, 'doing what, I can't remember though . . . he lived in another city . . . was something like the director of a shipping firm . . . Anyway you could tell from his manner that he'd made it – a man of the world he was . . .'

She paused for a moment as her thoughts lingered over the past, and then she nodded. 'Yes, I'm quite sure now that he was there waiting for me, but who knows why he didn't come up like you did!'

She sat opposite me – a severe woman with her elbows on the arm-rests, still upright in spite of her age – and I'm sure she could never have imagined the tumult her words had caused in me. So he was still alive! Somewhere in the world he was safe, with a career and a family, living just like any other person, as if that whole distant parenthesis had been wiped out for good.

'He looked as if he wasn't quite sure whether to approach me or not, then eventually he made up his mind and came over.

106

"Signora Fasano, I believe," he said. He was holding a little boy by the hand, who must have been about seven or eight . . . Listen, there's more . . . so he pushed the child towards me and said: "He's my son – the eldest." I patted him and said, "What a handsome boy. What's your name, then?" And then this child looks at me straight in the face, and in a shrill voice he says: "Giulio." Just think, my Giulio's name! I must say I was taken aback, because I realized that it wasn't just a coincidence. "What a fine name", I said. Then the father stared at me, and with great difficulty he said: "And it's no coincidence, either: it's in memory of your son, Giulio".'

She paused for a moment, then added: 'So that's why he came! Can you imagine – he called his first-born after my Giulio, and he came here to tell me that.'

'He came here to tell me that,' she repeated with emotion, staring at me as though hoping to glean a sign of approbation. But my agitation was due to quite different reasons: now I understood the reasons behind that encounter, and the thought of the little boy, innocently carrying that name around with him, gave me a sharp stab of anguish. It was as though the father had loaded the justification for his guilt on to the child; as if, instead of coming to terms with it, he was trying to hide it behind all that affection.

I looked around in confusion, unable to speak. There was still an atmosphere of that period in the house itself, with its faded damask curtains hanging in the doorways and windows, the worn carpets, the moulding on the stained ceilings. Trying to find an explanation for their friendship I tried to picture that boy, whom I could now barely remember, wandering through those rooms, redolent with the signs of a waning prosperity, in an attempt to imagine how he must have been thinking and feeling at the time.

She got up and, walking towards a little table beneath the window, she picked up a photograph framed beside a yellowing newspaper clipping. She handed it to me: 'That was him, my Giulio,' she said.

I looked at the old portrait, trying to compare it with the image I had of him in my head, when he'd stood before that foreign officer and said, 'We don't want to surrender! We want to go and fight!' But I didn't recognize him one bit: there before me was a stranger, someone I'd never seen. Was that Giulio Fasano? In my memory, with the passing of time, I'd transformed him into somebody much more mature and adult-like, attributing a kind of clarity of speech and ideas to him which we'd all been lacking – me, Fabio and Enzo Grama, and Blondie. Here at least was someone who knew what he was doing! It was amazing how much a two-year age-gap meant at the time. Yet there before me was the face of a boy who was barely twenty years old, little more than an adolescent; a product of those long-gone days with his hair cut short about the temples, an air of breeding, and an ingenuous, carefree expression on his face. And that, I thought, is how all our faces looked then. We were boys, killing and dying for those symbols; it was in our name that all that murderous atrocity was committed.

'He was always such a gentleman to me, so affectionate,' she murmured, sighing. 'He used to bring me flowers, like a sweetheart he was . . . there were no secrets between us . . .'

Out of my bitterness, I felt a sudden unreasonable thrust of rage against that woman. She was still alive, still mistress of herself with her bun, her air of severity, while that boy in the photograph, his shirt open at the breast, a childish expression on his face was gone forever – killed in a village square that foggy winter.

I almost blamed her for what had happened to him – she with her world and its values. I could imagine the kind of conversations that must have been going on behind those walls – duty, one's country, principles, morals – and he, swallowing it whole, had ended up in the square at Croce Mosso, a bullet in his mouth, surrounded by people who loathed and rejected him. An open window, one shot, and 'Take that, you son of a bitch!'

She picked up the photograph again, and looking at it for a moment, she brushed her hand over it once or twice, as though ridding it of a speck of dust. She shook her head.

'We buried him in the municipal cemetery among all the others who had fallen,' she went on. 'My husband and I decided to lay him to rest amongst his friends: there'll always be a flower for him here,' we said to ourselves. But when we came back in '45, he just wasn't there anymore. The grave had been opened, but no one knew anything about it. We begged and pleaded – even bribed – but no one would talk, until finally a caretaker took us to a field – Sant' Emiliano it was called, yes, Sant' Emiliano –

where they'd put all of them. Over two hundred there were, without so much as a name or a cross – nothing! He told us that he was the fifth one in the twelfth row.'

All that distant past was flooding back now, as I sat there on a summer's evening in Via Salaria, listening to the sounds of the traffic mingling with the faint hum of the buses. In fact I'd heard hugely exaggerated versions of this story when we first got back from the war: some said that they'd been dug up from their graves, others even claimed that they'd been thrown into the River Sesia. No one wanted them alongside their own kind, those unwanted dead . . .

Absently, I walked down the shady part of the street. Giulio Fasano and Lando Gabrielli. What did those names, and all they evoked, mean anymore? I looked around at people walking past in light summer clothes, at cars zooming along in the cool morning air, at the flower-seller at the corner spraying water on bunches of carnations in tin vases. The world had carried on turning, and life had gone on in a completely different direction from anything we could have imagined at the time. Now, looking back on it, how much bigger than us were those events we'd got ourselves mixed up in.

'D'you remember? D'you remember?' Fabio Grama would ask me, anxious face poking out at me from the bar table. Yes, I remembered all right, I remembered . . .

On that yellowing newspaper clipping next to the photograph in the silver frame, there were the words: 'Soldier Killed by Bandits. He Fell in the Line of Duty'. I remember that night on the lorry, and Giulio saying: 'One day they'll be a page in the history books for us – kids at school will read about those twenty boys, who, when all seemed lost . . .' That's how we thought history always turned out: something straightforward, with a predictable conclusion, just as we ourselves had learnt it back in the classroom.

And instead we'd ended up in that tangle of passions and hatred, violence exploding, your companions being killed, and their deaths to avenge . . . Blood, fury and Lando Gabrielli . . .

At the time I felt ashamed of my pity, of that icy hand on my heart. I tried to conceal it from myself and from the others: 'It's

109

only a question of physical disgust,' I'd say to myself, 'shooting an unarmed man who can't defend himself. I accept full responsibility for my actions.' Yet deep down I was glad not to have gone, glad not to have been a part of all that, with the burden of bloodshed to carry around with me.

I was frightened of losing their respect, of being thought of as weak, half-hearted, irresolute. You had to be seen as a man who'd hold out till the bitter end; it was only the firmness of your resolve that counted for anything. I had invented this persona for myself, someone who corresponded to a real person, whose job it was to throw any weakness back in my face.

'You can talk all you like,' he'd say, 'but it's what you do that counts. A few words go an awfully long way: Backs against the wall! . . . Wipe the slate clean and all that . . . You've sorted it out in your head, killed the whole damn lot of 'em,' he'd say, 'but only in your imagination! When it comes to actually doing it, that's when all your scruples – the "if"s" and "but"s" and "it depends" – start coming out. Because they're right there in front of you now, you see, and you've got to look them in the eye and kill them. No longer shadows, but men. And that's what you can't stomach: they're men, just like you. You expect someone else to do the dirty work, to get rid of them for you. And you don't even want to be there when they're doing it . . . Let Lieutenant Veleno get on with it, you say . . .'

Yes, I did feel the rub of that ambiguity, the weight of all those contradictions – yet I just couldn't bring myself to do it. Who knows where it would have led?

I tried to defend myself: 'But we joined to go to the Front . . . to fight the enemy with equal weapons, face to face . . .'

And then he'd retort: 'Oh yes, unto death – is that it? To die for your country, for the Great Cause . . . Do me a favour! It's a cop-out, that's all it is! Even at the Front you'd be killing people. To die means nothing, not a damn thing! No one can imagine their own death. Killing is the thing, crossing that frontier. Now that's a concrete act of will all right! Because in killing another man you live through your own death, and that's when you show that you possess something which you value more than life itself – yours or anyone else's!'

I'd look for bloodstains on their hands or something in their faces which made them different from me. The thought that they might be capable of performing the unequivocal act, of reaching the point of no return, both repelled and fascinated me. I could never bring myself to ask them what they'd been through, how it had affected them inside, what it was like over there. For example, when Blondie and I used to go to the pictures together, we'd talk about such things, but once we got to that point the conversation would just lapse. The world around us had returned to normal: there were people in the streets, women with babies, smiles, workmen . . . And once those events were free of all the gloom and passion that had been their catalyst, they became loaded with a kind of awful weight. It was as though a barrier lay between us, an obstacle which no one could ever overcome. Blondie grew silent, and I saw his face harden, sensed him withdraw into himself. Nervously, he rummaged in his pocket for a cigarette and lit it. I remembered what he'd said to me at the time: 'I joined the firing-squad for the experience: to make a man of myself.' But what was that supposed to mean – that you became a man when you killed someone? His silence held no answers. And walking in front of him, I could feel him locked in a shell which cut him off from everything else; I realized then that the act which, in his words, had been going to make a man of him had instead pushed him beyond a wordless frontier, banishing him forever into a terrible and futile solitude.

And yet there was a time when I would have done it. If things had worked out differently, it would've been my turn, and I would have done it. It was an order I would have obeyed: holding on to the butt, I would have fired those shots. I don't remember feeling anything in particular at the time, just a kind of practical interest in the mechanics of how I was going to do it. I must admit that I was also excited by the thought of actually shooting for real at a living target. The sergeant said to me: 'When he comes out of the hotel, act as though nothing's up; let him get a few steps away, and then you shoot. You shout "Halt", then fire straight away.'

There were sergeants, captains, uniforms: the war, positions-orders to be obeyed.

'Understood?'

'Yessir.'

'He's not to escape.'

111

'Yessir.'

I think he might have even slapped me on the back as though to say: 'There's a good lad!' And off he went, with all the confidence and elegance of a veteran in his walk.

Then the front door of the hotel opened, and I saw the square of light reflected on the opposite wall, diffusing into the street, as the sound of voices, grown unexpectedly loud, rose up from the well-lit hallway and into the silence of the night.

I never found out who he was: I had just had a faint glimpse of his shoulders in the dark as he was driven to our headquarters at the hotel. I noticed, too, that the two officers who accompanied him seemed to treat him with a kind of respect. The moment he crossed the brilliantly-lit threshold, I saw the outline of his profile as he turned for a moment to let the others pass. And I was supposed to kill him!

Perhaps the darkness made my task seem easier, less real to me, as though the black night had the power to somehow blot out the physical consequences of my act: the body lying a few feet away from where I was hiding, its features increasingly taking on the ineluctable stillness of death.

All I'd been told was that he was a Communist, an important one. And yet thinking back, not even that made any difference. The only thing that mattered was that I'd been given an order, there was a target, and I had to shoot at it . . . Before me lay the darkening square, where I was supposed to let him walk a few steps, then fire. A cold, cutting wind blew down from the mountains, as I sat behind my machine-gun, waiting.

But things didn't turn out according to plan, and at a certain point the sergeant emerged, yelling: 'What the hell d'you think you're playing at! You let him get away!'

I didn't understand: 'What? Did he leave? Which one was he?'

At least three of them had left together – two in uniform – and they'd headed off down the road, chatting. At the bottom they'd split up.

I heard the Captain bellowing from the hallway in a furious voice: 'For fuck's sake! What kind of rubbish of soldiers are they! They don't even know how to obey an order!'

A memorial plaque must have been put up at the spot, but I never once considered looking for it when, years later, I returned to the area. I'm sure I would have been able to find it though, in the labyrinth of alleyways which made up the old quarter of the city. It couldn't have been very far from the square where our headquarters were situated, because I seem to remember that when all the shouting and yelling broke out a few minutes later, it only took me a few minutes to get there.

A small group of soldiers, led by the lieutenant, stood in front of a closed doorway, while a little further on I could just make out the outline of a figure hunched over a darker shape on the ground. I understood at once what had happened, as two harsh shots rang out from the other side, accompanied by a brief spurt of flame.

'What's the point now?' I heard one of the soldiers mutter.

Standing in the doorway, illuminated for an instant by the beam of a flashlight, I saw that the lieutenant had a strange grimace on his face, his lips frozen into a kind of dull smile, as though under the circumstances it were the only thing possible. Then, from behind the closed shutters of a house, a woman's shrill cries rose into the air, followed by someone trying to calm her in whispers.

Our footsteps grew more distant, and the sound of our rumbling voices echoed through the dark alley-way, as a soldier paced up and down, slapping his arms against his body to keep warm.

What had happened was that, in a fury, the captain had sent for his men and they'd marched up to the man's house. They made him come down on a pretext, and as he reached the doorway, they heard him trying to reassure his wife. 'Come on now, give it a rest! Probably they just need some information from me. Calm down, it's all been sorted out.' Then they ordered him to move, and the lieutenant shot him in the back.

I remember a vague mist settling over the darkness, as we stood there with balaclavas under our helmets, wearing grey-green woollen gloves. The lieutenant walked on, reloading his tommy-gun: picking out a handful of bullets from his pocket, he rapidly slipped them one by one into the magazine. He couldn't have been more than about twenty years old, as he stood there, his entire attention concentrated on that one act: picking up the bullets and loading them one by one into the magazine with the ball of his thumb.

Over forty years have gone by since then, and he too has aged a lot.

I used to see him until quite recently. Almost every summer he'd return from the Caribbean with his rainbow shirts and his gaudy ties, and each time he'd dig out all his old friends – 'his' men, as he liked to call them. He'd ring up:

'How are you? Let's get together.'

He'd married a Spanish woman with enormous, black, kohl-rimmed eyes. She must have been in her fifties – plumpish, querulous, but well-preserved. He sounded like a Spanish *mujer* himself now, with a mournful, gossipy ring to his voice. They were the kind of couple you'd see getting off the coach at Villa d'Este with cameras and leather hold-alls around their necks. Still young and sparky looking, they'd go and dance the rhumba and the cha-cha at discothèques, hurling themselves around and sweating: *The king of Portugal/He likes to dance the samba/Swaying like a mamba/He thinks he's oh-so-cool/But to us he's just a fool!*

Mass on Sundays, too.

He can do it all because he is still alive: talking, eating, travelling, booking hotels, places to stay. And he laughs, too, a really incredible laugh: drawing back his upper lip and gulping as though there were something stuck in his throat preventing the laughter from bursting out. They are always touching each other too: 'When I wake up in the mornings,' he says, 'the first thing I do is feel around with my feet for Concepcion's feet.' If he doesn't find them, it troubles him. She lays out a clean shirt on a chair for him, along with his underwear and a pair of nylon socks.

And there are those hands of his – always on the table, touching you as he talks, always needing to be in contact. He's also picked up this habit of holding your face between his palms when he meets you, and standing there, scrutinizing you with those watery blue eyes of his, dilated behind a pair of thick lenses. It is as if he is trying to uncover who knows what, hoping to somehow place you with that fixed smile – as though all that touching is a means of possessing you, of establishing a link with the outside world.

They don't have children. Sitting at the head of the table, he reminds me of a statue of some archaic god which the sculptor hasn't yet managed to free from the stone. His wife places the food before him, taking away the empty plates. He eats in silence, bringing each spoonful to his mouth, chewing at length,

114

and swallowing. There doesn't seem to be any relationship between himself and the food: not even need – a satisfied craving – nothing. It makes you think he could go on forever like that: the years would pass, and he'd still be there, chomping away.

When you ask him something, he says 'What?', looking around in surprise. Then he makes you repeat the question, to give him time to dig out an answer from his bag of clichés.

And when he talks about those events, it's in a sing-song way, hiding a stubborn denial behind that flabby exterior. He speaks of it all in general terms, as though it were something he'd picked up from an illustrated historical weekly, submerging the events he'd been part of it in a mass of generalities – as respectable and inevitable as it all now seemed. If you happen to remind him of a precise name or episode – not those of course, not those – he looks startled, dazed, peering at you with a frightened, watchful expression in those dull eyes. The grimace is back on his face too – that smile which is perhaps just the sign of a mask trying to control the unexpected wave of terror welling up inside him, faced by details which are threatening to dislodge those events from the order he'd tidied them into waiting to confront him in all their terrible reality. Immediately he searches for words, gestures, anything to smother – as though with a handful of pebbles – that menacing pulse beating inside him, which has appeared from who knows where.

I sometimes wondered what would happen, if, in the middle of a conversation, you were to look him straight in the eye, and to say to him in a precise, cold voice: 'What about the one you went to get from his house at Varallo, the one whose back you fired a volley of bullets into, right on his own doorstep?'

I'm sure he'd be stunned for a moment then, letting out the scream of a wounded beast, he'd hurl himself on top of you, maddened by rage.

Or maybe he'd cry his first, humble tears as a man.

Chapter VII

THEY never mingled with us. We'd see them wandering around the courtyard in ill-fitting clothes, looking bored, as though they were asking themselves: 'What on earth did we come here for?' An order had gone out for them to take up arms.

In the mornings, there'd always be someone sitting by the misty window-panes: 'Look out – there's more of 'em coming.'

And if, strutting down the corridor in our usual high-handed fashion, we happened to run into them, they'd look at each other with incredulous faces, as though to say: 'Who *are* this lot? Are they off their heads or something?'

At times fights and arguments would break out because one of them had given us a dirty look, or hadn't let us pass in the corridor.

'Move it, blockheads!'

Their officers, however, dressed in faded, old-fashioned uniforms which recalled a bygone era (as though they'd been fished out of the bottom of some cupboard), would pass us uneasily, almost apologizing for the rank they'd never dream of pulling.

The storerooms were half-empty now, with piles of old rubbish – a few dented flasks, some blankets – heaped up in a corner. A warrant officer, wearing the badge of the 41st infantry of the 3rd Grenadiers, greeted us with a jolly wave and a smile, looking for all the world like any bustling, good-humoured civilian.

At mealtimes, they'd line up patiently by the thin rows of stunted trees, waiting for the soup caldrons – old petrol drums – to arrive, banging their mess-tins together, which made the cracked, clanging sound that aluminium always does. In the air there was a despondent feeling of people who were doing things without real conviction, grudgingly resigned to the hardship which even the jokes of the cook (standing there, legs apart in his big boots, ladling soup into the mess-tins in one swift movement) were not enough to dispel.

'Roll up, lads! Roll up! The feast's about to begin, and it don't cost a penny!'

They sat around the courtyard in little groups, eating in

116

silence, occasionally muttering amongst themselves in dialect – boys from the same village who already knew and understood each other as civilians. We didn't mix with them: we went to eat elsewhere, finding a stone or a step to sit on.

The smell and taste of your mess-tin became very familiar: the stench of old fat which had never quite been scraped away, of boiled cabbage-stalks and potatoes, which you thought must go back to the days of the First World War or even beyond. They were all there, your companions, bent over the soup, concentrating on each mouthful, chewing slowly and purposefully. It was good food, spoonfuls of slightly over-cooked pasta, still red from the sauce.

We threw them the occasional disdainful look, conscious of that passive, unwarlike manner of theirs, as though they believed it was fate that had led them there. 'What use'll that lot ever be?' someone said. 'What was the point of bringing them here in the first place? At the slightest chance they'll hop it – back to shovelling manure in the stable!'

At this they'd look around towards the great door which kept them shut in like cattle, as though they were waiting for it to open at any moment and set them free – free to return to the villages on the plains, back down wide roads flanked by poplars and mulberry bushes, back to those dark hamlets set in the midst of marshland, back to where they came from.

By contrast, the reinforcements from Ferrara were a noisy, arrogant lot. They arrived that evening, singing: standing in the dormitory with our faces pressed against the window, we watched them file past in line – bumptious and picturesque in non-regulation uniforms, which they'd livened up with an assortment of ribbons and badges.

Swagger-stick in his hand, legs apart, Commander Ussari was in the courtyard waiting to inspect each one personally.

'Where you from?' he shouted.

'From the Alps Chasseurs,' one replied.

At this he was overtaken by one of his bouts of rage: 'Don't give me that!' he bellowed. 'What sort of Alps or Pyrenees Chasseur are you! D'you know what you are?' he yelled in his face, 'You're nothing but a mosquito-catcher, a filthy mosquito- catcher from the marshland of Copparo! And just you remember that!'

Gnashing his teeth and hopping up and down before the stunned row of soldiers, he went on: 'D'you know where you happen to be? Do you realize what an honour this is?' he shouted, with a wicked expression in his eyes, the veins on his neck all swollen. And then he launched into a description of the Red M's badges awarded to those who had been under fire for six months at the front, and of the gold medal on the standard, and of the strongholds on the Don, and of the 25th of July –

'We've never taken off our badges! Never surrendered our arms! On the eighth of September, the day of betrayal, we were the only ones – the only ones – left to guard the faith!'

Groups of soldiers, sitting here and there on the ground, were making the most of the scene, while officers, looking casual and impassive, stood silently beneath the archway of the hall.

'And just you remember one thing,' he went on, 'once you're in – you don't get out!' He lowered his voice menacingly and the words came out in a gurgle: 'There's only one way out of the M battalions – and that's in a wooden coat!' He paused for a moment, then shouted: 'In a wooden coat with a zinc lining – d'you hear!'

Then out came the flat feet, the asthma, the prostate trouble. They listed their ailments, staring down at the toes of their boots, looking around stealthily for help which never materialized. Those who survived the ordeal took a step forward and were herded into a corner. The others – officers, NCOs and their men – were given one last volley of abuse, then shunted off by the worst of the corporals and left to his mercy.

'Quick march! Quick march!' bawled Blondie in a voice like a whip, beautiful as an avenging angel. 'Move it!'

Sweating and broken now, their fists clenched, elbows pressed close to their sides, they were forced to do another fifty laps, keeping time, around the courtyard: one two, one two, one two. Until nightfall.

Then on the following morning at dawn, before the notes of the bugler's trumpet lacerated the misty silence of the courtyard, we heard the ones with their flat feet, their stomach ulcers, their piles, running past the barracks towards the station, footsteps dragging, a little crestfallen, but glad all the same to have got away from that maniac.

The few of them who did make it through the selection process joined the companies. They came from places with strange-sounding names: Lagosanto, Commacchio, Copparo – full of swamps and lagoons, canals, mosquitoes, and miles of rushes.

'Where were you on September 8th?' the Cadet shouted at one of them, his fez streaming behind his neck. 'What were you doing on September 8th?' Then, without warning, his voice changed, and putting his arm around his shoulder, he led him towards his bunk, murmuring words of advice in his ear, until, equally suddenly, he just left him there, stupefied, and with the same volubility he launched into another victim.

On the whole they were good enough lads, always talking away in a throaty, full-blooded dialect, which sounded loose and conversational, full of open vowels and sucked-in s's – entirely suited to the cunts and hand-jobs they liked to spend their time discussing, and indeed around which most of their interests seemed to lie.

And it was they with their cheerful nonchalance who introduced us to the charms of the prostitutes in the brothel, over at the little green house by the railway track at the end of the avenue. With a jest or a quip they even managed to extract a smile from the Madame, who would sit grim-faced behind the cash-desk, a ticket-book in her hand.

Knowing more than what is necessary about life, they were above not only our awful business but everything that happened out there. And when you stripped off and stood there in the middle of the room, with your trousers around your ankles, you became what you were really worth: a frightened little boy who'd left all his big talk outside the door.

'Well, don't just stand there! Come here and let's have a look at it!'

She squeezed it decisively between her thumb and forefinger from base to tip, pulling it up and down a few times, until you drew back in pain and disgust. 'Okay, okay, you're a clean boy.' Then swivelling only her top half around, perched there on the bidet, she washed it in the basin with professional dexterity.

They'd been suspicious in the beginning, but that was probably only due to their astonishment that anyone could still actually want to be in uniform. A little uncertainly, they came down into the parlour, wearing those filmy voile dresses you could see their

119

big, button-like nipples through: 'Where you from then?' they asked us. 'What are you doing here?' In the end though, a spirit of professionalism prevailed – that and the knowledge that we too were on the fringes of society.

It became our refuge: just one bed, the wardrobe with the suit-cases on top, the wash-stand covered in brushes and face-powders you weren't allowed anywhere near, the fur rug, and the folded military blanket tucked into the end of the bed to protect it from muddy boots. You'd spend an hour there in the warmth, smoking the occasional cigarette.

In high spirits we walked noisily through the door, our weekly allowance in our pockets. Even the smell became familiar and welcoming – that combined odour of make-up, disinfectant and sweaty bodies, so different from anything you were used to: the ambiguous smells of home, the school, the barracks.

The feeling of awkwardness never changed though, once you closed the door behind you and found yourself face to face with another human being whom you didn't know, and with whom you had no chance of either establishing a rapport there and then, or of entering into any other kind of ordinary dialogue. And when, without any kind of preamble, I was forced to uncover that crude, naked erection, it wasn't just a matter of shame – it was that the whole business wasn't how I'd carelessly assumed it would be from the expressions we used: having a good fuck or a screw. And it was no good telling myself that that's what I'd gone there for, that I was in a brothel and that's why people went to brothels, that the woman in front of me was just a whore. I couldn't get away from the fact that here was this person whom I didn't know from Eve, who meant nothing to me, and with whom, any minute now, I was supposed to enter into total union – that special, unique relationship.

She was an older woman with dyed hair, a slack body and two big, dark nipples. She squeezed me tight and I could feel her breath on my neck: 'You're just a little boy, aren't you . . . come, come to your mamma,' she whispered in my ear. I'd have much rather just lain there without doing a thing, basking in her close warmth, and letting it rest there against her stomach. She caressed me on the nape of the neck, whispering 'Come, come.'

We'd got there through the narrow streets in the centre, my companions steering me with as much certainty as if they'd been

following a scent: 'This way, down here – no . . . don't worry. I
know where I'm going.' Standing in the darkened hallway, I felt
my heart expand, pressing against my throat, as though it had
crossed the threshold of some inaccessible sanctuary. After the
irritation of the lights, and all the men leaning against the wall,
came the sudden sense of shock at the sight of all those naked
women, their bodies thrown into high definition by the men's
dark suits – all that bare flesh amongst the grey cloth. They
moved about with casual ease, drawing attention to the most
intimate parts of their body.

She was standing by the cash-desk, tall and slender, with a fine
neck. It seemed impossible: how could she be like all the others?
Then immediately she became unattainable . . . I wanted to
devour her with my eyes, but all I could do was throw her quick,
furtive glances, terrified lest she notice. As soon as anyone shifted
from the wall, my heart leapt to my mouth: right, that's it, I said
to myself, he'll take her away now . . . I had to clench my teeth to
stop the hard knot of emotion from exploding. Now I'll get up
and go, I kept saying to myself, all I have to do is walk past, and
without looking at her, just say the word . . . Right, in one
minute, just one more minute –

And instead I went with the other one. She came up to me and
said: 'Come along.' Undressing in a second, she sat there waiting
for me by the basin. I didn't dare look at her – especially at that
thick tuft of hair beneath her belly which I just managed to
glimpse. But after all the fussing about – soap, water, toilet-paper
– that part of you, now that you'd actually got it back, seemed to
have lost all value, and indeed any sense of belonging to you.
The almost medical atmosphere pushed you further away from
what had first brought you there, and it was now an effort to
recall your need with any degree of urgency. You tried to appear
nonchalant, but you didn't have a clue how to switch roles in
such a hurry.

She lay down on the middle of the bed, her back resting
against some cushions, and she opened her thighs. As I passed
over her left leg, I saw that large slit with its dark outline – her
whole groin yawning before me, like a mouth with no appetite.

All those things I'd heard people talk about were now dis-
played before me – not wantonly but soft, damp, a little droop-
ing. It gave me a faint stab of fear and surprise: I never imagined

it to be so bold and defined. Intimate and imperious, it was the most important part of her body, and I couldn't not look at it, not be drawn to it. I had envisaged it being more like a hidden flower, secret and delicate. I'd heard stories of violence, of blood and screams, and there instead was this opening, so adult and ready, so accommodating.

I barely had to push: everything at the entrance of her body seemed predisposed to penetration. What surprised me though, something I'd certainly not expected, was the living, beating warmth in there – a deep heat which wasn't mine, but to which I immediately became privy. It was as though I'd penetrated right into the living flesh, but gently, as it was meant to be, with a sense of being welcomed. She held her arms behind my back, whispering words into my ear. Even the acrid odour of powder and sweat clinging to her neck and the cushions – which at first I'd found unpleasant – now smelt good. That heat down there, too, wasn't confined to the part that penetrated, but had begun rising up inside me, radiating through my body and turning my limbs to fire. I felt fine – relaxed and wanted. I would've liked to have stayed there for a while, peacefully bound to her, without stirring, but I realized that it was time for me to make those movements I knew.

The orgasm, too, came differently from when I did it myself: not tugged this time, but sucked out by her with a sense of easy liberation. Then all at once the other human being, emerging from the haze of that abandon, awoke me by tapping me lightly on the shoulder: 'Hey, what d'you think you're playing at? You asleep or something?'

The main hall was smoky and hot, still packed with people. The other girl wasn't by the cash desk – not that it mattered a great deal anymore. Outside in the street, it was dark and dank.

The only risk was the usual one, but on the whole you took it cheerfully: it was inevitable, a kind of certificate of maturity. Once three of us went. She was a little, shrivelled-up old woman wearing faded clothes and worn shoes. She might not even have been a professional whore, seen there for the first time in a smoky hotel. We drew lots as to who should go first, because those who followed would find themselves wallowing around in somebody else's semen, something which made you feel a little sick. It never occurred to us however that the last one, after having screwed her, would end up in bed without knowing what to do with her. He held her for a bit, then he got tired of it. He was a young lad, a student, blond and stocky with a well-fed body. I heard them arguing in the gloom. She was timidly trying to defend herself as she searched in the darkness for her clothes. 'But where can I go at this time of night? What am I going to do?'

Even if I'd been awake I wouldn't have done anything. I was withdrawing further and further into sleep now, and although I hadn't forgotten those moments of tenderness a few minutes back, it was precisely in order to savour them languidly right up to the threshold of sleep that I did nothing. I didn't give a damn about her now: she was just a whore again, and she'd have to deal with it alone. Her smell lingered in the room, sweetish and slightly sickly. It clung to her skin, to her slip, as I lay there holding her, wanting to remain in the warmth. It was only afterwards, as all your other senses were reawakened and everything fell back into its proper place – distinct and removed – that it began to bother you.

We were reminded of it a few days later when the bloke who'd gone first came in with a worried, anxious face, and started asking us all these questions.

'Oh, but that was actually the smell of blennorrhoea', the others teased him, saying that we should have done the lemon test on her: 'It never fails,' they said, 'just a few drops right on the cunt, and if she hollers it means she's infected!'

Instead we were lucky. Every morning you'd be there squeezing it, waiting for the dreaded yellow drop to appear. In the end, though, he was the only one to get it. 'The whore! The bitch! Wait till I get my hands on her!'

And out of that coincidence came the explanation: 'It's simple: whoever fucked her first got it. He sucked her clean, all to himself!'

And so the prophylactic service was started. Sergeant Gaiba set up shop in the brothel, complete with gauze, ointment and syringes laid out on a polished table. Before leaving, you had to drop by.

Then one day Commander Ussari got up on a crate and gave us a lesson on sexual hygiene. 'I fuck too – and how!' he announced, puffing up with pride as though fucking were the most noble – the most fitting – pastime available to man. All our sniggering merely emphasized the pride we felt in the sexual prowess of that commander of ours, who did it every night. He even told us about his testicles: two steaming balls which swung from side to side like bells. 'If God provides, every night I get my oats,' he declared. It was like a kind of sacrament: after a night of drunken singing and revelry with his officers at the Three Kings hotel, there was always some local woman waiting in his bed, ready to bear the weight of that full-blooded, thick-set body: *Fuck her, fuck her, like an ass/Make the fat cheeks wobble on her ass!*

All you had to do on your way out of the brothel was to drop by Gaiba's – once a hemp-grower from Lower Ferrara – who'd be there with his flat face, his trousers poking out from beneath his white coat, waiting for you in his makeshift surgery. He'd squeeze it clumsily in his big, purple hands, and clutching an enormous syringe with a nickel-plated plunger, he'd inject you with 10cc of permanganate solution. Then with a hefty forefinger he'd spread two or three blobs of ointment – black and sticky as tar – all around the glans. Tall and stocky, he'd stand there, displaying a set of fine, horse-like teeth firmly entrenched in his gums, yelling: 'Come on there, lads!' An assistant would put a gauze plug on it, and you'd leave the place, not knowing what to do with that reeking bundle inside your pants. On the way out, going through the corridor, you'd pass by a row of soldiers, waiting dejectedly behind the door for their turn.

In the mornings, skin glowing, freed of that dense burden of semen, the commander was quite a sight as he stood there in the still mist-swathed drill-ground, looking rested and well. Massive thighs poised in a triumphant swagger, he reviewed the sweating troops:

'I need soldiers I can send to die for the Duce!' he thundered. 'Not a bunch of plague-ridden morons!'

Colonel Ussari of M Battalion! He who on September the 8th had never laid down his weapons! He who never once removed the red 'M' of his battalion! I remember his huge thighs, the turbid blood coursing furiously through the veins of that slow, swollen body.

He frightened me with the charge of violence and rage he carried around with him: 'D'you realize where you are?' he'd thunder, 'the honour that's been bestowed on you? You only leave this battalion in a wooden coat with a zinc lining.' I tried to conceal my fear from myself, but that power of life or death – subject to his moods – which he carried over everybody, scared the living daylights out of me. Who'd refuse if he gave the order to shoot you? Who was he answerable to?

I remember when he went to report to the governor of the province on the first raid: 'What?' the governor yelled at him. 'You've shot Osella? Are you mad? Are you off your head? D'you realize who Osella was? Do you? An old comrade no less! I'll report you to the Duce for this!'

He didn't let him finish. Dragging the governor by the arm – there in his own office, the very seat of his power – he led him over to the window which looked out on the courtyard.

'D'you see that platoon down there?' he said, pointing to the escort he'd brought with him. 'D'you see them? Well, all they need is a sign – just one word from me – and they'll come running up and put you against the wall too!'

What an impression it made on me when I saw him for the first time, after our final defeat, in civilian clothes! The word had got around: the commander's here! He's back, says he wants to see us again, to reassemble the troops. 'Nothing's over yet, lads. Be on the alert – this farce won't last. This time we'll sort them out for good – they're all out in the open now!'

Down there, at the bottom of Via Nomentana, Blondie and I caught a glimpse of him and his adjutant standing beneath the shadow of some plane-trees. We barely recognized him: a man in dark glasses, thighs already turning to fat, suspicious-looking, as so many people were at the time. He'd shaved off his moustache and goatee beard, but even then we didn't want to see things as they really were. Walking over to him, we stood sharply to attention with our right arms raised in the air: 'All present, sir!' We wanted to let him know that in spite of all the blows we'd received, nothing had changed for us. We were still the ones: the never-defeated, the ever-ready!

And instead we saw the colour drain from his features, and looking around with a pale, stunned face, he shouted: 'What the hell are you playing at? Are you mad?' Who could ever have imagined such a total transformation? Then without a single word or gesture, off he went, turning his back, fleeing as fast as he could, the tails of his jacket flapping against his thighs. 'Get lost!' shouted the adjutant hysterically, as swiftly and uneasily he too vanished on the commander's heels.

We heard that when it was all over, they'd got as far as Revó, Fondo.

Looking through his binoculars, he cried: 'There's another valley over there! We'll cover the whole area, we'll stop at Fondo! The second company's to go on ahead.'

'Surrender, save your skins!'

'Forward! The banner ahead!'

'But it's all over now, colonel! It's finished!'

'On with our song!'

'*Battaglioni del Duce, battaglioni . . .*'

'But Mussolini's dead!'

'Who said that – who said it? I'll have them shot!'

'He's dead, dead, dead . . . . d.'

'We'll go to Germany! We'll return, rebuild, get our revenge!'

But at Fondo, on 5th May 1945, they were forced to stop. Berlin had fallen, and the Führer had shot himself. The German units dropped their weapons and fled towards the Brenner pass; meanwhile Carletto Ferrari was trying to get back on his 'colonels or not colonels' hobby-horse:

'For fuck's sake, what's happening round here? We're not having another September 8th are we? We'll go on . . .'

'Come on, Carletto, can't you see there's nowhere to go! We're at Fondo – the end of the road!'

Then came the final showdown in the dining-room of the tavern at the staging-post: all the high-ranking officers standing to attention, red M's, stripes, ebony-handled daggers.

'Brother officers,' he began, 'honour requires us to shoot ourselves! We cannot survive this defeat!'

But then up jumped Captain Ponton, who'd been on familiar terms with him since that time at Passo Uarieu, and who spoke with a lisp: 'No way, Ussari, my man, not a chance!' And in the end it was Captain Ponton – coward and realist that he was – who managed to break the tension:

'All this hot air's a fine thing, my dear Colonel,' he said 'but we do want to save our skins, don't we – get home in one piece and all the rest of it!'

126

And so with tears running down their cheeks, the officers burnt the standard. Then came the last speech:

'Legionaries, it has been my honour . . .'

But what about the wooden coat, Commander? What about the zinc lining?

No, he never got lynched by a screaming mob shouting: Death to him! Death to him! which might have shown us what he really had down there – the two balls that were supposed to swing like harness bells. Instead, he slipped away with Don Fulgenzio, the army chaplain, staying at convents and seminaries on the way. He ended up in South America, growing cabbage and watercress in the Pampa: back to nature, heavy siestas, a bottle of wine on the table for those long, hot nights . . .

He used to write pathetic letters in a minute, petty-clerk's hand, speaking of his distant homeland, nostalgia for the country of his birth, telling us as Italian soldiers never to let the side down. I never wrote back. An obscure rancour prevented me from doing so. Not yet having come to terms with the whole business, I was still groping around for the right words to salvage some of it. Not him though: I had nothing at all in common with him. I hadn't yet managed to extricate myself from the sticky tangle of memories, self-reproach, alienation, and the solidarity which could not be denied. But not him. I didn't see why I should carry on sharing that burden of violence and blood, the executions at Borgosesia, at Crevacuore, at Sassocorvaro, at Tavullia, at . . .

Then, after twenty years, he returned. Everything fell under the statute of limitation: the death sentence, jail, the lot.

It was Lidia, the auxiliary, who told me about it, sitting amongst paper patterns and half-sewn garments in her dressmaker's workshop, her mother bent over the old Singer, nodding 'Yes, yes' with her head, but only to keep time with her foot going up and down on the pedal. There was already something cagey and suspicious in the way they treated me, sitting there muttering amongst themselves. 'It's different now, you see, he's passed over to the other side . . .'

Apparently the word had got around, and a few of the ultra-faithful – dredged up from here and there – went to meet him at the airport. Sitting there with her sad face and discoloured hair, Lidia showed me a head and shoulders photograph of the com-

127

mander. He looked like a kind of Italo-Argentinian Bonnie Prince Charlie: a toothbrush moustache, his face grown soft and florid, the eyes startled and almost dead-looking. 'Oh yes, he'd put on a bit of weight, you know – wasn't the same man at all,' said Lidia in her nasal, slightly atonal voice, as she sat stitching a piece of quilting. All that flesh bulging out of his clothes, the fancy tie, that stupefied expression. Could it really be the commander? That man, the commander – Colonel Ussari of M Battalion? And even the ones who'd gone out of a kind of fatalistic sense of pity, even they began to see, if only in flashes. But they wiped out that image because it was easier to turn away, to continue lying to yourself. Why give up your own little corner of wishful thinking?

'You know how it is, he'd let himself go a bit,' she went on, in that sing-song voice of hers, drawing clouds of steam from a double-breasted jacket she was pressing with an iron filled with embers. 'One day after another, so far from his homeland, and all those disappointments . . .' The pedal of the Singer monotonously groaned up and down to the accompaniment of her mother's head.

Apparently, just a few days after his arrival, he was in the middle of telling a story about the Amazonian snake called an anaconda, so long it could swallow an ox whole, and the others were all sitting there, bored, listening to him (the visits had grown less frequent: 'Shall we go and see the commander this evening?' 'For crying out loud, I've got things to do – my own life to lead', etc.) – anyway, in the middle of telling his story he went purple, staggered, lost his balance and fell to the ground. A stroke it was.

At the sight of his native soil
And the embrace of his beloved friends
That heart which had suffered so much
Broke –
And found rest in the peace of God.

He died at home in his polished iron bed, the eternal flame burning under the picture of the Sacred Heart, a priest beside him, and that smell of dried apples you always get in old-fashioned country houses. God, country and family. Purified by the sacraments – *pax Domini nostri Jesu Christi* – he was confessed and given communion by Don Guglielmo, who'd known him since

he was a boy and who was repeating, 'That fine figure of a commander – *Corpus Domini nostri Jesu Christi.*' He placed the host
on a lip which dribbled slightly at the corner. 'A little drop of
water, signora! Quickly, a little drop of water so that he can swallow the host . . .'

And what about Signora Osella who'd stood there that terrible
night at Borgosesia, hugging her fur coat to her body, benumbed
by lack of sleep in the foggy dawn?

'No signora, the commander is unable to see you,' the adjutant
said, without looking at her. And she, with her aristocratic face,
had said in a firm voice: 'I am not going to move from here. You
will have to throw me out by force.' The body and blood of our
Lord. And there he was in his blue suit, lying spread-eagled in
the catafalque, feet pressed together in their woollen socks. And
what about the ones we left lying on the damp pavement, soaked
in blood in the midst of all that carnage? 'They asked for a priest,
sir.' 'A priest? Do me a favour! We haven't got time to waste!
Move it, I said – move it!' . . . His hands joined together over
his belly, a mother-of-pearl rosary between his fingers, flowers,
candles . . . His wife there, his children, his legionaries, the local
band at the funeral, the family vault, wreaths. Commander
Merico Ussari in his black service-cap with the silver eagle,
standing there in that mist-streaked grey dawn, not knowing
where to rest his eyes. Commander Ussari, with that hook-like
arm hanging from his shoulder, nickel-plated dagger at his belt,
ready to brandish it like a Sicilian puppet: 'Here, take that, you'll
pay for your crimes!' Zap! Biff! Pow! Wham! Colonel Merico
Ussari of M Battalion, who on September 8th never weakened;
he and his followers, songs of war, camp-fires, shooting, mottoes,
raids, pennants hanging from tents, piss-ups and threats, blood-
sucking officers, vicious company commanders – he with his
dagger and swagger-stick, fighting for the Duce till the bitter end!

And now at the cemetery at Ascoli in the Marches, the
mahogany coffin moving along at a slow pace: *Ecce Agnus Dei qui
tollit peccata mundi . . . Exaudi nos Domine . . .* incense, wreaths,
the widow, dignitaries dressed in black . . .

Chapter VIII

TAKING a machine-gun to bits, laying it out in little pieces on a regulation blanket, dismantling it before your eyes, seeing how it was put together – loader, feed-spring, deflectors – as though in doing so, you might discover in its mechanism the secret of that fascination which rendered it an almost sacred object. After that, you put it together again, fitting each piece back with sharp, precise movements.

There was talk of explosives, of TNT – 'It's called that, you know, 'cause it's triple-strength nitrate' – of fulminate, loaders and chargers. We'd open those crude hand-grenades – Breda's, Balilla's, O-T-O's – just to show off to each other our familiarity with explosives, the disdain we felt for the danger. Everyone kept some in reserve in their rucksacks.

One of the clearest memories I have is of someone sitting on his bunk during the rest period, and polishing his pistol with manic, intense thoroughness. Click! Click! Click! went the bolt as he slid it into place: removing the barrel, he lubricated it, looking around suspiciously as though it were a precious object he had in his possession, a treasure to be protected.

We'd witnessed the ruin of an army, seen weapons become useless, wretched, obsolete, disposed of from one day to the next. In our imaginations the guns acquired a kind of mythical quality: we'd go and steal them from trains loaded with scrap-metal, which the Germans were sending back to Germany, then fix them up. From attic to cellar the guns popped out – weapons of all kinds, from all periods. And as the unreality of the war grew more marked, and the aims and objectives which had led us there increasingly confused, we held on to our weapons more tightly, seeing them as the only thing left we could identify with.

We roamed the ravaged cities with machine-guns around our necks and containers stuffed full of ammunition, trying by that performance to convince ourselves and the outside world that we really were soldiers – soldiers who still had a part to play in a war from which the armistice had excluded us. It became almost fetishistic: weapons were worshipped like symbolic objects – the

130

more lethal, the better. Then there were the magical ones, with supernatural powers like the weapons of the epic heroes – Achilles' spear, Siegfried's sword – which rose high above the ranks of ordinary weapons.

I remember covetous eyes lingering on Lieutenant Mazzoni's automatic, which he'd wrested from one of them by throwing himself into the line of fire. Our imaginations were kindled, too, by Pinguino's stories: he'd been over to the other side, and he told us about a gun we'd never seen before – the *Taxun*, the legendary tommy-gun of the partisan leader, Moscatelli. 'Do me a favour, it's not Russian or American! I'm telling you it's a gun in a million, and he's the only one who's got one.' Capable of firing three consecutive rounds of forty, who could tell what planet it must have rained down from! 'As soon your first one's finished, you slip in a clip – away with that, and you're ready for a third!' All that without having to pause for a second!

If you got hold of one of those you became invulnerable, safe inside a cloud of fire and bullets which the enemy couldn't hope to penetrate. Like a feudal knight, you'd display it before the avid, reverent eyes of the others: locked inside your armour, you became as aloof and invulnerable as a god of war.

And instead, the real hero of that war was one of the shoddiest, most basic guns ever made: a rubbishy barrel soldered on to a bit of moulded sheet-metal, and fitted out with a percussion pin and striker. That was it: a Sten.

The first time we ever got hold of one, Carletto Ferrari picked it up and, turning it over once or twice, handed it back with a grimace. 'They're already free', he said. 'With rubbish like that they've already lost the war.'

But in fact Carletto's and Bonazzoli's war – a war of decent weapons, fanfares, piss-ups with your friends, the Front, strongholds – all that had been over for quite some time. All that remained was the aftermath, symbolized by an object which bore more resemblance to a primitive cooking-utensil than to a gun. Designed purely for the purpose of killing – ending the game, getting rid of the dross – it was an instrument whose very austerity expressed a rejection of all that was false or hypocritically gallant, or rhetorical, in the act of killing a man. You just positioned yourself behind a tree, Sten extended, tra-tra-tra, and that was it.

Another one down, a notch on the barrel of your gun, and off you went. All as it should be.

After a certain point, those bits of scrap metal began raining down from the sky in their thousands, filling the valleys and sub-urbs with angry rattles and short, vindictive bursts of gunfire. You could instantly recognize the sound of a Sten: a little slower, more staccato than a tommy-gun, it was made up of individual, muffled shots. Haunting, too, was that pretence of a personal vendetta, a settling of old scores: this one's for you, my Fascist friend, just one bullet, no trimmings, no regrets . . . After that you threw it away, just like a rusty old tin-opener or a used beer-can. It was the first consumer product we knew.

And when, at the end of the war, we saw them parading up and down the city streets, all spruced up in uniforms which had been unearthed at the last minute from some military ware-house, we immediately recognized the Sten – off-key and already out of date as it was – as the only authentic note in the entire battle.

If that shoddy weapon soon became their symbol, then there's no doubt that the dagger was ours: *A dagger between your teeth,/grenade in your hand!*

In our iconographic vision of the world, that most antiquated, provocative of weapons and all its associated ritual reigned supreme. At the altar of the Fascist martyrs, a dagger thrust into a block of stone took the place of a cross.

'Hail to the Duce!'

The blades glittered in the air.

'And to us!'

A dagger rose out of the flag-poles of our black standards like a challenge, a warning, to the heavens.

It was virile, phallic even – you gripped the handle protruding from your side: it felt hard and strong, then, 'baring' the blade, you flung yourself, 'man to man', towards the enemy. All units had started wearing them in their belts. They came in a variety of shapes and sizes: broad-bladed like swords, the haft shaped to the hand, with hilts like eagles' beaks, polished blades, nickel-plated blades, combat knives, parade knives. I'd seen old *squadristi* commanders' daggers with triangular blades – weapons that could cut you with a wound that would never heal; subtle and deadly as stilettos with their mother-of-pearl handles, they were almost like surgical instruments.

It was our trademark: consecrated by a political act, by the fury of taking sides, it was handed down by the *arditi*, bringing us back to the days of bitter factions, of Guelfs and Ghibellines, of old, sordid feuds. In our symbolism it evoked naked courage, a blind, plebeian violence that had no relation to the aloof, aristocratic sword. You faced your enemy with your dagger – close enough to breathe in his breath, to look him in the eye, to smear yourself with his blood.

The veterans who'd been at the Russian Front maintained that, deep down, the Germans were cowards. 'If they start getting too loud and big for their boots,' they said, 'just pull out your knife and see if they don't quieten down a bit.' It was our weapon, a southern weapon, evoking Sicilian Vespers and Corsican Vendettas.

The blades were rusty and corroded, spotted with bits of left-over food. We used them for opening tins or making holes in our belts. When there was a ceremony, we'd get them out and shine them as best as we could, so they'd gleam in the air.

There were some blokes who scratched the names of their girl-friends on them; one had even engraved his mother's pet name – Musi, it was.

Mother don't weep
When the advance begins . . .

Pino Mazzoni once finished someone off with his dagger. Following the trail of blood on the grass, he went after him on all fours, dragging his wounded leg behind him, until he caught up with him in the hayloft where he'd taken refuge. There he stabbed him.

After that, the 'Red' of Borgosesia – in order to avenge the seven killed in our last scrap – got hold of one of our soldiers during the ambush at Ponte della Pietà and, grabbing hold of his dagger, stabbed him seven times.

Weapons.

Weapons you carried around with you, dismantled, cleaned, greased, placed in position, drew back and reloaded from the shoulder, cleaned again, brought out, brandished . . . weapons you carried and carried . . . Heavy cumbersome objects that wore you out, covered you with bruises, hindered your movements. And which you could never be rid of.

We didn't read newspapers or listen to the radio. The outside world held no interest for us – either that, or we just wanted to ignore it. Only every now and then would the echo of some event reach us: the Russian Front extending to the Vistula, the Normandy landings, but it was as though it had no bearing whatsoever on our lives.

Word got round that ministries and recruiting offices had been re-opened: we'd seen recruits setting off reluctantly for training camps in Germany. Odd names would reach us – Pavolini, Ricci, Bufarini – which either meant nothing, or merely conjured up images of the tired, distant past. 'Long live the Duce!' said Sergeant Acciaroli. 'The rest are all shit – shit!'

The day they presented us with a new flag – the tricolour banner and an eagle with outstretched wings – in place of the one with the hole in the middle, all the companies were lined up in the courtyard, the officers wearing their decorations. And that's when Domaneschi (who was standing there clutching his dagger, right arm extended at eye level) asked timidly: 'What's this Social Republic meant to be then?' And it was Bonazzoli, his broad, serene face framed by the helmet-strap, who replied in a serious, mournful voice: 'A republic of rags, that's what!'

Sometimes you'd come across a group of German soldiers in a bar, huddled together in a corner, their heavy uniforms clinging to their bodies. They drank with great seriousness, bringing their glasses to a brief halt by their chins: '*Prosit!*' Sometimes they'd link arms and start singing, swaying their torsos from side to side.

We were fascinated by them: the way they looked so steely with their big pistols by their sides, their uniforms covered with all those hooks and studs for hanging accoutrements. Their way of talking – so that you could never make out whether they were angry or if it was just the way their language sounded – both irritated and intimidated us.

We sought their 'camaraderie' in the way we'd read in newspapers: someone would go over and, slapping them on the shoulder, say: '*Kamaraden, kamaraden, trinken*', hoping by that familiarity to appropriate, at least in part, some of their strength,

134

to lose himself in a common identity. They were unpredictable though, often taking refuge in curt gestures as though they were afraid of getting mixed up in something murky and suspicious, or as if they wanted to cling to the reserve which allowed them to assume their peremptory tone and manner.

Someone stuck our emblems, the red M's and the crossed daggers, under their noses. 'This means attack! D'you understand? *Sturm! Verstanden? Sturm!*' They didn't seem to be impressed as they sat there, watching us uncertainly, asking themselves what all our expansiveness and exhibitionism could be in aid of. They did thaw a little when they saw a ribbon from the Russian campaign on one of the veteran's jackets. They pointed to it, nodding their heads respectfully, as though the red ribbon with its black stripe and white border had established a point of contact – a kind of common ground from which we, the novices, felt ourselves excluded.

The Cremonesi listed the places they'd been to: 'Gomel . . . Kantemirovka,' then asked them: 'You, Gomel . . . Don?' almost as if they believed they might have met in those far-off war zones. They didn't understand each other though: '*Ich zwanziche division Panzergrenadier*', growled the one they'd asked, showing off his ribbons. '*Ja, ja, Panzergrenadier . . .*' he nodded decisively, making a few more incomprehensible noises as he turned to his comrades for confirmation. Their inability to communicate made them irritable: '*Nein, nein*', they said, waving a hand in the air as though to rid of something in front of them. The Cremonesi just shrugged their shoulders, indifferent to the incomprehension.

They may have been talking about the same places and the same events, but the names were pronounced in such different ways, the two languages were so utterly unlike one another, that they might just as well have been talking about other places, other events, from a different era, a different war.

Sometimes we'd force ourselves to speak, lying on our bunks in the bare dormitory, looking up at the ceiling. They were confused conversations though, composed of such poor, inaccurate words that they never led anywhere. You thought you had so much to say, but when it came to the crunch, the knot gripping

135

your insides would just dissolve into childish prattle, made up of shared places and a few odd phrases picked up here and there. Annoyed at your own uselessness, you just let it drop.

'Who needs words, anyway?' said Giannetto Lettari, sitting on the edge of the mattress, his feet dangling over Fabio who lay on the bunk beneath him. 'All words do is tie you up in knots and confuse your ideas: you want to say one thing, and something else comes out instead.'

Nodding his big head, Fabio added with characteristic seriousness: 'There are some things you can't explain,' he said, 'things you just *feel* are a certain way, and that's it . . . What's the point of trying to explain them – if they haven't got it inside them, if they can't feel it, then there's no point in trying to make yourself understood.'

We'd picked up the mottos, key words such as Honour, Loyalty, Combat. What good were they, though? They gave you a thrill as you said them, but there they remained, surrounded by all that emptiness. What did they have to do with what was actually happening, with the events we'd glimpsed here and there through the cracks in the wall of rejection we were hiding behind? The war we'd set out to fight certainly wasn't the same one that was raging throughout every corner of Europe, one which every now and then we'd hear scraps of news about. In fact it was more like those wars we fought in the municipal parks: scuffles, a rag hanging on a pole in place of a flag, and the dead being carried to their graves amidst bursts of gunfire.

There was to be no *afterwards* to the story, no sequel grounded in concrete facts and circumstances. At a certain point it would just end, there at the edge of the plain, with a cross and a helmet on your grave. It had all taken place within the realms of our imagination, and that's where it would end – in a void.

And if you tried to imagine a possible tomorrow, all you came up with was a vision of the past, only with all the shadows and errors wiped out. It was the world of childhood – all our idols restored to their positions, ready to protect and defend us – unwinding there before our eyes, like a film shot backwards; repeated every morning, always the same.

Yet even amongst ourselves there seemed to be someone who held a clear idea as to what that *afterwards* might hold: Mazzoni, the young officer whose example irrevocably mapped out Fabio Grama's destiny.

It was actually Fabio himself who told me, years later, sitting in my room. The big window overlooking the terrace was wide open, the mild evening air filtering in. At times he used to come and see me: I'd hear an uncertain knock and there he'd be, standing by the door, with a timid little smile on his lips.

He told me how sometimes Mazzoni would sit in the middle of their circle, trying to make them see that no matter how things turned out, there'd never be a place for them: 'We've had it', he'd say. 'Once this war's over, we won't be needed any more. We'll just have to disappear. After all we've been through, how could we possibly expect to go back to an ordinary, run-of-the-mill existence? Can you imagine me in a tie, going to the office every morning with my brief-case? Once we've fulfilled our destiny, we simply have to vanish.'

Years had gone by, and all the old threads began to weaken. Occasionally we'd meet up, by chance usually – one bloke here, another one there – but Fabio still used to come round and see me. Only much later on did I realize how important it was for him to keep up that contact, a single link between the present and those events. He saw me as somebody who could make those memories real for him – memories which were becoming increasingly blurred around the edges.

He was seduced by the fascinating air that young officer emanated. I remember that Fabio had put together a collection of photographs dating from that time, and how Mazzoni appeared in almost all of them: beret pulled down over one eye, that athletic body, the boyish face with its tight little mouth. He had a closed, adolescent beauty. Even at the time he aroused mixed feelings of admiration and fear. I could sense a sacred aura about him, the stuff of which our myths were made. A noble, implacable hero, who both fascinated and appalled us.

'He used to talk about blood,' murmured Fabio, 'saying that Italy "needed our blood", that our lives as men were worthless, that we Italians "had to die" in order to cleanse ourselves of the shame of that betrayal. There was only one way to redeem ourselves, he said – through death! It was as though we were all somehow responsible, and had to pay the price for what had happened. He said that "the earth must be made fertile again by our blood".'

Those words stunned me, even reaching me as they did from a period which was slipping further and further away into the imprecise limbo of memory with each day that passed. Branded forever on the mind of that solitary boy, they still had the power to transport us back into the atmosphere of desperation and death which we'd breathed in, grown drunk on. It was one of our obsessions – to die, to know how to die! The whole mystique of courage revolved around the ability to confront death. In the end, a man was valued for his ability to die.

'Yes, Mazzoni was his role-model . . . Mazzoni and Fabio's own moral rigidity, that uprightness of his . . .' repeated Enzo, shaking his head, a glass of whisky in his hand, when almost thirty years later I went to visit him on a rainy afternoon to find out more about his brother's death.

'Just like Mazzoni, Fabio couldn't stomach compromises.'

Enzo's suffering was plain to see, as my questions forced him to re-live events:

'D'you remember when Mazzoni turned up in Rome to enlist, and how he defended his stars, the symbols of the royal army, with a pistol in his hand? Everyone had gathered around him, wanting to rip them off: "Off with your stars!", they were yelling from all sides, "Off with 'em!"

'We'd pulled off those hated emblems even from generals' tunics, and the entrance-hall was studded with little metal pieces which we ground into the floor with our boots. But Mazzoni just pulled out his gun, and leaning against the wall he said: "I'm not taking off my stars – I'm not ashamed of them! If anyone comes close, I'll kill him!"

'He'd have done it, too', said Enzo. 'We realized immediately that he'd have done it.'

The rain was beating against the window-panes, and down on the garden. All those distant events were coming back now – Pino Mazzoni . . . Lieutenant Pino Mazzoni of Zara! Who was that young boy, just over twenty, as handsome and reserved as a dark avenging angel, who left a trail of blood in his wake? Deep down, what did I really know about him? An episode came back to me: one day, Fabio and I were leafing through the photographs he collected – which, from time to time he'd bring around to show me – when my mother came in. Picking one up, she looked at it and said: 'Of course, I remember him! He's dead

138

now, isn't he?' Then, as though she were talking to herself, she added: 'A good-looking boy, he was – a very good-looking boy!' And then she commented: 'He never smiled though', and searching back through her memory she said, 'I can picture him now, that evening when your battalion set off from the station at Rome. There was me, poor Signora Fasano, and the mother of that stout boy with the glasses. Anyway, he was standing there on the empty platform, it was getting dark, no one out on the streets anymore, just him – I tell you, it gave me quite a turn! And I thought to myself then; you know, it looks as though he were the last person left on this earth . . . just think . . . and yet! Heavens above what difficult times they were! What difficult times we've been through, my sons!'

Her saying 'he never smiled' struck me – in fact it was the only picture I had of him. And, thinking about it, she was right: he never smiled. An entire legend had formed around him, of how all his family – mother and sisters – had been burned alive in their house by Yugoslav partisans. Apparently he had a girl in Zara, as brave as he was, by all accounts, a kind of Valkyrie. He was withdrawn and severe, never joined in with his fellow-officers drinking and horsing around. Once he received an order he'd just say 'Yessir' and he'd be off with his platoon, as absorbed and aloof as a Greek hero. We never once saw him turn on a prisoner.

With obvious difficulty, Enzo told me about one episode he remembered. 'It was almost a case of murder', he said. 'We were very near the Front when we came across this bloke who turned out to be a deserter. Mazzoni told him to walk on, then without batting an eyelid, he shot him. After that he took a scrap of paper and wrote down that he'd been executed according to instructions. Then he lifted up one of his feet, stuck the note underneath it, and we went on marching.'

In the years immediately following those events, Fabio and I used to walk up and down Via Merulana, in the midst of all the people. How strange and different everything seemed to me! Green trams lurching towards San Giovanni, all those people who had things to do, who were part of day-to-day life that seemed to have no bearing on us. How ordinary that street, those people and their smells seemed to me, and how cut off from it all I felt!

I used to talk in order to smother the sense of unreality which threatened to engulf us. Where had it all happened? Fabio's pleasure was plain to see when he listened to me go back over the events. I sensed his need for that 'us', for something to cling on to in a world which seemed to be disintegrating around him. It was a vague identity, though, anchored to a negative state; indeed in the end we'd probably have found it easier to say what we were not – and what we had no desire to be – than what we were, and hoped to be. 'We're the ones who said "no" and left', said Fabio. And that's where we'd remained, in a blurred, uncertain region about ten centimetres away from reality.

Then one day I managed to get hold of the book I'd heard so much about, the one Mazzoni was supposed to have bought all the copies he could lay hands on, and distributed among his men: *I Proscritti*, it was called. It was said that in that precious book – which in our minds acquired the proportions of a kind of bible, an initiatory text for the elect few – you found everything we'd lived through but were unable to express ourselves. I devoured it voluptuously, drunkenly abandoning myself to its dark atmosphere of bloodshed and violence. So vividly did I live through it that it seemed to be a series of extracts from my own life, rather than a mere book. The desperate attack of the Free Corps in that godforsaken region of the Baltic, the clashes in the square, machine-gun fire rattling at street corners, Kern and Fisher and their lonely death in the abandoned tower by the Saale. *In life, bloodshed and knowledge must come together. Only then will the spirit be born* . . . So that's where Mazzoni had found his identity, where he'd learnt those expressions, absorbed that mystique.

Fabio told me about the circumstances of his death: 'It was all over – Milan liberated, Mussolini killed – but every morning he'd still come down, inspect the platoon, take a roll-call and review the troops. On his way out he'd stroke the machine-guns mounted in the middle of the room. He must've thought, you see, that as long as we still had weapons . . . who knows . . . Anyway, we should've realized that something had snapped inside him, because his stare had become distant and fixed, and he'd look at you without registering who you were. Then as the days passed, he must've realized what was happening, and one morning he made his decision. It was Foggia, his batman, who'd

140

unsuspectingly helped him get ready – he told us what happened. Apparently he put on his linen uniform and pinned on the M's that Matteo had given him on September the 8th in return for his stars. Then he stood looking at himself in the mirror, dressing very, very slowly; he kept adjusting and readjusting the black silk ribbon across his shoulder and straightening his belt, until he put on his cap as though in preparation for a ceremony. He even checked the bolt of his Beretta. Then he ordered Foggia to leave.'

He shot himself by the open window which looked out on mountain forests, where the trees were covered in new leaves, and the valley breathed out the scents of spring – all that life renewing itself . . .

Sitting by the desk, Fabio looked down at the ground, smiling bitterly as he recalled those events. Small and dark, he was, with that big head resting on a pair of fragile shoulders and two knobs sticking out on his forehead above the eyebrows. Now, remembering him like that, I realized it was as though he were being crushed by some enormous weight which he couldn't get rid of: the embodiment of solitude itself.

I lost touch with him: time passed, and reality began to permeate our closed world. Then one day, a few years later, I ran into him by chance. He seemed uneasy, bogged down by worries. He was working in a land registry, worrying about pay-rises, his tyrannical boss, all the things he wanted to do: lodge a complaint, get himself transferred. He looked different, enclosed in his dingy life, and we didn't go over old memories. We said goodbye as hurriedly as possible: 'Bye.' 'See you.' It was an autumn day at Largo Leopardi, and long rays of sunshine were turning the yellowing leaves of the great plane-trees into gold. I watched him disappear: that big head on frail shoulders, locked inside his tremendous solitude.

Then one afternoon, leafing through a newspaper, I came across a short, news-filler article: just a few lines, it was. Under my very nose was his name; and although at the time I couldn't take it in, it gave me a real sense of déjà-vu. Fabio Grama! Written like that I could barely recognize it, and yet it was really him – Fabio! Yes, Fabio! How anonymous and insignificant his name looked amongst all those news items . . . 'cause of death unknown'. How far the world had already shifted from those events! What could the writer of that article, or anyone else out there, possibly know about Pino Mazzoni, the blood that was supposed to renew us, and all our sickly fantasies. I was stunned, and a lump rose in my throat. What bearing did those events, all we'd been through, have on reality – a reality in which his suicide resounded like an extreme cry of desperation? I looked back, trying to recapture the atmosphere of those days. It was as though life were shedding all its lustre and illusions, I thought, contracting into a hard knot which was growing tighter with each day that passed. And as all warmth and gaiety withered away, the only thing that remained was the coldness of your gun, violent hands, and that seam of hatred. Fabio had never emerged from all that . . .

He had locked himself inside the broom-cupboard, and after a while his brother heard the shot. In desperation he pushed and pushed the door, but he couldn't shift the body which had fallen against it, blocking it from the other side. When he saw the Beretta on the floor – a Beretta Calibre 9 – that's when he knew what had happened.

Guns – guns and their awful fascination! You'd look at one, weigh it up in your hand, carry it, and you were a different person. Then maybe you'd shoot yourself.

I didn't even go to the funeral. They telephoned me: 'Yes, yes, of course I'll come,' I said, but I knew what those occasions were like – a few of your old companions dotted about, each one in the clothes and trappings of his social class. They'd park their cars: 'Oh look, Nello's here too.' Always in a rush, always full of things to do, schedules to keep. I heard they carried the coffin on their shoulders, the done thing at the time. If I'd been there, I'd have worn an appropriately gloomy expression on my face, clicked my heels, saluted. I would have trotted out one of the stock phrases, 'Another one bites the dust', or something along those lines. It was a kind of refrain, a way of finding a place for his death in the tissue of lies and rituals. But it was no use to him now; and what did I have left in common with the others – the memories? No, now that even Fabio was gone, I had them all to myself. The others had managed to weed out what was unnecessary, relegate them to a corner of their lives, available for pulling out with a flourish on such occasions. Then: 'Bye.' 'Bye.' 'Yes, let's meet up . . . keep in touch . . . get together for a reunion.'

Enzo sat on the dark leather armchair, glass of whisky in his hand, watching the rain beating insistently against the window-pane. He repeated the phrase: 'It was his moral uprightness,' he said, 'his moral uprightness.' Forcing myself to see what he meant, I thought of the withdrawn boy, his infantile seriousness, his inability to express himself. I remembered how worked up he'd get about the few things he was able to comprehend; his feeling of not being accepted, which manifested itself in his shy-ness, in that 'let's stick together' which he kept repeating over and over again in those far-off September days, when all ties had been severed, when the grown-ups had retreated into their houses, each one for himself, disoriented, shrunken, leaving us out there in the streets alone.

There was a magnolia-tree outside the window, and its big, hard, shiny leaves were wet with rain. I remember its being there when I used to go and see him in the far-off days when we first got back. It was a summer's day though, then, and the air was blowing freely through the window . . .

Those two had an awkward way of moving amongst the dark, severe furniture of that house, as though, thanks to the past, they weren't even welcome in their own family, in their own home.

Chapter IX

WE still weren't sure about him, even after he turned up on the radio; we were left with the feeling that he was from another planet, a bygone age. He seemed to be hiding somewhere, but no one knew quite where: Rocca delle Caminate? Gargnano? Where were those places? Once upon a time they might have had real geographical locations, but now they were just floating in a sea of vagueness, along with everything else.

In our eyes, he stood as a kind of distant hermit, a shadow of his former self, lacking any kind of real substance. A few photographs were circulating around the newspapers: one of him getting down from Skorzeny's aeroplane, dressed in civilian clothes with two mad eyes staring out from beneath the brim of a floppy hat, and another one of him wearing a creased cap and long, bare military overcoat, with a faintly pious air of suffering. But if he were no longer the Duce, the Founder of the Empire, the Field Marshal – what was he? What was he trying to be? It was difficult to find a place for him in our own private landscape.

Taking advantage of the camaraderie which prevailed in the waiting-room of the brothel, we'd exchange the odd word with some of the civilians there. That's when one or two of them would muster up the guts to insinuate that he was dead, that it was a double we were seeing. For them he'd become inconceivable outside his usual surroundings; or, who knows, it could have been a residue of the old affection they bore him, his fascination . . .

The transmitting of information had regressed to its most primitive state; news was travelling by word of mouth. There was no longer any reliable news or verifiable official truths. Real events and inventions mingled indiscriminately: reports were whispered, vague, contradictory. There were those, however, who'd seen him, who'd spoken to him, 'In the flesh, I'm telling you . . .'

A group of officers and wounded men went to see him; they returned in dusty cars on one of those grey, winter evenings, back from who knows where. Outside the main door of the barracks they showed off the presents he'd given them: cigarette-cases, fountain-pens. 'We saw him', they said; 'we spoke to him – he even touched that bloke's shoulder, right there.' But in their excitable voices, in the exaggerations which seemed to be a means of convincing themselves, of keeping their real impressions a secret, something remained unclear, something which heightened your own doubts and uncertainties.

In the deserted square the mist began to rise in long, whitish strips, thrown into relief by the bare trees which already appeared filmy, lacy, extraordinarily fragile. It came there, descending silently from the distant marshlands and suburbs which you could already imagine being empty: people tucked away inside the villages, uncertain presences lingering along the muddy banks of the river. Meanwhile, the guard at the sentry-box already had a taut expression on his face, prepared to face the night ahead.

Why didn't he show up? Why didn't he take up his position, all that he'd been before? Otherwise what was the point of turning up? He no longer defended us now, and yet we still had to carry around the burden of that hollow image, with all its accompanying demands, its denial of reality. A sense of ambiguity grew out of that strange position, as though in some way he wished to protect himself, to avoid being wholly responsible for the events which were unfolding – events in whose face he appeared to be utterly powerless. For us he never regained his true stature, not even when he came to inspect us at the Gothic line.

It was summer: we'd left the mountains and the misty plains, and we were at Tavullia in the Marche, camping in branch-covered camouflage tents. Then just like that, with no warning, he arrived on a lazy morning. The captain came running over as we lay basking in the sun in the grassy clearing by the little village church. In the beginning we couldn't understand what he was saying: 'Form ranks, form ranks!' officers were shouting. 'Move it! Second platoon to form ranks!'

'What's he saying? . . . the Duce? . . . Who said the Duce?'

We weren't able to conceive of that reality in concrete terms. As he stood there, surrounded by German officers dressed in summer uniforms of light colonial cloth and tight-fitting peaked caps, we could make out his lighter-coloured uniform, bare of all decorations, with the big cap pulled down over his ears. It was him all right: he came towards us nervously, with the jerky movements we'd seen on the newsreels.

It was a strange feeling: there he was in the flesh – as close as could be – and yet even then he didn't seem to be real. The German officers following him a few steps behind behaved very deferentially towards him: at any given signal there was always someone there at his side to respond. He even looked as though he might venture a smile, throwing back his head in a gesture of high spirits.

And so he reviewed the troops, coming to a halt every now and then in front of a soldier. Our daggers were unsheathed, and we held them outstretched at eye-level. Some German bloke was on one knee taking photographs, while marksmen scanned the sky nervously. Lined up in three rows, we stood there with our bare legs poking out of short trousers, and those big, square cartridge-cases hanging over our bellies. We were surrounded by deserted countryside, and in the distance the sea glittered. Stopping before a soldier he'd ask him a few curt questions; then pursing his lips in concentration, he'd answer – throwing back his head and fixing them with a stare.

All right, so there he was, but it was as if he'd appeared from nowhere. We'd covered almost all the republic's territory – Piedmont, Lombard, Emilia – and all we'd seen were bombed-out cities, silent, cowed people, deserted streets and those villages on the plains which gave you the feeling that time itself stood still, and was waiting for something to be over before it could go any further. Then out of that void, he emerged. Who was he? Who was that shrunken man in a bare uniform – reminiscent of those soldiers who fled the armistice on September 8th – surrounded by foreign soldiers: head of a defeated army, of the country he'd bewitched, and which now, deluded and disillusioned, refused him and didn't acknowledge him anymore as its leader. It was like being part of a postscript, a useless, apocryphal afterthought.

He left in a hurry, as quickly as he'd come; back down the sun-warmed road with an identical roar of engines, orders in German and marksmen holding four-barrelled machine-guns.

'Just think – the Duce in the flesh!' we cried, slapping one another on the back. There was singing, and special rations all round, with a tinful of cognac. We touched the cheeks of the blokes he'd cuffed: 'He touched them! Just think, there're people out there who think he's dead!'

146

He'd spoken in a voice we know so well, cutting his words with that Emilian accent of his, and yet there was something strange in his voice as if it didn't belong to the person who was standing before us.

'I know you've fought well,' he said, 'and that you'll continue to fight well! Remember, this is the gateway to the Po valley, territory of the Italian Social Republic – so defend it!'

It wasn't true: we hadn't seen the enemy yet, nor would we in the future. No one was willing to let that encounter take place, and yet the fact that those words had come from him almost made us believe the contrary, moving the whole mystification a degree further. We attached campaign ribbons to our jackets, and above them a little star denoting three months spent at the Front.

Every now and then, someone would escape. As soon as word got around that a unit was about to 'set off for the Front', the desertions would begin. They'd fill their rucksacks with a few rations, then during the free period, instead of going for a walk, they'd sneak off to the station and catch the first train to join that unit. Sergeant Acciaroli had formed a special team to go and look for them, all expenses paid.

'The only way you leave this battalion is in a wooden coat', shouted Commander Ussari from his makeshift podium, whiskers quivering: 'In a wooden coat with a zinc lining!'

I stood at attention and asked to be demobbed.

'I don't demob anyone!'

'I'm a volunteer. I joined to go to the Front.'

'What d'you call this then? The Front's all around us! They're the real enemies – the cowards and traitors who sold out! And that's what we're here for: to stand behind our allies as they defend the soil of the fatherland until the day comes when we'll be ready too! Understand?'

'Nossir.'

He was livid: his neck swelled and his eyes were popping out of his sockets. That kind of impertinence at his headquarters – right under the battalion's flag hanging on the wall, and with all the adjutants and clerks present! An armed guard came to the dormitory and put me under arrest.

147

During the Anzio landings, however, a few of them did manage to get away. Sergeant Acciaroli went after them, caught them and chained them up in a cell next to the guard. They sat on the bunks in scruffy trousers, no laces in their boots, their feet in irons. We'd go and visit them, bringing them cigarettes. They spoke of war-torn streets, of empty countryside, and ruined houses among the marshes. They got there by night, dodging German patrols, not knowing where they were, or which way to go. 'We followed our noses,' they said, 'a kind of scent – going by noises and artillery flares.'

It was Giannetto Lettari, Enzo Grama, and the tall, skinny boy with brown, ox-like eyes who'd been a stable boy – Bersante, his name was. A fine trio they made: him, Enzo, who was always so happy-go-lucky and Giannetto Lettari, watchful and nervous, unable to bear his imprisonment. Armed with the old '91 musket and a rucksack full of hand-grenades, they'd set off at the tail-end of the winter, the sun descending rapidly, and dusk settling damply beneath the trees. They'd made it as far as Rome, hitching lifts from German lorries, while Bersante, bandaging up one of his legs, pretended to be wounded. *'Mein bruder verletzung'*, Giannetto had learnt to say: 'My brother is wounded.'

In silence, they'd help him get up amongst rucksacks and cases of equipment: a few whispered words and roadblocks, the beam of a flashlight, swarms of soldiers and columns of lorries in the darkness.

'Subiaco?'

'Ja, Subiaca.'

They got on.

'Anzio?'

'Ja, Anzio.'

Thus they reached the outer perimeter of that great stain of weapons and soldiery which was contracting a little more with each day that passed. They had their own war to fight, one that had managed to coincide in time and place with the one out there only once, one that had been recounted to us like some kind of exhilarating fairy-tale, and from one day to the next had been snatched away from us. And so, obstinate and gay, they'd gone to look for it on their own.

'We had a good supply of ammo, and our rucksacks were full. We'd walk at night so as not to be nabbed by German patrols. It

148

was bloody hard too, with that lead weight we were carrying!'

They laughed at the thought of it as we sneaked in a tin mug of wine. Hopping because of the chains, they made a pyramid and climbed up to the square window set high into the thick wall. There they took it in turns to shout out cat-calls to passing girls, or to exchange a quick word with the guard standing in his sentry-box outside the main door.

They said that on the marshes they'd met members of the Decima Mas who were loaded down with machine-gun cartridges, singing *Rosamund, you're driving me crazy* . . . They didn't join up with them though – they trusted no one now. On their own, they'd have been sure to make it in time behind some embankment, to shoot their sixty shots apiece.

Enzo went back over the particularly funny incidents, like the time they'd fallen asleep in a kind of hay-loft, and woke up the next morning to find two dead men beneath their bedstead – 'And they'd been dead a long time!' Eventually they were caught in a ruin in the middle of some marshlands, where a German – an odd sort of bloke, an old hermit with a field telephone and stores of provisions – had taken them in.

'We were just a stone's throw away from the Front', said Giannetto, brooding. 'The night was like one giant firework – tracer bullets of all colours, and great bangs from heavy mortars!'

Then, handcuffed in a lorry, they'd crossed the city by night. More roadblocks and inspections. Sergeant Acciaroli patted them on the back: 'I'm sorry lads,' he said, 'but once a soldier, always a soldier. This time you could end up against the wall!' And he laughed. Passing through Rome, he hadn't missed the opportunity to pay his wife a visit, dragging them behind him. 'The bastard!' said Giannetto. 'He handcuffed us to the living-room radiator, while we heard him bonking his wife in the next room!'

Giannetto was a restless, independent type. The minute he was handed his kit, he lost no time in taking it to bits. He believed in the 'rule of lightness', because according to him, all a soldier needed was his gun. 'We're not out to fight the Hundred Years War, you know!' After a while he deserted again, and this time he wasn't caught. It was said that he'd raped a girl at a road-block in Pray. Her father came to ask Commander Ussari for compensation: a tall, wiry peasant with a pair of big hands poking out from the sleeves of a shrunken jacket. Giannetto sat dejectedly outside the office on a wooden bench, while a guard kept an eye on him. The girl was there, too, standing next to her father at a slight distance – eyes lowered, stringy, mousy hair, a pair of knobbly knees showing through her cotton stockings. His friends walked past, teasing him. 'You'll have to marry her now! No one'll save you this time – you can count on that!'

'You can imagine, I didn't even recognize her!' he told us. 'It was pitch dark: she was going past on her bicycle when one of the guards asked her for her papers. How was I to know she was a virgin! I told her to come behind a tree, and she just stood there not saying a word while I pulled down her pants. She didn't even utter a peep when I shoved it up her! How was I to know she didn't want to?'

He managed to get away though: a guard accompanied him to the latrine, only he waited outside the door. Then Giannetto climbed up to the window and slid down the drainpipe.

Years later, I saw him again in Rome. He'd travelled as a ship's boy on an oil-tanker on the Indian Ocean. We used to go to dark, smoky taverns where the floors were covered in sawdust, and sit talking for hours. He'd recite poetry, watched by the occasional bemused, purple-faced drunk, who'd sometimes applaud. His head was always full of hare-brained schemes and extraordinary things to tell me. He showed me a stateless passport made out in the name of one Peter Cibos. 'When the cargo ships pass through the Suez Canal,' he said, 'the sharks turn round and ask "Is Peter Cibos there? What've you done with Peter Cibos?" '

We saw each other for quite a few years, though I never found out where he lived. He was always out and about, and you'd run into him in the most unlikely places. He said that he lived with two spinster aunts of his, pensioners.

He'd arrive at the bar in Porta Pia with a bit of cash in his pocket, 'C'mon, get a move on!' he'd say. 'The world's our oyster tonight!' We'd wander round the city, then he'd disappear, and you wouldn't hear from him for ages. Then someone would say they'd seen him in Spain.

Lettari . . . Carletto . . . Giano Bonazzoli . . . Those faces

150

buried deep in my memory, and yet re-surfacing at times with extraordinary clarity, aroused by some forgotten incident – a detail or a prase – which at that moment you remembered having learnt from them. My companions – or rather, my comrades, because at the time the word didn't have a vile ring. It just meant being together: brotherhood, sharing the few things your life was made up of; a bond strengthened by the surrounding hostility. But apart from Enzo, Blondie and him, Giannetto, who were the others? What did I know of their lives, their interests, the thoughts and bonds that stirred them? The things that move me today: love, pity, sharing. There was nothing in their language or in their manner which allowed any glimpse of what they had once been: their background, their work, their past – did none of it interest me?

Just sometimes a fleeting curiosity would rear its head, a desire to know what lay behind their faces and gestures. It would soon vanish, though, as if I wanted to ignore everything lying beyond that experience, to cancel out the 'before' and 'after' as if the only thing that *should* count, that *should* be true were the heroic experience itself, severed from any connection with the common-place or the trivial.

For years that bond had held, an increasingly painful seesaw between everyday reality and the illusions you desperately clung to. 'He's one of us': immediately that mechanism would spring to life, automatically placing him on another plane from the others, in a different network of relationships where nostalgia, secret guilt and solidarity would mingle together, despite everything else.

Almost every evening someone would arrive at the bar in Porta Pia, looking mysterious and secretive: 'Captain Alimonti's back – he made it! He wants to see us – says he's got some news.' They came from other cities, and from the North – that accursed North over which hovered the shadow of all the violence we'd been part of, even more sinister for us now because of its association with the terrible vendettas which were taking place.

We'd turn up at those meetings – always in out-of-the-way places, like the deserted corner of a park or some remote cross-roads – with the secret hope that the man we were to meet could conjure up with his presence and the memories he evoked the entire background in which we'd known him. Instead, you usually

found yourself face to face with a bloke who was in civilian clothing like everyone else, and in fact, was a bit shabby, in ill-fitting
clothes, frayed tie, and with that cagey, uncertain look they always
had. They'd speak in whispers, and even when they were talking
to you, they'd look around suspiciously, with a kind of false
reserve. They brought news of comrades who'd been killed, of
people who'd been forced to leave their houses and hadn't
returned:

'You know they bumped off Bartolazzi as soon as he got
back . . . at Rovetta they massacred forty-three of 'em, five at a
time . . . a whole pile of bodies there was.'

It was done in order to stir our blood, to be accepted, but also
because we were trapped now in a murky substance from which
we weren't able to free ourselves. And nor did we want to: we
were afraid of losing something which was ennobling by its very
awfulness, as if once those events were liberated from the dense
atmosphere which enveloped them, we might see them in all
their sinister nudity – in all their futile horror.

But there by the newspaper stands, covered in the first maga-
zines; there amongst all the colour and noise and people who'd
begun to look normal again (having resumed all their interests,
no longer returning home at night with drawn faces), those men
began to appear in a different light.

Without the uniforms and gold stripes, the black peaked caps
with the red badges, without the rainbow of ribbons on their
chests, they began to shed some of the aura they'd possessed
until then; we were now seeing them against a starker backdrop.
Mingling amongst the crowds in their cheap clothes, with that
furtive, uneasy manner, how quickly they lost their glamour and
sparkle. They looked awkward and stiff beside all that life and
movement, the bustling *joie de vivre* which had exploded around
us. And even if you weren't yet ready to dig down deep and see
things as they really were, you couldn't miss the out of tune,
grotesque quality of their arrogant poses, their haughty manner –
accentuated by their lack of words, and the cynical jokes with
which we tried to stifle the unease that certain memories aroused
in us. And it was the very primitiveness of our needs – to get a
meal, find a bed for the night – which made our position as
rejects and pariahs all the more sordid. There was Lieutenant
Guadalajara with his mongoloid's face, thinning moustache, the

sleeve of his amputated arm tucked into his pocket, saying over and over again: 'I am a citizen of a state which has been wiped off the face of the map. I've nothing in common with these people.' Or Major d'Aragona with his Calabrese accent, his large, smoke-blackened teeth, whose only reason for coming was to borrow two thousand lire, which he'd pay back the moment he managed to sell his father's olive-groves at Cosenza and had 'got out of all this shit'.

What bound us together? How did we all end up on the same side when the crunch came? These were the questions we began to ask ourselves. All right, so we set off on that lorry – and then what? What did we have in common apart from all the singing and the marching, the gestures and the mottoes, the feelings of rage and rebellion, and now the sense of being excluded by everybody (which merely served to reinforce our rancour and desire for revenge), and, mixed up with all that, our unease at the thought of all the bloodshed?

We'd meet in damp, poorly lit basements; sometimes there wouldn't even be anywhere to sit. The word would get around: 'There's going to be a reunion – so-and-so's coming.' There were people you'd never met and couldn't imagine ever having been on our side. Apparently they had worked on newspapers, in offices and ministries. In their threadbare overcoats and tinted glasses they looked like old-fashioned conspirators, or provincial scholars as they walked through the narrow, down-town streets. They spoke the language of the newspapers we'd never read, of the kind of propaganda heard on the radio. Trying to indoctrinate us in their high, pedantic voices, they looked just like the middle-class fools we'd always hated and despised. They spoke of things which were alien to us, which rang false: of the Ethical State, of corporation and socialization.

Is that what had spurred us on? Is that what we'd gone and risked our lives for, killing and violating in its name? Is that what had been thundering away inside us, which we'd found impossible to express?

'Do me a favour! It's just a load of bollocks! What have we got in common with those words? That wasn't *our* Fascism – *our* Fascism was . . .' and out would come the usual infantile babble, the three or four disjointed phrases which didn't explain a thing.

All you could remember of those days was the misery, which, after all the bugles and banners, your life had suddenly fallen into from one day to next. All you could muster up were feelings of nausea and fury, an impulse just to leave, to abandon those crushed, resigned people (whom you felt had wronged you). Mingled with that was a desire to find a culprit at all costs, someone on whom to take out all the disillusionment and resentment you felt for having being deceived.

Many years went by in that fashion, with all the falsehoods either beginning slowly to fray, or crystallising for ever. Then the small groups began breaking up: people began retreating into their houses, taking up their studies – the ones who had high-ceilinged rooms, radiators, carpets in the drawing-room. Life went on, with just the occasional detail emerging to pull you back. The only ones left now were filth called the 'Black Mob'. You'd put them up sometimes, on a mattress on the floor, and they'd leave the next morning having nicked some household item, the odd sheet.

Now all that remained were the occasional evenings, the famous reunions with everyone getting chummy very quickly, the cheap bonhomie born of people who'd found their niche, that petty sense of security, and could therefore allow themselves the occasional lapse. Blondie had begun working in a notary's office, had designs on a mahogany-fitted sitting-room, complete with illuminated drinks-cabinet. Enzo had opened up a dental surgery, which was full of equipment.

Even though I'd realized for quite some time that it was just an evening's charade; that at a certain point they'd become distant (preoccupied with wives, businesses, contacts, career etc.), I still clung on to those reunions, because it meant one evening less to wile away, one more to add to all the others which had been wasted.

They'd play the part of hosts: a couple of litres of cool, dewy wine (that good, clear white wine), pouring it out of the bottle – let it flow! Go on, let it flow! And when the atmosphere had got all glittery, and there'd be a buzz in the air, that was when I'd launch my attack – out of a perverse desire to mystify both myself and the others, to revive the old ghosts, and to see their faces dissolving into nostalgia before my eyes, all those soft, easy emotions . . . D'you remember . . . Ah, d'you remember that

154

time at Passo Baranca? Who was there now? D'you remember Lieutenant Mazzoni singing the M Battalion song as he led out a platoon during the attack on Mortirolo?

But then a perverse desire to wound got the upper hand: a craving to see their bovine senses of security, their mundane forgetfulness waver a little – combined with the need to air my own doubts, aroused by reading books and by remarks I'd heard.

'For Christ's sake!' I lashed out at them. 'We put the members of the Fascists' Gran Consiglio up against the wall! We shot Ciano and his lot! And who were they? Fair enough, the traitors of July 25th, the ones who betrayed Mussolini! But weren't they also the figureheads of Fascism, the ones responsible for those twenty years? Weren't *they* the essence of Fascism? And we shot them! Apart from Him – just a shadow of his old self anyway – and that woman, who were the others in that heap of dead bodies at Piazzale Loreto? How many of those leaders were there, the ones who had been on the front pages of the newspapers until then? The ministers, the academics, the scientists; all the ones who gave lectures and speeches? What about the writers and journalists, the ones who went around smiling and shaking hands, or who were simply there? And the king we wanted to hang in Piazza Quirinale, with a lead ball around his feet as a dead weight? Were they there to pay the price? No – just a bunch of almost totally unknown nonentities! And of course, there on the stage for the final act, were us – me, Blondie, Giannetto and a handful of crotchety old bastards . . . After everything that had happened in those twenty-three years, all that remained was us: Fabio Grama, Giulio Fasano – with our grotesque posing, our wicked, adolescent faces. And Carletto Ferrari's piss-ups: "Colonels or not colonels, they'll be one for them too", and Giano Bonazzoli saying over and over again: "Ehi, Carletto, who's fighting this war then? Fuck me, it's us lot – that's who!" '

They looked irritable and disgruntled, sitting there with eyes clouded by wine and nostalgia, pleading for mercy. They didn't understand; they didn't want to, at least not beyond a certain point. What was I after? Why was I trying to jolt them out of their peace of mind? Now they too had begun to be involved in relationships, interests, ties . . . They'd barricaded themselves behind an air of normality, relegating memories to a little corner of the sanctified past (purged of anything that might cast a

155

shadow over their lives), but ready to pull them out for the right occasion: for a piss-up amongst old buddies. Beams from the lamp-posts were reflected by the misty plate-glass of the restaurant, illuminating a window full of food – splendid cuts of meat and fish – placed there as though on a high altar. I looked around at that circle of ageing faces, already as soft and flabby as old rubber, scored now by daily preoccupations and selfishness which rendered them almost unrecognizable.

At one or two o'clock in the morning you'd be standing in the deserted street, your temples going boom-boom-boom, damp pavements, headlights, a drunken babble of words, the group already beginning to thin out: 'Bye.' 'See you – I've got to get up early tomorrow morning – due in at the office.' We'd be the only ones left: me and Giannetto, the last.

Up and down we'd wander, past the house, along Via Poliziano, until about three or four in the morning, when dawn would begin to lighten the sky between the two bell-towers of San Giovanni . . . Backwards and forwards, talking and tormenting ourselves: *One man went to mow, went to mow a meadow* . . .

'And having dropped us in it, what kind of life was it that they were dishing out to us, day after day, full of all that cowardice and crap? A joke they wanted to foist on us at all costs, because they'd swallowed it themselves!'

His face was always tense, restless, and he had an agitated way of talking in short bursts. As he grabbed hold of my arm, I could sense a nervous vitality in his hands which troubled me. He stared at me with yellow, exultant eyes:

'And now they tell you that's what reality was! Reality! D'you understand – we were meant to accept it without question!'

Once we got to the gate of the German convent we turned around. In that quiet street all you could hear was the sound of our footsteps, our raised voices. From behind a half-closed blind I saw my father's face watching me. By that stage he almost never managed to sleep, what with his diabetes and worry. He'd stand there in his vest, bare elbows resting on the marble widow-sill, the sharp collar-bones poking up from curved shoulders, grown very vulnerable. If he dared hazard a whisper in the silence of the street – 'What are you doing? It's so late! Aren't you coming up yet?' – all he'd get from me was a burst of barely suppressed rage.

156

Giannetto went on:

'For as long as it suited them, you were meant to accept it – just like that, from one day to the next. One thing yesterday, another thing today.' He threw me a filthy look as though he had it in for me, then steam-rollered on in his usual aggressive fashion: 'And what about us – who'd been born in that parenthesis they wanted to wipe out? What were we meant to do? What were we to do with our shattered lives – destroyed by something which was just an interlude for them, a shameful episode to be forgotten? But for us it was everything: our whole life! They say, you'll grow up, it'll make a man of you. But how – with which words? What was meant to have matured us? Nothing, that's what – a page wiped out! They tell us that all that remains of what happened before today is the smear left on the blackboard by the sponge!'

It was like an eruption as he spoke: as though inside him there was bubbling, compressed magma just waiting to escape. He talked and talked, in a language stuffed full of metaphors, filled with shared memories and the most unexpected association of ideas. For hours he could talk, continually aggressive, launched on a never-ending invective.

'It was such a fine illusion: to wipe it out in a single day, all the frustrations, the petty cowardice, the delusions, and to start afresh, begin anew, wipe the slate clean. And instead we turned up; they hadn't foreseen us. And the few sounds we managed to utter, what could they be other than the distorted echo of words they'd spoken yesterday, words they didn't want to hear today? No wonder we forced ourselves to remember – what were you left with otherwise? Who were we? Where were we meant to find the raw material – the schoolbooks to invent new words for ourselves: words for survival, words to help us get beyond that dead-end, to take our first steps towards the tomorrow that was about to begin? We didn't have their ability or their will to survive because our life hadn't taken root yet: it was so green it seemed both arbitrary and eternal at the same time. And yet we weren't filled with their remorse, nor did we have their sins to forget. All we had was our childhood: a childhood that was part of a dead world, part of the brackets they opened and closed – it was they who did it!'

He grew passive, bitter, and letting go of my arm, he stopped

157

and stared down at the ground. Behind my back, I could feel my
father watching me from behind the half-closed blinds. It was as
though he wanted to soften me with his insistence, to find a place
once more in my world – a world he'd felt excluded from since
the night he hadn't defended his castle of cards. Giannetto was
off again:

'D'you remember the one we shot in Borgosesia – that classy
bloke? D'you remember him? What style, eh . . . what a way of
talking! You remember him, don't you? Well, he was a member
of the Fascist Action Squads in 1921 – d'you hear? He was one
of us, a mayor, he took part in the March on Rome – the lot!
And when things changed he became a non-person. He said he'd
invented all those honours out of vanity, to further his career . . .
In fact he maintained that he'd always been on the other side and
that was why, after the armistice, he had been sending out supplies, relief, information to the partisans. Then he became one of
their heroes, fêted by everyone . . . they even named one of their
brigades after him. And instead, who were we – we who'd gone
there in the first place because of what we'd heard from people
like him? We're the guilty ones now, the outcasts, the murderers!'

He wanted to become a writer, Giannetto did. We knew that
he used to write in secret: poems, squibs. He'd read anything he
could get hold of from the 200-lira stall – *Mandrake* and
Zarathustra – without any kind of choice or discernment. Then
for days and nights he'd be locked away, devouring pulp: days
and nights without food, just endless cigarettes, until he'd
emerge ashen-faced, with puffy eyes and a burning desire to
explode, to lash out. You weren't allowed to mention his solitary
ambition either: for him it was agony to talk about such things,
and he always defended himself from any kind of intrusion into
his private life. From one moment to the next he'd become
prickly, evil, full of jealousy – ready to hate you, to grab you by
the scruff of the neck if he felt he was being challenged: 'Come
on, let's fight it out', just so as to end the matter there and then,
to show that you couldn't put one over him.

For weeks and weeks he'd disappear, and if you happened to
run into him he'd sidle furtively out of your way, as though he
were being followed. You could never quite work out if it was out
of shame, or because old grudges which hadn't yet found an

outlet. Once he'd got it out of his system, he'd be back again as though nothing had ever happened: 'Hello', 'Hello', and off we'd go, roaming around the city, waving our hands and making exhibitions of ourselves, the conversations beginning once more. How silent and peaceful Via Merulana was in that hour before dawn! The two rows of plane-trees running along the edge of the pavement so massive and still, and the double line of railings snaking their way along the slope of the Esquilino, descending towards Viale Manzoni, crossing that flat stretch, then rising up towards Piazza San Giovanni. It was only then that I felt as though the city belonged to me in any way, that it made some kind of sense. We said goodbye at the corner, then off he went with that nervous walk of his, brooding on all his fantasies and gesticulating to himself. He waved at me from a distance.

I went back: the big grey paving-stones, worn and uneven, the pile of wooden tables outside a restaurant smelling of wine and mould. His words were still ringing in my ears: 'And what are you to do with this severed life of yours? What's left once you wipe out your childhood and adolescence? What are *you* now?'

I, too, couldn't accept that mutilation. It was like agreeing to a situation that held no place for me as a whole person, like being obliged to say: 'No, I'm not what you see – I'll be whatever you want me to be.' I was filled with such a sense of sadness and dejection, there in the empty street, the water gurgling monotonously out of the fountain at the end, the street-lights swinging on cables in the middle of the road. It was the same sadness I'd felt on that distant afternoon, when, like a lame duck, I'd gone to the study filled with pictures and books in the hope that my professor-uncle might be able to give me something more than just words. Instead, he'd even prevented me from asking that question: us, what about us . . . ?

All he'd done was to try to convince me not to go, flattering me with those five words: '*We* too were taken in. We too got it wrong . . . things worked out differently. . .'.

Those words had stirred us up, others would have deterred us. That's why he'd sent for me: to appease his conscience, to silence the mute reproach of our presence. And I was supposed to take him at his word – which word though? The word which now denied everything I'd been expected to believe until then? How? How could they, in the moment when, to preserve their

159

credibility, they should have been standing as tall as they'd claimed (and instead merely appeared small and bewildered, in the face of events *they'd* put in motion) – how could *they* ask me to believe the opposite of everything I'd been told until then?

There was Sor Amedeo's shop, with its faded advertisement for Brill polish, past Signor Turchi's, the orthopaedic shoemaker, and the rusty blinds of the tobacconist's shop. All my infancy and adolescence had been spent in those streets, in that humble little quarter. The school was up there, just round the corner from Via Ruggero Bonghi. On Saturdays there were parades in the streets, and we'd march up and down with drums and fanfares and our black banners! And everybody cheered us.

His intelligent, easy-going face grown so absorbed: 'Responsible men don't make rash decisions', he said. 'It's their duty to preserve themselves for the future, for when they'll be needed.' How well I now understood all the rage and rebelliousness that had been building up in me in those days! Responsible, I said to myself . . . for what? Towards whom? Towards those books of his maybe? Towards the whole history they contained, which I couldn't know? But for us – me, Blondie, Giannetto Lettari, Giulio Fasano – who was responsible for us, for Christ's sake? Was there no one – no one prepared to take responsibility for what we were, for the pain and confusion we were carrying inside, for our overwhelming rage at all the disillusionment and deceit we'd suffered?

I climbed up the dark, stinking stairs – the smooth iron bannister encrusted with dust and grime, the worn steps. Past Signor Lastrucci, the tram-conductor's door, then Cavaliere Pelosi's, clerk at the post office, and Sor Ubaldo's, the baker. There were faces behind those walls, a monstrous cycle of habits, words, interests, now lacking any kind of warmth.

Opening the door, I walked into the house which was stuffy with their breath. I heard him stealthily return to bed, settling down by her side without making a sound, so that I wouldn't realize he'd been standing behind the door, waiting for me to get back.

The blame I'd heaped on him for not having been up to events that distant evening had turned into a painful awareness of the bewilderment that simple man must have been feeling. From one day to the next, he'd been thrown into a world where all his

160

'decency', his 'sense of duty', had become obsolete – useless to him now as a means of understanding life. And who was responsible for him, for that good faith of his which had been duped and deceived?

I went back into my room with its old furniture, the bed squashed between the wall and the cupboard full of winter blankets. I heard them whispering in their room, her saying: 'Let it be Tonino, go to sleep and get some rest – tomorrow you've to get up early to go to the bank.'

'His' office, 'his' clients, clerks, the cashier Perrella, double entries in the ledgers, the boss's trust, and his unquenchable optimism which lingered till that very last evening:

'You'll see! Just wait and see! Things'll sort themselves out. You've got to have faith! The Duce is there – he'll be there to look after us.'

And just at the moment when I should have rejected him, freed myself of his shadow, the world handed him back to me, crushed and bedraggled, in that wreck of a father of mine . . .

Once he'd got over his queer turn, Giannetto Lettari would be back in the bar at Porta Pia – everything forgotten, bursting with gaiety and *joie de vivre*, ready to drag me around the city. 'Come on, let's go!' he'd say, pulling onto my arm. 'The world – the whole world – is our oyster!'

We'd head towards the centre of town, full of brightly-lit shops, meeting places, people, crowded streets. In Spain he'd learnt to bull-fight with cars. Quick as a flash he'd whip off his jacket, and suddenly throwing himself into the road, he'd stand there in the path of a moving car, waving his improvised cape and shouting: 'Aha! Aha! Toro!' then there'd be a screech of brakes, cursing, as laughing and happy now, he'd return to the pavement.

We'd enter a café full of noise and voices: women, elegant people chattering and ordering aperitifs. Giannetto would stand at the counter, looking around with his spirited, laughing eyes, making comments and sparring with the bar-man. Then back to more aimless wandering in the streets, his aggressive streak gradually beginning to get the upper hand.

'You see these people here?' he began, pointing at the passers-

161

by. 'The ones who walk on as if they didn't even know we were here? Well, they've wiped the slate clean for good – they've got things to do, a life to enjoy, while us – they don't even see us!'

He paused in mid-flow for effect: 'Because we're transparent, you see! Fleeting as shadows!' He began to gesticulate with his hands to show just how insubstantial we were. 'Don't be fooled into thinking that you're a man you know, a concrete human being like one of them! You're nothing but a shadow, a ghost. We're the spectres of something which never was – the faded mark on a page which has now been erased!'

He stopped, all hunched up on the pavement, looking as though he was about to hurl himself on top of me; then with that unexpected fickleness of his, his expression suddenly changed, and he became distant, absent:

'Tell me,' he said, 'Who Priam really was. Do you know? And who were those people behind the walls of Carthage? What language did they speak – not Greek or Latin surely? Who *were* they? What were their faces like – the ones they told us about?' With insolent glances, he pointed at the streets and buildings, aiming his finger at the occasional passer-by, who stopped in embarrassment, uncertain how to react.

He went on: 'All the defeated ones, all those overcome by history, stand there together in that dark recess, with their blurred faces, their incomplete gestures, their lost words which have never been retracted.'

In the deserted Piazza del Campidoglio, he stood tracing the geometric shapes on the ground made by the paving stones. Then scrambling up the statue of Marcus Aurelius, he scaled the marble pedestal, up the hind legs of the horse, so that he could sit on the bronze saddle and 'depart from history', as that emperor-philosopher had done.

'You see them,' he said from his position up there, 'the ones who were on the other side – well, now they've gone back. The Grignaschesi, the ones from Coggiola and Pray! Life has taken them in again: habits, affections, work. Time's gone by, they're grown-up now, different, part of what happened *afterwards*. For us that wasn't possible: we were left hanging, pinned up against that faded landscape by the defeat, with all our vague gestures, our incomplete sentences – cardboard cut-outs posing as men! And all we can do is keep repeating the same acts, acts which

162

belong to that interrupted story – and get more grotesque and futile with each day that passes. Because our story has no sequel, you see: for us there's no way out of this weird mess.'

Settling on the back of the horse, his beautiful voice resounded through the empty square.

'And it is their story that continues,' he added, 'the one which went on behind our backs, removed from our story which was so abruptly interrupted out there. Back and forth, returning to square one – finding reasons, meanings, motives in that whole damn chain of cause and effect! All we severed ones can do is to shrivel up a little more each day, withering away behind our gestures, all the rituals becoming increasingly empty.'

The few cast-iron lamp-posts scarcely managed to illuminate the darkness inside the porticoes of the Palazzo dei Conservatori, while from the stone tower, the glowing clock face gazed out at us like an immobile cyclop's eye.

We hurled ourselves at breakneck speed down the stairway of the Tabularium, chasing one another, spurring each other on. In the distance, the Arch of Septimius Severus loomed darkly ahead; while further down lay the paving stones of the Via Sacra: tall columns and the scent of laurel-trees rising up from the darkness of all the ruins. In one leap, agile as an acrobat, Giannetto made it up to the wall which looked down on the Forum, and from that prime position, he took up an orator's pose: *'Friends, Romans, countrymen! Lend me your ears! I come to bury Caesar, not to praise him!'* He winked at me as though to say: nice one, eh? Mark Antony coming up on the sly like that and doing his business! *'He was my friend, faithful and just to me!'* Then little by little he tells the whole story, his own story up to that moment . . . When they dump us here on the quiet and turn over the page!'

The moon shone down over the ruins, throwing them into stark relief. Fascinated, I watched him gesticulating against the dark backdrop of the distant Palatine, following his every change of expression and tone. He smiled at me in satisfaction: 'It's anti-history, that's what it is! The counter-story, our own story! We're the ones who wouldn't give in, the ones who said no! We of the *gran rifuto*, we who'll retreat with the passing of time, obstinate and arrogant, rejecting the imminent future with weapons clenched.'

Then his expression became ironic and, tightening his lips, he looked at me through half-closed eyes, without hiding a gleam of mockery and triumph.

'But with what words, though?' he went on. 'Where'll you get hold of the words to do it? From them – that lot who didn't give a damn?' He shook his head. 'How can you describe events which were made up of emotions and feelings, not of words? That blind, instinctive revolt: *With the illusion that songs/Could fill the void/ Left by those words which betrayed us.*' Gesticulating, he declaimed to the empty street, oblivious to the way his voice rang out in the silence, 'How can you tell the story of those who were nobody's children?' he said, then jumping down from his podium, he took my arm and we went on.

We skirted the high walls of the Curia, then past the newly-trimmed hedges of the Via dell'Impero, and sat down on one of the little benches in the gravel-covered path. All that quiet space and hush, the Colosseum standing illuminated in the back-ground like something not of this world. For some minutes we sat beside one another in silence, as Giannetto followed the dis-ordered train of his thoughts; until lighting a cigarette, he began scratching around with his foot in the white gravel of the little avenue. We began to walk, and he was off again.

'For a lost cause – a cause we knew was lost from day one! An absurd and useless testimony!' He raised his voice: 'A death-wish, d'you hear? A death-wish – that's what it finally boiled down to! D'you remember Strazzani, who wanted to sew a tri-colour ribbon on the sleeve of his jacket, so that *when we were dead*, people would know who we were? "Here they are," some-body would say, "Italian soldiers they are." We wanted to die – we didn't want to survive into the end of a world which had spawned us, and which was the only one we knew! Pino Mazzoni was articulate: bang!' He stopped, and gripping my arm, he stared at me as though he wished to spit those words into my face: 'Why?' he asked, pausing for a moment. 'Why? Because accepting that defeat meant accepting everything which had led up to it: the hypocrisy, the lies, the cowardice! D'you see? We didn't want that – why should we? What did we have to do with all their shit? We weren't the slightest bit responsible for it. I'm telling you we weren't! We were seventeen or eighteen years old at the time – sixteen even! Get hold of any of the photographs taken then and look at those faces . . . Of the forty-three who

164

were shot at Rovetta – after it was all over – the eldest was Lieutenant Panzanelli, who was twenty! Then the officer-cadets at Oderzo, and all the others who were slaughtered after the war. In our ears we had only the echo of the songs which had filled our adolescence. And those things – the rhetoric, the false myths, the pomp – they ranted and raved against them after the fall of Mussolini, but for us they were the only reality we possessed! It was all we'd ever known, so that sacrificial death – the ritual suicide, the battle cry before the enemy: *Merde! La garde meurt, mais ne se rend pas* – became a way of denying history, a testament to the truth – to our illusions!'

Then suddenly he became silent, distant, and watching him walk up and down, kicking a stone with ever-increasing restlessness, I sensed the approach of one of those abrupt changes of mood.

'Yes,' I said, 'that was the idea all right when we first set off from that little village in Agro Pontino, the very first days with Carletto Ferrari and the others. How simple and straightforward it all seemed then: "Just pick up a gun from the pile, and off you go to the Front – the enemy's in that direction." But then what? Things didn't work out like that: that last desperate battle didn't take place. All we got was that lousy ending, with Him fleeing, disguised as a German. And the execution squads, the hatred, the violence. Where's all that supposed to fit in, then? What about Lando Gabrielli and Lieutenant Veleno? And then there's us – the wreckage, the survivors – only fit for stirring it all up, without ever finding –'

He didn't let me finish: 'Things didn't work out,' he shouted, 'because of history, history and the old words – the only ones which meant anything to us! The only ones which seemed to have the remotest connection with what we were feeling! Only the gesture which was meant to be a sign of our refusal never came off, because history came along and swept us up in its tide! History – the same old story begun all those years ago, before we were born, by other people, for reasons we weren't even aware of, and which it was then up to us to finish!'

We went on down the narrow streets of the Suburra: the stench of poverty rising up from the higgledy-piggledy doorways, washing hanging from windows, dark corners, piles of rubbish. He became more and more gloomy, until it was obvious that my presence jarred on him. I watched him grow mistrustful, suspicious, no longer listening to me – not even in his own fashion, which was just a way of taking a cue, an excuse to launch into one of his diatribes. He became watchful, ready to discover hidden allusions in whatever you said, ready to dump you there and then with just a cold goodbye; then he'd disappear with that hurried walk of his, as though fleeing from something. Giannetto the dreamer! That hard, coiled body, the unexpected flashes of gaiety, the sudden changes of mood. We just thought he was an extreme type – extrovert and reserved at the same time, full of vitality and contradictions. 'Ah, Giannetto's a poet', people would say. He may well have been, only he was schizoid too. And as his illness grew more marked he became touchier and gloomier, his absences ever longer.

Who knows what became of him, what he did, whether he found his peace? Someone said that he'd been cured, and only every now and then did he have to admit himself as a voluntary patient into a psychiatric clinic. He'd stay there for a while, then discharge himself. People had seen him, said he was leading an almost normal life. A woman was looking after him, a nurse he met inside. They had a house somewhere.

Chapter X

WE were supposed to be going to the Front, to the war: something clear and unequivocal, a long line of helmets on the other side; you and them, the enemy . . . Hurling yourself forwards, you'd face them once and for all . . .

The Legion was ready: the eight companies, the standard, the mortars and artillery. And instead they stuck us out there. For a while we fooled ourselves into thinking that things were quiet, that this time we'd really wiped them out, really got rid of them – until something else would happen, maybe in some far-off village, and we'd know that they were still around: perhaps one, perhaps ten, irrepressible.

Then some names began to circulate: Moscatelli, the 'Red' of Borgosesia, Chiodo, the Australian . . . Where were they coming from? How did they manage to scale the wall of unreality to reach us? Details began to emerge as though through a randomly-torn veil of mist – a voice growing louder and more precise by the minute.

'Yes, I'm telling you I saw him! I really did – it was him, no doubt about it! We jumped down from the lorry, then he came out from behind the bushes wearing a big hat and holding a Thompson!'

'Who, the Australian?'

'Yes, it was him!'

There was no doubt about it, all the signs were there: the cowboy hat, the tommy-gun, his big build.

Commander Ussari was standing yelling at us from the bonnet of the lorry: 'We've got to wipe them off the face of the earth! Only when we've got rid of the lot of them will we go to the Front! We're not leaving deserters scattered around the mountainside!'

And yet we were unable to picture them as actual human beings, ordinary men like all those around us, people on the streets, our companions. Instead of making them more real, the voices and the uncertain scraps of information merely heightened their aura of unreality. You felt outraged: everything was so normal and innocent-looking – the mountains, the bare trees –

167

when all of a sudden one of those apparitions would materialize then vanish, and you'd be left with the traces of the encounter: voices, the odd name. Who were they? What did it mean?

There was that bloke – Pinguino, his name was – who'd been with them and swore he'd met him in person: Moscatelli himself.

'No way, you'll never put one over him', he said. 'You lot are all right – I'm not denying it – but he's something else.'

'But have you really seen him? Have you really met him – spoken to him?'

He didn't give any clear answers which might have dispelled our doubts: 'Yes, he did turn up once, but where he is now is anyone's guess. You never catch him in the same place twice – he appears out of the blue, then just vanishes.'

We were off again; the courtyard rang with the sound of heavy boots tramping on gravel, orders, swearing:

'Roll-call for First Company! Mortar platoon on this truck!' Still dazed with sleep, we bumped into one another in the gloom, weapons cold, feet aching in our hard boots. Outside, in the misty square, the row of lorries stood waiting.

And we were back on the road.

Caresanablot, Oldenico, Lenta . . . high above the opaque squares of the marches, driving up towards the mountain. There was a river, a thread of current rushing between silt banks and tongues of sand. Back now to the villages and that obsessive refrain – Arborio, Ghistarengo, Carpignano – names tied to images and memories which you'd rather stamp out for good, but which instead launched you back into the horror of something you couldn't understand, which you were unable to find even the terms to define.

You threw yourself on to a blanket, and lit a cigarette. There they all were: Blondie, the Cadet, Enzo Grama . . . Romagnano now, the valley opening wide before your eyes, a stone bridge, a row of willows and plane-trees on the rocky slopes . . . Serravalle, Borgosesia . . . the deserted square, the wall where it'd all begun . . . In the distance the mountains appeared, a line of peaks and undulations beneath which all illusions, had crumbled. You saw the tension renewing itself on those faces, a blind rage over expectations which constantly frustrated, at the hostility which you could sense in the very air itself . . .

It was a physical sensation, like a dog's scenting game: lingering traces of their hostile smell, their mountain boots which had disturbed the pebbles on the path, their voices which had resounded among the trees. Stragglers and cowards they might be, but they hadn't keeled over like the people in the cities. And although they refused to meet us head-on, they hadn't given in either.

We penetrated the villages by stealth, smashed down the doors of isolated huts. Just a moment before, they'd been there; they'd spent the night in the warmth, huddling close to one another on the dry straw. Their heat still lingered in the air.

We entered with baited breath, barely touching things for fear of dissolving that essence of theirs we were after: the empty hut, an old rucksack tossed in the corner, a used magazine.

We gathered up such objects, decking ourselves with them as though they were magic trophies or symbols that possessed something of theirs: 'Look, this belonged to one of them, to one of those bastards – and now it's mine.'

A handful of crumpled messages: 'Went down into village for shopping. Encounter with Fascists; general escape up to mountain. Cino turned up, all shifted – marched at night. Courier not back.' A wealth of meaning lay behind those few phrases. You went outside into the biting cold: mountains all around, and there they were, somewhere in that open space, possessing everything you wanted to lay your hands on . . .

If we ever caught one, we'd all gather round to look at him, touch him, get physical proof of his existence. It was always an illusion though: they were exhausted, frightened men, who wouldn't meet your eye, who had the faces and looks of ordinary men. Could *they* be the ones? If they'd stayed in their houses like all the others, who would have given them a second glance? Wiry, mountaineers' bodies, faces darkened by sun – no way! It must be one of their tricks, another one of their little games! They should be made to talk all the same, made to come out with it: names, places, the lot! What names though? Hell, they'd know, and they should be forced to spill the beans: where they hid the weapons, their suppliers, who were the people they were in league with, what they did. Yet that was still not enough! There was something else, something vague which we sensed, which we knew *must* be there. Outside, night was falling; patrols were being withdrawn, bodies hoisted on to lorries, orders shouted in the darkness; shots, our presence, that tension in the empty streets . . . Right this minute they should be made to tell us what it was: the whys, the wherefores, down to the very last detail! Make them throw some light on it all, dissolve the obscure knot of terror, so that we could depart in peace without leaving any shadows behind us.

Determined to remain silent, they nevertheless allowed us glimpses of blind alleys, of areas smothered in ever-increasing gloom, hoping to fool us with their insignificant faces and half-truths, trying to drag us into their inescapable game, filled as we were with even more doubt and uncertainty. It was as though in our presence something inside them seemed to disintegrate, as if the truth we wanted to know and grasp lay elsewhere, and was no longer part of them, as if they managed to shed that secret the moment they were in our hands.

Every now and then there was a brief engagement, a sudden tra-tra-tra, the occasional drop sprayed on to the snow. Then one of those dark shapes flopped down against the back lighting, and you realized what was happening when you saw a box of ammunition gliding along the crust of ice, astonished – fascinated – by the insignificant event. At first it came slowly, uncertainly, then once it hit the slope it got faster and faster, leaving a spray of white specks in its trail, sliding and bouncing off the pristine snow.

'Heavy machine-gun up to the front', went from man to man, down the line. 'Heavy machine-gun in the front.' And so up you went with your weapon, tearing your roots out of the ground with each step you took. The snow you'd hurled yourself on was slowly filtering through your clothes, as you scanned the hillside through the rearsight for the target.

We were near enough for our voices to carry. 'Deserters! Cowards!' we shouted. 'We're here – just you wait!' The echoes chased one another, swelling in the open mouth of the valley. Wait . . . ait . . . ait . . . We could see them disappearing beneath a ridge of rock over on the other side of the pass: a short line of them struck by the rays of the setting sun, swift in their snow-shoes. They were out of range of our weapons. They left one of their wounded behind a boulder – someone must have heard his wheezing. Mazzoni went over, and I saw him return with that tireless tread of his, reloading his tommy-gun, up to the knee in snow.

'He was bleeding from the mouth and arse', someone said.

We carried ours on our shoulders: we knotted a tarpaulin, and sliding a pole through the holes, our lot took him on their shoulders. One in front, one behind, we stumbled on, the bundle in the middle bending the sticks. With all the jolting and jerking the road seemed to be getting harder by the minute.

In the beginning we were careful not to bang him against any protruding rocks – as though he still retained a spark of what he'd once been – and you caught yourself saying over again: poor Cinti, he got his. But then tiredness overcame everything else: it no longer mattered if he were dragged along the ground, or if he got caught up on a root, or if the bloke in front of you, tripping over a stone, lost his balance and, holding on to the pole, sent you flying forwards so that you began to swear and curse at him, the corpse.

Those places – valleys and villages – belonged to them. They were theirs, and they defended them: they knew where the paths, huts and ravines were, and where to find a refuge. They knew how long it would take us to march to the ridge, which route our dark line would have taken along the bare hillside, the obstacles and uncertainties we would have encountered on the way. They had informers – runners who would scramble up to their hideouts – and mysterious alarm signals: while we had to manage on the strength of marching, roadblocks and gunfire – threats.

Reloading our guns, we climbed back into the lorries. Caresanablot, Oldenigo, Lenta . . . 'This time they won't get away', somebody said. 'This time we've definitely got tabs on them.' The column spread out along the road: Villarboil, Carpignano, Gattinara with its dark hillside and ruined tower, scene of our first ambush. We drove by in the lorries, pointing out landmarks to the new recruits: this is where so-and-so happened, that's where the trap at Roccapietra was laid – they were hidden up there behind those rocks.

A road, or one long, tortuous furrow along which memories were constantly set in motion?

If it wasn't there, it must have been further on by the next bend, or the one after the valley narrowed down, forming a long gully. Something in the pit of your stomach became hard and taut. Freeing your feet cautiously from the tangle of rucksacks and cases slung carelessly under the benches, you sat there mentally repeating to yourself the movements to be made: let down the side, jump down, and throw yourself on to the hillside so that at least you get the satisfaction of grabbing hold of one – of being able to look him in the face and pit yourself against a man, not a shadow.

The landscape was changing now, gradually acquiring the contours of a nightmare. The track grew narrower as it ran between the bare hill-tops, then making a sharp turn, it was crossed by a bridge.

And that's where the 'Red' was.

A still, skeletal landscape, watched over by that terrible ghost. We scanned the slopes with bated breath, as though from one moment to the next we expected to see him appear out of the bushes – that awful, flame-haired minotaur, brandishing a Sten and demanding his pound of flesh.

Obscure childhood terrors rose to the surface, re-echoing names of places redolent with horror: the massacre at Sarzana, the slaughter at Empoli. In my mind I saw a picture of my mother's face as she paused at her work, lowering her voice to a near whisper: 'Be silent, my son, be silent; what terrible years we lived through, what fearful memories my son!' Her eyes, suddenly grown uneasy, flickered over the corner of the room as though afraid of evoking them:

'Thank the Lord you never lived through those days, that you were born in this new era of order and peace.'

Instead, the monsters which seemed to have been driven away in the mythical days before your birth were re-surfacing between the mountains, and this time it was your turn to confront them.

Within the shadow of their helmets you saw the faces around you contract, the eyes set into chalk masks, beginning the never-ending game. From the movement of their pupils you could guess at the fugitive images they'd been struck by: a sudden gleam in the shadows, the indistinct outline of an object.

And it was the faces of those very boys which, twenty years later, I forced myself to recall as I returned to trace that itinerary of memories and heartache. It was as though I believed that by remembering their features – Blondie's thin lips in his sulky face, Fabio Grama's eyes searching me out beneath the brim of his helmet – I might somehow be able to bridge the gap of the intervening years. Sitting beside me in the car was the foreign woman whom I'd met such a long way from there, the woman with whom I'd decided to share my life, and whose presence reminded me of the gulf of events and years which lay between those days and the present.

It was a silent, empty road, flanked by bushes and trees. Cars had to pass the trout-farm by the dam, then carry on down into long tracts of fresh air and shadows.

Then I suddenly stumbled upon it: there before my eyes, a cement bridge crossing over the road, right on the curve where the cars were forced to slow down. That was the one – it must be! I pulled up and switched off the engine. I felt almost dazed by all the silence, sitting in the shady field with warm sunshine criss-crossing through the branches of the trees. She was sitting there, her blue eyes so serene and joyfully absorbed as she played with a blade of grass, watching the movement of her hands, as was her wont.

I tried to force myself to connect everything I carried around inside me with what lay out there, yet I couldn't. There were just a few phrases floating here and there in my memory: 'That's where they stepped down on to the road to finish off our wounded comrades – the ones that hadn't been burnt on the lorry . . . "Red" booted them out and shot them.' It was no use, though – they couldn't superimpose themselves on the years gone by, the following seasons, the leaves piling up on the grass beneath the trees, the rain rotting them.

I didn't talk about it even to her: those days were so separate from her, from the life we'd shared, all our wandering around the world. They had no bearing on those hands, which had never struck a blow, never snatched anything away from anyone.

We left in silence, a little troubled by all the open space, as the river gurgled softly among the trees, mingling with the faint rustling sound of the reeds along the bank swept by the current.

I didn't recognize a thing: a radiant sun shone over the valley, there were vines and gardens along the road, houses dotted about the hillside. It was like another country, a place I'd never been to before. She sat beside me, watching me, smiling at times as she pointed out a feature of the landscape that struck her.

I didn't even recognize the square at Borgosesia, it was so vast and open, so full of traffic and people. I'd ended up there by accident, just by following the road-signs. And if it weren't for the little chapel built against the church wall, I'd have got straight back into my car and driven away. People were hurrying past, there were shops and buses circling the little oval-shaped garden in the middle of the square.

Had I really been there?

Then those ten memorial stones: I read the names and, looking at the faces on the varnished plaques, I wasn't able to recognize one of them. Could they be the 'cowards and traitors' we'd shot that distant morning, in order to avenge our 'murdered comrades'? Ordinary, everyday faces, belonging to the kind of people whose footsteps I could hear trotting along behind me (the kind of people you run into everywhere over the years), captured in the rather unnatural poses of formal photographs: weddings or Holy Communions? What about that artisan in his best dark suit? And the other one – a clerk perhaps, or a tradesman? And this one here – could he have lived in the block of flats across the road?

I was appalled, stunned.

At a certain point I even considered going into one of the shops, stopping a passer-by, just to ask – to have it confirmed: 'What? . . . that morning? Which morning?' Who knows, though, perhaps someone – just about managing to tear himself away from his own thoughts – might have been able to go back to those days. 'Wait a moment now, let me see . . . oh yes, of course – that day!'

But what would have been said if I'd picked on someone who'd been able to come up with a personal recollection: words, stories, tales maybe, standing out from all the others?

You see, for the people in their shops and offices throughout the city, for them, those dead men had been taken away, had grown remote; with the passage of time they'd become just a few names inscribed on some blurred memorial stones, lost now in everything that had happened since.

I had this lacerating sense of time passing, of life going on in

174

other directions without me, of my being rooted to the spot where the page had been turned, chained forever to those memories and emotions at the point where the cord had been severed.

A road, or one long, tortuous furrow along which pain eternally renewed itself?

They had their homes, their lives, their preoccupations. There were houses, hotels, multi-coloured shop-signs. What had brought me back to those places? The absurd hope that maybe if I returned to where it had happened, I might find it all as I'd left it? Out of all the passions which had exploded at the time – which then seemed to have impregnated every man's gestures, to have filled every corner of the valley – the only remaining signs were a few lines on a plaque on a wall, and a fading crown of laurels hanging from a nail.

Once again life had flowed through the streets and villages, people had re-emerged from their houses, filling the space with their voices and presence, their small daily gestures. How and when had those events taken place – events I had carried inside me for all those years, fixed in an anguished reality which seemed to have lost all ties with the present? Where were my companions: Enzo Grama, from the gap in his balaclava maliciously winking at my filthy, down-at-heel appearance? Carletto Ferrari, passing around the bottle, saying 'Your health!'; someone picking it up and returning the compliment: Your health!' Where were those obsessive presences, the ghosts who watched over the mountains and villages, the faceless faces, the elusive shadows which surrounded us, spied on us and struck out with such terrible ruthlessness?

Then, coming up to a bend, a detail would catch my eye – an old stone roadside-post maybe, a little garden wall – and out of the blue, something would return: an image of those days superimposed on what lay before my eyes: 'Yes – that's it! We passed through here, now I remember! Of course, this is where the lorry skidded and almost overturned, and in a minute we'll come to that path where we all jumped down and made a run for it!' Slowing down, I forced myself to return to the past, as isolated scraps of memory gradually began to float to the surface, a word, a face . . .

The road was uphill now, and you could look down on the

river glittering in the sun, currents of clear water flowing between the white pebbles. Then there were the road-signs – Rimella, Fobello – and yes, that was it: right behind that big building is where we'd placed the last road-block; the machine-gun hidden behind a pile of logs, its barrel aimed up at the high valley, and your companions muffled up inside their greatcoats, stamping their feet on the ground.

'Hello, lads.'

'Hey – look who's here! Where're you off to then?'

'Rimella.'

'To Rimella – are you off your head? Rimella's where *they* are!'

Yes, them! In the end you'd meet them face to face, there at the highest point of the valley: where else would you expect to run into them, if not there?

Now I would cross the Ponte della Gula, where the water roared around the foot of the precipice, turn right along the road cut into the living rock, up into the Val Mastallone, and there I'd surprise them at some point in their day. There they'd be, patrolling the alleyways, Stens around their necks, red flag hanging from the iron railings of the town-hall balcony in the narrow square, clouds gathering beneath the mountain tops – and there at last I'd see them, seize them, meet them.

We returned as the rays of the setting sun turned the peak of the Magugnaga to gold, drawing the reflections from her eyes. Back along that road we went, crossing the city filled with lights, footsteps, and the sounds of people rushing past the shop-windows of the arcade. Then we stopped at a tavern: there were faces all around, smells, the hum of voices. We had returned to the life of the present.

A life in which people work, meet, travel. Where my daughters are, my friends, the colleagues I see every afternoon, bent over their work at their desks. Those familiar, ordinary, true faces, illuminated by a circle of lamplight from the table – so in tune with one's day-to-day life. Marta and Petrilli, Francesco who was preparing his university lectures – people with whom I'd discussed books and politics, whom I'd joked with, whose interests and ambitions I knew.

And one day, after thirty years, it was right there amongst the old, scratched desks, the shelves full of proof-sheets and books, redolent of the smell of cigarette smoke, that Gabriella, the young scholar of modern history (sitting at the edge of the table with her legs crossed, a cigarette between her fingers) began to talk of those events. Still excited by the holiday she'd just spent in the mountains (where, with other colleagues of her own age, she'd been doing research for an institute of historical studies), she suddenly came out with the names of 'those' places, 'those' people. And the events themselves – the ghosts of the distant past amidst which my memory floundered – emerged from that confused tangle of memories and blank spaces, and were made concrete by her matter-of-fact tone of voice: the people acquiring faces, life, actions, words, as you saw them taking their place in a real world.

She'd met them while gathering evidence, spoke of them by name.

'They took us everywhere – "Stay as long as you like," they said, "free hospitality all round!" They were generous, and grateful that we wanted to gather information about them. They gave us fondue and bottles of Grigolino. Everywhere we went there'd be people who knew them: "Ciao, Pierino" – embraces and greetings in village squares – "Ciao, Vinicio".'

Glancing at her from time to time, I listened to her speak in her vivacious way – pleased by all the attention she was attracting – and tried to force myself to maintain my usual expression. But there was an uproar raging inside me, as though those things had been ripped from the most intimate part of me, where they'd been jealously guarded, and were now exposed for all to see.

She sat there smoking nervously, her dangling legs illuminated by the lamplight, making little moues with her mouth as she described the men: the one who spoke in such and such a way, another one who was so meek and mild that 'you'd never have guessed he was one of the toughest of the lot'. She sat there shuffling through the notes she'd made from interviews and oral testimonies she'd gathered in her encounters, reading out the odd extract to add a bit of colour. And out of those stories, those testimonies, a picture began to form which was not only vaster and more real (shot through, as it was, by a whole network of reference-points and landmarks, circumstances and people) than the one anchored in my memory, but also utterly different; and it was with great difficulty, and only through place-names and the occasional detail, that I was able to connect those events with that nightmare I'd lived through.

It was another story which, unbeknown to us, had been unfolding behind our backs, and which was now coming into the foreground and grabbing all the limelight. We appeared only negatively, as it were, flattened in the background like confused shadows, faceless ghosts whose actions lacked sense or justification, marked only by evil and shame.

'Then they took us to this place,' she went on, 'a kind of bridge or overpass it was, where they'd wiped out a whole platoon of Fascists.' As she spoke, she filled in the details: the number of wounded who'd been finished off with a gunshot or stabbed with their own daggers, the lorry they'd burned.

'Hang on a sec now – what was it called?' she said, looking around and frowning in an effort to remember. 'Yes, that was it, the Ponte della Pietà; it was called the Bridge of Mercy.'

The blood roared in my ears; unable to control the trembling in my hands, I didn't dare look at her or my other colleagues. So that's what that place was called – Ponte della Pietà! I remembered the boys of the platoon ambushed there: curly-haired, dark-eyed Southerners who'd always be first in line at meal times, noisy and patient. Here and there throughout the countryside we'd gathered them, separated from their families by the Front which had divided Italy into two. Not one of them survived.

'It's a cement bridge that crosses the road between Quarona and Roccapietra', I said. 'The road curves, there's a slope, and there on the right-hand side, beyond a clump of trees, runs the Sesia.'

The words came out almost unawares, and the sound of my voice startled me.

'Yes, you're right, that's the one', she said, and she flashed me one of those smiles that could so easily be replaced by another emotion. 'That's what it was called: the Bridge of Mercy.' But then, with the same rapidity, an expression of astonishment crossed her features: she went back over it, she thought about it, and looking at me with surprised curiosity, she said:

'But how did you know?'

That's right – how *did* I know? How could she or Marta Alba (who was sitting there, her little face craning forward) have known that I'd been 'one of them', that on that terrible night I could have been on the burning lorry, that I – the colleague who had shared their room, participated in their discussions for all those years, whose wife and daughters they knew, whom they'd been able to joke with – was one of the black figures outlined against the appalling backdrop of those distant days!

As her voice continued to murmur from afar, I could see, as if through a mist, Petrilli rolling a cigarette between his lips. In the midst of my confusion I asked myself, what if I were to interrupt her right now and say: 'I was there – I was one of them'; what reaction would I have got? 'What's come over you – what are you saying?' Or, if I'd told them about the little Sicilian boy, 'who had burned like a human torch on the blazing lorry' as she had said, and who'd cried out in a heartbreaking, plebeian way: 'Don't kill me – I have a mamma in Sicily'; and that I'd known him? Yes, I had known him; I could have even told them his name, how he talked, how he laughed. He was called Cattania Alfonso and he came from a village in the Palermo basin, and his mother was a little old woman with a black shawl around her head, who was leaning against the low wall of a well in the tattered photograph he kept of her inside his waxed, canvas wallet.

How would they have reacted if I'd managed to tear those shadows and ghosts away from the vagueness of her voice, restoring to them the features of people – of living men with faces and gestures? Would they have been as perturbed as I had been, standing in front of the memorial plaques on the wall in Borgosesia? Such ordinary faces – the run-of-the mill kind you meet all the time in the street, in shops, or at the next desk in your own office. You hear them speak, watch them move, breathe, smile . . . that one who might have been an artisan, in his best suit; this one here a clerk; that one there, who, for all you know, might have lived in the block of flats across the road . . .

Chapter XI

SPRING was here, and suddenly nature became more important than anything else. Looking out of the open window of the mountain hotel where we were stationed, I could feel the harsh air grow balmy as I gazed at the four houses with their glittering slatted roofs up on the other side of the valley; and, next to that, the bell-tower rising up between the green of the beech trees, which – overnight it seemed – had suddenly sprouted new leaves, glistening in all that light. No one felt like guard-duty or marching or ambushes any more; we sat on the stone pavement, backs against the wall, faces up in the air, intoxicated by that first sunshine. It was as if, with the reawakening of nature, everything were over, really finished with: they'd disappeared to goodness knows where and were forgotten about, swept away together with the winter cold and the wind which blew down from the pass.

It was the one gleam of hope in those eighteen months – a moment when it seemed as though something really might be returning, as though we'd almost managed to break free from that exclusion: people were beginning to get used to our presence, and the war was contained elsewhere, in some other distant place.

At the dusty drill-ground in the city, a merry-go-round was playing that stupid song, carillon-style, about swallows returning to their nests, *the sky getting bluer by the day*, while girls and idle young men were prowling the streets once more. With the big dormitory windows wide open, I'd spend hours lying on my back, gazing up at the ceiling, as the air swept freely through all the things now beginning to lose the desperate taste of misery and death.

And sometimes, on a mountain road, you'd become aware of the company's footsteps marching around you; and looking up in the clear air at the high line of mountains, you'd be conscious of being young, carefree, together, and you'd forget the reasons that had brought you there. In a minute the Paduan's clear, confident voice would rise up from the last line as he sang the song about *the pilgrim who came to Rome, with broken shoes on his feet*, and you

180

didn't have to turn around to know that he'd straightened his back in that insolent, mocking way of his. Someone called out; everyone was egging him on, and even the Cremonesi were going for it in their out-of-tune voices.

And so we set off for the Front. At last we'd made it, shown them what was what, and the remaining few survivors had fled to Switzerland. He was there on his white horse, stiff arm dangling; over his saddle was a black cloth with a red M in one corner:

'Forward march! Eyes left!'

What a way to leave! The fresh morning air, the façade of the barracks illuminated by sunlight, and Sergeant Acciaroli, happy as a sandboy, with his boxer's face poking out from the head of the line: 'Keep in line lads! Close together!' The big-wigs were all there too – the lord mayor, the CO – while towns people lined the route, clapping their hands. A military band was playing: 'Goose-step on parade! . . . Tan! Tan! Tan!'

Crossing the endless plains by train we saw deserted fields, razed cities, silent rivers . . . Piedmont, Lombard, Emilia . . . And then, after Sant'Angelo di Romagna, we packed our kits and set off on foot.

You heard it grumbling from Urbino, out at the edge of the horizon – a continual blind thrumming. It was as though some enormous illumination had been lit against the blackness of the night, a painted red line reverberating against the face of the clouds, expanding and contracting with a flow which at intervals would grow more intense. That was the Front, and it was exactly how we'd imagined it to be that very first night on the lorry – me, Enzo and Fabio Grama, and little Strazzani: a rumbling line of fire advancing inexorably, devouring everything in its path as it flared up and melted all impurity.

We put up tents, camouflaging them with branches and twigs, and we spent most of the day in the shade of some poplar trees, smoking and lubricating our weapons. The only ones to go to the village were those on fatigues, who would climb the tree-lined slope every morning and collect the day's rations in an army blanket.

From up there, looking east, you could see the sea: a long stretch of pale, sunlit sand as far as the eye could see, then a glittering expanse of water which was never once ruffled by a sail or the outline of a distant boat. For hours we'd sit on a low wall, admiring that extraordinarily tranquil sight.

Wandering aimlessly through the countryside, we'd cross never-ending orchards which German engineers were cutting down to clear the way for guns and anti-tanks. All you could see along that undulating landscape were the stumps of trees, and beside them yellowing clumps of foliage turned upside down like severed heads. There wasn't a beast nor a shadow of a man in sight in those deserted hayfields, not even the creaking of a cart on the white, sunlit roads.

What a sense of freedom and space! The feeling of being able to take hold of, to grasp, whatever you needed; use it, then just throw it away, because by this stage nothing mattered any more apart from the imminent encounter. That's what war was all about! Sergeant Acciaroli's eyes grew small and gleaming.

'With one kick, you scatter the embers of the last bivouac, you pack your kit, and off you go! Whatever you leave behind is no concern of yours. Don't even think of it. Let the others – the cowards and dodderers who go picking amongst the scrap heap – let them worry about it! Once again, the unknown lies before you: the risks, everything that makes you feel alive again, like a king of the world!'

It was as if all those bloody memories which, until now, had so burdened and tormented you, were over and sealed forever in a closed bracket. All that belonged to another era, to other places which had become so remote and strange as to appear almost unreal. Nothing could remind me of them here; with the sunlit hills, the sea down below, the warm nights. The turning point had come: the purifying, restorative experience I'd set out for was getting nearer all the time, and would soon absolve me from everything else.

Sitting in the lounge of the vet's house like a nabob on the brocade armchair where he'd installed himself, Sergeant Acciaroli was telling us about his life as a civilian: soubrettes, smart cafés, well-cut suits – then bang, off he'd go in search of adventure.

'It's like a disease,' he said, 'and if you've got it, there's no cure. After the Russian campaign, I said to myself, right, that's it – enough. This time I'll go back home and be done with it. The retreat from the Don to Gomel was no joke either, I'm telling you lads: thousands and thousands of kilometres in the snow. But then you get the itch again, it's inevitable . . . petty irritations, the wife, the office . . . you sense this buzz in the air, and you begin to prick up your ears. You've had it with your life: days and nights, all the same, your colleagues' faces in the ministry getting greyer by the day. Then comes the moment when you can't stand it any more! Throwing it all out the window, you present yourself at the office: where's it to be this time then – Africa? Spain? Always find the same old faces – they never change. "Hey, you weren't at Malaga with the *Tercio Bandera* were you?" "By God, you must be Acciaroli of the 29th!" Embraces, piss-ups and the same old songs: *Come on you old skin/Serve me well again . . .*'

You'd have taken Sergeant Acciaroli for a boxer all right, with his flat face and squashed nose, and yet he had such delicate, well-tended hands. When he dealt cards, he'd hold them between his thumb and forefinger with all the gusto and dexterity of a professional player. He treated us familiarly, offering round cigarettes. When he spoke, he'd draw in the smoke, exhaling it with his words:

'Then there're the nippers,' he continued, 'lads just like yourselves who remind you of how you were when you first set out. It makes you feel young again, doing the same things – marching, singing . . .'

The entire rainbow – the whole firmament of glory – shone on his chest: blue decorations, ribbons from campaigns, clusters of stars:

'What's that one, sir?' we asked him.

His face lit up as he touched the ribbon: 'Ah, that's the *medalla militar* lads! Teruel, Ponte Ebro, Guadalajara,' he said dreamily.

Beyond the open window, we looked out at orchard and vineyards, at distant hills fading into the mist. The Sergeant shuffled the cards, making them snap: all aces, three queens, flush. Little cylinders of ash flicked on to the ashtray as five-lire chips were dropped into the silver plate.

'And don't think it's going to be like the civilians imagine, either,' he went on. 'If you know your stuff, you've got a chance of coming out alive! A grenade falls, and it looks as thought the whole stronghold might be burned. But then wait: you shake the dust off and begin to look around. Look, there's someone getting up, a bloke nearby's moaning . . . you count them – a couple dead, one or two wounded . . .'

We often still came across women and peasants in those closed-up farmsteads, sitting in vast, bare kitchens. Following the Cremonesi, we'd walk in ceremoniously, and Carletto would begin his German act: '*Arbeit stighen . . . rudoich!*' Bonazzoli would interpret: 'He says he wants bread and salami.' We sat and waited, surrounded by their astonished faces. It was strange seeing them gripped by enforced idleness: they were so clumsy and gauche, people who were made for being outdoors in the fields and on the threshing floors. Every now and then, they'd raise their eyes from the floor and look at us without much surprise. Carletto was enjoying himself: '*Garbait fon Machenzen ghefrait!*' Po-faced, Bonazzoli explained: 'He says he wants wine and eggs.' The women moved around getting the food, then they stood at a distance, leaning against a stone sink or chimney-post. As we drank the tart white wine, conversations were struck up. With real know-how they questioned those peasants about the land and the harvest, ignoring the fact that we were intruders. It was as if we were there by chance, travelling, on holiday perhaps, and would eventually pay up and take our leave. They answered our questions a little reluctantly, uncertain what to make of us.

We left the moment Carletto turned gloomy and started muttering threats. With an air of complicity, we winked at them behind his back, to show how much our idiot of a companion got on our nerves too. We waved at them from the threshing-floor, then once we were past the bend we began to run, laughing our heads off and taking the piss.

And I even had an amorous encounter – my first! One evening, it was, in the last inhabited house by the edge of the village where three women lived, the only ones who'd stayed behind. We hadn't spoken, only at some stage we ended up next to each other. She let me hold her, consenting to my kisses through half-closed lips. I just remember this little, unripe figure standing in the half-light of the room, her black curly hair, the faded shawl, and her body which gave off an acrid smell. Her mother and sister were in the other room, standing by the window which looked out on to the archway to the village. We heard them whispering and laughing with some soldiers on the road down below. Then, at a certain point, I felt I should venture more, and sliding my hand along her flank, I lifted up her skirt. She held my wrist to protect herself, insistently muttering 'No, no, no', without raising her voice – nothing else, just that 'No, no, no'.

She was all wet between her thighs, and even the rough cloth of her pants was damp. I didn't know what to do with my hand there – besides, I thought that her resistance was only feigned, and that after a while she'd stop. Instead her grip grew increasingly angry and stubborn and I felt that she was no longer amenable, as she'd been before when I was kissing and holding her, but hostile, hard and withdrawn.

I left the room with two wires of agony rising up my testicles and along that tall erection; but running downstairs, I still felt overjoyed and incredulous: in a single evening I'd managed to kiss her and touch her there! And it was a girl we were talking about – a fresh, graceful, sixteen-year-old girl whom everyone was courting!

On the way back to camp, I ran into someone clattering noisily along the cobble-stones of a deserted alley-way. I couldn't contain myself any longer: 'Smell that,' I said, sticking my finger under his nose, 'that's the smell of cunt!'

Each day, the rumbling on the horizon grew louder and steadier. Some evenings, we'd spend hours lying outside our tents, watching the streak of fire expanding in the sky.

From dawn till dusk, columns of Germans would pass by on their way to the Front: boys from the most recent call-up, young faces drawn with fatigue beneath their helmets. On they marched, loaded down with gear, black leather cartridge cases attached to their belts, gripping the straps of their square rucksacks. Every now and then they'd stop at the edge of the road, Mausers between their legs, to cut up their black, brick-shaped bread.

Beneath their rough uniforms, you could sense a homely air about them – something in their manner, a kind of curiosity in their eyes. They hadn't become *soldaten* yet; they could still be interested in some feature of the landscape, or make the effort to communicate in that language of theirs which consisted of onomatopoeia and miming gestures. Then the inevitable '*Sigenstaghen!*' would come and, picking themselves up, they'd begin marching behind their dust-covered, taciturn officers.

We crossed endless mine-fields, marked out by red tape tied to stakes and *minen-gasse* written on sign-boards. Bare-chested beneath the burning sun, German soldiers were moving cautiously among them. Looking at those vigorous, bronzed bodies glittering with sweat, you might be fooled into thinking it was a game they were so intent on, or that they were on holiday somewhere. Occasionally there'd be an explosion, and we'd scan the sky in search of a column of smoke.

One time we rushed over: two of the bloke's friends had already brought him to the road and were doing their best to help him. It was extraordinary to think that such a mass of bleeding flesh still possessed enough strength to suffer and cry out in that way. They managed to bind the stumps of his legs with their belts; on the pavement we saw scraps of burnt cloth and flesh. In the midst of his blackened, devastated face, his eyes – which were a dazzling blue – were rolling furiously from side to side in a frenzy of pain and desperation.

It was only a torso and yet, even ripped to shreds like that, it was full of incredible vitality: strips of torn muscle continued to contract amidst the blood, and there was vigour in the legs which had been there until just a moment before. He looked as though he wanted to get up and move about, as though he still had the use of his limbs.

All around, the light lay over the deserted fields, and there was utter stillness on the asphalt road which wound its way between the hills as far as the eye could see. There was a fiery sense of summer; the chirping of insects beneath the golden stubble was interrupted by unexpected pauses so precise they might have been orchestrated.

Then at one point he stopped yelling and thrashing about; looking at his companions with imploring eyes – all the while agitating those horrific stumps – he kept saying something over and over again, which we were unable to understand. We realized what it was when one of them suddenly got up, and rushed over towards the pile of jackets, belts and pistols which had been dumped at the side of the road. The one on the ground looked at us with bewildered eyes and shouted something at him. The other one had already pulled his pistol out of the leather holster by the time we threw ourselves on top of him. I remember the feeling of that vigorous body trying to free itself from our grasp, muscles tense beneath the light shirt, his alien smell, and the raucous sound of his words rendered even harsher by all that rage and struggling.

By the time the ambulance came, he'd calmed down a bit, and we'd let him go. They stuck the wounded one, who was lying there wheezing, on a stretcher, and rushed off at top speed towards Pesaro. His friend remained by the edge of the road, which was deserted once more. We didn't know what to say to him as he sat there subdued, sobbing quietly, his head bowed beneath the glaring sun. So alone, he looked – so foreign.

Assuming a self-important air before the Ferrarersi, Corporal Travagli stood there, moistening his lips:

'You're still young lads,' he said, 'you do it like rabbits: zac! zac! zac! – two strokes and you come!' Slipping his hand through his shirt, he squeezed his breast and looked at us through half-closed, heavy-lidded eyes:

'Women know it, too: they prefer discreet, mature men who can give them pleasure.'

The air had lost some of its fierce daytime heat, as we sat on the worn town-hall steps opposite the slope to the archway, waiting for our food.

He smacked his lips beneath his shiny whiskers which were parted by a little triangle of shaved skin: 'You've got to know the right spots,' he continued, 'which bits to play on. Personally I like having them underneath so I can watch them thrashing about, crying yes, yes, yes – I like that . . . Yes, even a whore'll enjoy it if you know how to do it right. "Just wait a little, my precious, it's not time yet." I have to hear her shout, enough – no more!'

In their pockets they kept paper wrapped condoms, worn out through so much handling. They'd pull them out and show them around, trying to console themselves for their enforced abstinence. They knew all the positions too: from the side, doggystyle, or with her on top. Even their dialect was sensual – that

187

way of pronouncing certain words, of sucking them almost, salivating over them, savouring each one in the mouth.

Strutting before an audience of his fellow-villagers, the corporal ran a hand through his bristly hair, which was plastered to his temples with brilliantine.

'A seasoned prick,' he said, 'that's what they want – a seasoned prick. I can even get it up against a pair of woollen underpants.' He smiled in satisfaction.

The hours would pass, and not one person would walk along the deserted road which coasted along the remains of the old wall. The only sound was our voices: you'd have heard anyone else approaching from a distance, even before they appeared around the bend.

Then the sun began to go down towards Urbino: slowly, stopping at the horizon where it grew large and fiery; then, when it was half-down, it appeared massive and red, extraordinarily close. There were vines which hadn't yet been cut down, and cane-fields all along the ditches.

Gathered there together in a group, they began to sing:
'Like fish we'll act, like fish we'll act
We'll even die together . . .'
They drew the notes out in plangent voices:
'Together we will die
United we will die . . .'
So sensual and gay the Ferrarese were, with those strutting poses, their curling pomaded hair, the uniforms they'd livened up with multi-coloured ribbons. Then, melancholy and swaggering, they began to sing again in those rousing voices, as though making a declaration:
'Lift up your leg – and let's see what you've got!'

The Front was getting nearer: Spitfires flew above, spinning around with an angry roar and shooting at anything that moved – men, beasts, the lot. They even got one bloke behind a bush with his trousers around his ankles.

Noses in the air, we'd stand in the shelter of the trees, watching the formations of flying fortresses as they passed above us, filling the air with that continual roar.

'They're heading for Milan,' someone said.

High up on the air, swarms and swarms of silver aeroplanes crossed the sky in compact, silver formations. An airborne duel looked like a harmless carousel in that summery sky. We watched them soar, whinny, slide on a wing, throwing off such a dazzling glare from the aluminium fuselages you couldn't tell the opposing sides apart. Only the abrupt changes in the sound of the engines gave us any indication as to what was happening up there.

Once I was told to sit in the lorry by the edge of the road with my machine-gun to watch out for one. 'Aim high!' the captain yelled at me as, bent double, he ran off, while the others dispersed among the stubble-plains. With my cheek resting against the bakelite grip, I tried to keep that distant insect buzzing in the sky somewhere between the sight and the backsight notches. All around lay the summer morning – that luminous countryside and in the distance the calm, deep blue sea. At one point it looked as though that narrow shape might be heading straight for me like a blade. The Paduan was beside me, panting furiously with his machine-gun belt in his hands. Close as anything, I heard him whisper in my ear: 'Now we're going to die.' Such a strange, fervent, gurgling voice he said it in, too, as though it gave him pleasure. But the plane reared up, then rumbling and flashing its glittering belly, it made a kind of S-shape and disappeared calmly into the horizon.

He walked down the dusty road between the broom, accompanied by a warrant officer who chattered to him; all that marked him out was the fact that he wasn't wearing a belt, and that his tunic was unbuttoned. It was only when he got to the blackberry bushes – where we were lined up in rows of three – that he saw us and gave a start. The warrant officer was about to grab his arm when he ducked, smiling and waving at us. They walked on a bit, then, almost as an afterthought, he stopped, turned around, and with the permission of the NCO approached the rows of the company. 'See you', he said, going down the line and shaking his friends by the hand as though he were going on a journey. 'See you', we replied.

The whole thing was like a monstrous game – an absurd, passive farce which it would have taken just a single gesture to halt,

189

a gesture which you knew would never be made.

As he found his place beneath two cypress-trees, he carried on chatting earnestly with the warrant officer as if he were really interested in what he was saying. Then, stating quite firmly that he didn't want to be blindfolded, he even asked for a cigarette. We saw the NCO fumbling with his packet, getting one out with a little tapping movement.

All alone, he stood at attention with that little lit cylinder in the corner of his mouth, effortlessly erect in his non-regulation uniform, jacket undone, staring them straight in the face.

Dragging their feet on the ploughed earth, the platoon moved reluctantly, stumbling over upturned clods as they raised their knees out of time.

'Platoon halt! Eyes right! Front!'

And in the parched air heady with the scent of dried grass, beneath a brilliant sun, the lieutenant's voice seemed to have regained a kind of normality as he stood there shouting those everyday words.

Gently he fell, down on to the sun-warmed earth between two cypress-trees: the cigarette, the elegant uniform, his insolent bearing – nothing now, just a small shape huddled on the trampled grass.

Then the lieutenant went over to him with a regulation pistol in his hand – a Beretta calibre nine. A big man in riding-breeches, cowboy boots, red M on his jacket collar and a black cap. He was young, vigorous.

At sunset we went up to the village to eat, just as we always did: a mess-tin of pasta with a piece of boiled meat in the lid. We ate in silence, sitting there and there on the clearing by the town hall, with meaningless clichés ringing in our ears: 'The military code in time of war' . . . 'Desertion in the face of the enemy'.

And it wasn't even true: he'd only gone away for a few days, and he would have returned of his own accord. They found him at home in a little village not far way, where he'd gone to say goodbye to his family before leaving for the Front.

The order came from headquarters. It was unequivocal: he was to be executed within twenty-four hours. Nor were the captain's efforts to any avail: an example had to be set to the troops.

Sitting in the square the warrant officer was singing his praises in a querulous voice. 'What dignity!' he was saying, 'What spirit!', moving from one group to another, his petulant nasal voice ringing out, little brush moustache twitching above his mouth. He related with satisfaction, how 'watched over by the military police, he spent the night laughing and boozing with his friends, as if he didn't have a care in the world.'

Frowning darkly amongst his subalterns, the captain stood by the door of the officers' mess, at the foot of the slope which led up to the village archway.

'All I hope,' he said, 'is that when our turn comes, we can pull it off like he did.'

Together we will die
United we will die . . .
Lift up your leg
And let's see what you've got!

At one stage, endless herds of cows began climbing northwards up the hill, prodded on by peasant soldiers leaning on sticks, wearing short, dusty boots, and old Mausers around their necks. Whistling and yelling, they urged the stragglers on, throwing stones to keep the herd together. They were animals who'd travelled a long way: night and day, mile after mile they'd walked, driven on by the war. We spent hours sitting on the parapet of the bridge, watching them pass. Some blokes could tell which region they were from by their size and the colour of their hide:

'You see those over there with bent horns – well, they're from the Marches.' Apparently they were bent like that deliberately when they were young, but he couldn't recall why.

In those long afternoons, amidst the dust raised by their cracked hooves, you'd see them from miles away, massive heads dangling, coming from the direction of Urbino. Then you'd hear one big bellow made up of all the little bellows, a good deal of grumbling and huffing and panting, with one moo rising higher and more mournful above the others. Hooves stamping, they filed down the wide road between rows of acacia-trees, as the acrid smell of sweat and dung filled the village . . . Masses of unexpected, hot, animal life in the narrow, silent streets, devoid of any human presence.

Faces still soapy, we'd come out of the barber's shop – situated in a kind of volcanic cave – in order to watch the sea of rumps

191

drift by. They were stable animals, still marked by traces of the care they'd received, more accustomed to quiet barns than to walking in open countryside. They looked exhausted, disoriented, with big frightened eyes. Sitting there watching them pass, we'd throw the occasional stone or make the odd comment: 'Cripes, look how many!' someone said. 'Makes you long for meat, don't it?'

Once outside the village, the herd began to slow down and spread out, while the odd no-hoper would curl up on the ground. No amount of beating or cursing would get it to budge. We watched the big white patch descending slowly down the hill, and along the deserted plains.

They passed by in baggage trains – crude, trough-shaped carts with sides made of roughly-hewn planks. Stuffed full of rucksacks and bundles, they were drawn by heavy, big-hoofed horses who minced along the stone road-bed. They were reservists: old men with sun-baked faces, bristling moustaches, and ancient green-bordered berets, who conjured up images of bygone days. Like animals exhausted by their load, they walked resignedly amidst the dust of the carts, loaded down with all their accoutrements: emblems, iron crosses, medals, and faded, tarnished silver ribbons. And there was something in the colour and cut of their uniforms – in the load they carried – which was redolent of a dim life, a life comprised of repeated acts and passively-accepted habits, lacking in any kind of spirit or sparkle. The craftsmen of the war, they were, with their shaved heads, short necks and resignation in the face of such an absurd fate. Apathetic and indifferent to what was unfolding before our eyes, we were the unknowing witnesses to some appalling tide – to the finishing touches of that immense tragedy which had begun five years before. How vividly it returns to my nostrils; the unique smell of leather and felt, of boots never broken-in enough through use and sweat, of harnesses of beasts of burden, of laces and studded belts, of buckles and hooks – a smell known throughout every farmhouse, every stable and storehouse of Europe, a stench of blond, masculine bodies nourished on margarine and sausages (tired out, whacked, yet still prepared to get back on their feet and keep marching), and mixed up with all

192

that, the smell of weapons, oil, explosives, engines and metal. These were men who, for six years, had travelled the world with square, goatskin rucksacks on their backs full of stinking under-clothes, day and night the same gun by their sides, a little black leather case full of shiny bullets, steel helmets (for by now the German helmet had become a symbol) bayonets with knurled handles, chubby buttocks in tight khaki trousers, gas-masks in zinc, tubular cases, kitbags . . . War, war and nothing but war; war for five years in a row, traipsing along roads sodden with mud or beaten by the hot sun, repeating the same things, the same acts: '*Sigenstaghen!* . . . *Rudoich!*' and thinking the same thoughts: food, tiredness, fear, orders . . . Soldiers, soldiers, *soldaten, panzer, machingever, patronen* – hand-grenades stuffed into belts, trenches and bunkers, parades, ranks, rucksacks on backs, the trampling of steel-capped boots – forward march: '. . . *Aiden Marie . . . Maaria . . .*' For five autumns, winters, springs and summers they'd started out again with the advent of each season . . . that stench of vomit and desperation, of weapons, of brutality . . . Dragging their boots in the dust, they filed past, occasionally leaning on a stick as they followed those bathtubs on wheels . . . Down the last road in the hills they travelled, carting all their strange, obsolete equipment with them – those miserable, useless objects: the rolls of telephone wire, the pliers, the shovels and pickaxes; the camp-stoves, the pots, the smoked kippers and darned socks; the old clothes which had lasted and lasted through good care, and which they continued to look after and patch with that dogged meticulousness of theirs. They were like a herd of tamed beasts being driven back to the heart of their vil-lage – back to the fold. We stood there curiously, watching them file past, making the occasional wisecrack: 'Cripes! Look at that one there – what a bumpkin, eh!'

They'd begun the war in one era and ended it in another. Out of date and anachronistic now, within the space of five years, the whole baggage of their values and words had been irrevocably swallowed up, their entire 'culture' run down and perished in a blaze of their own making. It had happened once before, thirty years ago, yet this time, even after digging deep into reserves of courage and stubbornness, they were being pushed back to the sty – the debris of the pestilence which finally struck their herd in *feldgrau*. Time passed, while behind the line of fire we heard

193

getting nearer each day, there were not only armies and victors to reckon with – along with an immeasurably superior economic force – but also a whole world of values and ideas, a brand new culture which would darken once and for all the already murky world in which we lived.

By now the rumble of the Front had turned into a continual roar, which was approaching menacingly with the passing of each day. Even the landscape seemed to have undergone a subtle change: bare and impoverished, it had become stiller, almost static-looking, as if parched by that fiery breath which had turned it into a kind of lifeless backdrop – appropriate to what was about to take place.

More serious and yet less formal now, the officers would spend their time talking to us in chummy voices, while even the captain – usually so dark and taciturn with his sooty, puritan's beard – seemed to have softened up his manner a little, and every now and then we'd catch him looking at us in an absorbed, paternal way.

The order to leave came at night: 'Wake up, wake up – we're off!' whispered the platoon commander, going around from tent to tent. In the dark, we rolled up tarpaulin sheets and emptied out our straw mattresses. 'We're off to the Front for a counter-attack', the rumour went around. 'They've broken through.' Some were worried about weapons, but word had it that they'd be waiting for us there. Others were better informed: 'No – we'll be used as assault troops! We'll be carrying grenades and daggers. There's been an infiltration, and we've got to eliminate a whole pocket of 'em.' All the old words, the communal places, were slipping away . . .

Bumping into one another in the gloom – rucksacks packed, machine-guns hung around our necks – our flashlights illuminated haphazard piles of weapons and equipment. Gathering in the square filled with fugitives and their carts, everything seemed to have sprung to life: the countryside hummed with swarms of presences, with subdued voices and noises. Who were those people? Where had they sprung from? There were old men and children, but also frightened men trying to make themselves invisible. The captain paced nervously up and down, shining his torch every now and then on to the troops: two platoons of infantry carrying Breda 30's and a platoon of machine-guns.

In the distance, behind the first row of hills, shone the glow of the Front. It was really there: a great fire burning high in the sky which filled the entire horizon. Now you could make out the rumble of each individual weapon.

The lines of fugitives were heading north: from other areas down South they'd come, wriggling out of secret hideaways in the countryside. Silent and mistrustful, they passed by us in the darkness, hunched mutely over carts filled with household goods, some pulled by animals and others by hand. There were women holding children by the hand, wrapped tight in cotton shawls, and old crones with dresses reaching down to their toes – all with that air of resignation which marked them out as veterans of pain.

Every now and then scattered companies of Germans carrying munitions and weapons would descend swiftly and silently from the other direction. I remember their alien smell in the darkness – that sense of compactness, order and efficiency which belied their small numbers.

What was holding us back? It was as though we found it difficult to leave the place, until the captain thundered out the order to march.

And so off we tramped down the curving, hillside road in the direction of the refugees, threading our way amongst women and carts.

'Stick together!'

We still found it difficult to believe: 'We have to join the other companies of the Legion. It makes sense: only when we're united will be able to attack. Sant'Arcangelo is the concentration point!'

Unwillingly we went, with ever-increasing scepticism, irritated by the forced intimacy as we mingled with the chaos they'd created.

'For Christ's sake, get out of the way! Keep your distance – move it!', or 'Hey – you look strong enough! Come here and give us a hand!'

Crossing the plains, we ran into blokes from other companies: 'Hey, Enzo', someone shouted, recognizing his sharp, good-humoured face. 'Hello fleabag! – see a runaway soldier's good for another bash!' We greeted each other gaily in the darkness: 'But where's Blondie?' Then the fourth company went past. 'We were attacked by Spitfires on the road – the captain's dead.' And then explanations: 'The German command . . . differences in weapons . . . how were they meant to get us ammunition? What we've got to do is form an independent unit . . . It's only a matter of days now . . . the other units are waiting . . . three legions'll all join up together.'

Then the photographs appeared in the papers: 'Italian Soldiers Back at the Front: First Blackshirts to Reach the Action'. 'Blimey, look at that – it's us! There's the support troops, and look, that's Blondie!'

And so we, convinced now, also began to cultivate the airs and graces of veterans. 'D'you remember that time at the Gothic Line?' we'd say loudly in the taverns, so as to be heard by all those around.

Then, crossing once again the devastated territory of that Republic, we saw wide rivers glittering beneath the sun, increasingly deserted cities. We were a little subdued at first, truculent, until back on the lorries we began to sing:

We're not afraid to die . . .

Mountain-tops peeping out beyond the haze at the edge of the plains then more Blackshirt roadblocks – 'Halt – who's there! Stop!' – faces fierce beneath their peaked caps, their black sweaters, their silver skulls. But now the barracks were surrounded by cheval-de-frise, and the machine-guns positioned behind sandbags. And there, in the humid air at the foot of the hills, stood those notices:

'*Achtung! Achtung!* Rebels in the area!'

That was the war that awaited us.

Chapter XII

THAT escape from reality which was supposed to have lasted one day, and come to its conclusion in the war cemetery at the edge of the plains, instead dragged on for eighteen months. The Republic was filled with stragglers like me who spent their days wandering around without knowing what to do next. One day you'd be forming a unit to 'go to the Front', by the next, it wouldn't exist. The ranks would break up, and you'd be back to roaming around in search of a non-existent place, of an army that never was, of an epoch that had never come into being. All you were left with were the emblems from your last unit.

Blondie, the Paduan and I left M Legion, and one night we deserted the officer cadets' course. Lying at the bottom of some icy ditch in the middle of a vineyard, we could hear the voices of our pursuers: 'That way – they went that way!' We recognized them too: 'Look, that's Acciaroli – can you hear?' We thought to ourselves how easy it would have been just to pull them down, as we watched their dark shapes silhouetted against the white of the snow, there amongst the shrivelled shoots hanging from bare trees. Then, at Treviso, we boarded a train filled with women carrying bundles.

There was no money coming in at all now, and our only hope was to beg a meal from wherever one turned up, or a bed in some barracks – a dry place to sleep. Every morning we'd find a bloodstained corpse lying on the pavement, with passers-by making that all-too-familiar detour: steering a wide berth, they'd walk on, pretending not to see.

On the façade of the barracks was written in Gothic or Latin characters: 'For Italy, for Honour'. Once you had passed the hallway and saluted the guard, after a few minutes it would hit you that it was exactly like the last barracks you'd left – the same makeshift feeling, the same precariousness. The myths never changed either: 'It's just a matter of few days – all we're waiting for is weapons: machine-guns, Tommy-guns, anti-tank guns.' Only the uniforms varied – tunics, bush-jackets, jerkins – and the badges too: gold swords, skulls with a rose in the mouth, grenades sprouting vermillion flames. It was as though the whole firmament of illusions – of real deeds and invented ones – were tumbling down on us like a shower of shooting stars for that one, final, grotesque spectacle; and in the meantime the futile battle we'd originally set out for was getting more remote and unattainable with each day that passed.

So you'd hop on to a lorry and travel to another city, and there, sitting at a roadblock in one of those dusty suburbs – windswept and solitary, all spindly trees and heaps of rubble – you'd wait for the MP with a silver disk on his breast, swaggerstick in his hand, to assign you a place on one of the transport trucks.

It was always cold and dusty on those ancient, open-topped lorries, driving along twisting, pot-holed roads and over shaky plank bridges. Silently the villages slipped by, barely glimpsed in the darkness: outlines of tumble-down houses, piles of rubble heaped alongside the pavement. And there was a continual roar, filling the entire sky from east to west, which made the air tremble as if from a distant earthquake. It was a futile display of strength: explosives, bombs, fragmentation bombs, incendiary bombs; while machine-gun fire, spraying the land which had been devastated by war, left piles of debris in its path.

I have a memory of misty plains, of continually travelling behind the Front. At Pontelagoscuro, German engineers were building pontoon bridges; then at dawn the next morning they'd take them to bits, hiding the boats in the reeds along the river bank. Crossing over, by the fitful light of the sentries' pockettorches, you could just make out the dark water swirling against the pontoons.

The rain beat down as we drifted around that countryside, sometimes losing ourselves. Blondie clung to me, saying over and over again: 'It doesn't matter during the day, but please be with me at night – please be with me.' Soldiers would spring out of the ditches alongside the road, huddled in rubber mackintoshes which reached down to the toes of their boots, heavy helmets dripping with rain: *'Papiren? Papiren, bitte!'*

Ferrara: a dead city, almost no one out on the streets meandering awkwardly through rows of gutted houses – walls propped up by girders, doorways blocked by sandbags. We wandered around the filthy suburbs, entering bars, where the one or two customers would scarcely bother to look up from the rotting wooden tables. But even then we didn't make it to the Front: cold, tired and lost, we spent our days roaming the deserted, rain-sodden countryside, to the accompaniment of artillery roaring in the darkness like some distant thunderstorm.

Once, we stopped at a little row of abandoned houses by the side of the road, and there in a downstairs room, we found these figures – an old man, a woman and two German soldiers – sitting on the floor with their backs against the damp-stained walls, faces illuminated by the orange glow of the flame burning in the smoky grate.

As we entered, one of them – who'd been standing by the fire in a pair of muddy boots, his sodden greatcoat steaming in the heat – turned around and stared at us, eyes glazed through lack of sleep. Then, in a nasal, sing-song voice, he began to speak:

'Tomorrow it'll be Pierino *kaputt* . . . Then Angelina *kaputt*!' He paused for a moment, his eyes wandering around in search of his audience: 'Why Pierino *kaputt*? Why Angelina *kaputt*? . . . why?'

On hearing their names, two children who'd been dozing in the shadow of the chimney post, heads resting on the woman's lap, lifted their faces and looked at his uncertainly. The rain continued to beat a frenzied tattoo against the shutters.

'I must to know – yes, I must to know,' he went on in that lamenting voice, placing one hand on his heart: 'I must to know.'

Pointing at our uniforms, he shook his head and turned towards his comrade, who was sitting on the ground, head dangling drowsily on his breast.

'Me . . . you, tomorrow all finish! Understand? Finish! Tomorrow, *nicht* – nothing! Understand? *Verstand* – nothing!' he shouted, slashing the air with his hand to emphasize that nothing – the annihilation which would include us, him, our uniforms, all that he was, all that he'd once been. Nothing.

Passing through Verona under fire, I remember lying on the stone kerb, feeling the flagstones roar and tremble beneath us, as the pavement shook with a tremendous underground force which jolted and knocked us to the core.

In Milan, even the desperate desire to appear more numerous, to fill the empty streets with gestures and songs, had given way to dumb apathy, a kind of furious resignation. Under a faint wintry

199

sun that warmed the half-deserted city, battered middle-aged faces mingled with those of gloomy youths who stalked the streets showing off their peaked caps where the old *squadristi* skull had been replaced by a little one that looked like a silver button, a tiny, ruthless metallic eye; the black of their uniforms was even darker and more dismal, even more oppressive. The odd passer-by would still automatically give way to us, but without the same uneasiness that our presence had once aroused; they seemed merely absent now, as if they were part of another reality which we were not able to comprehend.

Some nights, straining our eyes by the light of shielded street-lamps, we'd go out in search of cigarette-butts, down Corso Venezia and along towards Piazza del Duomo. Walking along in his crumpled overcoat, the Paduan – his furtive, mobile face like that of some nocturnal animal – was swearing at the top of his voice in his nasal Veneto accent: 'Those pigs haven't left us a single crumb! They've even smoked their fingers!' And Blondie, with his sulky, bitter face, followed behind us, glued to our footsteps. Every now and then a searchlight would suddenly come on and dazzle us, while behind the brilliant disk of light we'd hear the 'Who's there?' of the sentinel – the voice of a man with his finger on the trigger. The beam would follow us for quite a while, illuminating our backs which shuddered at the thought of the hole at the end of the barrel of the Tommy-gun, which we sensed was aimed at us.

Those last days in March dragged on slowly, as the sun struggled to warm the grey flagstones of Corso Monforte and along San Babila. Running into people here and there, you'd get to hear the odd scrap of news – the Front at the Oder attacked, the Rhine crossed – but those bits of information conjured up no precise images. They merely offered us sudden glimpses into a reality beyond our landscape, populated with forms which – chilling just because we couldn't decipher them – we felt we had to stamp out at all costs.

The Paduan was still managing to nick the occasional blanket from the last barracks to put us up, and these we'd sell on the black market: with the proceeds we'd go to the Party canteen at Piazza Cordusio for a meal.

In that bare hall, amongst the cracked plates and damp table-cloths, you'd see clerks, civil servants and secretaries of the

Fascist organization sitting there, watching their shabby families with gloomy eyes – little Southern wifies, wretched-looking children; all were marked by a communal misery, yet branded by a sense of exclusion which prevented them from sharing their misfortunes with the others. They were really the dregs: people who hadn't pulled out in time, who'd remained tangled in a web of minute considerations and petty opportunism. They barely bothered to greet each other as they left, just giving the faintest wave, each man locked inside his own weary reserve. 'All right,' they seemed to be saying, 'so things worked out as they did – but do me a favour and leave me alone, will you? What's the point, now, anyway?'

Outside lay streets and squares down which their footsteps followed a particular sequence, travelling along an invisible path which had been set aside for them, and which no one else would dream of treading.

Now, in the cities, there was only one reality open to us because of our uniforms: a shot from the barrel of a gun waiting around the next corner – bang! – then the sound of fleeing footsteps. And that vision, too, which had seduced us for eighteen months, was now slowly revealed as an illusion. Even the four divisions of conscripts we'd seen leaving for Germany, apathetic and reluctant, were back now, bearing the odd *feldwebel* or *oberfeldwebel* on their uniforms, and carrying a handful of Mausers. They too, along with our companies of excited adolescents, had been caught up in that civil war where you didn't even have time to ask why or where; but, bent over your rear sights, you just had to shoot – tying to get the other bloke before he got you.

Blondie, the Paduan and I would spend hours sitting on a park-bench in the still-damp air, watching a child crouched on the ground, playing a game (yes, there were still some around!), listening to the light rustling of leaves which were beginning to turn green on the branches of the trees. Then Blondie – rooting around furiously in his pockets for a string of stray tobacco, which he then carefully separated from any bits of fluff before rolling a cigarette – suddenly burst out, as though ending a long monologue:

'For Christ's sake, we've still got the secret weapons! Have we forgotten about them! The Duce's seen them with his own eyes, he swore to that . . . They're meant to be amazing, mind-boggling!

Wasn't it the Führer himself who said: "God forgive me for the last ten minutes of war!" '

Excited by that apocalyptic vision, the Paduan shook himself out of his torpor:

'Anything could happen now,' he added thickly. 'We'll show them – we'll show them!'

Instead came that day. There we were in the guard-room at Villa Mozart, while the Tuscan captain who was meant to be submitting designs for the new Blackshirt uniform was pleading not to miss his turn.

'All I need is five minutes,' he was saying, 'just enough for the Party leader to sign his name – then I'll be off.'

Standing by the window with rolls of paper under his arm, he was keeping an eye on the door of the large, still deserted house across the garden. He showed us water-colours of 'country outfits', of 'fatigues outfits', and also an officer's gala uniform, complete with red stripes and badges. All agitated, he went back to the receptionist, begging to be given 'absolute precedence'.

'All I need is his approval,' he said, 'then I can give the go-ahead to the workshops.' Outside, along Corso Venezia and San Babila, the balmy air was charged with a feeling of spring, which seemed to be melting and giving new life to it. Even people on the streets didn't look so drab and colourless any longer; they'd meet your eye without flinching, as if everything they'd been intimidated by until now had vanished all of a sudden.

Then at noon came the thunderbolt which turned everything on its head: no more audiences, no more protocol with doormen and clicking of heels. Instead, there was a chaotic coming and going of officers from the garden gate. In the shadow of the laurel hedges, they were bumping into each other, yelling: 'Where's the Party leader? What are the orders?' Climbing up the short flight of steps they burst into the hall and in raised voices demanded explanations; they wanted clarification. All that black cloth: skulls, caps, berets, those weary faces, boots, jerkins, daggers – a veritable mass of violence . . .

The effect of the uproar was to drag me further away, so that the din of voices in my ears became a kind of backdrop . . . Remnants of dispersed units and disbanded garrisons were bivouacking in the meadows: the Manganiello Black Brigade – Tuscan voices, wooden expressions . . . and here at last were the famous Ferrara 'Tupini': lean, lugubrious men with lazy bearing and black-gloved hands.

Then dusty cars with armed soldiers riding on the mud-guards arrived outside the gate with a screech of brakes. They came from other cities, from distant garrisons, and in their eyes – reddened by wind and lack of sleep – you saw images of roads now grown dangerous, roads you crossed with one finger on the trigger, of stretches of deserted villages redolent with a sense of anguished finality. Still stiff, their faces drawn, they jumped down and began looking for him: 'Where is the Duce? Has he got here yet? What's he doing? What's he saying?'

At each arrival, a shiver of desperate longing would run through the little groups scattered about the garden. Then more embracing, as men recognized each other; their names whispered from mouth to mouth had the magic power to reawaken sudden memories of past exploits, along with visions of new bloodshed. They were the old *squadristi* leaders, men of violence, carrying little burnished metal pistols in their belts and strange daggers, accompanied by their latest followers, who were adding their own fury and bewilderment to the mixture already fermenting inside. The excitement caused by their arrival soon subsided, however, their bad-tempered faces quickly lost in the crowd.

Then the awkward figure of the Party leader appeared at the top of the stairs. Dragging his boots reluctantly, he came down the few steps, eyes glued to the ground, He responded coldly to their salutes – almost as if he wished he could be rid of everyone who was trying to get noticed, to get their word in – struggling to be free of the hands which sought him out.

'Where's he going – what's up?'

'There's a meeting in the town hall.'

'The Duce'll be there too.'

Berets pulled down over one eye, they rushed off, shaking their heads menacingly: 'What's there to decide? We'll barricade ourselves in Piazza San Sepolcro and hold out till the end.'

We heard the wail of engines disappearing down the half-empty streets.

Feeling the need to get away, I managed to lay hands on a bicycle, pedalling and pedalling until I reached another district of the city, wheels rustling on the pavement in the unexpected quiet of the streets. Turning a corner, there they were: massive buildings with portals and balconies, stucco, moulding, and the sun illuminating their high cornices. You see, it wasn't all confusion and dark despair: there were other things around us – space, and all that freedom to move about.

The wide, half-empty streets were unusually clean, as if during the night they'd been doused by non-existent hydrants; or as if the city, extricating itself from the mist which had smothered it until now, were filled with new, sharp outlines – a hitherto unknown clarity. Beneath the precariousness and violence of the times, it had reserved a dignity of its own, an unexpected decorum, which was now emerging as if out of a spell. You were aware of people behind those doors and walls – of people whose feelings and hopes, you sensed, were not only new and incomprehensible, but part of an arena of existence you felt was utterly foreign to you.

In short the circle of my evasion was closing, and an irresistible attraction was drawing me back.

Blasts of orange flame leapt from open furnaces at the bottom of the garden, as they burnt files and documents from the archives. Doormen and clerks, laden with boxes and cases stuffed full of papers, were heading for the camp kitchen down by the wall, their faces swallowed up in the crowds. The Tuscan captain, standing sweating and incredulous in that madhouse of a hallway, greeted me with a flash of pleasure:

'You can't follow a damn thing,' he said, 'but this time I'll wait right here and nab 'im!'

I flitted amongst the groups of armed soldiers, stopping every now and then as I was drawn by a voice. What was this I was living through? Which road had led me there? There was no one who knew what was happening yet, no one able to issue an order or make a decision.

Climbing down the narrow stairs to the cellar, you were hit by the heavy, dense feeling in the air. All around lay weapons: machine-gun belts, upturned helmets filled with red hand-grenades, windcheaters, black cloth jerkins and those little silver skulls on berets and caps. It only lasted a moment, though, that sense of being sheltered and protected by those walls, the heat of the voices around you. Sitting down at a table, images from a film – seen who knows when and where – drifted through my mind. One was of a boy with an unripe, adolescent face, sitting in a corner by the window cleaning his nails with a penknife, eyes fixed and absorbed, his expression aloof. Another was of an old man crouched over a bowl of soup, dipping the spoon into the liquid, holding it to his mouth, closing his lips around it. After that, someone else walked in, a man with the ravaged face of one who'd left behind scenes of abandoned villages, of streets swept by silence. Then, throwing himself on to a bench, he lay there with his head resting on a bulging rucksack.

Rumours were flying around: 'What? What's that they said?'

'Apparently he's been killed . . .'

Silence, questioning looks.

Beside me, a wolfish-looking warrant officer narrowed his smoke-reddened eyes, letting them wander over his 'boys'.

'Hey lads,' he said, 'we don't care when we leave, do we? We've already done our bit – and no one's said who'll be carted off to hell at the last minute either!'

In a corner of the room, right beneath the shutters, sat two magnificent creatures. No one dared sit beside them, and around them the babble of voices dissolved forming a zone of silence and making them appear even more aloof and unreal: beings from another planet, who'd somehow ended up there. Our eyes devoured them with a kind of helpless lust. Tall and blonde, dressed in auxiliary's uniforms, they sat there with their legs crossed, their lazy, indolent bearing arousing fantasies of smooth bodies and silken underwear beneath the rough cloth of their uniforms.

The wolf-like warrant officer sat smoking fiercely, looking around with his red-rimmed eyes:

'That is flesh for champagne, lads! Stuff for generals!' he said. 'Getting hold of one of them is Paradise!' Drawing on his cigarette, he nodded restlessly: 'Just one night – I say, just one night! Then put me up against the wall!'

An image remains stamped on my memory: I saw them jumping out of a dusty civilian car, then coming through the gate: an older, aristocratic-looking man with white hair, the other two younger, but bearing an extraordinary resemblance to him, following close behind. All three, dressed in simple black pullovers and jodhpurs, with the same bronzed faces and haughty bearing, had Tommy-guns around their necks. Cleaving their way through the crowds, they headed towards the house. Who were they? Where had they sprung from in that operatic fashion, with their hard faces and manner, and the archaic carriage which seemed to have nothing in common with our age, or those events? Were they real, or ghosts from a bygone era? I pictured them as turbulent vassals, who, locked in their feuds, had remained aloof for twenty years (more like centuries now), until picking up that desperate appeal on the radio, they'd come to carry out one last act of loyalty, remaining faithful to some ancient feudal pact.

That night, pushed on by an avenging tide, the lords of war and violence had come to join together for a final rendezvous – a time when all the ancient bonds would be dissolved, all the old scores settled.

Then came the Black Brigade of Lucca. We pricked up our ears the moment we heard the singing, and went out into the road to wait for them. We heard their voices, magnified by the silence of the city, travelling down Corso Venezia and along the empty streets like a summons – something unexpectedly returning from the past. We stood there fearfully in the bare street, guns in our hands. Then the first lorry headed slowly towards us from the top of the crossroads at San Damiano: the dense blackness of their uniforms, guns jutting out, and the pennant with its silver skull, streaming in the wind. It was like an old oleograph: *The Last Expedition*. Their angry voices grated along the façades of the buildings in that narrow road, and up to the high, barred windows, as old trucks with flattened-out suspensions followed on behind, packed tight with men and luggage. One, two . . . then a couple of cars . . . a lorry, and a chunky armoured truck. The distances between them grew narrower as they began to pull up to the kerb. Every time a car stopped there'd be shouted greetings, and the singing would fade out, disjointed, only to be rekindled with each new arrival. We carried on waiting, eyes glued into the distance, but the crossroad was empty once more. And so that was it: the last 18BL which had left twenty years earlier.

206

The singing went on at a distance from us, close to the trucks and those hard mouths, while the exhausted engines, breathing their last, finally died. Then, shaking off the dust, they jumped down in a disordered mass, dragging along weapons of every shape and size.

The Black Brigade of Lucca
The Black Brigade of death . . .

Exultation and despondency, giddy hopes and instant disillusionment, delirium and reality ran through that crowd like a sudden gust of wind – capable at once of kindling their hopes or smothering their desires, of throwing them back into an instant torpor, of stirring their souls, of lighting up their eyes.

Surrounded by a huddle of people, a young officer was shouting above the din: 'A Rome Battalion! A Rome Battalion!' Dull faces, young and old, stood in a circle around him, staring impassively: 'We did it!' he went on. 'Look, here's the Duce's decree! Red and gold badges with the emblem of the she-wolf!'

Wild and excited, triumphant-faced, he was almost a boy as he stood there in his brand-new uniform, waving a piece of paper around, trying to reassure them, to draw them into his euphoria.

'This is it!' he shouted. 'All you've got to do is prove you're from Rome, and you'll be enlisted immediately! Drop by the office and you'll be straight off to the Front!'

The faces around him looked incredulous, uncertain: 'Apparently he's already given out orders . . . Romans will be the first to re-enter the eternal city – Romans! Down Ponte Milvio and straight on to Piazza Venezia: The Roman she-wolf, d'you hear, Mistress of Rome!'

There was something in his face, in his bearing and manner, which I recognized: it just had to be him! Back down those long eighteen months, more like centuries, to Captain Tannert's ante-chamber, where I'd first seen him. Thousands of years had passed since then, thousands, and it seemed amazing that now he too could be here! That same evening when Fabio, Enzo, Blondie and I, with all the others, had set off on the lorry and left him at the abandoned studios of Cinecittà, standing alone in the midst of some bare flowerbeds . . . It was definitely him, standing there in the dusk, waving, surrounded by cardboard backdrops:

207

'No wait! Stay here!' he was shouting, running along behind the lorry. 'Don't go! We'll form a battalion just for Romans to defend the city! Come back! . . . red and yellow badges! . . . the she- wolf! . . . the Front! . . .'

And he'd gone and done it. Now he could give the signal for new recruits to start – order uniforms, provide weapons. Rome will rule . . . back along Ponte Milvio, the fanfares ringing in his head! We'll reconquer, reconstruct, restore . . .

O long live Rome battalion
You're the best of all the lot:
Out of all of the Republic
You're the finest that we've got!

Pedalling, I turned the corner, and look – more empty streets! What had happened? At some stage, quite unexpectedly, the streets had simply emptied, almost from one moment to the next: a few footsteps scurrying along the pavements, then bang – nobody! It was painful now, walking between the tall, mute buildings, down wide streets which were deserted from one end to the other. At the Porta Venezia crossroads, two avenues stretched into a boundless space as far as the eye could see. How much longer would we be able to cross them, guns levelled, to keep the void at bay?

It was the final signal: the moment when, by a kind of common consent, they too – the ordinary people, the civilians – had disappeared, retreating into their houses. The fence-sitting, the waiting, was over now – even though the choice had been made long before. Out of necessity and cunning they'd remained there, rooted to an uncertain, equivocal frontier. And now, with the end in sight, they'd retreated. The last, inevitable events awaiting us out on the streets no longer held any interest for them, not even as spectators. Afterwards they'd emerge with new faces, new expectations, ignoring any little spots of blood left on the steps of public buildings.

The exercise did me good: suddenly I felt overcome by a quite unreasonable surge of euphoria, excited by the silence and empti- ness which seemed to open up endless new possibilities of play. Pedalling and zig-zagging between the tram rails, doing wheelies on the pavement and making the bell shriek – I imagined that I'd stumbled into a kind of no man's land: 'Oh yes – who's that hiding behind the corner? Halt! Who's there? Stop!'

But out towards the suburbs something quite different seemed to be brewing in the air: isolated, furtive footsteps, faces peering between half-closed doors, whispering – faint beginnings, yet dense and insistent. It was emanating from houses which were poorer and less shuttered than those downtown, and yet precisely because of this, they seemed to be shot through a network of voices, of understandings and agreements.

It was then, in the silence of those empty streets, that you had a physical intuition of the advance drawing near. Beyond the outskirts and suburbs, down there at the foot of the plain, and as far as the imagination stretched, you heard the rumble of divisions already spreading out along the Po Valley, proceeding towards the city in one long, unbroken, grey line. With nothing more standing in its way, it was drawing nearer and nearer, while the space inside me began to contract at a dizzying rate, and along with that, my capacity for evasion. It would soon be time for me to face something which until then had been denied and repressed, and which now – magnified and bent on an implacable course – was ready to make itself known.

In the meantime, amidst the bivouacs and all the excitement, hour by hour that long April day dragged on inexorably. Their gestures, although more feverish than usual, nevertheless seemed to be losing their vigour, increasingly unable to keep pace with the heightened speed with which time seemed to be flying past. By now, two sets of unrelated events were taking place: the one I was living through – indeed the only one I was aware of – was unravelling into the past, losing any kind of intensity or concreteness. Fading away, fraying, it had all been swept away by the crushing din of the reality which surrounded us.

I have a vivid memory – one of those unexpected thrusts of clarity which lies beyond the times – of feeling that I was witnessing a scene which had taken place at other times, in other days and places of my country's history, as though I were reliving its ancient past but in modern trappings. How many states, kingdoms, principalities had crumbled like that, had arrived at their final day with the same rhythms, the same linking of circumstances? Modena, Naples . . . senseless upheavals followed by words, movements, incidents, intentions – the same inability to control events, and finally a sense of futility, followed by collapse. Any old ending would do, though, because time had finally run out.

When he arrived, the sun was already setting and shadows were growing dense beneath the trees. A soldier came running in through the gate, shouting his name: 'It's the Duce – the Duce's here!' We were surprised for a second, trying to give substance to his words, and it was a few moments before they acquired any meaning. How strange and unreal his name sounded! So absorbed in misery, we'd forgotten about him! But after a while the old mechanism sprung to life and, knocking against each other in our haste, we hurled ourselves outside in great confusion. If he was still there, still around, then it couldn't be over yet!

Standing on the back seat of an open-roofed car, framed against the background of the deserted street, he was there, waiting for us, dressed in an old uniform bereft of all decoration, a beret pulled down over his ears.

Calling out his name we surrounded him, forming a circle around the car. But the shouting – once upon a time so familiar, and now suddenly rediscovered – lacked any kind of resonance.

Lapping it all up, he even managed to muster one of his old smiles, stretching his lips and nodding his head as he stood with his hands on his hips. But when he made the signal for hush, the silence that followed was like the silence of the entire city, of all those empty streets and squares (not a footstep to be heard), the silence of all the closed windows, the bolted doors, the people locked away behind them – all those mute faces and turned backs. It was the silence of the whole country, of the streets which traversed it, of the countryside and villages – a silence which even the agitated breathing of the few hundred men thronging around him was not enough to keep at bay.

Perhaps in that moment he saw us: saw the circle of old daggers pressing around him, the ferocious, enraged faces, the melancholy death-masks, the old grudges, the final vendettas. And in that extreme hour, he finally found himself face to face with the very essence of his adventure, with the men of blood whom he'd stirred

210

up, and who were now locking him within their circle, as though to hold him prisoner: 'We followed you this far,' they seemed to be saying, 'and you're not getting out of it now! Us and you – you and us, it'll be for one final showdown!'

The faint echo of gunfire reached our ears, spinning along the emptied streets and suburbs without encountering any obstacles. Maybe it came from some isolated garrison, from one final road-block to have been attacked, travelling in waves until it reached us. Suddenly disoriented, he looked around with a questioning expression on his face, as though he couldn't quite piece together what he was living through. Oh yes, I saw it flit across his face all right, that sudden change of expression, the flash of bewilder-ment in his eyes, which I remember to this very day. But what else did he expect to find in that moment, with all the faces and events of his past brought together? What did he have left apart from his name – grown so alien and remote now – and us, crotchety old men and shiny-eyed adolescents, forming a circle around him in the street?

You see, he hadn't accepted what we'd known right from those first days in September, that the only thing in store would be a desperate final end, a pointless barricade for those who'd taken advantage of his shadow to screen themselves from reality. The only way of those people's showing their rebellion was to gather together all the symbols that he'd given rise to in the first place.

He rejected us, and by doing so pulled off his last swindle. He even deprived us of the heroic, futile *beau geste* we'd set off for: a glorious death.

Going through the usual motions, his face was settling into an expression we knew so well: chin up, mouth sticking out. Lifting his face, he looked straight ahead without meeting our glances, and there, standing before us like a shadow of himself, he man-aged to muster his old voice:

'Comrades!' he said. 'Do you still believe in me?'

'Ye-e-e-e-s, Duce, ye-e-e-e-s!'

A long, silent pause, then, stressing each syllable:

'And so, comrades,' and here, gathering sudden strength, his voice grew louder and more pronounced, 'and so, comrades – victory is still in sight!'

Dazed, we stood there for a while, watching his car disappear around the corner of the San Damiano crossroads, our faces all turned in that direction. Then, in silence, we began to trickle back into the garden. He'd gone; he'd led us that far, then gone. Our common destiny was over; from now on each man would work out his own fate according to his lot. For him, stripped of all that he represented for us after his obstinate flight, all that lay ahead was a miserable, shabby death against an orchard wall.

One memory rose to the surface: he was standing on the balcony at Palazzo Venezia, surrounded by dazzling floodlights, looking satisfied and exulted by the rising heat of the crowd – all that violence and desire for possession! I was still a child, and suffocated by all the trembling bodies around me, deafened by the shouting and singing; I remember feeling my father's hand shaking in mine. Then, looking up, I saw that his kindly, familiar face was streaked with tears, which trickled down his cheeks as though he'd been transfigured by that exaltation. Now the two pictures mingled, overlapping each other as if they'd become one: Him and my father, my father and Him . . . fanfares, anthems and songs were sounding all around: *Life goes on, life goes on/Drawing us all in, with the promise of future years!*

And so that's what the future held in store for us: his head rolling on the cobblestones, kicked along by people's feet the night he was overthrown! An inner force was pressing down on me: exposed to a world which had grown so hostile, I *had* to get out of there, *had* to escape! An obscure feeling of vertigo rose up from the dark street, a desire to lacerate – clutching the window-sill, I called His name. And that cry, hurled out into the night, put up a barrier between me and them, a rift between me and the world, drawing me further and further back to infancy, back to . . . this point.

It was the *afterwards* we certainly hadn't been expecting that September evening, the lorry taking us further back into the mythical world of childhood; nevertheless, it had happened. The only thing the formless revolt of that initial gesture had led to was blind violence, useless and evil: little Strazzani, who fell on a lorry in a mountain road without a tri-coloured badge sewn on his sleeve; Giulio Fasano, killed as he sang in the square at Croce Mosso. All right, so we'd got the 'cowards and traitors' up against the church wall at Borgosesia – only none of it meant a thing.

The night grew dense, wiping out all traces of our presence as it advanced silently along the city streets. Shadowy figures moved cautiously amongst the sparse trees, at times stooping to speak to someone hidden in the darkness down below. I saw the red tips of their cigarettes reflected in the burnished barrels of their guns, as a subdued whisper ran between the trees. I was conscious of it as a physical sensation: the weird current of history running dry. What lay on the other side, beyond this day?

At the bottom of the garden, I saw enormous shadows moving by the glow of the cookhouses with their immense ranges. I tried to think of the future, but it was impossible to look beyond that night. What did we have to replace everything which had been destroyed? I didn't know. I didn't possess the images or the terminology or the symbols to imagine a landscape which held no place for us – no place for the only words and signs I was familiar with.

The Black Brigade of Lucca had placed roadblocks at each corner of the building, defending us with rusty muskets, old as their grudges. There weren't many of us left now, just a few figures dressed in black pullovers, eyes weary. The moment night fell in the midst of all that confusion, they'd begun to sneak out, one by one: 'I'm just popping off home to check on the family' – and you'd never see them again. Away – far away from that slaughterhouse atmosphere – to freedom! Furtively, pursued by terrors, they'd sidle along the walls in deserted, dusk-filled streets, back home to the shelter of domestic walls, to wives and children, where you could feel like anyone else, like an ordinary man, with the neighbours saying: good morning and good evening when you ran into them on the stairs. The last of the deluded they were, really the very last – the ones who hadn't yet realized that time had run out, that the frontier was closed to them, and that whoever had made it had made it: end of story. They didn't realize that by tomorrow there wouldn't be a single place on the face of the earth to run to, no one to show you the way, to open a stable door. Tomorrow they'd come and drag you out of your hole – in pyjamas, in uniform, it didn't matter – pulling you down the stairs with everyone out on the landing watching, the neighbours and all the usual faceless people. Because you'd become a fated symbol, responsible for everything – the final scapegoat upon whom to off-load all the hatred and the vendettas, the remorse and those accursed memories.

No, comrade, the only thing we can do is barricade ourselves behind this dreadful night, praying that it won't slip away despite all its terrors – terrors which stare out at you with a thousand eyes beyond the barrier of our refusal. Hold them close to you, those hideous voices and grudges, don't let this night slip away into another day!

Feeling the seconds ebb away, I forced myself to condense and highlight each moment, hoping in this way to make the night last.

I remember some men who'd gone to make the last radio broadcast, and how when they came back they brought in the smell of the night with them, clinging to their clothes. Somewhere in the darkness we heard their car speeding along, but we couldn't work out where it was coming from. For a while it seemed to be getting nearer, then the sound of the engine grew distant again, as though it were unable to find its way in a city which no longer belonged to us.

We managed to get a good look at them under the lamp, once they made it into the ante-chamber. Civilians, they were, collars pulled up, sitting there in silence, blinking in an effort not to look at us and our uniforms. I remember one bloke, his face utterly ravaged by fear, sitting huddled on a sofa in the corner, as though trying to keep the maximum possible distance from us. Mechanically pulling his cigarette in and out of his mouth, he couldn't stop his eyes from flickering incessantly towards the door which he and his companions had just entered, as though on the other side lay some terrible being which had followed them in.

Then someone began to answer questions: yes, there'd been a broadcast, but that didn't mean a thing anymore, not even to us. All we could feel was the icy terror which had gripped them in the deserted buildings: a line of their shadows flickering across the long, candle-lit corridors, the murmur of a car engine still running in the dark courtyard, their voices echoing in the microphone in the empty rooms. Then, as the door thudded shut for the last time, resounding through the deserted buildings, they drove off with a guard hanging on to the footboard of the car. A desperate race through the city, all the crossroads illuminated by the sudden flare of headlamps, menacing shadows rising up in corners, unforeseen terror in those narrow streets, a sudden screech of brakes . . .

214

I went out once more that night. Was it curiosity perhaps, a need to actually touch a reality which I was only just beginning to perceive? Or to flee the nightmare that lay inside?

Who knows where I ended up that night, which streets I traversed; all I know is that at every crossroads it felt as though it were my own fear I had to get past. The air itself was heavy with menace and violence – directed against us, it was, against us . . .

Every time I came to street corner I saw a picture of myself lying there in a puddle of blood and, although I tried to avert my gaze, each step seemed to be bringing me closer. And those people, all those Blackshirts with their lugubrious faces . . .

A car sped by, wailing desperately in the darkness, and I pictured men sitting their clutching their guns. Those hateful weapons! Why couldn't we just throw them down? What use were they to us now? They might be glued to you, but they didn't stop anyone getting killed. Streaks of flame flared through the darkness, like a shower of bullets through the air. What was happening down there? Gripped by a kind of anguish, I clung to the walls, asking myself what was this thing I was living through. The engine sped by, and suddenly the air was lacerated by the sound of screeching brakes and a car smashing against the wall. Then the high screams of rampant terror, more isolated blows, running footsteps, and voices grown subdued. They'd finished them off.

Was this the glorious death which awaited us – dying in the shadows, full of despair?

Death comes by,
Sneaks in on the sly;
So you'd better get up and run
'Cause he's after the king's son
And he'll get you one by one
Yes, he'll get you one by one

I took off my socks, and as they fell on the floor behind the sofa, I heard them go crack! First one, then the other – crack! Crack! – that's how rotten they were! Figures laden with guns and baggage were flitting hurriedly past the door, not taking any notice of us sitting on green velvet armchairs in the twilight of the Party leader's ante-chamber.

And when, later on, he appeared at the door, he'd changed so much in just one day that we barely recognized him. He was no longer the minister now – the secretary of the party, the commander – standing there nervously clutching the Tommy-gun around his neck: his shiny black hair, the purplish stubble on his cheek, the big, balding head perched on narrow shoulders.

'What are you doing here? What are you doing here?' he squeaked in his Tuscan accent, the voice of a man who knew he could no longer command, or even pretend to.

'No one's left in Milan!' he went on. 'Everyone's going – we're leaving now! The column's on the move!'

We didn't give a damn – it meant nothing to us. His words were unable to make the slightest dent in our apathy.

He realized that too. What were we to him? Where had we sprung from? How had we, and all the others out there, reached the same point? For a moment I saw those thoughts flicker disturbingly across his face until, shaking his head, he made one last effort to snap us out of it:

'Can't you get it into your thick skulls that we're abandoning this city? D'you hear – by tomorrow morning they'll be here! Them!' he shouted. 'Them!'

We were tired; we'd fought hard for the warm space amidst the shiny, comfortable furniture, illuminated by dim greenish lamps; and no we wanted to stay put, no doing anything or going anywhere. Everything out there had shifted into the remote background, and no longer held any interest for us.

For a moment he looked as though he were about to threaten us, or even use his gun, but resigning himself at once, he shrugged his shoulders and disappeared the way he'd come. We heard the gigantic echo of his footsteps disappearing down the corridor, crunching the gravel for a long stretch.

Farewell Comrade Minister.

Stretching out each toe luxuriously, I remember dragging my sweat-hardened feet along the thick carpet, and the fresh, clean feeling of my bare soles on the soft wool. The other two, stretched out more comfortably now, had loosened their belts.

In spite of the detour I had to make around the boxes and crates spread out on the corridor floor and next to the open cupboards, I still couldn't come to terms with what was happening. I kept going from room to room repeating mechanically to myself: I'm going to leave now; I, too, am going to go away from here. And yet I couldn't bring myself to do it, as though somehow my presence might keep that final end at bay. And nor did I dare touch those objects, fearing that my contact might dissolve an essence they still possessed. Heading towards the stairs – the echo of my footsteps magnified by all the uninterrupted, empty space – I remember the painful sense of something closing inexorably behind me, something that would prevent my ever returning. All the obsolete things no one would need any more, the raised voices, the feverish excitement of just a few moments back – and now nothing! Where are you? Where have you gone? . . .

I stood in the dimly-lit hallway, staring fascinatedly at the big black square of the open doorway, while the cold night air rushed in from the garden beyond.

By the time those amassed smells had dissolved, the imprint of the hands which had touched those objects removed, the atmosphere and thoughts which still hovered in the air disappeared, then the others would be there with their firm hands, their resolute ways, to change things – to put it all in a different light.

I tried to picture them coming in: singing, perhaps, on a lorry, or on foot maybe, a little uncertainly at first. I imagined them cautiously approaching, one bloke walking in through the gate, his finger on the trigger: up to the main door now, sidling past the walls, then all of them hurling themselves in through the door – hearts in their mouths, guns held out – only to be surprised by that now deafening silence.

Examining their surroundings with curiosity, they'd wander through the corridors and rooms: opening drawers, moving objects, rummaging through desks, hesitantly at first, then with increasing confidence. I could imagine their strangers' voices – orders, exclamations – the still nervous laughter, their foreign ways. Them – finally them! Here, like this, as masters and victors, getting their hands on the lot!

In one room, piled up in a corner behind the door, I found bundles tied up with string, containing brand new black shirts – abandoned along with everything else. I just couldn't resist it – a good, new, flannel black shirt, all clean and soft. I took off the khaki pullover I was wearing *The whole world knows/you wear your black shirt/to fight and die in* . . . As I did up the buttons, tucking the tails into my trousers, I was filled with a sense of well-being,

217

a feeling of warmth spreading along my arms and neck. *A black cloth closing in around you:* a magic garment, like a charmed suit of armour which rendered you invulnerable; all the coldness and hostility in the world will never get to you now!

Or should you perhaps deny it all, push everything that had happened even further away, hiding behind the one last illusion: It's not true! Look, I'm still here! Everything which lay beyond those symbols was unknown and hostile to me – it was the other side, the enemy. Only they could keep it at bay, could exorcise it.

Just before I reached the gate, turning around to take one last look at the place which had been the theatre for that last day, I was surprised at the sight of the deserted villa, all the windows wide open, the illuminated doorways casting squares of light on the stillness of the trees and shrubs beyond. How empty and silent it looked, so exposed from all sides!

That's where it had begun, all those years ago, in the days of the myths: *Be on your guard, we are the Fascists* . . .

Turning down Corso Venezia, there was still no one to be seen behind the windows and doors: the road stretched out empty and wide as far as the eye could see. Everything I hadn't been able to bring myself to imagine had gone and happened: one little event leading to another, with the same inexorability that all things occur.

You felt almost liberated by all that had happened – events which you knew could now never be undone. The whole lot, all the things that had been put in motion over those last eighteen months, would go up in smoke; and with those gone, vanished, what else would lie in store? The only thing to do was to start afresh in a new world, where everything had been forgotten and wiped out, as in a nightmare. Now, all I had to do was creep off the stage and go off on my own.

Instead, there was that day to face. And the only means I had at my disposal were obsolete now; while inside me, there was just a bare, defenceless emotion. That's when, picturing myself as the sole survivor of some catastrophe which had emptied the city streets of the world, I invented an imaginary period of time which belonged to no one else, an unreal period in which all obstacles had been removed and I had total freedom to do as I pleased. Seized by a whim to act out my part, I began to drive right down the middle of the road, giddy with all the fresh air I

218

could feel blowing in towards me from the countryside's wide open spaces. It was a game, a performance: I was the only one left – they'd all disappeared, and there was only me now! I was the King of Milan, and I could do whatever I liked: take potshots at the street-lights which hung from steel wires, or lie down between the tyre-tracks which stretched as far as the eye could see, calmly smoking a cigarette. Not worried about the danger, I was no longer tormented by the uncertainty of what lay in store. All that remained was the pleasure of making those gestures, their ability to create a reality in my imagination in which I could place and visualize myself. Who could contradict me now – who? Kindly step forward! It was my grand moment, my performance on an empty stage. But where were they? Was I the only one left on the streets of Milan? Come out right now! They'd all gone, but I was still here – I, the King of Milan!

Stop! Who's there?

Chapter XIII

WE listened in astonishment to unknown voices rising up in the silence. Who were they? Where were they coming from? There wasn't one word or accent in that chorus which was familiar to us, and yet everyone seemed to understand and participate in it all. They were suddenly back, the anonymous masses – hurling themselves into the empty streets, where we'd once marched surrounded by a ring of silence. Where were those songs born, those links formed? It was the other side of the moon emerging from the unknown – a shadowy zone which, unbeknown to us, had risen from a darkness our glances were not able to penetrate. Huddled against the walls, guns pressed against our bodies (as though, in a flash, we had been hurled on to another planet), we gazed upwards, fascinated by the spectacle. Everything which had existed until the day before – filling our eyes and our ears, and still evident on our uniforms – was now disappearing at a dizzying rate.

The streets of Milan held no escape, while dream-like images continued to float before our eyes: a road opened ahead, a deserted road filled with taut morning air. The car picked up speed, and our hopes began to rise once more: 'Quick! Quick! Maybe we'll make it! Accelerate!' Holding his breath, hands clenched around the steering-wheel, the man hit the accelerator, his eyes flickering from side to side. Then suddenly we had an intimation of danger from that direction. Was it the echo of voices or lorries? Physically sensing their presence, we didn't dare look towards those streets . . . A face appeared at the mouth of a crossroads, terror-stricken at the sight of us, then there were more quick footsteps and human shapes freezing on the pavements. Behind me, in the backseat, I heard one of my companions shout: 'They're over there – over there!', and as the car gave a start, I pushed my pistol into the driver's side. 'Quickly, turn right! Right, I said!' He braked, swerved, and as we hurled into a side-street, we heard the crackle of gunfire whizzing past our shoulders. In that narrow, silent road, hemmed in by old buildings, we found ourselves back in our element, back in an area where that dawn had not yet exploded. Our weapons gleaming dully, we could dominate these streets again; it was like a moment of respite, a glimmer of hope.

Purely by chance, without any kind of foresight, the chase had led us to an area where everything was different: there was a strange light, wide open spaces, flags hanging from the windows and people out on the streets. It was like breaking into another element – a different air filled with forgotten sounds, as though the city were divided into quite distinct areas. Their expressions, the fleeting smiles on people's faces, the incredulous gestures; then suddenly, like a flock of birds in flight, they began scurrying towards the doorways; shouts, footsteps, windows slamming, and words ringing out – those words which sounded utterly alien in their mouths, 'The Fascists! The Fascists!' . . .

'What the hell are you doing? Where are you going? Turn left!' I heard myself shouting at the top of my voice. You saw the same images all around, red predominating over everything: the drapes hanging from windows, the handkerchiefs on men's shoulders. When had all those red flames been ignited? Each one wounded us to the core – it was an unstoppable wave, spreading further and further, while the area where you could rest your gaze was shrinking all the time. Look! another one up there – hunting you, hemming you in . . . A hostile, evil colour, red was, the colour of hatred and revenge, blinding us, throwing us into confusion. We were frightened, really frightened, with a cold, implacable fear which gripped our insides and prevented us from thinking straight . . . go on, quick! down that cross-roads! Where could we run to, hounded and pushed about in a city with a different heart, a different face? Was there any place left for us – a refuge to head for, somewhere to stop for a moment and absorb what had happened? We wore the uniforms, we carried the weapons – but what had happened? How many centuries had gone by? Where were we? I asked the man next to me, but he didn't know either: he just shook his head, unable to speak, so frightened that I knew he meant it. We forced ourselves to look ahead as the car began to pick up speed, tearing down a wide deserted road towards some side-streets. It was quiet and still down there, and our spirits rose a little . . . Where to, now? No time to think about it though – just run, run – get away from there! But what was going on down there at the end of the street? We could just see a knot of people standing in the middle of the road, shouting and applauding as vehicles filled with armed men drove past the crossroads. It was them! Them! 'Stop for Christ's sake, stop!' but it was too late: a hiss of tyres, and we were surrounded by their fiery breath, their faces, their voices . . . the colours were more vivid here, the noises slamming against us with all their unknown resonances. Then the line of people gave way, he braked, trying to steer his way through (Watch out! We'll run them over!), and we hit a bus-load of armed men: shouts, fleeing . . . we jumped down in a flash; quick, run, get away! Were they after us? Would they shoot? The bus was moving again now . . . At breakneck speed we hurled ourselves into the first road we saw, but who's to remember now which places and streets we ended up in? Only that we ran and ran, sticking close together, breath getting shorter all the time – on and on for as long as heart and lungs held out, until suddenly we ran into this young boy in civilian clothes who was panting along beside us. Who was he? Where had he sprung from?

'What the hell d'you think you're doing?' I heard him say. 'Are you mad? Take off your black shirts – throw down your guns! If they catch you like that, you've had it!' He was running along, waving his hands about, repeating those words over and over again, until he grabbed hold of one of us, as though to bodily hold him back. I heard the Paduan say in his stubborn, cracked-sounding voice:

'I'm not taking it off! I'm not taking it off! I've worn it for four years, and I'm not taking it off now!'

Then the boy slowed down; he wasn't beside us any more, and soon we heard his footsteps getting further and further away until they stopped. All you could hear now was the thud of our feet hitting the pavement, getting slower and heavier by the minute. We couldn't go on: like hollow-flanked animals we were . . . But the end was in sight: only the last few blows, and soon the finger which had been searching us out through the streets of Milan would come to a halt . . . Then suddenly a screech of brakes, and looking up towards the crossroads on the right, we saw a car skidding along with armed men riding on the mudguards . . . They'd found us. I got a good look at one of them as he jumped down: a young, agile boy, running past a wall. Then he knelt to the ground, Tommy-gun outstretched, and you heard the rattle of gunfire as the air suddenly vibrated with steel-shavings snapping and whistling past.

That unexpectedly cold feeling in your back; an unbearable sense of being surrounded by emptiness, which made you stagger; a desire to retreat, to turn back . . . You just couldn't bring yourself to cross the threshold, to descend the short flight of steps . . . It was suddenly knowing that you were worth nothing, a creature at the mercy of everyone . . .

Forming a semi-circle outside the door, they stood there watchfully, guns levelled:

'Hands up!' they shouted in their vibrant voices. Then those first steps, your legs almost buckling beneath you . . . Oh yes, it was them all right: the dark hole of the barrel of their guns, the red kerchiefs . . .

And still they hadn't approached: they stood there warily, eyes darting all round the place, fingers on the trigger. Shivering in the empty air, we descended the short flight outside the main door, hands held above our heads. More tight-lipped men rushed past: straining eyes, confusion – 'Is that the lot of you, then?' – while beyond that emptiness, standing at a distance against a teeming backdrop, there were other people – curious civilians who had gathered in a group.

After a moment's hesitation, one of the armed men cautiously approached us: you felt their hands touching you, searching you – hot, sweaty, living hands, which, after an initial diffidence, grew hard and confident. They shook us and hit us randomly, realizing that we'd been reduced to nothing. There was a violent fury in them now, a desire to lash out, to wound, to let you know that you were at their mercy and that they could do whatever they pleased with you.

Wounds rather than images remain: the flesh remembers, and still you feel the pain. One of them, wearing an Alpine cap, a long pistol in his hand, was pushing us jerkily towards the road – proud of his strength and infinite power.

The space between us and the shouting crowd was decreasing; now you could actually understand what those monstrous, ranting mouths – (spitting as we walked past) – were saying, it was quite unbelievable:

'Judases!' they were shouting. 'Judases who sold out for a

handful of coins! Cowards – for a handful of coins, and look how you've ended up! Pigs!'

The cold, the effort of dragging your body along in that sea of evil, the physical resistance of that hostile mass . . . What a hideous birth! The hatred, the fury of the entire world all around me, on top of me . . . As a piece of living flesh, vulnerable to every insult, I didn't know where to rest my eyes. I tried to avoid their gaze: come on, chin up, look straight ahead! One of my companions was beside me, others at my shoulders, and yet how far away they seemed! Meanwhile behind our backs, Alpine-hat had begun to shoot, aiming his pistol between our feet.

Then someone grabbed hold of my arm, and without looking, I tried to resist, tugging from my end. Lacking the courage to turn around, I could just make out a breathless figure hanging on to me with incredible strength. It was a woman – an old woman, too – who wanted to pull me out of the group and drag me back into the throng.

'Leave them to me!' she was shouting in a harsh voice. 'Let me be the one to kill these pigs! Just one – leave just one to me . . .'

Like sleepwalkers we went, pushed on by a mass of people, trying to keep our eyes fixed on the distance. There was a roaring in my ears, as though all the blood in my body were rushing towards my arms and legs, giving me pins and needles. I had the feeling that if it weren't for the crowd supporting me, I'd have probably just buckled at the knees.

'Kill them!' they were shouting. 'What are you waiting for? Kill them!' The wounds that those words left . . .

'Who know how many those bastards have done away with! Don't show them any mercy!'

Even at the windows – seen almost through a veil of mist – there were people ranting and raving, waving flags, shouting. Hands were raised to strike us, fists whistled through the air, as red handkerchiefs and machine-gun barrels sailed confusedly amidst that swollen, screaming mass. Now, all you could hear was the occasional fragmented insult, floating high above that din.

Quite clearly, above the heads of the crowds, I remember seeing them appear around a corner. Exultant and gay, waving red flags and banners, they were responding to the shouts and greetings

224

coming from the windows as they proceeded down the street. A kind of giant in shirt-sleeves was leading the way, gesticulating and waving his fist in an attempt to incite them. Then, like a sudden blade of ice came the thought: 'Right – that's the end now.' They had seen us, and after a moment's confused incredulity, they began running towards us, shouting: 'It's the Fascists! It's the Fascists!'

We were surrounded by their breath, their voices; around us the fury of those alien, pitiless hands, a fury which gripped you and shook you, rocking you from side to side. 'Not the big shots any more now, are they?' The only resistance left now was the inertness of your body, which was being pushed forwards in fits and starts. 'Hey, what are you doing? Where are you taking them?' I heard them shout, as the line of armed men began to break up. Then, as if through a screen, I saw them swallowed up by the crowd, until all you could see was the occasional figure dotted about here and there. I remember one boy beside me, a red handkerchief around his neck, his face tense and drawn, trying to free himself from the crush to make some room for himself. 'No no!' somebody shouted. 'Do it right here! Get them up against the wall this minute!'

There was the clamour of the crowd like a distant roar, the fiery breath of their hatred . . . And the space which separated me from the wall was getting narrower and narrower; while my terror – heightened though lack of an outlet – was washing back over me in waves. There wasn't one friendly face or object in sight – just their hard, pitiless loathing, their twisted faces, their screaming mouths: 'Come on – move it, you cowards!' Pushed and shoved about, I remember tripping over something, and almost stumbling. I would have fallen if they hadn't grabbed me by the shoulder: 'Come on, move it!' someone said in a cold, merciless voice. But what were they doing? Where were they taking us? There was an iciness inside me, and my lungs found it difficult to take down the air which, filled with their breath, had turned into a kind of dense, oily fog. As they pushed you on, their hands couldn't sense that your body was void now of everything which had led them to do those things in the first place. One fleeting memory of the other three has stuck: an image of the Cadet's blind, dazed face being swept up along above the other heads like something washed up by the tide.

All that remained now was an impossible terror, a desperate and futile desire to escape. No resistance left, not one iota of will . . .

Then at a certain point, the noise around us suddenly stopped: all contact ceased and they no longer held us or pushed us around. Actually, there had been a moment when those hands – wearied by the struggle – had slackened a little, and a well of silence had formed behind us. I just remember the faint, distant hum in the air; beyond that empty space, a group of them standing in a circle, illuminated by the sun. There was silence, and all the expectant faces had suddenly grown serious. Only a few armed men remained beside us now. Another uncertain pause, and one of them raised his left arm as though to say: 'C'mon, let's go.' He held a machine-gun over his shoulder – the last image of them which remains . . .

But I couldn't hear them now; they'd gone and left us, and we were alone. Having taken us that far, they'd retreated – just like that! Where were they? It was colder now, as we stood there listing to their footsteps filling the void behind us . . . Why are you leaving us, why have you suddenly gone quiet, why have you stopped venting your hatred on us? Come on, shout! Keep hitting us! Don't go away like that! Keep us with you, don't leave us here! All around lay the silence and emptiness of the whole world, and there you were standing right in the middle of it, a palpitating mass which was supposed to have been destroyed . . . There was nothing to hold on to now, nothing to stop you from falling. They'd gone and dumped you, retreating behind the frontier of colours and voices where the world lay. You didn't belong any more; in fact, they'd really have to get a move on now, because even the bond of their hatred had been severed in the face of that violence – the worst possible thing that could happen for both of you and them. They had become very distant and remote, hiding behind their screen . . . No brothers, no! Don't leave me! Come back! Just for a moment – please come back! What use is this miserable wreck of a life to you . . .

'Load.'

Oh God, I've had it! They'll kill me! Who'll stand by me through this business, what word or gesture can reach me now? I am alone – just me and this incomprehensible thing . . . It wasn't the bullets or the physical pain that got to me, but the thought that whatever was about to happen inside me would never – *could* never – happen again, ever! In a second it was going to happen, in one single instant, so that all that would remain was that moment – my entire life reduced to that one moment . . . For the time being I was still inside myself, still part of my life, but in a second from now it would be all over, finished with for good . . . I looked around in desperation: I could do it – yes, I could still do it . . . What purpose would my death serve? What could they do with this extinguished life, this irrevocably dissolved image?

I watched a row of identical brown ants moving along a crumbling wall, millions of little legs all in action . . . *They'd* still be doing that afterwards . . . after what though? No! No! No!

It was as though an immense force, rooted in the very essence of my being, were going to be ripped out and tossed aside. My life – light years away from the point of my birth – had reached this second, and was now going to end. And out of everything that had happened in the intervening years, nothing was left now – absolutely nothing.

Chapter XIV

THEIR footsteps rang above our heads, mingling with other sounds we were unable to decipher. We had been reduced to a kind of base, animal state, no longer in a condition to move or utter a sound, where all we could do was drag ourselves around amidst piles of scrap-iron. Who were those people? Where had they sprung from? In the first few hours, not daring to look at them, I was unable to distinguish a face or establish a set of features in my mind. They were just bodies bursting with violent and exuberant vitality, enormous hostile presences whose very essence represented my negation. We weren't looking for answers; devastated and empty, all we wanted was to be left alone in the dark. Huddled against the walls, I heard my companions moaning in the gloom – one long, ceaseless lament.

And when the trap-door opened, that rectangle of light not only hurt our eyes – accustomed as they were to total darkness – but it was as if they were uncovering us, handing us over: Look! Here they are! In the darkness we'd felt protected, even kidding ourselves for a while that they might have forgotten about us. Up there must have been a garage or depot. When we first entered, shoved in by kicks and rifle-butts, we'd seen, across the almost dream-like state of drunkenness we'd fallen into, bits of engines and car parts scattered around the place. We heard noises coming from the road: cars zooming past, hurried footsteps, orders, call-ups and sudden bursts of gun-fire exploding in the distance.

Every time they opened the trap-door to come down, we felt violated by their presence – by their bodies, which glowed with violence and animal spirits, by the horror of their weapons, by their open-throated voices. And, from down below, their legs planted on the stone steps rose up towards the fork of the groin like tree-trunks, massive and hard.

Striking him from behind, they pushed that man down the stairs, the thwack of their blows resounding deeper the harder they hit.

Arms crossed behind the nape of his neck, he was trying to protect his head as he crawled down on his knees, careful not to fall on the slippery steps. They carried on hitting him until he got to the bottom step, then as huddled on the dirty floor amidst the rusty scrap iron where he'd tried to take refuge, they began to beat him with obvious, primal satisfaction, ignoring his cries as they struck his body with their feet and rifles. Then a new guard arrived: we heard an angry voice and hurried footsteps coming from a kind of courtyard up above:

'Have you got him? Where is he?' he yelled. Running down the steps he hurled himself on top of him.

'Here, take that you bastard! And that! The Buffalo Bill of Porta Vittoria! This one's for you, arsehole! You used to go around with a pistol on each side, didn't you: "Hey, move it, guys," you'd say, "let me through!"'

We scuttled into our corners like mice, while on all sides a kind of wailing, moaning chorus struck up, almost like an accompaniment to the beating. Letting them vent their anger uninterrupted, no one interfered or tried to make them stop. They'd found him at home in civilian clothes, thinking he'd got away with it. Every time the trap-door opened to let someone else in, there'd be another round of kicks and rifle-blows on that pile of flesh and rags.

We heard him moaning and snivelling in the darkness: he hadn't done anything, he hadn't killed anyone – everyone knew that! . . . He was calling someone by name: 'Angiulín! Angíulin! You know I never done nothing!' He knew who they were, that they were Reds . . . and yet even when they lashed out at him with their blows – had he buckled up under that crazed fury – he continued to defend himself, obstinately shouting out and pleading his innocence. He knew that evening when the Blackshirts stopped him, Angiulín was armed – he knew it!

'You remember Angiulín! You remember!' he kept saying. 'I stuck up for you, Angiulín, I stuck up for you!' He was shouting beneath the blows: 'And if they'd caught you with a calibre 9 in your pocket, you'd have had it – you'd have had it . . .'

I don't recall when it was exactly that they dragged us out of that hole, when they came there with their flashlights, picked us out among the others, and pushed us up the stairs. I just remember we found ourselves in the pitch dark outside a tin-roofed shed, shivering uncontrollably in the incredible, biting cold.

Surrounded by their guns and their silence, we huddled up close; and yet now I don't remember even one of my companions' faces or expressions. We were together, touching each other, and yet each man was alone, locked in his own private anguish. I noticed their fleeting glances, not aimed at us or anyone in particular, and I understood. Then one of them, a boy, roughly pushed a bottle of wine at us with a hard, forced gesture: 'There, drink this,' he said, 'it'll do you good.' The Paduan snatched it furiously from his hand, and bringing it to his lips, he drank, gurgling – mouth stuck to the neck of the bottle, desperately overcoming his nausea as he choked. 'Yes, yes, I'd rather be drunk.' His eyes were white, dilated, as he held his head back to gulp it down, the wine trickling in rivulets down his cheeks and along his neck.

Scattered about the city, distant gunfire travelled through the night: isolated bangs and short volleys, calls sent out and answered from various points. For an instant, strips of sky were illuminated by flares. They all shared a common sound, so different from any other weapon I'd heard until then: other guns, born by other men, all pointing in the same direction; finite, clear-cut, inexorable, they were, the last and the most pitiless; and they were aimed at us.

Looking up beyond the columns of bricks which held up the roof, I could see, through a crack in the metal, a patch of sky pierced by millions of stars. It was an unexpected, unbelievable sight, that little slice of sky – so distant and remote, impassive in the face of my suffering – and it remains one of my most anguished and desperate memories.

Prodding us with their guns, not violently but with a terrible sense of resigned determination, they pushed us in silence towards a closed door. We heard someone talking over the phone in a firm, authoritarian voice, then, in the half-light of a crowded office, we found ourselves before him. A tall man, illuminated by the light of a desk-lamp, he was standing behind a table with a red handkerchief around his neck, a big pistol tucked into his belt. Watching our misery and terror bounce off his impassive face, we heard him say:

'I've just telephoned to HQ for permission to execute you.'

230

Standing there, distraught faces a few inches apart, each man was trying to out-shout the other. And as battered as he was, he just wouldn't give in, wouldn't let go; he kept coming out with furious, desperate responses: 'Angiulín!' he was screaming, grabbing hold of him and shaking his arm: 'Angiulín!' It was because he sensed that the other wasn't telling the whole truth that he was weeping and yelling in that way:

'Oh Angiulín! You've got to be careful here – it's life we're talking about; life! D'you hear?' He stared at him with eyes which were bulging out of their sockets: 'Life!'

'I warned you, I did!' the other replied. 'I told you, you and that damned bald-headed Duce of yours, what would happen to you! I told you – you and your crazy black shirt!'

And it was precisely because he knew he wouldn't be able to help him, that Angiulín – an old, white-haired anarchist with a black cravat and locks reaching down to his shoulders – would get enraged and rebuke him in a raised voice:

'Idiot!' he used to say. 'They'll kill you! Don't you understand – they'll kill you!' He had warned him that they would kill him, just because he wouldn't be able to save him, even though he was a friend. He had told him to snap out of it, to get all that 'crap' out of his head, to forget about that 'bald-headed fruit cake'. But even so, every time they turned on the radio down at the bar and he heard Mussolini's voice, he'd make them all get up, shouting 'For Christ's sake, be quiet! Shut up, will you!' sitting there in ecstasy like a complete idiot.

Holding each other, we lay on our bunks – two above, two below, while the others stretched out on the floor with their backs to the wall. When the new group were brought in, and they saw us huddled on our bunks they put a struggle to resist coming in.

'No! Not with them! Don't put us with them! We don't want to be in the same room as that lot!'

Now they were trying to keep their distance, to emphasize their desire not to be mixed up with us, terrified of being contaminated by the fate we had written on our faces. They were still ranting and raving even after the door had been shut, and silence had fallen outside. It was we who had wandered arrogantly around the city, we who had shot and killed . . . how could *they* – law-abiding citizens who'd never once put on a uniform or carried a gun – how could *they* be mistaken for that scum!

We were their guilt – a living image of their guilt – yet we could also become their salvation . . .

Backing each other up, as if there were still someone outside to hear, they were shouting:

'You've got to kill them, d'you hear, kill them! They're the ones still in uniform! Look at them lying on their bunks without a care in the world! Can't you see the difference between us and them!'

One memory remains particularly: a spiteful-faced, elderly, well-to-do looking man in a black wool coat. Even under those conditions he was acting superior towards the others, insisting that they keep their distance and allow him space, air. Yelling loudly, so as to be heard by those behind the door, he kept on trying to incite them against us, sitting there smoking and accusing us over and over again; until, the Cadet looked at him menacingly and said to him in a cold voice,

'Enough! That's enough, now, D'you hear – enough!'

When he heard the sound of the bolt being drawn back, Buffalo Bill dragged himself along the floor and hid in a corner. 'No, c'mon no, no,' he kept saying over and over again, 'Don't do it! Don't do it!' looking around him with terror-maddened eyes. Meanwhile, the old man's wrinkled, thin-lipped face was peering out from behind the half-closed door: 'Ssh, ssh, be quiet! Ssh,' he was saying, enjoying the spectacle of that animal terror.

'Come, come,' he whispered rapidly, 'come outside, my Fascist comrade, and we'll have a little chat', sidling clumsily towards him in his patched shoes. Then his voice suddenly changed. 'Come outside, you piece of shit', he shouted. 'Bastard! Son of a bitch! Come outside, Blackshirt!' Taking hold of his jacket, he pulled him along the floor like a pile of rags, his rifle slipping down from his shoulder. 'Come outside', he shouted, as the others drew back against the wall.

The bloke's yelling and swearing was the only indication of what was happening out there. He began in a subdued voice: 'Right – over here now,' he said, then you heard a few blows and a moaning sound. 'Where's your black shirt now?' he went on. 'The Buffalo Bill of Porta Vittoria! Not such a big shot anymore, are we? In your black shirt, I want you! In your black shirt, you bastard! Son of a bitch – you son of a . . .'

But when he brought him back, grimacing with exhaustion as he pushed him by the shoulder, he had his falsely kind voice on again: 'Off you go then,' he said; 'we'll be seeing you later.'

His continual, obsessive lament rang out as silence fell over the vast, deserted cellar. Even on the floors above, and in the dark streets, the noises and voices had ceased. Then he came back. Opening the door, he poked his ferocious face around it, and at the sound of his yelling outside, the terror which had been circulating around the cell suddenly exploded, and everyone began screaming and crying, shouting, wailing and clutching their heads in their hands, while those two miserable wretches held each other close, sobbing quietly.

He was sitting in a corner now, moaning softly and fingering his wound – a blow from a bayonet had pierced his thigh from the buttock downwards. Holding the laceration in both hands, he was showing it to himself: 'Look,' he was saying, 'look what they did to me.' He turned towards us, as though for help, then he gave a start: 'Kill me!' he said. 'I can't take any more. Kill me – I want to die!' His hair was plastered down by the sweat which trickled along his ravaged face, while his eyes looked as though they were no longer able to see.

All night long we lay listening to his wheezing breath, at times slackening off as though he might be silent, then beginning once more.

Cum subit illius/tristissima nòctis imàgo

It was there inside you, an infectious germ like a fever which you couldn't shake off, a long continual shiver. The cells in your body were full of it: millions of little terrors all vibrating together until you'd become nothing more that a trembling mass.

Prostrate with exhaustion, I managed to doze off – for minutes? seconds? – beneath the dazzling light of the lamp which was never switched off. It was a feverish sleep, though, shaken by tremors and punctuated at sudden intervals by a thought which would cut through my slumber like a blade of ice, dissolving it in an instant, and I'd awake to find myself sitting up on the bunk, eyes open wide, forehead dripping . . .

Blondie was weeping uncontrollably on the bunk beneath me, while the Cadet, his face all twisted, was swinging his head from side to side, emitting a kind of inarticulate wail.

Rocking and shivering, the Paduan was huddled up on the cot opposite me, swept up in a wave of terror which had loosened all the stops, shooting through his veins and turning his body into something without a will of its own. Shaken violently by that uncontrollable trembling, gripped by a fanatic terror, he was gesticulating at intervals with his long, dislocated arms like some kind of grotesque puppet.

I was sure that when they took us there, he would begin shouting and screaming and begging for mercy.

The others had changed cells, and he, with his monotonous voice pleading for respite in a long, pitiful lament, he had gone too. No longer would our glances meet those wildly staring eyes, prisoners of their own sockets.

They were back already: we heard the clear, staccato sound of their footsteps in the deserted alleyway, their carefree voices ringing without resonance in the damp air. We heard them coming in through the door and exchanging a few words with the sentinel, followed their footsteps up the stairs and into the rooms above our heads. Each noise was familiar by now: the thud of guns laid down on the table, the screech of chairs being pulled out. It was still dark outside, as silence began to fall over the building, filling the cellar down below.

When they came to get him, and he realized that there were others waiting outside, he understood at once what was happening, and he didn't want to go. In an instant his faculties had returned, and he became watchful, determined to resist.

'What d'you want? Where're you taking me?' An unexpected will to survive had sprung to life. 'I'm not coming! I won't come!'

It was the fact that they called each other 'tu', that they'd once sat at the same table, which made it all so appalling. And there was an expression on those faces in the doorway which by now I'd come to know well, the look of people whose minds are made up, who've come to take a man to his death. 'Come on, come along outside', the old man was saying in a sugary voice, luring him on with a repulsive smile.

Retreating among us, he was hanging on to our clothes,

searching us out and pleading with his eyes. We could feel his hands on our bodies in a desperate desire to mingle among us, to lose himself in our fate. But it was him they were after – him! Our terror-hardened bodies were pushing him away while the others, pressed mutely against the walls, had turned to stone.

He was looking for Angiulín, calling his name in a furious voice: 'Angiulín!' he was shouting. 'Angiulín! Where's Angiulín!' But Angiulín wasn't standing among those outside the door; he couldn't hear him. Who knows where Angiulín was that night . . . Then they came to pull him off, to prise open those hands and drag him away. They pushed and pulled him as he struggled, shouting: 'I'm not coming! I'm not coming! No . . . o . . . o.' He must have wriggled free on the stairs, because we heard a commotion of shouting and swearing, and the old man saying in an enraged voice:

'Alive I want you, you son of a bitch! I want you alive – I want you there alive!'

We knew what happened next: walking uncertainly by the light of their torches, they dragged him to a place – chosen in advance – where a wall stood. We understood what he must have been going through, feeling the night air and that tight circle of men around him – his ravaged face looking from side to side, the unexpected heaviness in the legs which no longer seemed able to carry him. Then someone gave the order to halt, and pushing him against the wall, they laid into him.

They left him on the pavement, his hands and clothes sodden with all the blood in his body which had made him shout and struggle. He lay quite still in the silence of the street, huddled up in a position we knew so well, that enormous weight crushing him into the ground forever.

He'd become a thing of the street – a dark mass lying on the pavement, which the first passer-by would unexpectedly stumble across in the morning: something ugly, unmistakable, unutterably alien. And he'd have to make a detour around it, or maybe he'd stop and look out of curiosity (a curiosity which would never be satisfied) and mingled with all that, feelings of guilt, bewilderment, horror. Look at that: another Fascist getting his just deserts!

They, on the other hand, came away in silence, shivering a little now in the cold night air, trying to muster up an expression, a demeanour, that was appropriate to the occasion, to the emotions that were raging inside them, and yet unable to find one that would do. We knew, down to the last detail, the images that must have been flitting before their eyes: the disillusionment, the rage, the bewilderment on suddenly realizing that the object of all your hatred was no longer there; and that the very reason for doing all you'd done up to now had suddenly disappeared along with your rage, your toughness and the very gun you carried – all wiped out by the act you'd committed.

Then we heard them go upstairs, moving around a bit up on the upper floor, putting their weapons down on the table – slower now, with just the odd word spoken here and there – until they too became silent. Even the old man, who'd been up for two nights, went to sleep.

I held on to the thought: I didn't do it – I never went! No, I'd always refused. Each time I'd felt this hand holding me firmly on the step, preventing me from moving. It was that thought which gave me a few moments of respite – not that it lasted long. And watching Blondie's face, I knew it was that idea which was creeping up on him, racking him to the core. They must've known it would be like that though: after all, he who lives by the sword, perishes by the sword. Looking at Blondie, I thought to myself: now he must be remembering every moment of that day, every last detail. And they weren't things you could extract from the murky substance they floated in, one by one: you'd be thinking about something quite different when bang – they'd emerge, as vivid as anything, and there was nothing you could do to prevent it. It's our turn now – our turn! And that's when Blondie would start twitching helplessly from side to side, holding his head and moaning. There was no way out – except for me. I hadn't crossed that point of no return . . . They clung to me, casting sidelong glances in my direction, as if searching for confirmation: he'll be saved, and we'll be right there with him . . .

And yet it was precisely the knowledge of our shared fate that plunged me into despair: if it could happen to them, then it could happen to me, too!

In a faded, greasy Alpine cap and the wellington boots he'd got from Blondie, he stood there, legs apart, in the middle of the doorway, relishing the effect of his entrance. With a thin smile on his lips, he'd come to tell us the details – how he'd delivered the *coup de grace* with his P38. Pulling it out of the holster, he aimed it at the floor, making us wait a while before firing the unloaded gun. Then he looked at us and laughed, scrutinizing us, weighing us up with ironic eyes as though to say: just wait till your turn comes! But then he worked himself up into a kind of rage (yes, that's really what it was), furious because all of a sudden it had dawned on him that we were hardly in a position to congratulate him or share in his satisfaction.

He closed the door behind him. We heard his footsteps disappear into the cellar, as a sense of anguish rose up in us – soldering the hours, the minutes, the seconds into one long continual, unbroken suffering. Then the door swung open with a crash.

It was him again.

A breath of damp air blew from the door, as we suddenly emerged from the feverish, dream-like state we'd fallen back into. Leaning against the doorway, he stood watching us with obvious enjoyment.

'The People's Tribunal has reached its verdict.'

At this, all four of us leapt to our feet before his smiling, mocking omnipotence. Then, brushing his hand meaningfully over his big pistol, he added:

'You'd begun to think you'd got away with it, eh? A few of them might have gone soft – said they're only young . . . well, in the end we won!'

Night time still . . . one of those nights! How ever did the hours go by, as I lay hunched up and trembling on my bunk, dazzled by the yellow light? One minute I'd seem to drop off, then all of a sudden I'd awaken to a ferociously lucid consciousness.

We didn't speak: there was nothing left to say, each one of us locked in his own private suffering. That was the night the Cadet began to rail against Blondie:

'It's your fault! It's all your fault! I was already back in civvies!' he wept, holding his head between his hands.

Leaping up from your stomach to your throat, it was something you couldn't get rid of – not for a moment, not for one blessed moment! Sudden wounding thoughts cut through the flesh like blades . . . Just one hope to cling to, just one word . . .

An old monk came, exuding a smell of wax and incense: his words, too, had a whiff of the monastery.

'Resign yourselves . . . ask for forgiveness . . . free your souls from all bitterness . . . Think only of Heaven.'

You could tell he wanted to leave, to return to his cell – to long, twilit corridors and the silent refectory.

The Paduan didn't want him to go: taking his hand and holding it tight, he was saying:

'Father, Father . . .' He even gave him some money with a trembling hand, for him to say mass. 'For Saint Antony of Padua, Father.'

You see they could still do these things – believe in certain acts, involve themselves with the priest, in the masses. Their terror was still on this side; while for me, all that remained was a blade thrust inside that white fear, nothing else. Nothing I was familiar with – nothing of what there'd been before in the world, of all I'd believed in, which made up the very essence of my being – could help me now, could give me a moment's respite. Nothing – not one word, not a single word I'd ever been taught – could penetrate the roots of my anguish. Nothing could accompany me to that point and beyond, into the annihilation which awaited me.

When Blondie took his head between his hands, and began beating it against the wall, that's when I got down from my bunk and struck, hitting him mechanically on the cheeks. 'Pack it in, will you! Pack it in!' But it was only because my terror was buried so deep that his outburst looked like showing off, like exhibitionism. And so, of course, was my reaction.

Each time that door opened, or we heard a noise outside, my heart leapt to my mouth.

Who is it? What do they want?

Jumping off our straw mattresses, we'd stand there leaning against the bunks, eyes glued to the doorway. What could it be this time?

I didn't hate them anymore. I no longer felt anything for them, for their symbols, their words, their insults and their threats. I no longer felt anything for anyone.

Just fear. Fear of their footsteps in the unknown rooms I couldn't picture; fear of being offered a cigarette, of the noise out there which made us jump every time; fear of a look, of a smile even. Fear: a tight knot at the pit of your stomach which consumed everything else.

We weren't able to give any answers, to make any signs, to string together a single thought. We no longer felt like men – like human beings similar to them or to anyone else. We'd become empty, fragile, naked. They could demand any kind of behaviour from us: 'Do this!' and we'd have done it; 'Say that!' and we'd have obeyed. We were nothing now: things at their mercy, whom they could order around as they pleased. Masters of our lives and feelings, they could make us laugh, cry, suffer, – or restore a crumb of hope to us. Straws in the wind, scraps of torn paper . . .

To whom would they be accountable for our lives? Who gave a damn about our four lives, about my life?

But then what did my life finally boil down to? My awareness of it – the tattered remains of the fabric it appeared to have been woven from?

It was simply the crude existence you sensed in your refusal to die, to be wiped out. All that remained was that contraction of the living substance – the spasm of beating flesh, the blade thrust deep into the pit of your stomach.

Life meant being able to say: tomorrow. Being able to sleep and think tomorrow morning, and everything which lies ahead of it. Afterwards: life was that afterwards – the possibility of avoiding this anguish, the possibility of deceit, of illusion . . .

Who were these people? What did they want from me? Which ties had ever bound us together? I didn't know them, I'd never seen them – and now there was a terrifying intimacy! They came in and insulted me, they were free to question me, touch me, to laugh at me . . . But what did they know of what I was inside, of what I was thinking and feeling, of where I came from?

Later in the evening we heard them coming down the alleyway, laughing and singing a few notes of an unknown song in raucous voices. The, coming down to us, we heard them arguing outside with the guard; opening the door, they walked in with the excessive, exaggeratedly arrogant manner of all drunks. They looked at us with eyes grown misty through alcohol: 'I'll break your neck like a chicken! Tell me, where's your black shirt now!'

They were so confident, so full of life with those exuberant bodies of theirs: bodies that breathed, gesticulated . . . They seemed to be expanding in the space around us, annihilating us in the process. Free to come and go as they pleased, to walk out into the street, to talk to people, to do as they pleased, they were no longer human beings but in our eyes had acquired the status of giants, of divine presences.

At times they even brought others with them – workmen, ordinary people – as if we were beasts in a cage. When they first appeared at the door, their faces were full of uncertainty and curiosity, which soon gave way to indifference as if they'd been disillusioned. In spite of the red handkerchiefs, and the weapons which they carried so awkwardly, a few of them had such run-of-the-mill faces that we could actually sense how uneasy they felt in those clothes, clothes which they'd only just donned in the first flush of euphoria. One of them was getting impatient now, and he began tugging at their sleeves: 'C'mon, lads! C'mon, let's make a move.' Then, staggering a little, making a few inarticulate grunts and threats, they left. The smell of wine remained, though, mingled with the bitter smoke from their cigarettes.

Those days haven't left a single trace in my memory: all I remember are evenings, nights and sunrises, as I emerged from that feverish daze called sleep. We were safe during the day, though, for those things happened only in darkness.

And how long did it all last? I can't pin it down with any degree of accuracy, but it felt like a vast tract of time, days and nights like some terrible illness . . . Could it really have only been four days? At some point their behaviour began to change, but we were only aware of it after a long time had passed. Their vigilance began to slacken a little, too.

I remember one guard coming into the cell, and sitting himself down on a stool. As he smoked, inhaling with pleasure, he began to talk. A young man, almost a boy, it was he who told us about that spectacle. And out of his words a picture was born of some kind of celebration or popular festival: thousands of people,

240

whole families holding children by the hand, walking down Corso Venezia and the wide, adjoining thoroughfares, shouting from one side of the street to the other. Then the tramping of all their feet, returning triumphant:

'But have you seen Him?'

'You bet I have! It's really him – they're all down there!'

His face was happy, and he was telling the story with passion, as if he too saw it as something out of the ordinary. All that had remained was that vague, lingering, shadow, and now it too had been done away with. The monster terrorizing the city had been finally caught and slaughtered: what further proof did they need to confirm the end of the long nightmare? The news spread along the street from house to house, passed on by word of mouth: yes, it's true, they've got him! He's down there – everyone's there! It still seemed incredible, though – incredible that he ever existed, incredible that he was dead. All that babble and feet going to and fro.

Days later, they brought us photographs of the four corpses strung up by the feet, arms dangling. The woman's skirts were tied with a length of string. There was one, too, of their spraying the pile of rotting bodies with fire-hoses: a local policeman dressed in a black uniform, with the city's crest on his cap.

But from his words and manner, he seemed to be telling quite a different story as he sat there, joyous and euphoric, offering us cigarettes, and enjoying a great chunk of bread. To me, too, it seemed such a distant thing: how many millions of years had gone past in those few days? The whole building seemed empty, as if it were some kind of public holiday.

'D'you want to come and see it?' he asked us with a complete absence of malice. They'd all gone. 'I'll take you – we can pop out in the late afternoon.'

But there was already a feeling of melancholy in the air, a vein of regret and disillusionment. It was Him all right – there was no doubt about it, no mistaking him even as deformed as he was, dangling there with that petrol pump, hanging from his boots . . . Yet what was left for them now? Somehow those twisted remains managed to dwarf everything, so that he, too, standing there with his gun and a red handkerchief around his neck, felt shrunken and useless.

There was a pain inside me, an imprecise ache which was not

for him, or how he'd come to his end – he no longer held any kind of concrete reality for me. After all I'd been through, a kind of terrible illness, it was as though the past had been entirely wiped away by a cleansing tide. The pain I felt was for me, for them, for the world – a pain that marked a new awareness of the desperate futility of bloodshed. It was for all the atrocities, for the violence and brutishness of what had been unleashed in those years, of which that display was both conclusion and symbol.

Leaning on his rifle, he filled us in on his nocturnal adventures, telling us about the 'trials' he'd taken part in with other divisions. His face grew animated beneath the yellowish light of the lamp cutting through the gloom. And from his words, we guessed at a whole network of places like the one we were in: cellars, garages, makeshift prisons. The minute they found out a trial was going to take place, they'd be over there as quick as a flash to be a part of it. 'A Fascist, d'you hear? One of those bastards, pissing himself with fright!' And he looked around, honestly expecting us to share in his loathing. The smile which his good nature had aroused remained frozen on our lips.

Of course I could picture it, but quite differently from how he'd described it all: the swift, back-street executions taking place early in the morning when you could just begin to see, out there on the city outskirts beneath high, crumbling factory walls; the feeling you could hardly confess to yourself, let alone to anyone else. Imagining them, it was impossible not to identify with the bastard 'who pissed himself with fright'.

Who can remember it now? Who kept track of the solitary bursts of gunfire exploding at intervals through the silence of the suburbs, of those nights, now deleted from memory, when you knew for a fact that hideous death was wandering freely through the streets, no matter how hard you tried to ignore it. They just turned over and went back to sleep – events which no longer concerned them any more; while we sat rigid in our bunks, foreheads dripping with cold sweat, staring at each other with whitened eyes.

It was the other side of that story, the forgotten face which belonged to us in those terrible nights; nights when, locked in cellars, you suffered and died in that sordid way without means

242

of escape, without a crumb of comfort from anyone. We were crushed, defeated people, ravaged by history . . . while they just turned over and went back to sleep: 'Go on – let them get it out of their systems . . . Let them get it over with . . .'.

Around dawn, before people left their houses, old lorries from the municipal rubbish department would go around collecting the useless remains, the dross of their haul, picking them by the arms and legs: one, two, upsy-daisy, and on to the lorry. Then they were piled up under the wall at the Musocco cemetery for people to identify the bodies: haphazard rows of corpses in shabby outsize civvies and army boots, or sometimes as naked as newborn babies.

For days on end Blondie's mother – a little, doll-like lady with badly dyed hair – would go to that meat-market to look for us; every morning she'd be there, with each new arrival. Other women, she said, would wander amongst the twisted objects, rummaging in the pile in search of a detail – the colour of a piece of clothing perhaps, or the shape of a shoe. And they didn't even have the courage to weep, surrounded as they were by those people – some armed, others with hard, hostile faces – just waiting for a flicker of reaction in order to lash out and insult them.

It was warmer in our cell than in the vast, damp cellar. He offered us cigarettes, wanted to know about us – about our lives as civilians and students. Which one was he? What was his name? I get them all a bit muddled now. I remember he was very young, even younger than us: sixteen or seventeen he must have been. He told us what he'd got up to: how many times had I heard the same words, the same boasting, only in completely different circumstances? Apparently he'd killed a German captain at a bus-stop, creeping up behind him and firing at his head from down below, because he was 'a great hulk of a man – this tall, I'm telling you!'

How many do I remember? Two or three, but very vaguely – figures tied by association to isolated episodes or sentences; no faces, though, no even after a few years would I have been able to recognize one. And yet, now I come to think of it, I did meet up with one bloke – another one of life's coincidences. It can't have been more than about three or four years later – on a train it was, when a conductor opened the carriage door: 'Tickets please!' Behind him I saw this railway policeman with a white, enamelled holster and a red stripe down his trousers, looking, staring really hard at me: I'm telling you it's got to be him! Look who's here! It's him! I couldn't believe it was true. We embraced like old friends, while the people in the carriage took up this air of emotional complicity. All excited, he sat down beside me, and we held onto each other's hands: so, whatever happened to that bloke? And how did what's his name end up? And how come he'd become a policeman? At this he looked embarrassed:

'Well, you know what it's like . . . They made us an offer – whoever wanted to, could. No work to be found, and all the rest of it . . . By the way, talking of that, d'you remember the old bloke who was with us, the one dressed in overalls?'

Like hell I remember him.

'That poor old man,' he went on.

'What about him?'

The train rushed through the Tuscan landscape: vineyards, plains, fields, villages, past lines of cypress-trees along the hills and avenues which led to the farmhouses.

That's all it took, a chance meeting – a word or detail which you thought you'd wiped out of your mind, when bang! you were back in the torrent of emotions and memories as if the whole thing had only happened yesterday.

I must have told him what I thought of that poor old man in overalls, along with other things I remembered, because when we said goodbye, I had the distinct impression that he was colder, less pleased with himself. He'd been shocked to discover another point of view – an unexpected, reverse side to that story, one which he never imagined existed. Most vivid of all, though, is the feeling of liberation which overtook me on suddenly realizing that neither he nor anyone else had any hold over me any more. He and all the others were just like me now, like the rest of the world. We could sit like equals and talk: I was free to tell him what I felt, to contradict him or to chat with the other passengers, to ask their opinion. That was the real significance of what happened in the intervening years – something which he, yes he, couldn't begin to understand. I no longer had to lie to ingratiate myself with him, no longer had to make him pity me or show mercy, no longer had to fake anything.

Clumsy in his heavy uniform, he sat there beside me on the wooden bench. He'd taken off his felt cap and, wiping the sweat off his brow, he was casting me aggrieved looks, offended by what he was as ingratitude – a kind of disapproval or pettiness – on my behalf. What he didn't realize was that I – a man who was free to talk to him in that way, who as able to reproach him for those events – was in fact living proof of exactly the opposite.

In neat handwriting which still smacked of the schoolroom they wrote down their names in an old notebook: 'We'll keep in touch – see each other – write,' they said. At the time, it seemed possible.

Then they took us to the market to buy some clothes: 'You can't leave dressed like that,' they laughed, pointing to the uniforms we were wearing. All those people! All those new faces, there amongst the stalls beneath the parched tarpaulins! We were stunned to find ourselves still alive – just think, Blondie, we're still alive! Alive in the midst of all these people! Our companions' eyes twinkled: who cared about what had happened! All that counted was the tremendous awareness of being there in the thick of things, amidst all the movement and noise: life itself. Everything seemed new, unknown, waiting to be discovered: people wandering about freely, chatting, choosing things, haggling – it was a new world out there, full of open windows and doorways, of people shouting out to each other, getting around on bicycles and all sorts of makeshift transport. We bought cigarettes – those limp, damp cigarettes you got then, which tasted of grass – which we smoked like Turks, fingering the packets in our pockets. I remember when I pulled the money out of my sock, his eyes nearly popped out of his head to see such riches. 'If you'd killed us, you'd never have got hold of it!' and we all laughed. As he steered us about the city, the red scarf around his neck was already losing some of its special lustre and significance in the face of everything which was springing to life again: that hunger for life, for what tomorrow held, which you could sense in the air itself. Carefree and gay, he hardly seemed aware of it: 'Go on, buy this! Look at those great shoes over there!' he was saying, as if it were his merchandise, or as if he were personally responsible for its existence.

245

It even crossed our minds to remain with them; to throw in our lot with theirs, to forget how it had all begun.

'Hey, Blondie – what's say we don't go back home? What about if we stay here and begin all over again. We'll find work, and on Saturday afternoons we can meet up for a chat in the cafe with them, and then we'll go out looking for girls!'

Wandering arm in arm with me amongst the stalls and confusion, Blondie looked at me incredulously, yet fascinated by the prospect. I bought a cloth suit and a pair of black shoes, which I couldn't wait to get back to headquarters to try on. How blithe and free I felt in my light jacket and my shiny pointed shoes! Sitting on tables they looked at me and gave me their verdict. Christ! We are twenty, too, the eyes of the Cadet and the Paduan seemed to be saying, amongst those of all the others. We've survived this tragedy, so why shouldn't it be our turn to begin afresh like them, like everyone else? Why not? Brand new, carefree, we'll forget everything – start from scratch! Face life like people of our age should!

The sun shone in through the window, illuminating the weapons which were thrown haphazardly about the place. After waving them about in the first few days, like some proud symbol of their power, they seemed to have grown cumbersome, and now they lugged them around awkwardly. Life was opening before us: all that life which had now been restored to us. We were doing everything we could do to push all we'd been through into oblivion, and from their behaviour it seemed that they, too, wanted to put all that behind them, to wipe the slate clean and rise above the morass of memories and passions.

Was he there too? What was his name now? Luciano, yes, Luciano . . . a thin, serious boy who'd been in charge when we were captured. We didn't see much of him after that, but we noticed that he was looked up to by the others, that he seemed to have a special ascendancy which had been earned in action. Saying little, he watched with surprised curiosity as we began to emerge from the abyss, divesting ourselves of the role which circumstances had thrust upon us, beginning to acquire the individuality of men, with faces, minds, feelings and a faint glimmer of hope. Later on, we found that it was thanks to him that we were still alive, that even during all the upheavals he'd always been opposed to our being shot. He'd given us his word when we surrendered.

I remember when they put on the parade, although I can't actually put the various events into any kind of chronological order. Bringing in the parcels of khaki uniforms – so as to put on a good show in front of the Allies – they tried them on, laughing. That smell of the military in the midst of all the confusion! Some of them even put on stripes! Apparently there were English and American generals there, along with their bosses, some of whose name they didn't even know – middle-class types in civvies with tricolours on their arms.

Their stories and the pictures in the papers made a real impact on me. Look! It was them! the ones who'd come down from the mountains with there bronzed faces and Alpine hats – so different from how I'd imagined them to be! Roaming through the city on foot and in old trucks, with machine-gun belts around their necks, they filled the streets with their presence, their tales and their boasting. Watching people hail them and drag them into bars, I couldn't believe that I wasn't with them – aware that there was a parade in which neither I nor Blondie nor the Paduan, who'd gone along for the flags and the singing and the fanfares, could take part. Immediately afterwards, I realized with sadness that every word – every one of their symbols – was in opposition to all that I'd been until then, was celebrating a victory that we had fought against.

Even then they didn't really seem to fit in; the cities hadn't changed, nor had the people in the streets, in spite of their new, overjoyed faces. Right from those early days you could sense that it was just an interlude, a parenthesis, and that those streets had been built for other parades, other processions. The quaint rusticity which still clung to the fighters felt out of tune with the architecture and respectable façades of those streets, with their heavy doors, their balconies – as though just for that feast-day another culture had descended upon the city, a rupture in the passage of time which you felt could not last.

Even at their place, less frequented now, you got the feeling of things winding down. Restless and unwilling, they wandered from room to room, while the May sunshine filling the streets shone freely through the open window, leaving a trail of sloth and languor in its wake. Life seemed to be picking up according to its own, secret, immutable rules – and all this in such a short space of time! I remember that by this stage they treated us as if we were one of them, and spoke freely in front of us; one or two of them even confessed to having belonged to one of our military units.

Then the order came through to hand over their weapons: 'Our weapons? But now what?' Discussion upon discussion. Even Luciano had lost his air of calm and seemed tense and nervous. When it came to the crunch, his word still counted above anyone else's. Then, after long talks with the chaps over at the offices – the lawyer, the engineer – he grudgingly conceded that this wasn't the moment.

That's when I felt his authority quietly ebb away – the fascination, the air of quiet calm which that thin figure with the Tommy-gun around his neck emanated. He was back on an everyday plane now. They hid their favourites, the ones they'd become attached to – machine-guns, Tommy-guns – for when their time came, for the second uprising, the Revolution.

It was a real disillusionment for them, over something we felt we had sort of shared, even if we didn't dare admit to ourselves that we were actually pleased with the outcome. It was a kind of easy nihilism: look, you see, in the end you were screwed too! It always works out like that! They shook their heads: no, ours is a different story. And yet they too were downcast, dazed almost, as though they'd already resigned themselves to it, as though all along they'd never intended to make any claims once it was over.

Those sun-fulled afternoons, the building getting more deserted with each day that passed, women and children in the streets, and the old problems resurfacing: where to go, what to do, how to live. In the offices there were certain types we'd never seen in the early days, grown men dressed in civvies, who wielded a different kind of authority that wasn't born of that place. They were full of things to do, of outside contacts and meetings.

When we left, we got our travel rations too: a little kitbag containing tea, rice and sugar. But where were we going to? Back to what? After our experiences on that vanished planet, how remote the world seemed to us! I no longer remembered my parents or my home; I hadn't given them a single thought during the whole, harrowing period, so that now they too seemed light years away.

They gave us documents – Partisan C.M. who collaborated with such and such HQ – and accompanied us for some of the way. No more roadblocks, no more sentries shouting *Papiren! Papiren!* The streets were still full of dust and rubble, but you didn't see taut-faced soldiers on lorries anymore. The flux of life was beginning again, made up of people, meetings, chatting, warmth and human presences – so different from the dim, stultified world from which I was emerging.

I remember their waving as we turned the corner at the bottom of the road:

'We'll keep in touch! We'll write!'

'Yeah, you bet!'

Chapter XV

YES, there and then, in the giddiness of those first days when everything seemed to have been swept up in the current of events, it did seem possible to us. But why should we want to see them again, why should we be reminded of the events in which they'd played their part? Anything to do with them left us with feelings of inferiority and submission. Despots of our lives, they'd known us in humiliating circumstances, reminding us of a frame of mind upon which it was impossible to build a life.

After that moment of drunkenness, there were too many things that would surface again, dividing us and placing us on different shores. Even then, returning home on the lorries and trains amongst people with their bundles and parcels – still wretched, but gripped by a feverish *joie de vivre*, a desire to be together, to talk, to smile – we sensed the depth of that fracture. The only way we could be part of their stories and discussions was by remaining cagey, by keeping a reserve full of sudden silences and loopholes.

No, we were denied the youth one thought was owed to people of our age – the chance to prick up our eyes at the sound of those first words with their new meanings, to develop along with the ideas gradually being put forward. There were involvements, ties, duties and habits waiting to drag me inexorably back into the closed circle of rejection and fear which I'd fooled myself into thinking I'd broken by running away.

She was there waiting for me on the landing, ready to clasp me in her arms and pull me into the back room as though it were some kind of rabbit's hole: 'Be silent, my son! For pity's sake, be silent!' The old furniture all around, those musty smells stagnating in the rooms . . . When I tossed and turned in my sleep at night, she would come and wake me. I asked her to – 'If you hear me talk or move, then whatever you do, wake me up!' – because otherwise I'd find myself in it again, sunk deep in that well of anguish.

I'd awake to her calling me by name, shaking me, to her hot breath and anxious face hanging over me: 'What were you dreaming about my son? What did you see?' It was as though she didn't just want to free me from those visions but actually to take possession of my dreams, to cancel out everything that had become alien to her in the intervening years.

And then there were my friends, waiting for me at the bar in Porta Pia: all that commotion of noises and voices, the windows lit up, people out on the pavements, and us – still shaken by what had happened – with our old grudges, our nostalgia, our plans for revenge. There was Captain Alimonti with his threadbare clothes and thick accent, Major d'Aragona spitting as he spoke: 'Be on the alert, lads! This won't last! You just need four from each village, a couple on every city street, and this time we'll show them!'; Guadalajara with his Tartar's moustache, who, despite his mutilated arm, hoisted up a rucksack with twenty kilos of rocks and, dripping with sweat, every morning hiked thirty kilometres along the sunny beach from Ostia to Nettuno, so as to be in shape for when the time came. And Enzo, Giannetto, Blondie.

A sadness filled me, returning home in the evening along the deserted streets, my mouth sour with wine and cigarettes, and questions began to take shape. All the old things were there, waiting to attack with all the weight of their past. Turning the corner, I only had to look up to see my father, standing in his vest behind the faded blinds, bare elbows resting on the marble sill, his thin shoulders bent now. Who could tell whether his irrepressible optimism could lead him to believe that the outside world still held something in store for him – a world which, one evening at the same window, had turned against him, toppling his castle of cards and throwing to the lions his three sons, whom he'd 'always taught to do their duty'.

The day I returned, I remember his voice breaking over the receiver.

'Don't come back,' he said. 'Don't come back my son! If they see you and recognize you, who knows what might happen!'

So I waited till nightfall, creeping along the walls of the Via Poliziano, my jacket collar pulled up so as to conceal my face. They'd hung a towel from the window as a signal that no one was out on the stairs, and that it was safe for me to go up.

So there'd been the flight, and now the return. It hadn't ended in that cemetery at the edge of the plain as we had imagined it would, that first night on the lorry. And now life had to be faced – but how? It was no longer just an unknown, hostile thing suddenly gaping before my eyes, as on that far-off evening when, with shouts rising up from the darkened street, I had decided that I would throw it away. No, there was also the past to reckon with now – all the bloodshed in which I'd been personally involved, the hatred which had been unleashed, and that sentence with no grounds for appeal, ever ready to pull you down. There was no one willing to offer you a word or a helping hand now that your blame, isolated from any context, was fixed there for all to see, conveniently concealing a whole tangle of responsibilities and involvements which no one was prepared to shoulder.

It was in the avenue of oak-trees, outside his beautiful house with its luminous study, that I happened to run into him. Back to his disinterested, free and easy self, with a newly-kindled vitality, he couldn't resist saying to me, his expression careless again:

'You see, I was right! It didn't do any good at all.' Not bitterly though, because by now his life was chock-full of engagements again: seminars, conferences, literary articles.

'Come on! Chin up! You've got to forget about it – that's the ticket!'

Waving to me from a distance, he made an expansive gesture with his arms, as though to say: 'Just look around you! This is what life is – a life you've got to lead!'

It was true: it was bustling with people and activity, life had returned to everyone else. But where was I supposed to fit in? A whole me, with no holds barred, with nothing suppressed?

Okay, so I'd survived, but now what? Should I throw myself back into the business of living like everyone else? Friends: the small circle of their faces contracting a little more with each day, the occasional evening in a tavern with anchovies, sour olives and a litre of wine glistening with drops. 'D'you remember the time when so-and-so happened? And so-and-so? Then that other time . . . ?' By now they had relegated the whole business to some personal, sanctified little corner of their beings (all the ugly parts obliterated), ready to dust and bring out for the odd occasion, after which they'd blithely return home to sleep among clean sheets . . .

One or two in the morning, and me and Giannetto the last ones left: *Two men went to mow, went to mow a meadow . . .*

Backwards and forwards with no way out, like the vicious circle of the thoughts we were grappling with. Crossing the darkness of the Colle Oppio, we went to sit on the balustrade of the terrace which looked out on Via Labicana. There, in the silence of the park, you could hear the water trickling down the long tufts of moss on the fountain and into the basin below.

That's where we'd first met, in those days of bewilderment after the armistice: me, him, Blondie who'd volunteered for the execution squad, Enzo Grama, and Fabio, who a few years later would end up killing himself. It had filled me with such happiness to run there and see that little group of them waving from a distance, to be among them in the midst of the desert which had formed around us.

'What's there left for us?' Giannetto used to ask himself at that time. 'Tell me what left for us if they have wiped out everything we've ever know?'

People had run away, shouting:

'The Germans are attacking! The Germans are attacking!' and all you could see were little huddles of curious boys, standing at deserted street-corners, outside half-closed doors, and weary soldiers in leather jackets beneath the arches of the Colosseum. But where had the grown-ups been – all the people who'd once filled the streets with their voices, with their singing, their speeches, their articles, their flags and music?

There was Giannetto, with his contracted features illuminated by the reflection of the street-lamps of the Via Labicana.

'How many of us were wiped out?' he muttered. 'Tell me, how many young boys – twenty thousand, fifty thousand – when the war was all over and the tragedy had come to an end? How many were slaughtered during the upheaval in that bloody April of '45, when the war was over, I repeat? No one has counted them – no one wants to take that on! The *pharmakoi*, that's what we were, the *pharmakoi* who paid for everybody!'

Looking down at the street below, scored by tram-lines glistening beneath the moon, he went on:

'No, you see, we weren't innocent anymore! Not a chance! We'd killed, raped, the lot! But then in the end, how many people could go back over everything that happened in those twenty years of Fascism, could look themselves in the eye and say: "I've got nothing to reproach myself with, I was never involved in anything in the least bit shady or ambiguous, any kind of weakness or laxity"?'

Looking at me with eyes which were growing confused, he took hold of my arm, almost as though he needed that contact to reassure himself of my presence: 'How many?' he repeated. 'Tell me, how many could really say they were innocent? Were not compromised, were not involved in the dictatorship? I don't know, but if there was someone who could say: no, not me, I had nothing to do with it, I carry no blame – well, even their innocence founders on the face of the massacre which took place after the war!'

There were years, illusions, poses and gestures to be got rid of: '*Friends! Romans! Countrymen! Lend me your ears!*', there, in the dead silence of the Forum, with the moon casting shadows of the columns on to the grey cobblestones of the Via Sacra, while a heavy perfume rose up from the darkness of the laurels.

Now to find the words, those missing words *to fill the silence/which the songs left behind*. One after another, and another. And you throw away the old ones – no easy task, because underneath each one you almost always stumble across a wound or a falsehood. Or a void.

You had to return to Borgosesia and stand before those ten memorial stones; to Cossato, to Crevacuore, to the Ponte della Pietà where your teenage companions were killed. You had to return to those places, and once you'd got hold of the rope, you had to go down deep, to the bottom, with no more fooling around – no more pirouettes, a few funny faces, a joke or two, then walking off the stage.

And that lasts a lifetime.

But ten years later, I did go and look up Angiulín in Milan. Yes, really him, Angiulín, the old humanitarian anarchist with his black cravat and flowing locks. He who had clung desperately to that reproach: 'I warned you, I did; I warned you about that bald-headed Duce! I told you!' Because he knew that he wouldn't be able to save Barzaghi, the Buffalo Bill of Porta Vittoria, who went around with a pistol on each side: 'Hey, you guys, let me through!' 'I warned you, I did!'

I don't recall exactly when it was, but I remember feeling very remote from those events already, as though I were a different, more adult person, who'd somehow managed to emerge from that viscous mess. My first studies, lectures . . .

I went on the off-chance, without knowing the name of the street, although I did more or less remember the area. How astonished I was to see that those places really existed! I found the church we'd fled to, the attic where Blondie suggested we shoot ourselves: 'You're crazy! You're crazy!' the Paduan had shouted, maddened by terror. I turned into the dead-end alleyway where their headquarters had been. It was a luminous Sunday in summer, and the streets were empty. They'd built a razor-blade factory in there, one of those little Milanese outfits with a workforce of about ten or so. It was closed, though, completely deserted. From a little window at street level I looked down into the basement: a vast, spotless room with machinery dotted about the place, rolling mills and presses. The cells had been knocked down.

And yet Angiulín was still there. I'm not sure if I knew at the time that I'd find him in his old haunt, as neither his name nor address were in my address book. Was it a chance inspiration that had led me there? I leant against his secondhand-books stall in the tree-lined avenue near Porta Ticinese. A stifling afternoon it was, and the heat was suffocating. He was sitting on a straw-covered chair under the shade of a tree, a book on his knee, not taking any notice of the solitary client who, in the heat of the sun, had crossed the square at that unlikely hour, and was now browsing amongst his old books. Every now and then a car wold drive past in that furnace, the windows open, the tyres roasting on the asphalt.

I watched him covertly as I pretended to leaf through a book I'd picked up at random: he hadn't changed much, just a little older with his black cravat and that other-worldly air about him. You sensed that he was someone who'd remained aloof from things – a solitary bachelor figure or an old, childless widower.

Then at a certain point I made a casual comment. He looked at me irritably, then starting, he rubbed his eyes. He couldn't believe it, he was stunned:

'It can't be Carlo . . . bless me, it really is! You of all people!'

Whoever would have imagined he would react like that? He embraced me, and holding my shoulders, he kept touching me to make sure I was real, hugging me and holding me close as he looked at me with tears in his eyes.

'But the others – what about Blondie and the Paduan?'

He wanted to know where they were, whether they were well. 'But are they alive? Are they alive?' he demanded. Then he began to talk, and his memories and mine – grown equal now – mingled. We remembered them in the same way: they were just men, no more – people I'd once known and were tied to my memory.

He was so happy – so happy! You saw that happiness in his eyes which kept looking me up and down.

'Really, you can't imagine what joy you've brought me by coming to see me! If you knew how many times I've asked what became or you – how you'd ended up, whether you made it home, whether you were still alive!'

We went to the bar next door for coffee; just an ordinary local bar full of loafers, the smell of mould and washing-up water in the air. I can't remember if anyone greeted him, whether he was known there or not; and yet he was an old anarchist and partisan, a member of the Resistance in a working-class neighbourhood. No, if that impression remains it must have been because I really did notice a feeling of indifference in the air, as though he were a stranger there. It really hit me, the thought of his going on with his solitary life after it was all over. There was a notice-board hanging on the wall, with the dates of football matches, an espresso machine belching out the occasional cloud of steam, flies following each other and settling on the dirty floor.

We drank our coffee and left. I asked him how things were going, about his old friends, politics. At this he shrugged his shoulders, and shaking his head, he grimaced. How remote it all seemed. He kept out of things now, didn't see anyone anymore . . . He'd been disillusioned; things had worked out differently. The section had closed down, and new people had moved in. I only remember bits of it, though – how he smiled, as if I'd taken him back to far-off days and events which had been wiped out now. It was then I realized with a pang how much more alive and important it was to me, how the people and events stamped indelibly on the painful substance of my memory were almost-forgotten episodes to him – episodes which only my words could drag out of oblivion. It was the other side, the other face of that story which would always remain in the shadows. For them there'd be an afterwards, something beyond all that, memories growing more frayed with each day that passed until they were re-absorbed into everyday life. He gave me news of people he still ran into occasionally, but his thoughts were elsewhere.

'What joy! Just thank the Lord you're alive! . . . You were good boys.' Then, suddenly struck by an idea, he grew pensive, as though a cloud had fallen over his thoughts. And impulsively, with a sense of liberation, he added: 'Just think – we could have killed you!'

Shaking his head, he looked at me: at the man standing before him, a man whose smiles and gestures were filled with the capacity for life, who could move and greet people, a man whose very being was made up of a whole network of affections and interests.

'Just think, Carlo!' he repeated. 'Just think – we could have killed you!'

And that terrible possibility of death – a possibility which had been within a fraction of an inch from turning into reality – was now all that mattered, the only thing he retained from everything he'd lived through.

Shaken by emotion, I looked down at the ground, unable to speak or answer him.

'You were good lads!' he suddenly burst out. 'Good lads!'

But were we, I asked myself, were we 'good lads'? I pictured them in my mind: Blondie, the Paduan, the Cadet – good lads? No, maybe today's young men could be good lads, but not us. We were 'that lot' – youth gone adrift, the final dross of the tide. Turned wicked through disillusionment, we'd committed acts of violence and abuse, filled with rage and a burning desire to find something upon which to vent the misery and despair into which our lives had fallen.

When I turned to wave to him from a distance, I saw him standing there in the sun, next to his stall, waving. A bitter shadow had crossed his face, though, and his lips were tightly pressed. I sensed then his private grief, the pain caused by those words: 'Just think – we could have killed you!' Yes, that's what it was – it was that! He hadn't managed to save that bloke, Buffalo Bill! But even if he too had survived, how would it have altered things? He would have become an ordinary man, like him, like me, like anyone else out there in the everyday world. So what was the point?

Angiulín stood there, waiting – a thin figure in a black cravat his white hair reaching down to his shoulders – waiting to see me go, so as not to miss a single movement, a single detail of the utterly normal, utterly inimitable step of a living man.